Six Days to Zeus:
Alive Day

Based on a True Story

Samuel Hill

BookLocker

ISBN: 978-1-63263-804-5

Library of Congress Cataloguing in Publication Data
Hill, Samuel
Six Days to Zeus: Alive Day
Fiction: War & Military | History: Military - United States | History: Military - General
Library of Congress Control Number: 2018905554

Published by BookLocker.com, Inc., St. Petersburg, Florida.

Printed on acid-free paper.

BookLocker.com, Inc.
2018-2020

DEDICATION

This book is a fictional account of a real soldier's life. Although every day was filled with highly classified missions and sub-compartmented special access intelligence, the heart of this story has nothing to do with classified information. This book is not a kiss and tell, but rather a book about the lessons in life we all must learn and about the often times expensive tuition we must pay. Life lessons about success, failure, betrayal, heartache, pain, suffering, dedication, persistence, survival and ultimately, learning to forgive but to never forget because in the end, *life is about what you do to other people.*

Every effort has been made to sanitize classified information out of this book. Non-disclosure agreements signed by Intelligence Professionals are there for a reason. A very good reason I support wholeheartedly. There are mission tactics, technology and methodology that U.S. Intelligence Professionals use on a daily basis, that if disclosed, would cause severe damage to the American people, the U.S. Government and give an unfair advantage to the enemy, subverting the hard earned successes that have made America the greatest nation on the planet. With that said, the reader should know that every effort has been made to ensure those tactics and mission essentials have been changed to ensure nothing is given away to enemies set on destroying us.

This book encompasses the sacrifice, trauma and the bad things that happened to "Chief", a Chief Warrant Officer in the United States Military, and the group of "Quiet Professionals", that work tirelessly behind the scenes. These are the men and women who make America strong by guiding decision makers, providing sound moral compass headings and impeccable service through

Intelligence and other specialties. But this book also demonstrates and emphasizes the good things that transpire when Chief recovers and learns from what life has thrown at him.

At times in his life, there seemed to be no end in sight and no sane reason to continue fighting. But through perseverance, faith and primal instinct he learned that only those who tolerate the pain and get through the storm become better persons in the end for having lived through it all.

This book is dedicated to the concepts of Peace, Strength, Humility, Loyalty, Integrity and Selfless Service. This book is dedicated to those men and woman who work in the shadows who have made those concepts a lifestyle choice. There are men and woman who work daily in a thankless, often times hazardous environment performing the most difficult job known to man. They dedicate their lives to this work in an effort to predict the future, keep the peace and save innocent civilians from the death and destruction caused by evil men. They help prosecute United States Foreign Policy and provide, time sensitive, real time intelligence to decision makers at the highest level of the United States Government.

While the world went into a panic after September 11, 2001, pointing fingers and assigning blame, many of the "Quiet Intelligence Professionals" never skipped a beat and went to work. Quietly. Silently. In the shadows. They proceeded to pick out "critical node" intelligence in order to prosecute foreign policy with a ferocity and professionalism never before seen in the history of mankind. All the while balancing their actions with humility, self restraint, integrity, loyalty and selfless service. These *are not* the men and women who lowered their standards because it was easier. *Not* the ones who degraded themselves by resorting to despicable physical violence at Abu Gahrab prison simply because they could. These men and women worked tirelessly in pursuit of Actionable Intelligence. These are the men and women who stuck to the plan, did the hard work and can look in the mirror knowing they never once tarnished the honor of their profession by taking the path of least resistance. Not once.

The resulting personal sacrifices these men and women endured are incalculable, elevating their status among the warrior population to that of "Tier One". What most American's will never understand is that the sacrifices don't end when these men and woman retire from, or are released from Active Federal Service. That is when the consequences of their service and the adverse impact on their lives usually begins. The lifetime of consequences and sacrifice goes on until they themselves leave this earth.

To those "Quiet Professionals", the Silent Warriors of the United States Intelligence Services, I say, " Thank You, Cheers, Semper Fi, Airborne and God Speed". In a single word, "Whooah!"

ACKNOWLEDGMENTS

To Julie, Michelle, Mike, "Jesus Christ Landis", Frances, Lowell, Kent, Donna, Kate, George, Marciel, and all the other members of "My Writer's Group" who gave me encouragement, brutal critique and comments that kept me writing. Thank you for putting up with my growing pains, my therapy and my never-ending epiphanies of who I am today, because of who I was yesterday! I never could have become the writer I am today, without your steadfast friendship and encouragement. I will never forget you. I will forever cherish the words, "It's emotionally STERILE!" Your kind criticism made me look at my writing from a different perspective and helped me grow. Thank you. I truly, deeply cherish your friendship!

"Chief"

To my loving wife and soul mate, Jeanette…

Thanks for believing in me, for standing by me through thick and thin through so many surgeries and recoveries, through the healing process of my own PTSD and Moral Wounding.

I never knew what love was until I knew you. I am a much better "ME" because of you!

Thank you for loving me in a way no one ever has.

You truly are my personal "Tier One" Teammate.

CONTENTS

Introduction

Chief and his Team were running on empty as usual, completely unaware that another 72 hours transpired. Time was a strange beast. Although everything in a normal soldier's life revolved around what time it was, when it came to the missions of Joint Task Force Arc Angel, the days just flowed into each other. Time seemed to be inconsequential.

Barely 30 minutes after mission success, "Zeus" as it was known in Tier One inner circles, Chief and his six man Team entered the air conditioned aircraft hangar at Sanctuary Base being briefed en-route, on yet *another* mission that required their expertise and attention. Mission tempo increased in the Middle East, leading Chief and his men to execute up to 25 missions a day, when just a few short years earlier everyone complained they'd still never done ONE real world mission.

Special Ops was considered the "Ferrari in the barn" that everyone was afraid to use because it was expensive and cost so much to run. But now, that "Ferrari" was running flat out, with barely any down time for maintenance. These were heady times. Egos ran enormously high with such great mission successes. But Chief learned from his earlier days conducting missions all over the planet, that life didn't always throw roses your way. He was careful to keep his Team both highly motivated, but grounded in reality as well.

No one died yet. The egos among Special Operators was running high, simply because they were kicking ass and taking names. No one was dead yet, but the golden BB moment was waiting. Until Marc Lee died, the first Navy SEAL to die in combat in Iraq, there was a surreal aura amongst Special Operators. Detrimental to combat operations, Spec Ops was just too used to winning without paying a price. That would come to a screeching halt very shortly. It was time to get serious and understand that life changes in thirty seconds.

There were only two types of mission in the world of Joint Task Force that Chief concerned himself and his Team with. Hostage rescue and High Value Target (HVT) take down. Sometimes the missions Chief was involved with were both. Intelligence collection was just a part of standard procedure when his Team got on the ground. This job was all about selfless service, dedication, loyalty and persistence. Only here, within the Inner Circle of Tier One Warriors, the mission was a lifestyle, a conscious choice, not just words.

"Zeus" was called on the mission they just finished, a huge Intelligence and Operational success that no one in the free world would ever hear about. The mission particulars were a "Need To Know" only basis and very few people had that "Need to Know". Even fewer knew the mission had ever taken place. Only those hostages whose lives were saved knew and appreciated the real impact of his Team's professionalism and expertise in execution. The certain and imminent death of these American civilians was suddenly averted when Chief and his Team showed up in the middle of the night to snatch the American Hostages from the jaws of death. All of the unsuspecting hostages were brought back to Sanctuary Base instead of having their heads removed for propaganda value on social media.

These Evangelical Christian American civilians took it upon themselves to believe they were "Anointed by God", and decided it was their mission in life to convert Muslims to Christianity, never realizing they were not just putting their own lives in jeopardy, but the lives of Tier One Warriors as well.

Like spoiled children, they never looked in the mirror long enough to understand that what they were doing was sacrilegious and against Allah in the minds of fanatical Jihadis, just as much so as the fanatical Muslims were violating Christian beliefs by trying to install Sharia Law worldwide. The tit for tat struggle between Islam and Christianity was centuries old, going as far back in history as the Crusades.

The concept was completely lost on the Christians that they themselves were off the reservation in a Muslim land, feeding the flames of radical Islam. It always surprised Chief to learn that these people never understood that their actions would put the lives of good soldiers in jeopardy. The very lives of those soldiers who vowed to give their lives for others. "So Others May Live" was one motto they lived by. And they came to rescue anyone in harms way. In this case, simply because the Evangelical Christians made some very stupid, very naive, very selfish decisions based on their own religious fanaticism.

Judgment of such people who got themselves into this kind of trouble came too easily. To the men of Joint Task Force Arc Angel, successful mission completion was all that mattered. The medals, awards and recognition were nothing more than trinkets without any real value. The grateful look and tears in the eyes of those they'd spared was all the "thanks" any of the men needed.

The seven-man team was barely awake, running on pure adrenaline and looking forward to some much deserved sleep, food and down time. They dropped their gear in the secure fenced compound surrounding the air field hangar, slung their weapons and sensitive items on their backs and trudged into the air conditioned aircraft hangar completely unaware that another 72 hours was gone. After so many repetitions of the same operation set, "where they were" really didn't matter anymore.

To the uninitiated, the sight of these well muscled men walking around in their underwear and combat boots with weapons slung across their backs, night vision dangling from their necks and web gear dragging from their tired and aching forearms, these men looked more like a band of undisciplined, uncaring beach junkies than a well oiled terrorist take down machine. Looks can often be deceiving! These were Tier One warriors assigned to ISA, the "Intelligence Support Activity" otherwise known around the world as "The Activity" or "Those guys".

No words were shared as they walked. Words had to wait until they were inside the secure walls of the Sensitive Compartmented Information Facility (SCIF). Cautiously they let out a sigh of relief, allowing their unconscious to relax if only for the few moments it took to walk from the Blackhawk to the SCIF that awaited inside the hangar.

Subconsciously they were taking inventory of what hurt, what was numb, what mattered and what didn't matter anymore. In a remote region of their minds, each man took inventory of his own personal priorities. Some thought of their wives, children, girlfriends or parents. Others about their dog or where they intended to go when they got a break in the action. But each and every one of the men kept track of where their minds were, taking care not to allow things to teeter too close to that emotional danger zone that every man cordoned off. The boundaries were different for each man, but they all respected the unspoken code of never trespassing into another man's "Zone" unless invited.

As the Team walked towards the SCIF, something told them it was too soon to celebrate. There was always that chance something would get screwed up this close to going home. Every time they'd planned down time, or celebrated, thinking they were out of the shit and could spend time at home, something would flop right in the middle of it all and change everything in an instant.

Inside the hangar, the Team dropped their sweat encrusted, stinking uniforms on the concrete floor and sprayed their bodies with a garden hose hooked to a bathroom sink faucet. Instinctively they choked down the remainder of the MREs they'd humped up and down the mountains of Afghanistan and Pakistan over the past three days as they made their way into the SCIF. Food was now scientifically received. No one liked the MREs or how they tasted. It was more about the nutritional value and keeping energy levels up, completely ignoring the taste whenever possible. With the exception of "Tabasco" of course, the only thing that had any real flavor that could cut through the paste that perpetually developed on their tongues and roof of their mouths. A mix of dried saliva, desert dirt and dehydrated goat shit dust constantly cycled from re-hydration in their mouths, to desert dry, leaving their tongues feeling like an old shoe and tasting even worse. Tabasco was the only relief. Yet even that was reserved for special occasions.

The SCIF was a "need to know" access area where Sensitive Intelligence (SI) information was discussed. SI was information deemed above Top Secret that needed special processing, special handling through special communications with the utmost urgency and secrecy. Every wire had special filters on the incoming voice and data lines. The electricity was monitored and filtered for inadvertent bleed over of sensitive data and everything inside this specially manufactured "box", was highly sensitive equipment used for Top Secret Compartmented and above intelligence conversations, communications and data transfer. TS/SCI, or Top Secret Special Compartmented Intelligence was the Tier One level of Intelligence. And not many people were allowed access at those levels.

The SCIF was basically a metal meat locker type of enclosure, flown anywhere in the world and erected inside of any other building, or simply dropped on the tarmac at Sanctuary Base, surrounded by razor wire and armed guards. It looked like a walk in freezer and had it's own cipher locks, computer systems and communications connected to all the higher echelon commands including the White House Situation Room, the Pentagon War Room, the CIA Operations Center, along with a number of other "Classified" consumers who were allowed to know what the Intelligence Support Activity was all about.

Along with all the high tech stuff inside the SCIF, there was one thing that remained constant no matter where the "meat locker" was deployed. Chief's desk. The simple metal desk was bolted to the floor in the same place every time it was deployed. The difference between that desk and every other military metal desk was the small 4 by 6 inch photos taped to the desktop. Photos of the only thing that mattered in Chief's quiet, secretive life. His two sons.

ISA was a clandestine Intelligence organization that very few people ever even knew existed. It's named changed every 30 days anyway, so most people never really knew if they were talking about the same organization or not when the conversation came up. Only those who knew the Tier One primary operators by their first names knew who the ISA really was and what they did. To the high level inner circle of the US Government, only the Commanders were known. The Team was perpetually anonymous.

The mission always remained the same. Classified, on a "need to know basis". The only thing that anyone outside the inner circle ever really knew was that when ISA got involved, the mission was serious and those conducting it were absolutely the best at what they did. There was no room for bravado or bullshit, nor was it tolerated.

Many Presidents had come and gone whose very lives, careers and Presidential legacies depended on that small number of highly trained professional intelligence personnel assigned to the "Activity", one name it was known by. Very few of those Presidents or their Cabinet Members ever heard the name, but were highly grateful to those few men and women whose lives were consumed with keeping continuity on the elusive targets whose sole intent was the complete destruction of America. These men and women were Warriors who owned the shadows and lived a lifestyle very few ever knew about. Some referred to this unit as "the Farm". Others just called it "that unit" or "those guys". Chief called it "his Team".

The FBI and CIA were constantly pissing on each other's turf, pointing fingers, trying to make each other look bad, all the while trying to make themselves look good, and in reality, were making it easier for the bad guys to win. The Activity didn't play politics. So, if no one knew what to call them and never knew where they were, they could hardly be sucked into the drama and bickering between governmental agencies inside the D.C. Beltway. The perpetual finger pointing was unprofessional in Chief's mind, which eventually caused ineffectual performance and impotence among those who were supposed to be defending America against all enemies, foreign and domestic!

* * * * *

The entire team was walking in a zombie state, somewhere in some desert environment. After so many mission sets, "Where they were" just didn't matter anymore. The entire Team was in a sort of comfort zone right next to being primal as they left the aircraft and headed into the hangar. Food and water was the only priority they concerned themselves with at the moment. Every man acted in unison. Patient. Calm. As if a silent voice and familiar robotic routine controlled them, urged them into the perpetual, well rehearsed action of feeding the body while their brain, numb and detached from the physical pain that was always present, subconsciously absorbed the new mission particulars spewing from the mouth of the JTF J2 Intelligence briefer. In this case, the man babbling as they walked was a well rehearsed and professional briefer carrying the rank of Lt Commander. But to Chief and his team, this guy was just another "talking dog" who should be in the civilian world reading news from a teleprompter on some TV channel, not getting in their way.

Chief was on year 26 with Joint Special Operations Intelligence, (JSOC-J2). He'd been there since the inception of "joint" operations, a result of absolute catastrophe in the deserts of Iran during the

American Hostage Crisis of the early 1980s. Eight Special Operators died that day, simply because no one checked the weather to see that a monster sand storm, known to the locals as "Haboob", was on the horizon. Either they hadn't checked, or they didn't understand the devastating impact of what a real sand storm meant to rotary winged aircraft. Three meters of sand was coming straight down every half hour. The weight of that sand alone would crush any aircraft that flew in the vicinity. But in the case of Operation Eagle Claw, the C130s fixed wing propeller driven aircraft and Sea Stallion helicopters assigned to that mission flew directly into the storm and were totally consumed. A fuel tanker on the ground tried to take off and immediately met a fiery fate when a Sea Stallion helicopter flew into the side of it. The Achille Lauro was Chief's first mission. Eagle Claw was his second. At age 19, his life changed in thirty seconds. The impact of two devastating outcomes would shape his mentality and his life forever more.

Joint operations were born as a result of that aborted mission. The Special Operators of Joint Task Force Arc Angel were trying to get out of Iran to regroup when the accident occurred. Subsequent finger pointing led to some level headed senior men figuring out that it wasn't a good idea to have three different services involved in the same operation, each service using three different types of radios so that the men on the ground couldn't actually talk to anyone in real time. Operations of this type were an absolute fiasco and good men died because the Admirals, Generals and Commanders of so many different services wanted their own piece of the pie.

A new organization would need to be formed, led by men with second echelon thinking and combat experience. Rangers, Seals, Green Berets, Marine Recon and Air Force Para-rescue types with a no bullshit attitude who were fearless, professional and, above all, competent. Joint Special Operations Command, JSOC, was born. And ISA was the Intelligence asset that supported these clandestine operations.

A "Commander" assigned to this small team, routinely transferred in and out, staying six months or less on station. The short time frame these Commanders spent at the unit was not due to the fact that they couldn't take the physical stress, or that they didn't like the missions. Usually, the insane tempo of both training and real world operations wore them out too quickly, as well as the fact they were trying to climb the ladder of success, *not* dedicate themselves to a cause. There was a real difference in tolerance between men with leadership aspirations and operators.

Chief was the hub of the wheel. The only Chief Warrant Officer assigned to this highly specialized unit, his years in Special Ops was the only real continuity in this chaotic and high risk environment. Yet the men who did the real work also considered Chief the outrigger that kept everything steady. All the other Commanders and Officers were there for their own reasons, other agendas like a quick promotion, limited time in the driver's seat with limited experience that gave them high visibility when it came to records review for promotions. Being dubbed "Commander of a Terrorist take down unit" meant rapidly rising within their peer group. They hoped to be quickly reassigned and move on to bigger and better things. Bigger and Better things was "Enlisted speak" for desk duty and an easy kush future climbing the ranks until they reached the top, or were forced to retire. Although there was mandatory respect of their rank, most of the soldiers saw the Officers who dashed in and out, as politicians who were out to get the patches and badges to put on their "I love ME" wall.

Chief was different. He didn't have an "I love ME" wall. All his medals, awards and recognition were in a box somewhere in storage. Until his new wife found them, had them framed for the kids to see. Chief had been there the longest with no end in sight. Literally hundreds of missions. Over sixty men died while Chief worked there. Some died in training accidents, others on real world covert operations missions.

Chief was a walking legend that carried things deeply and quietly, especially the scars, torn ligaments and hardware that kept his spine in one column. Those who died that were "worth a shit" held a special place in Chief's heart. The rest who died were just part of nature's inevitable herd thinning process. They were assholes when they were alive, now they were just dead assholes.

If a person had their head on straight and spent enough time with Chief in a room they could come away with a treasure trove of wisdom and knowledge about life in general. A younger soldier could tell there was a lot more than met the eye when it came to this big scary guy with the hard heart they called Chief. He was a man of few words most of the time and even less words during mission prep or when a Real World Operation was on the horizon. The warriors around the compound always knew when something was up. But as with all things, a person had to be perceptive enough and present to find out. Chief didn't offer his experience, wisdom and life lessons for free and not to just anyone.

This team of seven men had only been together for a little more than a year. Their combined Special Operations experience was considerable and contributed immensely to the fluid mechanics and un-canny ability to predict what Chief was thinking. More times than not, someone would say, "I'm on it Chief" without any other words being spoken. Just a look, a twitch in body language and everyone knew not only what needed to be done, but whose responsibility it was to get it done. Everyone was connected on a different plain. The unspoken communications plain of the Special Operations Warrior.

The selection process that Department of Defense used to find these Elite Warriors ensured they were highly motivated self-starters, pulled together from every branch of US Military Service. Thousands applied every year to get onto the Special Teams that America used to fight the War on Terror. But of those thousands, less than one percent would actually make it to training, and most of them would be weeded out. "Wannabes" was the name they were given. The ones who "Wanted to be" but just didn't have the heart and soul required to become part of the inner circle. Many excellent warriors from all the services, applicants with a minimum of ten years time in service, were dropped from the rolls simply because they did not have what it took for the long haul. The endurance required for a lifetime. Special Operations was not about the "sprint" from one mission to the next. It was a lifestyle intended for those men and woman who had the long haul in their genes and the long strand muscle texture of a marathon runner, not the big bulky short fiber muscle of a weight lifter or boxer.

Once a man was selected, it was a given that any task received would be executed with the same immediacy and professional calm that any other task mandated. Taking out a terrorist, or taking out the garbage resulted in the same physiologic elements being present - a moderated heart rate, controlled slow breathing, attention to the smallest detail and execution with satisfactory result in the most efficient manner possible without drawing any attention to themselves. The only aspect that changed from one task to the next was the level of ferocity and ruthlessness required.

The current mission they were being briefed on would be double. Double everything. Double the length. Double the danger. The standard mission set was three days. Some nerd, with all their medical and scientific studies had determined that the limit of human endurance was just more than 72 hours without pharmaceutical enhancements. But they had not taken into account the determination, the heart and shear perseverance of the Elite Warriors within the Special Operations world who were assigned to the ISA. Without chemical or pharmaceutical assistance, these guys were literally head and shoulders above the rest of the Green Berets, Navy Seals and Marine Recon men. They were the best of the best, with no bravado, no flash, just silent efficiency and perfection with just the right touch of humility. They were all brawn with the requisite brains included. Anyone could be trained to have the strength and stamina. But not everyone could be taught the brain part. That had to be there at birth. The number of men with both was an extreme limiting factor. There just were not that many who also had the patriotism and loyalty required by this elite organization.

This mission could take up to six days from wheels up to *ZEUS*, the code word often used for mission completion. Staying on the air too long usually meant someone with radio direction finding techniques would rain mortars down on your head. The less one said on the radio, the better. "ZEUS" was simply spoken to say, "Mission Success" on the designated operations frequency.

Chief and his team had already been up for over 72 hours and it was someone else's turn, some other team's time to take a crack at it. However, there was no one else. Twenty eight Special Operators were killed with one RPG strike less than three months earlier, the result of poor planning and a total lack of attention to Security Protocol. Millions of dollars in equipment was lost, but many more millions in training time and money were wasted just as well. The death of these highly trained Operators who fell victim to "the Golden BB moment" was devastating to the Special Operations Community. Direct-Action Insertions into hostile territory almost ALWAYS had preparatory fire by artillery, A-10 close air support cover fire, Spectre Gunship or Apache Helicopter cover for security on the drop zone. But in this case, there was no air cover, no preparatory fire, no surveillance and no advanced planning for the QRF mission to extract the Team. As a result, an RPG went up the tailgate of a CH-47 flying into a hot drop zone without killing everyone on board. The mission was a disaster from the planning stages, with no satellite communications, no air cover and no Plan B. Too many good men died that day over stupidity, emotion and complete lack of professional leadership. The Ferrari in the barn was due for a total and complete overhaul.

It would take years to fill those slots and decades more to fill the shoes of those men lost. Because even after the replacement men were trained, they still needed combat experience. Those who died would be remembered forever more within the Special Operations Community. America had all but forgotten the incident, never knowing their names, nor ever really understanding what went wrong, or why they died.

As Chief and his Team were tapped for yet another mission, Chief knew it was now time to find some more "suck it up" and go out again. There was no relief Team. There were no additional personnel so Chief and his men could take a break. Mission creep and operational tempo was at a staggering pitch. Chief and his men could sleep on the bird and the clock would reset to zero when they lifted off.

Someone in the Chain of Command estimated this mission would require six days. That set off internal radars in Chief's head. His internal compass, the personal "gut check" that saved his life and that of his men on more than one occasion was telling him that something was wrong. For the longest time during his storied career, Chief hadn't listened to that inner voice because he couldn't explain it. But years of real world experience had since taught him to listen to that quiet voice from within and to listen well. This time, that mysterious inner voice of his was telling him that something was seriously wrong. He'd been on longer missions. Some missions were as long as a year in duration, others more than that. But most of them were the standard 72 hours for Special Operations. After that, conventional military units came in to mop up and conduct extended mission tasks. But this time, as Chief listened to the mission particulars coming from the JTF/JSOC briefer, there was an un-easy glitch that made Chief repeatedly shake his head, look at the floor and try to keep his stomach under control. He couldn't put his finger on what exactly bothered him. But in the near future he would learn that "glitch" would change his life and that of his men, forever. Simply because the missions statement said, "Six Days to Zeus!"

Chihuahua Child

*"Just because you don't understand something, does
not mean it's false!"*

Life Lesson Nr. 1

A dark alleyway awaited the seven man Quick Reaction Force
(QRF) Team as the distance closed rapidly between Sanctuary Base,
somewhere in the desert of Iraq, and the location of a elusive bomb
maker. Chief and his Team, now designated Joint Task Force Arc
Angel, supported by the Night Stalkers helicopter squadron of Task
Force 160, had already spent nearly three years of research,
interviews, Intelligence collection and processing trying to mitigate
the seemingly perpetual bombings in downtown Baghdad, all
without success. This specific bomb maker had a signature, as did
most bomb makers. Only instead of some sort of wiring sequence, or
repetitive type structure or chemical explosive composition. The
signature this one use was children.

The initial assault team consisted of three seasoned Operators.
Chief, the Team Leader and Officer in Charge, a U.S. Navy Special
Warfare enlisted man, (SEAL) with expertise in Explosive Ordnance
Disposal (EOD) and over sixty classified missions, and a U.S. Army
Special Operations, Green Beret, Medic. Anticipation among the
Team was at it's peak as the highly modified Blackhawk helicopter
followed a sharp turn off on the main road leading out of the city
and into a small, walled in enclave in North Eastern Baghdad.
Barely 30 meters to the rear in flight, a second Blackhawk followed
loaded with four additional Operators, every man U.S. Army
Ranger qualified and experts in perimeter security for High Value
Target (HVT) take down missions.

Over the past six months inside the secure sanctuary circle called "The Green Zone" of Central Baghdad, a bomb maker contributed immensely to the chaos, terror and complete lack of peace and security by supplying dynamite vests to the Insurgency resulting in the death of eight suicide bombers and over four hundred innocent civilians. The tactics used were as sinister and deadly as was the result of their home made suicide vests.

Security forces, suspecting nothing from innocent four and five year old children, allowed them to walk unhindered through checkpoints into the town square, a local open-air farmer's market. At the busiest time of the day when civilians performed the mundane task of buying produce, these children walked past security and under the threat radar completely un-noticed. Under the guise of innocence, these children walked among their victims. The people had no suspicion that these small children were walking death incarnate, their tiny bodies strapped with high intensity explosives with several pounds of metal debris attached to the vests, intended to inflict maximum injuries and casualties to every human within the blast radius. With absolutely no warning and with no real understanding for the consequences of their actions, these small children from the age of 4 years old would robotically stroll into the crowd, and scream to the top of their lungs the Islamic rhetoric which they had rehearsed for months every day at the Madrassa under threat of whipping: "Allahu Akbar" (Allah is supreme).

With all the fervor and boldness of a much older, warrior Jihadist, they pushed the ignition button concealed within their clothes, detonating the dynamite vest which vaporized their bodies sending ball bearings and shards of cast iron shrapnel into the crowd. The death and destruction was enormous, caught on video cameras emplaced before hand throughout the city and around the farmer's market by Jihadi handlers. The physical injuries alone would devastate the population. But the realization that a young child caused the carnage was something so psychologically paralyzing it affected everyone in the country and indeed, around the world.

Civilian Liaison Group (CLG) provided real time, time sensitive intelligence information about a bomb maker's lab. Intensive Intelligence efforts had finally supplied information about the person, or persons responsible for thirty bombs that had gone off inside the "Green Zone" over the past thirty days, nearly one every single day, but often times, more than one a day further heightening the resolve to find this maniac and stop the slaughter.

Fragile relations between Coalition Forces and the Iraqi people depended on such things as electricity and running water. But peace and security were also at the top of everyone's list. After all, the Americans were being held personally responsible for the current state of anarchy that persisted within the country, which *was not* present during the last forty years under Saddam Hussein. Everyone knew Saddam was a butcher who murdered scores of people simply because he could. But his behavior was tolerated simply because everyday life was more tolerable with electricity, running water and fuel while Saddam was still in power. Now, since the Americans had come in and destroyed most of the city's infrastructure during the Shock and Awe campaign, the never ending issues that made daily life miserable were causing enormous political pressures on a very unstable new government. After all, Baghdad was in the middle of the desert. And most of the inhabitants were accustomed to having running water, electricity and even air conditioning.

The culture of the Middle East was to over exaggerate their misery, especially in front of video cameras, or when they had an audience. Complaining loudly, using small children to accentuate their agony and discomfort, often worked to enhance their position when they were considered by the local government for redress of their grievances. Acting mortally wounded usually meant more money, more food, or more attention. Any way around it, the result of their Oscar Winning theatrics meant more of something. For government officials, it was bad enough dealing with the mass complaints over power outages, lack of running water, no sewage or trash pickup, and food shortages. The constant bombings however, were just unacceptable and had to stop.

After months of sensitive intelligence collection, Chief and his team were sent in without any prior notice, to verify and to eliminate the problem. To say that no one inside Iraq could be trusted was an understatement. Everyone had their own agenda. Finding real, actionable intelligence brought back memories of the Cold War when Chief was stationed in Berlin a long time before the Wall ever came down. Things were the same in Iraq now as it had been in the East Bloc during the Soviet Occupation of East Germany and Berlin. The local population had broken into factions. And plenty of them. They were split into geographic location by century old tribal boundaries and religious beliefs. The problem was knowing who was on what side, what their agenda was and if they were telling you the truth or not. If you picked the wrong side, you very well could end up dead. Saddam was gone, but the in-fighting among factions and tribes was rampant now. All the control mechanisms that had kept the peace under Saddam were gone. Death was inevitable, but in this day and age in Iraq, it could come without any warning simply by going to the open air market to get food.

Preferred tactic for Chief and his Team would have been to wait till oh-dark-thirty to strike, a time when most of the local civilians were either asleep or at least inside their homes, limiting the exposure of Chief and the Team to hostiles in the area. Things could get messy in these parts. No matter where they went, U.S. Soldiers were constantly on the razor's edge knowing full well that they were either loved by the people or hated with a passion. Sorting out who was who never was an easy task. The job of showing up on someone's doorstep unannounced with the intention of stopping them from blowing people up had an inherent risk. Conducting this type of mission at night was intended to mitigate some of that risk. U.S. Special Operations had an enormous tactical advantage via night vision devices. An advantage they put to good use on many successful missions! But on this night, the Intelligence report indicated the bomb maker would be gone by morning. So the window of opportunity now dictated when Chief and the Team would strike instead of Standard Operating Procedures, which historically proved to be the key to not only mission success, but also the extremely low casualty rate Tier One teams enjoyed. To everyone on standby, going in without prior surveillance, in the daylight, without backup, was a classic case of the tail wagging the dog. Totally ass backwards.

In less than 30 minutes flight time by Blackhawk insertion, Chief and his men had boots on the ground. As they exited the aircraft, Chief had the Team Explosive Ordinance expert on his left, the Team Medic on his right. Too soon for night vision equipment, all three heads were on a swivel as they proceeded into the fading light of the alleyway. Lacking the luxury of pre-mission surveillance, time and darkness, Chief and his men hustled to get into the shadows and the relative protection of mud walls and concrete block buildings the local people called "home".

The second bird touched down meters away and the remaining Team members dispersed into the shadows setting up perimeter security and surveillance points surrounding the target grid square, a small cement block house near the center of the town. With a perimeter established by the remaining four men on the team, Chief plus two were inbound to investigate the situation. The element of surprise was even more important now since the cover of darkness was already sacrificed. They were moving at a full run into the darkness of the alleyway when everything suddenly changed for the worst.

With all the ferocity of a sledgehammer at full swing, a 7.62 mm round struck Chief in the back. His body lurched forward as if carried by an invisible linebacker, smashing his face into the mud brick wall in front of him. The shock and surprise of the situation was not unfamiliar to Chief. Training and experience took over as his body and mind absorbed the adrenaline, felt the heat in his face dissipate, responding by transitioning into survival mode. In an instant, the Ordinance man was slumped in a lifeless pile on his left, brain matter and blood speckling the dirt wall in front of him. A split second later, the Team Medic was down on his right, balled up writhing on the ground in agony, pulling his legs to his chest, screaming at the top of his lungs. Chief watched through a pain induced fog as blood spewed from the man's lower back and legs and a sudden sick feeling hit Chief in the guts telling him that maybe he'd just made a really bad decision by taking this QRF mission. An AK-47 machine gun round had torn off half of the man's buttocks. In a few more seconds, both the screaming and motion ceased.

Chief scrambled to stay conscious using the fighter pilot technique of grunting, holding his breath, contracting muscles and forcing blood to his brain. He fought hard to remain conscious between rapid, intermittent inhalations, straining to focus his eyes. His body and brain were in full warrior survival mode now and nothing responded to his will. Ears ringing, Chief strained to hear anything audible. Training took over as he keyed his headset and spoke calmly into the microphone.

"Contact rear. Three friendlies down. I need backup and Medics ASAP. Scramble DUSTOFF. One man is dead. I repeat, ONE KIA. The other needs some serious medical assistance!"

As he released the mic, Chief noticed the faint scent of blood in his nostrils. Licking his lips and tasting the combination of mud and blood made him realize the blood was his own. The salty taste made his jaw hurt as dry saliva glands spasmed in his mouth. His upper lip, cut cleanly in the middle, flowed heavily with blood where he'd pushed his front teeth through it. Instinct took over and Chief scrambled to his feet. He was fully inside his head now. Adrenaline insulated his brain, made him painless and super human as he forced himself to focus and recover from the ground. A violent growl grew within his chest.

The slow motion video footage he experienced as he struggled to his feet was familiar territory, a result of trauma conditions he'd experienced so many times before. The time warp in his brain slowed everything way down and allowed Chief to record unbelievable details that would later play out in his nightmares and dreams. Only the weirdest and most out of place things, smells, thoughts and observations stood out in time with seemingly endless minutes allotted for analysis and recall.

In this extreme trauma state, Chief's retinal focus was intensified. His vision was suddenly capable of supreme clarity, enabling him to watch slow motion bullets zip by. Chief could literally watch the dust in the air being pushed aside by an enormous pressure wave preceding the metal encased, lead projectile. His hearing was superhuman as well, as his mind recorded the unbelievably clear sounds of the metal on metal, automatic firing mechanism of the Kalashnikov as it reverberated off the mud walls with every round jacked into the firing chamber. Thirty rounds seemed to erupt in perpetuity as time stood still.

As Chief tried to recover, he got to one knee and caught a glimpse in his peripheral vision of a white cotton robe fleeing past. Bare feet and the brief but unmistakable aroma of goat manure struck Chief's consciousness. Was this the bastard that had just shot him in the back? It was payback time!

The robe and bare feet were fully on his radar as Chief blocked everything else from his mind. For some reason, the feet seemed to be out of place. Chief struggled to focus, fighting off pain, breathing through the bloody mud in his nostrils. He caught himself fighting for more air as he tried to prevent the inevitable inhale of mud and blood into his lungs, causing him to cough and lose valuable strength. He found himself trying so hard to keep his legs from folding under the weight of his body and the extra 80 lbs of Kevlar and ceramic trauma prevention vest plates that had just saved his life.

Instantaneous reaction to the passing feet cleared Chief's mind and fueled an almost cat-like strike as he reached out to grab a human form by the neck as it tried to flee. The vicious growl building in his chest released in such violence that it fueled every second to come. In one smooth and practiced martial arts, muscle memory move, Chief rose to his feet holding a human's throat in one hand, while pulling a well used K-Bar knife from it's leg holster with the other hand. In one more second, the blade would cross over his left wrist and severe all the vital tendons, wind pipe and arteries encased inside the human flesh that he now held in his grip. Neurons fired split second calculations in Chief's brain. A weird sense of calm and comfort came over him as he relaxed and let his primal instinct take control and go through the motions of a well practiced Kata he worked on for so many decades. A dance of Warriors that had saved his life on numerous occasions comprised of part Krav Magaw martial arts moves and part Ninja. He anticipated the coming adrenaline spike that accompanied hand to hand combat, yearning for the huge endorphin release that normally accompanied the rage! There was nothing more pure, nothing more addictive. One of them was not going home.

The more his brain relaxed, the more Chief knew there was a problem. There was little or no weight to the body he'd lifted so deftly from the ground.

"Could my own adrenaline mask the weight of a grown man?" Chief wondered in anxious anticipation that something might be out of whack!

Chief wasn't perfect by any means, but mistakes really sucked. Especially those errors when human life was terminated prematurely. Those were the mistakes a man never got over. Life lessons had to be paid for, just like college tuition had to be paid. But the life lessons a soldier learned while in combat were lessons that cost way too much tuition, especially if they got it wrong.

Chief's peripheral vision showed him that what he thought were a man's feet, were somehow dangling in mid-air, frozen in space without so much as a toe touching the dirt below. A fraction of a second later in the inventory process of Chief's mind, yet another warning signal flashed! *No beard!* Then came a sick feeling in his gut and a painfully burning question.

"Did he have the right guy?"

His muscles burned deeply as he hauled on the internal brakes attempting to stop himself from completing the terminal cut across the human's throat. As painful and disappointing as this turn of events was, Chief had to make sure he had the right guy.

Finishing his ascension from the ground, overcoming the smell of blood, cordite and brain matter, fighting off unconsciousness as he held this human figure by the neck, Chief felt the strength come back to his legs as his heels landed on solid ground beneath him. He shook his head from side to side like a dog coming out of the water, trying to clear his brain. As the fog slowly lifted, pain replaced adrenaline, tears cleansed dirt and goat manure from his eyes and Chief came face to face with what he had gripped so tightly in his fist. It was a five year old little boy, eyes as big as dinner plates. Words of some sort were coming from his mouth, his lips moving a mile a minute. But still all Chief could hear over the ringing in his ears was the barking sound of a scared Chihuahua dog.

Later he would reflect and comprehend the lip reading taking place, currently muffled by the persistent ringing in his ears from a close proximity AK-47 muzzle blast.

"Allahu Akbar! Allahu Akbar! Allahu Akbar" in rapid succession was all the child could manage, "Allah is supreme!" over and over again, the pitch of his frightened voice heightened by Chief's grip squeezing his throat and tightening his larynx. The only noise emanating was that of a frantic and petrified, Chihuahua dog, fighting to stay alive!

"FUCK!" Chief yelled at the top of his lungs, releasing the primal growl, breathing hard to expel dirt and blood from his injured face and packed nostrils. His brain was back in charge now and just in the nick of time. He'd damned near cut the throat of a child. A child who still gripped an AK-47 with a hot barrel and an empty 30 round magazine that had just killed two of his men and severely injured Chief's spine in the process.

"What the hell is going on?" Chief thought. His brain tried to process the situation. Without warning, there was another set of hands on top of Chief's, prying to release his fingers, allowing the neck to go free.

"It's OK Chief. I got this!" came a familiar voice barely audible over the ringing in his ears and the slow calculated heartbeat he knew to be his own. A few more seconds would go by before Chief's muscles complied with the command from his brain and he finally released his grip. The child dropped to the ground and collapsed in a ball, holding his throat, coughing and gasping for air. Anger seeped in and Chief's body morphed from a super-human door-kicking warrior into that of a mere mortal. His body was suddenly that of a stinging, painful, earthbound weakling. By the time he'd taken two more breaths, another surge of adrenaline filled his blood stream and Chief was pissed off beyond words. He fought off yet another wave of adrenaline as he grappled for control, searching in vain for his Team-Leader military bearing.

"God Dammit!" Chief yelled grabbing the boy by the scruff of the neck, kicking down a simple wooden planked door in the alleyway. Visions of his own son, barely six years old now, swarmed into Chief's head and heart. What the hell was this child, this poor young Chihuahua Child doing out here in this god forsaken alley, shooting at him and his men? Where were his parents? Why did he have a fully loaded AK-47 with a 30 round clip and why wasn't he just being a kid somewhere playing? The fact that Chief damn near killed this kid resonated to his soul and made him angrier. The impact from his combat boots rendered the door into splinters. As he threw the young boy through the open doorway into the inner sanctum of the mud building, Chief suddenly found himself in the dark indoor living quarters, standing next to the boy again as he lay slumped in a pile on the floor. Chief's eyes were still adjusting to the darkness of being inside the building when a shocking realization struck him deep inside his brain. Chief somehow was standing in the middle of the bomb maker's lab. Mission planning brought him to the correct grid square, but Karma brought him to the exact bomb maker's location.

Seven dynamite vests, prefabricated and ready to go lined the floor next to the inner mud wall as if on display, each bearing a name tag much like backpacks intended for grade school attendance. A single wire connection to a battery was all that separated Chief, his team and everyone else in a city block radius from a certain trip to the afterlife. Through the mental fog of trauma, Chief realized that the boy's mother was the bomb maker. She had sent her five year old son into the alleyway with a fully loaded AK-47 to stand guard. He'd done his duty as a Chihuahua with the determination of a pit bull.

The Team Interpreter translated everything into English as the mother of eight babbled something in a dialect that Chief could not understand. His entire head rang now and the sudden realization he'd been shot in the back at close range registered in his brain as well as his back muscles. The "chicken plates" in his vest saved his life. There was no bullet penetration, but the impact gelled his scapular muscles, tore tendons and made his left lung bleed. Two vertebrae were fractured, a career ending injury for certain, if anyone found out. The kinetic energy from the impact of a bullet traveling at over 2,400 feet per second was enormous. But all that paled in comparison to Chief's knowing two of his men lay dead just outside the doorway. The doctors would never hear of Chief's injuries. His men came first and he was intent on making sure his own non-fatal wounds would not diminish their honor.

What could possibly make this woman sacrifice her own children? When Chief got the final translation, the answers did little to clarify neither the situation nor the mentality so foreign to Americans who believed in life and prosperity. It was obvious now just how opposite this Islamic culture really was. Their entire goal in life was to die for Allah and this Islamic woman was extremely upset that Chief had not killed her son. Her Muslim faith required her to sacrifice her sons in the name of Jihad, but she also stood to acquire $10,000.00 U.S. for every child she martyred and she had seven of them left. She would earn an additional reward for every U.S. Soldier she or her offspring killed and this child's face, that innocent Chihuahua, would be painted in a wall mural on the side of a building in the town square. She stood to gain a lot and was willing to martyr her seven remaining children for whom she'd already made fully functional dynamite vests. She already murdered at least eight children from the surrounding families in the past six months alone, sending them into the market in downtown Baghdad to detonate themselves all in the name of Allah.

As the CLG team arrived to claim the glory, collect the vests and whatever other Intelligence was available at the house, Chief walked away in utter disbelief and total silence as he headed for the Blackhawk. The mission was over and it was time to return to Sanctuary Base. Only now, he had two more dead men. He winced, swallowed hard, and held his breath as he gathered his gear, knowing full well the adrenaline was wearing off fast and he only had a few more minutes before the pain would be too obvious to hide. As Chief climbed into the Blackhawk, he keyed the mic and spoke softly.

"Sanctuary Base, this is Arc Angel Six. Zeus. I say again, Zeus." Then he reached over, turned off the radio and slumped back against a rucksack for the ride home. The intended recipients at the White House situation room, the Pentagon War Room and the CIA's Tactical Liaison Office erupted in celebration at the news. Maybe now, the Iraqi agenda would gain some traction. At a minimum, the U.S. could claim the high ground once again. Back at the Tarmac in the Iraqi desert, the sun was down, the stars were bright in the night sky, and Chief had a lot to think about. But for the moment, all he could remember was the familiar rant that always came into his head when missions went badly.

"I should have been a cook!"

＊ ＊ ＊ ＊ ＊

The cool night air was a welcome relief as Chief sat in the back of the Blackhawk for a very long time after the rotors ceased rotation on the tarmac at Sanctuary Base. The 30-minute return flight was made in total silence. The team was out of harm's way now, back inside the wire and the somber task of respectfully unloading the bodies of his dead soldiers was at hand. It was never easy when the mission was over and casualties had to be reckoned with. These were the times he had to bury emotion, put on his "Team Leader" face and keep the men focused on recovery operations from this mission, and incoming parameters for the next one. There was no time to grieve. Not now. Maybe later, but for the moment, there were so many more things that required his full attention. Besides mourning just meant he would lose precious strength. Mourning those who did not survive this mission would have to wait like all the other deaths. Years, indeed decades later, Chief still hadn't mourned any of his lost men and women. He didn't know when he would have time to do that. What he knew for certain was, it wasn't going to happen tonight. All of that was shoved in a box, locked in a closet and pushed aside for some other time.

Chief sat in quiet solitude listening to the high pitched sound of the Emergency Broadcast tone in his ears he remembered hearing as a child on the television every so often. Only now the persistent, high pitched ringing was inside his head, a permanent result of an AK-47 muzzle blast so close to his ears. As he tried to ignore the noise and fight off exhaustion, he was trying to think of what he would say in the letters he needed to write. Letters home to the loved ones and families of his fallen men. How would he explain to these people that their soldiers, their husbands, their sons, died on a mission trying to take out a very religious woman hell bent on blowing up as many American soldiers as she could by sending her own children to their death with a dynamite vest!

How could he explain the Muslim belief that dying by suicide was an act of heroism! That killing Infidels and dying while doing so, was preferable to living a full, happy and productive life! How could he explain to them how contrary this woman, this mother of eight children was to Western woman who would give their own lives to protect their children. Everywhere else on the planet, innocent lives were precious and protected by any means necessary. There was no explaining that this woman loved Allah enough to martyr her own children for Jihad. After all, isn't that what Christianity preached? That God loved mankind so much that he gave his only son to be crucified? How could he console the survivors and explain to these families that which he had yet to wrap his own brain around.

Addiction to Poz One

"Life is short... Live fast!"

Life lesson Nr. 2

When a group of soldiers line up in an assault force to take down a location, especially in denied territory where resistance is assured and hostility is imminent, that group of men is called a "stack" in tactical terminology. Poz One, or position one in the stack, is the name given to the first man in the lineup, the first man to go through the door after breaching. No one ever wanted Poz One. Except for Chief. As a soldier, back during his enlisted days, that was the position he preferred above all others.

The doorman was responsible for knocking down the door or blowing the charge that took the door off its hinges, depending on which way the door swung. And depending on the mission, any number of men was lined up to sequentially go through the door with specific responsibilities upon entering the room to secure the location. Poz One was historically believed to be the most dangerous and fatal of all the positions. But for Chief, in his demented and compromised brain, it was the comfort position. The position that gave him the most freedom to conduct hostile fire, and he loved being there, up front, first one through the door. He often joked that he had the best seat in the house. If you had to be there, might as well be in Poz One.

Every position in the stack had advantages. But there were also disadvantages to consider. Not everyone understood that concept. Disadvantages, in Chief's book, most men thought of as advantageous to their survival. While most of the men concentrated on their own personal protection, using the man in front as a shield, using their equipment in differing ways to defend themselves. From Chief's perspective they were all disadvantages. Any place other than Poz One was restrictive and problematic when operational tempo exceeded someone's capability to move, shoot and communicate.

Poz One, on the other hand, was completely exposed to enemy contact. Just the way Chief liked it. Poz One gave him freedom. Pure, unadulterated freedom in a chaotic and extreme situation. Each subsequent position in the stack effectively limited the zone of fire the man in that position could use. Every man in the stack had to be concerned with preventing friendly fire. No one wanted to injure a Team Member, nor be accused of shooting their comrades in the back, or lower extremities and feet. So any place behind Poz One had it's own set of problems to consider and mitigate.

For Chief, Poz One was the only place to be. It gave him the freedom to pick targets, gave him a free fire zone that included the entire room, gave him the room to move, advance and accelerate at will and engage the hostiles with everything he had. There was one other secret to Poz One that he'd never shared with anyone else. Not even others who enjoyed and routinely volunteered to take the first position. He dearly enjoyed the adrenaline. Facing fear, taking it head on and living through the consequences of being the first one through the door, is what made him tick. That was what he lived for. He knew the feeling of having his ears burn, blood draining from his face and overwhelming heat being released from his soul in a Nano-second. That is what the adrenaline did for him. It made him painless. He felt alive, invincible, and confident. He knew that physically he was vulnerable, but it no longer made sense to hide from the inevitable. Death would come to every man. To Chief, the only thing that mattered was how honorable that death would be.

The mission was simple and required very little thinking. Go to a specific grid square, find the bad guys, set up a perimeter so no one could get away, and take the bad guys down. That meant kicking down the door if necessary and bringing the bad guys out dead or alive. But preferably with no casualties or injuries on the side of the good guys. That was the routine every soldier on Tier One would practice throughout their lives. Law enforcement the world over did the exact same thing, regardless of echelon, County, State or Federal. Things were no different with Tier One HVT takedowns.

On his very first mission, Chief was in Poz One when he was shot in the chest immediately upon entering the room. An AK-47 round from less than twenty feet away slammed into his chest and it scared the living hell out of him at first. At over two thousand, four hundred feet per second, the 7.62 by 39mm round's kinetic energy was staggering. The full impact hit Chief dead center of his ceramic trauma prevention plates. It felt like someone had thumped him in the chest with a jackhammer, sending him staggering to the rear by a few feet.

Although the plates had stopped the round from penetrating into his thoracic cavity, puncturing organs and causing catastrophic and fatal damage, his body absorbed the full impact. Had the round impacted slightly off center, some of the velocity and kinetic energy would have dissipated as his body rotated. But this was a full on, head on collision with a projectile destined to kill him. And he survived. The man who fired it didn't.

The term "Baptism by fire" took on a whole new meaning now. His body armor had done its job and stopped the bullet. The physical damage to his body was limited to deep tissue and bruises, some internal bleeding, but the damage to his mind was irreparable. Chief was hooked. It was a religious experience he would never get over. In a blink of an eye, too much transpired for the human mind to comprehend. But what Chief experienced in that brutal, life changing moment, cauterized the warrior into his soul and sealed his fate. Maybe later on he could articulate what it was that captivated him so deeply, so securely. But for now, the only thing he could say was "Fukin Whooah!"

The sound was so loud Chief's ears and brain went into defense mode and shut down. He no longer heard the explosions coming from the muzzle, but he felt the supersonic shock waves hit him as the skin on his face flexed, relented and allowed the shock waves to pass through to his soul. The reverberation was devastating at first, but later became the object of his obsession. All he could hear was his own breath, his own heart beat and he craved that impact feeling, daring each target to shoot him as he entered the room. Chief verbally taunted each target as he entered the room, begging them to lock horns and take him on. He craved the smell of cordite and gunpowder in the air. The sounds, the smells, the anarchy and the monstrous endorphin release all combined in a split second to quench the overwhelming fear and anxiety that built up in his soul just prior to going through the door. All those things combined to feed the animal within. A monster that grew bigger, badder and more uncontrollable with every mission. The monster that eventually would require his full attention. But for now, that animal within, that monster was a welcome addition to his war chest. Black and enormous were the only words to describe the demon they all knew as Fear. The internal monster in each man's soul needed grooming to become the equivalent and cancel the Fear. To be overpowering and conquer Fear. There had to be balance. Yet at this young age, each soldier had to find it on his own and bring it forward.

The bullet to his chest released Chief into a new realm, a realm where Fear no longer existed. The unintended consequence of which had given Chief a sense of peace and calm that he would crave forever more the same freedom he felt as a boy when his own father shot him with a 12 gauge shotgun during a fit of rage in the fields near his home during hunting season. That night, so very long ago when Chief was merely eight years old, he slept like a baby. The best he ever slept in his young lifetime. At 8 years old, Chief was too young to understand, but now he was in his mid twenties and he knew for sure that the impact he just experienced from the 7.62 AK-47 round was what had given him the peace he so desperately sought. Other missions, when he didn't take any rounds to his vest, left Chief wanting, depressed, unimpressed with his adversaries. And he couldn't wait till the next mission came. He was on the Gerbil Wheel of endorphin seeking. Others knew the same sickness. Adrenaline junkies that went sky diving, rock climbing and big wave surfing. But when it came to the most addictive type of action, getting shot was as good as it got.

Chief's new nickname soon spread like wildfire in a high wind. "Psycho". Everyone assumed, since Chief had taken a round in the chest, that on the very next mission someone else would be assigned to Poz One. But Chief would have none of that. Poz One belonged to him now. And everyone soon knew it.

Kick Starting a Blackhawk

"Ya can't fix stupid, but you can laugh at it!"

Life Lesson Nr. 3

A nine-hour flight over endless desert sand was finally coming to a close. The 130 degree heat was exhausting, the bird needed maintenance, the Team was ready to get out and stretch and Chief was on his last nerve with the constant vibration of the overhead rotors and noise of the huge, twin, 1400 horse power turbine engines. There was still plenty more flying to do to get to their target destination, but a much needed and much welcomed overnight rest stop at King Khaleed Military City, KKMC, was in order.

U.S. Air Force personnel at the brand new facility knew a "Ghost Flight" was coming in, the cover term for something out of the ordinary that had no flight plan, no set arrival time and nothing would be kept in the log books to reflect that any aircraft had actually landed. The ground crew waited impatiently for the bird to land so they could refuel the aircraft, check the air filters and rotors for any sand damage or lamination failures. The Air Force personnel didn't like doing maintenance on rotary winged aircraft. That was for Army personnel. They preferred fast movers, jets. But they didn't ask question either. They just found the qualified personnel, even if that meant hiring civilians for a few months. It wasn't worth the hassle fighting the system. So they resolved themselves to doing whatever was needed. Even for "Spooks".

The airfield was not fully manned yet by Saudi Arabian military personnel. Nor was construction even complete. The white marble buildings were brand new and an army of foreign workers was finishing the final touches on windows and doors, adding reflective film to all the glass to ensure cooler internal temperatures and scurrying around cleaning everything in sight. Outside temperatures soared since there was absolutely nothing in this part of the desert for shade.

The remote location wasn't chosen strictly for the relative convenience to other parts of Saudi Arabia, but rather to keep prying eyes of the locals from seeing who came and went. That was a constant concern to the Royal family under continual scrutiny by the deeply Islamic fundamental Wahabbi tribe of Saudi Arabia. The Royal Family built this place and it looked like a five star hotel, something that irked the Wahabbi leaders as contrary to the word of Allah and the message of the Prophet Muhammed. Gold plated ornaments inside stood in stark contrast to the goat manure and sand outside. King Fahd and his royal offspring and siblings were used to having their way. Their oil rich heritage dictated their lifestyle. Keeping the peasants at bay and uninitiated to the comings and goings of their visitors was paramount to keeping peace in the Kingdom as well as to their own personal survival. KKMC was critical to that survival. And Chief and his Team were there to exploit that weakness.

The runways were recently finished in smooth concrete. U.S. Air Force units had taken over the real estate and Commanders were still getting used to all of the foreign workers on site. Almost all of them were North Korean nationals shipped into Saudi Arabia and three quarters of those were forced labor serving jail sentences. They'd been bought and paid for by the Saudi government. Not a problem for the Saudis, but exponentially complicating the problems the U.S. Air Force encountered.

It was important to the House of Saud security that foreign nationals build this airport. That way, the Saudis could control every aspect of construction and every aspect of the workers' lives from what they saw, to whom they spoke to. The added benefit of having a North Korean/Saudi language barrier was fine with everyone involved until the Americans showed up. Then it became a serious problem to operations intended to protect the Kingdom against the impending Iraqi invasion.

There were cultural differences besides the obvious language barriers. But the biggest problem was trying to get the workers to understand intricate technical details about lighting and electricity. The American and British electrical engineers had complicated schematics in front of them, but the problems got worse when everything was translated from English to Arabic to Korean and back into English. How was anything expected to work when the electricians working to power up the airfield light systems, radars, and air traffic control towers had no idea what each other were saying?

The fact that they were not very far from Babylon made Chief snicker under his breath. Listening to higher Command bitch and moan about being so far behind schedule and hearing the "underlings in charge" try to explain the translation problems made Chief come to the conclusion that this entire thing was a bad idea after all. He knew this airfield was a critical node for combat operations that were most likely being planned as he listened to the ongoing Keystone Cops routine at the tarmac. Maybe it would just be better to bring in the combat engineers used to dealing with lighting and approach radar issues in a combat environment. After all, those were the combat experts who were used to dealing with power problems, lighting and approach radar issues where there were no airfields. That was their specialty. That's what they did for a living. But it wasn't his call. It just made Chief wonder what he was getting into as they boarded the Blackhawk Helicopters and headed into the desert. At least with the helicopters, he wouldn't have to worry about air traffic controllers or landing at night! Tom Kennedy was his taxi driver again, one of the experts from Task Force 160, the Night Stalkers.

U.S. Commanders had a mission. And that was to get the place operational so the lead wing of A-10s, F117s, B1B and B2 Stealth Bombers had a place to land and refuel. Since nothing was complete, other agreements had to be made with Yemeni Government Officials. Usama Bin Laden offered to secure the two Holy Cities within Saudi Arabia with his "Mujahideen", warriors of Allah. But after several top-level meetings with the US Secretary of State and Defense Secretary, the King decided to let the Infidels into the Kingdom. And that really pissed off not only Bin Laden, but also the entire Muslim world especially the Wahhabis of Saudi Arabia. The house of Saud was charged with protecting the two holy cities of Islam. Mecca and Medina. And now, the King universally known as the "Custodian of the two Holy Mosques" was allowing Infidels to enter into the country by the thousands. There would be repercussions for this transgression. The consequences of this blasphemy would be staggering.

Written off as fanatical fundamentalist posturing, the Saudi Government turned its attention to Desert Shield and Desert Storm. But the Yemenis took the cake when it came to psycho, fanatical Jihadist behavior. The Saudi government made sure that Yemen would only see the overflow planes. Only those that wouldn't fit at KKMC, or those that needed specialized bunkers. Very few in the US had even seen the new F117 Nighthawks. The rest of the world had heard the rumors, but not too many believed it. So these top of the line Stealth Fighters really were received as "UFOs" outside the country.

American Military Commanders, now in charge at this far away place, were used to giving orders and getting results highly professional and efficient results. But they were all "guests" to King

Fahd and the people of Saudi Arabia. So they were expected to politely accommodate ALL the cultural differences with a smile.

The female issue however was almost a deal breaker. The locals didn't believe in women in their armed forces, so when a U.S. Air Force Dolly Parton look alike with a 45 triple "D" set of boobs in a T Shirt came walking by, she damn near shut down Desert Storm simply by walking past several high level dignitaries who were coordinating with the U.S. Commanders over the Muslim tradition of tea. They were all obviously very impressed initially. She was a knock out. But the resulting silence was a huge indicator that their Muslim sensitivities had just been insulted. Especially since they were in public and were caught gawking at the very impressive mammary glands. From that point on, everyone, men included, were required to wear a complete uniform at all times, buttoned to the neck, sleeves down and buttoned at the wrist. In 130-degree heat, things were about to get uncomfortable. The unexpected consequence was that fewer soldiers got heat stroke and sunburn. A lesson the locals learned centuries ago, not lost on Chief and his men. Keep your skin covered and you have a much better chance of survival in the hostile desert environment.

The baby powder consistency of the dirt and sand that swirled below the low flying Blackhawk changed from time to time as topography changed. There were real problems with composite rotor blades de-laminating as the sand granules blasted the leading edges that swiped through the air trying to gain lift. As long as the aircraft was in a tail positive attitude during flight, most of the rotor wash would go down, back and away from the open doors of the aircraft. But every once in a while, headwinds and low altitudes would force those sand granules into the passenger compartments of the bird, sand blasting the occupants, stinging their skin and leaving grit in their mouths to crunch between their teeth when they talked. It didn't take long for everyone to automatically shut their mouths and cover their faces with scarves. It was too hard to talk over the noise of the turbines and rotors. Everyone was bundled up against the penetrating sand anyway, so any conversation other than instructions from the flight crew was just not worth it. Eventually, the pattern became habitual. No one ever talked. And when something needed to be said, there were long pauses between sentences, consciously deciding what to say in the fewest words possible.

Human comfort was compromised in this area of the desert by high temperatures. Chief and his Team had trained for that, and after so many mission sets in the desert, they were used to the sand and heat. But the toxic fumes and disgusting smell of the JP4 jet fuel compounded the heat. Frequently, soldiers on board the Blackhawks would vomit from the hot exhaust gases of the huge turbine engines reaching into their stomachs, making them nauseated, burning their lungs and esophagus. No matter how long a man conducted Airborne or Air Assault Operations, no one ever really got used to the JP4 smell.

Medically, the smell was a real concern. Vomiting contributed to even more dehydration. Eventually everyone got diarrhea on top of that, just from being in the desert environment, but more often because of the bacteria in the sand. So dehydration and heat stroke was a real concern as well as keeping everyone healthy enough to conduct missions. The Team Medic had his hands full keeping track of everyone's water intake. With the ever-looming threat of Chemical Weapons attack, donning personal protective equipment, charcoal suits with rubber boots and gloves became more frequent in practice and a greater concern causing more unwanted stress throughout the day. The ever present threat kept everyone aware of where their protective mask was, and more often than anyone liked, the chemical alarms malfunctioned causing everyone to startle, don their MOPP gear and wait out the process to determine if it again was a false alarm, or if there actually were toxic chemicals in the air.

The realization that most countries in this region didn't have an Environmental Protection section in their governments meant that anyone could and did dump anything they didn't have a use for, out in the desert. This seemingly uninhabited and pristine desert environment in reality was a toxic waste dump. Things were beginning to suck more and more each day.

Coming to King Khaled Military City (KKMC) was a true pleasure at times. The very first trip Chief made to this "Disneyland of the Desert" was impressive. Huge swirls of sand dunes, scalloped at the top looking like huge piles of frosting on a cake, decorated the horizon to the East as the Blackhawk approached the tarmac and runway surrounding the expansive military compound from the West. As Chief and his men came in for final approach, less than 30 minutes of daylight remained until sunset. The rapidly diminishing sunlight played vivid color games on the scalloped dunes. As the Blackhawk came in, making the mandatory approach dictated by the air traffic control tower, the Blackhawk lost altitude and flew just feet above the desert floor. From that angle, the light changed quickly and dramatically from minute to minute. The kaleidoscope of desert color was awe-inspiring.

The mood on the combat Helicopter suddenly changed as the bright orange sunset reflected against the brown and tan hues of the desert sand, casting an amazing pallet of colors onto the landscape below. Everyone on board seemed to perk up and chattered about the view after the seemingly endless flight in near total silence. The scenery out the windows of the Blackhawk doors was literally the most beautiful thing anyone had seen since coming to the Persian Gulf. Ripples on the tops of the dunes and gentle westerly slopes reminded everyone on the team of training days in the sands of

Silver Strand Beach outside of San Diego California and brought back a flood of memories. For the first time in a very long time, Chief heard his men start cracking jokes and telling stories of sharks and the misery they'd endured in the cold Pacific Ocean waters.

Chief slowly drifted into his own head as he watched the eastern view of these dunes and considered just how serious the winds could become at times, dropping off sand in piles that were up to a thousand feet high in some places, with steep overhanging ledges that would not support the weight of a man, never mind vehicles or aircraft. Smack in the middle of this amazing and color filled landscape seemingly immune to the wind and sand, was the huge white marble complex dedicated to King Khaled. The white marble, now immersed in bright orange light of the setting sun, stood in stark contrast against the purple, tan, orange and yellow colors of the dunes. Combined with the ever-changing brown hues of the desert sand, the view was truly something to behold.

Behind the complex lay a six thousand foot long runway capable of supporting any aircraft the world had to offer. Lined up along the concrete runway was yet another view to behold. One hundred and ten of America's finest close air support aircraft, the A10 Warthog, lined up over the mile long Tarmac frontage.

"Fuckin' WHOOOAH!" came a voice over the intercom as the Warthogs came into view, their huge shark grins painted across the front of the aircraft from wing to wing with bright white, razor sharp pointed teeth contrasting against the red background and the dark grey green paint on the rest of the titanium honeycomb fuselage.

"That's what I'm talking about!" came another voice, followed by more animated chatter.

"Talk about a force multiplier! I'm damn glad those guys are on OUR side!"

The awe-inspiring sight brought a new level of enthusiasm to the very bored, very tired Team. A10s were lined up wing tip to wing tip with support equipment beside each one for almost a mile along the runway. Everything was pristine and set up as if on display at an air show. The crew chief's stand-alone ladder, which they used to get into the cockpit without touching the skin of the aircraft was mimicked next to every aircraft down the entire runway. Support vehicles full of batteries, used to run up the engines and test out the aircraft before each mission, were parked perfectly aligned in front of each Warthog. And along side the starboard side of the plane, six-foot tall red metal tool boxes stood, filled with specialized equipment to maintain, fuel and arm this beast of the sky. At the nose of the bird, directly under the cockpit and near the ladder, stood large red fire extinguishing canisters on standby in case anything went bad. The logistics alone for shipping all of this ancillary equipment to Saudi Arabia was staggering. But it was also an indicator of just how serious things were getting. Regardless of the Intelligence ISA had, indicating that an internal military coupe could topple Saddam without any military units being deployed to the Persian Gulf, everything Chief saw indicated his collection and analysis was falling on deaf ears. The US was going to war for the first time since Vietnam. And they were going all in!

During the Cold War, the Soviets called the A10 the Devil's Cross based on the aircrafts unbelievable maneuverability. The pilot could turn the aircraft on a dime at almost full speed. When they pulled such a maneuver, reversing direction on one wingtip, the plane's silhouette against the sky looked like a large crucifix. The firepower and devastation that this Mach 1 capable ground support aircraft rained down on tanks, anti-aircraft weapons systems and personnel was truly menacing and helped it earn the reputation among U.S. forces as a "Pepto" dispenser. One of several sick humor referrals to the pink foam explosions the aircraft left in its wake that were formerly humans.

* * * * *

Catastrophic dune avalanches just outside the airfield perimeter were reported by the local military assigned to KKMC. Keeping the runways clear of sand was a full time task similar to what most airfield maintenance crews were used to in places like Alaska and northern states in the U.S. with one minor difference. The Temperature. You didn't go out there unless you knew what you were doing. A few rednecks from N. C. had decided the dunes were their personal playground and had taken two Hummers to the top of the dunes for pictures and some off-road four wheeling fun. They paid dearly when the sand gave way, tumbling the 100 thousand dollar tactical vehicle to the bottom of a 500 foot valley, then decidedly burying it with it's four wheel drive, quickly followed by tons more sand from the resulting avalanche. They were damned lucky no one died.

Chief decided their punishment, after losing this very expensive combat equipment, was to recover the sensitive items they'd left in the vehicle. The vehicle alone was worth over 100 thousand dollars US. But the radios, encryption devices and weapons put the price tag close to half a million.

Every waking hour they were not on duty at the air base, they spent out in the sand digging with their tactical folding shovels trying to recover what clearly would be a prize to any foreign national living in the area. Most of the locals knew it was a lost cause. Allah himself would have to move those dunes in order to get to the trucks. The night time winds routinely filled in whatever headway the soldiers made during the day, and the relentless 130 degree day time temperatures kept the men humble. But it was better to press on in an attempt to recover said equipment than face a Courts Martial, a permanent copy of which would stay in their records, halting any career advancement and registering high dollar fines they'd spend the rest of their careers trying to pay off.

Chief had given them an option. Dig, or face a Courts Martial for dereliction of duty and Conduct Unbecoming a Non-Commissioned Officer. He could have charged them with much more, but decided that digging would be therapeutic, giving them time to reflect on their stupidity and impulsive behavior. So now, it was all on them. They made the choice and Chief made sure they got the message. There were consequences for losing focus on the mission!

In the end, Chief would write everything off as a "combat loss", report the crypto gear as being destroyed vs. compromised and since no one was dead, the mandatory accountability reporting criteria was localized to the immediate Chain of Command. There was a silver lining to this problem after all. Higher command could change the encryption codes so even if by some chance the gear was recovered, it would be useless. The soldiers who had taken the joy ride learned their lesson, and in turn, they were a shining example to everyone else of what happens when you're on Chief's Team, or associated by being in support of his Team, and didn't take their presence in a foreign country seriously. They were ALL there for a reason. And it was not to have fun or go blow around the desert burning up fuel, nor surfing Hummers over sand dunes.

* * * * *

Chief was looking forward to a few hours down time without the constant drum beat of rotors overhead. He had a headache now. His body complained about things he didn't understand anymore. There were too many old injuries, scar tissue, and stab wounds, bullet holes, burning joints, and cramped muscles to contend with. This was a young man's game. He was 32 now. Most of his Team were barely in their twenties. Where had the time gone? The fast paced lifestyle of Special Operations, training, the East Bloc missions, the War on Drugs, all filled his brain storage to capacity. But he never had time to process it all. Some day he would have time. But not today.

The Blackhawk finally touched down with a gentle thump and relief suddenly overwhelmed everyone on board as the turbine whine ceased and the rotors came to a slow grinding halt. Comments about the much welcomed silence seemed to dominate the conversations as everyone exited the aircraft, stretching their legs and arms, yawning as they unconsciously scanned the perimeter for hostiles. Some habits were never intended to be broken. Everyone was exhausted. But they were still warriors. And muscle memory dictated their unintended actions.

Chief was the last one to unplug his headset, a routine he'd come to practice after many a mission. He'd learned a lot listening to both pilot and air traffic command and control over those headsets during the past several years on deployments.

Every man on this team knew how to exit a Blackhawk, with or without the rotors moving overhead. They were trained to always move 90 degrees straight out away from the aircraft doors, limiting a man's exposure to the relentless rotor wash and ensuring they didn't come into contact with the nearly invisible tail rotor that spun to the rear of the doorway at the end of the boom. More than one "newbie" had experienced either a near miss or been chopped to bits in seconds by ignoring this simple yet seriously important ingress and egress technique. By the time soldiers got to this level, to Chief's Team, the muscle memory was ingrained deeply. It was time to get some shuteye. Daylight would come too soon and they all knew it.

* * * * *

The sudden realization and consciousness that the sun was rising struck Chief as he went to find Gunny and jostled his shoulder to wake him. Six hours of down time had come and gone. Power naps were precious now at his age. After only three hours sleep, Chief unconsciously groaned like an old dog and raised his tired body from the cold concrete floor of the hangar. He went into the SCIF and logged in, allowing everyone else to sleep a bit longer. Once inside, time flew by as he downloaded orders and "Request for Intelligence Information" (RIIs) and studied terrain, satellite images and the "Black, White and Grey" lists of personnel they were sure to come in contact with on the next mission. After three more hours of intelligence work, Chief made his way to the SCIF door, walked outside the hangar and moved towards the six inch PVC tubing and gravel that stuck out of the ground in a nearby clearing. These were makeshift urinals intended to contain sewerage in a single location. Although the waste fluids would evaporate in seconds out here in the desert, the left over particulates eventually would build up and become a problem if every Joe Schmuck decided to just whip it out and take a leak anywhere in the area. Especially since the very near future plan included tens of thousands of soldiers and airmen eventually occupying this place.

The sanitation regulations were not lost on the Team after what they'd experienced with toxins out in the desert and so many cities around the world that had no sewerage whatsoever. But Chief made sure everyone followed the rules. After all, they were being watched. Maybe these stone aged heathens that called themselves "locals" would learn something from watching their conduct. Probably not, but there was no reason for Chief or his Team to do anything different than what they normally did.

Chief returned to the hangar and was met with a cup of coffee, something he hadn't seen in over two months. The aroma caught him off guard and made the hair on the back of his neck stand up. Comfort and self-indulgence were human traits that Chief and his men shied away from. This coffee was a genuine luxury and it took Chief by surprise, something that didn't happen very often. He hated surprises. But this surprise even Chief had to admit was pretty nice. The gesture from Gunny, Chief knew was heart felt, which made things all the more appreciated.

"Damn Gunny, ya make me wanna marry you man!" Chief said surprising even himself.

"Chief musta had a wet dream last night, he's in a good mood today." murmured someone still yawning and trying to muster the gumption to get up and get moving.

"Won't last. Enjoy it while you can." came another low, sleepy voice in nearly a whisper. Suddenly, with the words barely exchanged, the space within the hangar erupted as if an incoming mortar had blown the roof off.

"On your FEET!" bellowed Gunny in an explosive voice.

In seconds, every man scrambled to his feet, stood at attention, with utter shock on his face. They didn't expect soft-handed treatment all the time, but they were not expecting this either. Whatever set Gunny off, it must be serious. He was pissed!

"Front leaning rest position... MOVE!" came the next command. Every man dropped on his face into the push up position.

"In Cadence... Exercise! One, two, three," came the cadence. The Team sounded off loudly, in unison.

"ONE!"

"One, two, three...." Gunny continued barely able to contain the hostility that raged in his heart. He heard what was meant in jest. But it wasn't funny. It just pissed him off. No one got to talk shit about Chief. The entire Team didn't know Chief's background the way Gunny did. They didn't "need to know". The bottom line, Gunny had Chief's six. And these young pups were going to learn a very painful lesson this morning!

"TWO!", they were louder now. At the end of fifty, four count push-ups, the desired effect was obvious. The men were panting, heart rates were up, blood flow and oxygen to the brain increased, and attention... Well, their mental state had radically changed.

Gunny had the undivided attention of this Team as well as the ten or so Air Force maintenance men inside the hangar. Known as Zoomies, a pet name all the other services had for Air Force pukes, they were considered outsiders to the Tier One Team. The contrast between services was not very noticeable, especially at the "regular unit level", until it came to physical training. The Air Force left it up to each Unit Commander to decide if they conducted PT as a cohesive unit, or if each man was left to his own devices. As long as the men passed the annual test, most Air Force Commanders relented and allowed individuals to take personal responsibility for their physical condition. The end of year PT Test would answer the mail on their integrity. Most of them passed with flying colors having spent the entire year doing their physical training on their own. But for Special Operations, everything was done as a Team. Esprit De Corp, the underlying competition and the participation as a unit was well defined in the history of Warriors. This was a rare spectacle that didn't make much sense to the Zoomie onlookers. Corporal punishment, after all, was an entirely different mentality from the Air Force. The Zoomies watched with genuine interest and humor, knowing instinctively they would gain the wrath of Gunny if he heard them snickering. What the Air Force pukes witnessed, profiled in their minds as punishment, not Esprit De Corps or team building.

"Now, which one of you maggots has a problem with Chief this morning?" came the rhetorical question everyone knew was coming, from a man who already knew the answer.

"One of you maggots think you can disrespect our esteemed leader without repercussion? Without facing him and looking him in the eye? Which one of you dirt bags thinks its OK to talk shit behind his back?"

Everyone knew who mumbled the lame joke about Chief. Two of their team mates, one instigator, another sucked into it. They were just bantering back and forth as they tried to shuck off the mind numbing feeling that very few hours of sleep left within their brains. There was no malice intended. But allowing their mouths to run without their brain fully engaged was how problems began. Innocent comments or disgruntled opinions sucking in another, then another, eventually breeding discontent within the Team was tantamount to treason. Stopping the bullshit in its tracks was essential. Situations like this were not the norm. But this Team was relatively new, they were still sorting each other out and even though they respected Chief, Gunny was there to impress upon them that Chief was "God" in their lives. He knew after all that everyone on the Team was a human. But now, in view of what he's just heard, Gunny was here to make sure nothing like it ever arose to be stopped again.

"Next time I hear anything close to resembling disrespect to your Team Leader and Commander will be met with unspeakable pain and suffering. Are we CLEAR?" Gunny demanded in a clear, level, stern voice that echoed off the hangar walls. He didn't have to yell. Everyone was focused now.

"Whooah Sergeant!" responded the entire Team in unison between short intervals of breathing.

"Fall out for Church!" came the next command, referring to the daily religious experience. Eyes rolled, but no one said a word, knowing full well they were in for a fifteen mile run. Not everyone was ready for the run. Their eyes were barely open when they were jolted into consciousness. Only Chief had gotten to take a leak. The unspoken lesson here was that everyone would endure the agony of running with a full bladder without comment because of the one wise ass that had spoken out of turn with disrespect in his voice. The two "newbies" never intending to be disrespectful, were just documenting what they thought to be reality. Now they were learning that their opinions didn't count, no matter how accurate or truthful.

Chief hardly ever smiled. That was a fact. But making snide remarks about it was NOT going to be tolerated, especially by Gunny. He already picked out the weakness the newbies brought to the table. Bitching was one of them. They would pay dearly later on. If not today, soon. Everyone knew who it was that had let their mind wander and speak out of turn and aloud. There had been prior occasions. Although Chief commanded respect simply by his presence, men got tired, bored, angry, sore, and verbalization of mundane whining was part of the human condition. Chief's Team Sergeant didn't put up with that kind of bullshit. No one on the Team was human in his mind. Not like the rest of the herd on the planet anyway. And whining was not tolerated, no matter how you dressed it up.

"Gunny, do a short one and get back here. We are wheels up in an hour" Chief said in a low tone, ensuring no one heard him or could mistake his command as taking sympathy on them. He was genuinely enjoyed the morning sunrise. Very seldom was there ever time to just live in the moment. His mind drifted to his two sons as he read the Intelligence Update that came in overnight instead of a newspaper, drinking what was obviously instant Nescafe' coffee left over from an MRE bag. Seldom did Chief ever have time to heat up water, mix the coffee, or add cream and sugar, never mind have time to take in a morning sunrise. He was usually in the SCIF, or four floors underground by the time the sun came up. The normal routine while deployed was to keep a stash of MRE coffee, chocolate beverage powder, cream and sugar in the outside pocket of his ruck. It was a stash he hardly ever used for his own personal comfort, but kept it as part of his incentive packet, right next to the Tampons and Superglue he carried in case of bullet wounds. The upper right hand pocket on his ruck was reserved for his Team, the left one for local nationals and kids he might run into that needed schmoozing. That's where the cocoa beverage powder came in.

The routine copied throughout the military was to stuff a wad of instant coffee into the lower lip along with some Red Man tobacco and Winter Green Snuff, mixing it with saliva into a wet ball of brown goo. This gave a man the caffeine and nicotine his body craved, but also acted as an appetite suppressant keeping hunger pains at bay. Instead of spitting out the juice from the snuff and tobacco, it was swallowed. The instant coffee gave it a slightly less bitter taste going down, and the wintergreen gave it all a better aroma and taste when burped back up. The long-term effects were still to be seen. Chief already had several perforated ulcers, a medically disqualifying condition he convinced the doctors to lose the paperwork on.

It was rare that Chief actually got to *drink* his coffee. This was a special day. Gunny knew it to be special too, and honored it by surprising Chief. It was the closest thing he could manage to breakfast in bed. No one else on the Team had a clue that Chief was celebrating his "Alive Day" in total silence and remembrance to all those fallen soldiers Chief accumulated during his career. Everyone had a "Birthday" to celebrate. Only the lucky ones had an "Alive Day".... the day they died and came back to life. Chief already had one of each. But very few knew about it. Too many years and too many bad habits were catching up to Chief now. The writing was on the wall; he just didn't want to read it yet. The end of his career was near. After all, life was short. It could all be over in a second. The "golden BB moment" awaited them all, something Chief had told every man on the Team more than once. And when the new soldiers came in, the youngest man on the Team was tested again having to repeat the story to the new guys.

Many years prior, he'd had a discussion with an old British SAS Major while conducting Counter Terrorist missions behind the Iron Curtain. Chief was in his late teens or early twenties then and like all soldiers that age, was tired of the constant operations tempo that kept them deployed, in harms way and incessantly alert to the life threatening situations they found themselves in. The men had been sitting around talking about their mortality and how to deal with the strong emotions that crept into every man's dreams, knowing any one of them could die at any time. Major Bone, the old grey haired one with too many covert missions to count, had listened to the banter go around the group of fairly new soldiers to Special Operations, listening to theories of "when your number is up" and other such rhetoric when he decided to insert his considerable mentorship, personal opinions and theory on the subject.

"We are *all* subject to the Golden B.B. moment gentlemen!" he said in a strong Scottish accent, accentuated for effect in this case.

"You could be flying in a super sonic fighter jet at Mach 3 anywhere in the world when some cunty fires a BB into the sky with no intended target in mind, straight up into the air, and you could fly directly into it and nail yourself between the eyes at Mach 3. That would be the end of it. And there is absolutely nothing you can do to prevent it. So, make up your minds. You are either going to bemoan and worry yourself into a frenzy about your time and dying, or resign yourself to the Golden B.B. and get on with it."

That speech stuck with Chief forever more, along with the "How long is a piece of string" comment and a few other life altering statements Major Bone had gifted to Chief.

"It's as long as you make it... you have the option of cutting it to any length. So is it with bullshit in your life. How long you put up with it is totally up to you!"

Now that was pure wisdom and mentorship worth keeping!

The noise of turbine engine whine brought Chief back to reality from his daydream state of mind. It was time to shake off the lingering fog that the very few hours of sleep left in his head and get into combat mode again. Although they'd been on the ground for six hours, by the time Chief finished his nightly routine of cleaning weapons, sensitive items checks, communications to higher, reading and sending intel updates, he was lucky to close his eyes for three. He was up again before anyone else. Most nights, it was just easier to stay up than to fight off the sleep while trying to get re-started the following day.

The rotors slowly began to turn, responding to the electric over hydraulic starting mechanisms that wound up the rotors until the turbine engines could take over. Pilot and crew were busy getting the aircraft ready to deploy, checking radios, radars, instruments along with every other aspect of the now refueled Blackhawk which was now dressed out with an extra four hundred gallons of fuel, contained within twin external fuel tanks. No one on the ground crew knew where this bird was going. But the external fuel tanks were an indicator they were going somewhere a long, long ways away. Within minutes, it was fully operational and working it's way up to operating temperature. The maintenance crews had been awake and working throughout the dark night, checking filters, attaching the external tanks, looking at leading edges of the rotors to ensure nothing would come apart in flight, replacing whatever needed to be replaced, priding themselves on a ZERO failure rate within their Aviation Wing for two years running. The Night Stalkers worked side by side with their Air Force counter parts, but instead of a myriad of specialty aircraft, they focused on rotary winged aircraft that were direct support vehicles to Special Operations. Not only were the pilots second to none, the crew chiefs and maintenance personnel were world class as well. Chief had been around long enough to know who was who and had seen several of the men come up through the ranks from Private E-Nothings to their current positions as Senior Non-Commissioned Officers.

Two of the pilots on this mission had been Chief's taxi drivers on many prior missions in places no one ever talked about. Today was a special day, and it comforted Chief to know that some of his closest confidants were in the cockpit this wonderful morning.

"Hey! Do I know you?" came a voice immediately after Chief plugged his helmet into the intercom port.

"It was an elevator in Chicago back in 1963 wasn't it?" the dry humor, a signature of Chief Warrant Officer Tom Kennedy, callsign Extortion One One, now the senior W4 in the Army Aviation Regiment. His callsign came from the incredibly brave feats of flight during some of the hairiest missions, "Extorting" the air to his will as he dropped into extract "Teams" under heavy hostile fire. With nearly 32 years of Active Federal Service, Tom retired twice already, only to be called back to Active Duty in time of war. He really was the best of the best having served multiple tours in Bogata, Colombia, Honduras and the Middle East. He'd been in Somalia with Chief too, something neither man ever discussed.

"Yeah, the elevator... something like that...." Chief responded not wanting to get sucked into a long drawn out conversation these seemingly endless jokes always led to.

"Hey, what's the difference between the Army and the Boy Scouts" Tom started babbling over the intercom.

"Knock it off man, I'm having a really good morning believe it or not, so don't fuck it up. OK?" Chief spoke over him.

"Happy birthday by the way" came an honest and heart felt congratulations from the second seat pilot.

"The Boy Scouts have adult leaders!" Tom finished into the microphone anyway, instigating a snicker from Chief, forcing him to involuntarily shake his head.

"Thanks guys. I do appreciate it. Let's just go do this thing...." Chief responded ignoring the mistake about his birthday, hoping no one else on his Team would notice and try to engage him in conversation.

"WTF Gunny. I thought Chief was born on the fourth of July?" someone asked as they dropped their ruck into the Blackhawk and sat on the door sill waiting to be assisted with the rest of his gear getting past the door gunner and the massive mini-gun ammunition pod and belt retaining system.

"He was." Gunny responded without much interest.

"So WTF?" persisted the newbie. "It's not July!"

"You're a genius my man" replied Gunny, not letting on to the unspoken aspect of why Chief was being congratulated.

"Shut the fuck up and get in." Gunny said, refusing to expound any further on why it was a special day. "You don't have a need to know."

With that, the pilot rotated the collective and increased engine speed. The noise level increased as well. And Chief was thankful to use the noise as an excuse not to discuss the situation. Within ten seconds, the wheels were off the ground and the aircraft attitude changed. Nose down, tail up, forward momentum slowly took over and the bird followed the runway as if tied to the painted white center lines somehow. It was routine flight procedure on airport runways.

Two hours later, the Blackhawk was again over terrain that only GPS and instrumentation could differentiate from the hundreds of miles of terrain they'd already flown over. Although Chief completely trusted his pilot, co-pilot and crew, there were no contours, no terrain features, no buildings, anything to recognize or associate their position from. And the bland, sandy terrain made him wonder for a second if they were going in the right direction. Every once in a while, they caught a glimpse of a Bedouin tent sticking out of the sand. Brightly colored material propped up by poles and ropes sitting in the middle of nowhere duplicated the lifestyle of their ancestors from centuries prior. Chief smirked to himself when he overhead someone in the back ask, "What the hell is THAT doing all the way out here?"

"Goat herders tending their flocks. They live in those tents their entire life time." came an answer from one of the others, another Intel guy who'd taken the time to research the nation they were deploying to in an effort to understand customs and traditions. Simple things like learning the local customs always was a good thing and in several cases had meant the difference between a successful mission and one that ended in disaster.

Mogadishu was a prime example. The simple task of flying around with their boot soles showing to those on the ground had instigated a mass hysteria among the locals. An Imam at the local Mosque told everyone that the Americans were insulting the Muslims by showing the bottoms of their shoes. The American soldiers had no clue what a huge insult that was to Muslims. They were simply doing what they always did, sitting inside the Kiowa helicopters with their feet out on the landing skids. That was how the Kiowa deployed Special Operators and Rangers in an efficient and lethal manner. But the interpretation as an insult was more fuel on a nearly inextinguishable fire.

"So where the hell are the goats?" came another innocent question.

"Where the hell do you THINK they are you dumbass? In the tent, out of the heat!" came the answer with obvious impatience for stupidity.

"Damn. That's nasty man. How the hell do they tolerate the smell? Don't they shit on the carpet and stuff?" More of the same ignorance.

"You wonder why they all smell like goats?"

Chief just grinned as he listened. No one could see his face. No one knew he was listening. It was all he could do to keep from busting out laughing, and it warmed his heart to listen to the idle banter.

"You pulling my crank man? How many goats you think are in that tent?" The latent competition awakened and the bets were on.

"I bet there's at least twenty in there," said one.

"I bet there's more goats in there than people" said another.

"I'll bet you the guy has goats in the tent and his *wife* is outside somewhere instead of in there with him."

None of the banter had anything to do with anything. Chief let it go, simply because it broke the monotony. *So did the sudden alarms going off in his headset.*

"Break right, hit the dirt" came a calm yet firm and direct voice over the speaker. The aircraft suddenly lurched to the right and descended several hundred feet in altitude, rapidly into the desert sand.

"Where the hell did *that* come from?" came the voice from the co-pilot as he scrambled to ascertain the origin, type and location of the signal that had thrown the cockpit into disarray in an instant.

Tom Kennedy suspected, but waited for his second seat to bring up the automated recovery display on the dashboard.

"Fucking lock on. Some sort of camel jockey out there fucking around." Kennedy responded. "Replay the target master and give me some grids."

"Roger that", said the co-pilot without thinking. Training was kicking in and things were moving fast. Emotion and personal opinions cast aside as the data came up on the screen.

Kennedy pulled back on the stick and slowly but cautiously climbed in altitude, attempting to peak above the horizon without being completely exposed to the threat radar. The intense look on his face told Chief this was not some sort of lame practical joke Tom was famous for. Tom's face was dead serious with a glimpse of controlled ferocity he'd seldom seen. There was nothing to hide behind so Kennedy had to be careful. The lives of every man on board were in his hands and every decision he made could turn out to be his last. As the target master replayed the event, Tom got a completely different perspective and that changed the look on his face dramatically.

The initial data indicated that the weapon threat radar lock on signal had not come from above. That was a good thing. At least they didn't have to worry about some fast mover coming up behind him, or launching a missile from twenty miles away taking him out of the sky. Tom had several Hellfires on board at his command, but he really wanted to keep those for insertion and extraction time. The guys in the back were going to need them for cover fire, just in case. He calculated the amount of ammunition he had to feed into the nose canon. 30MM Gatling guns were really good for up close and personal engagements. But at the moment, his second seat was still trying to sort out who and what had locked onto him, so they could associate a plan of action to protect the aircraft and Chief's Team.

"Looks like it's ground based. Approximately two kilometers at heading 265 degrees left. Possible U.S Stinger Missile signature. Who the hell is out here fucking around with our stuff?" came the question no one was going to answer.

In ten seconds, Kennedy had the Blackhawk back up to 700 feet above the desert floor. In two more seconds, the alarms were going berserk again. Everyone in the back was at full alert.

"Get ready to bail gentlemen" Chief yelled over the engine noises. "We may have company."

"If this gets any worse, we're gonna have a long day ahead of us humping in on foot the rest of the way." Chief warned in that same low, controlled voice everyone knew. He only used it when the pucker factor was increasing. And right now, the pucker factor was way up.

"I'm gonna set her down till we find out what the hell is going on Chief. I'll call it in and have HQ determine via AWACS if we've got Indians in the area." Kennedy said over the mike.

No one but Chief, the crew chief and the second seat knew what was going on. They were the only ones with headsets plugged into the intercom port. Everyone else waited for the aircraft to land, and then instinctively did what they always did. They bailed out and set up a perimeter around the Blackhawk with fully locked and loaded weapons. Their heads were on a swivel now. All the banter was gone and the bullshit ceased. Until told otherwise, every man was in full combat mode. This bird was their ride in and out. This large chunk of metal alloy, specially constructed composites and massive turbine engines was the most critical item on their minds at the moment, their tie to the civilized world and their life support system while they were in hostile territory. Being on the ground made them vulnerable. And every man understood that concept. Their intention was to protect the bird at all costs. Their body language and facial expressions reflected just how serious they took this. The bird was their ride home, their survival. And whoever was locking on with a heat-seeking missile had just jeopardized their trip out of hostile territory. Someone just fucked up. Seriously!

As the Team deployed in a circular formation around the Blackhawk, everyone's eyes scanned the desert looking for hostiles trying to figure out what the hell was really going on. It didn't make sense that the radars set off the alarms, yet there was no smoke trail to indicate someone really was trying to shoot them down with a missile. Chief was talking to Tom and the co-pilot about the target master replay data when suddenly a small human appeared from the sand, his munchkin voice seemingly coming from nowhere, being absorbed by the sand and hostile environment as he yelled cordially across the desert. The crazy accent told every man on the Team that this hunyak must be an American who'd been raised in the deep South of the United States.

"What in tarnation you boys doin' way tah-hell ot cheer?" came the hick sounding inquiry.

"Contact left, 30 meters" Gunny said into his radio.

" Possible friendly" he followed up. "But debatable" he threw in, just to keep things light.

Chief's mind was spinning now. Who the hell was way out here, and why were they locking onto a U.S. Blackhawk Helicopter with a Stinger Missile System?

Someone was fucking up, and Chief was going to get to the bottom of it.

"Who's your Commanding Officer soldier?" demanded Chief as he hastily exited the aircraft. The engines were still winding down and it was difficult to hear this tiny man's voice over the whine of the turbines. Kennedy made the decision to shut down the engines and to keep his heat signature to a minimum, just in case. It was standard operations procedure to keep the engine running to retain maneuverability. But in this case, the radar index showed Kennedy that "heat seeking" was the primary mode of the threat weapon system. He shut down the engine without even asking Chief what he thought. Didn't matter. Kennedy was the Aircraft Commander, not the Mission Commander. And as long as the Team was on his aircraft, what Kennedy said was gospel.

"Lt Spindergrass is the Commander. He's somewhere over yonder. I kin gits em if you needs me to" the young U.S. Marine Corp Private responded.

Chief was pissed. Not how he wanted to be at the moment, but it was becoming quite obvious that some dickhead was really screwing up his perfect morning! One thing Chief hated was someone twisting his perfect day into a dog turd pretzel.

"What's your name son" came the next stern question out of Chief's mouth.

"Private Purdy Junior! Purdy K. Purdy... Junior. United States Marine Corp" came the response, giddy hillbilly southern drawl and all.

"What's the "K" stand for son?" Chief asked, regretting the question as soon as it came out of his mouth.

"Klemintine...with a "K".... Why? What's ur name dude?"

Dude. Another pet peeve Chief hated. This was turning bad faster than he ever imagined possible.

"Go find your Commanding Officer and bring him here Marine. We got things to talk about."

Chief watched the young boy fired himself up and took off like he was on a real mission.

"I can't wait to hear this one" Gunny mumbled into the microphone attached to his throat. "This ought to be good."

"Knock of the chatter gentlemen."

Chief had that tone. Everyone was on edge now.

"Get that bird ready to fire up. I think we found the problem, like that old saying goes, 'I have found the enemy, and he is us!' Get those rotors spinning. We're not gonna be staying long"

In less than a minute, Private Purdy Junior Purdy... Jr. had returned.

"LT said you come to him. He's in Command and don't take kindly to being told what to do. I kin show you where to go if ya wants me to."

Suddenly, the private stepped backward with fear on his face as if he'd just walked up on a rattlesnake. Chief watched the young man's Adam's apple snap in his throat as the Private swallowed hard, immediately recognizing a dramatic change in the air and realizing Chief wasn't in a very good mood. There was no rank on any one of the uniforms that dropped out of the sky via helicopter. No patches, no indicators anywhere for Private Purdy to glean any information about who was standing in front of him. Other than the fact there was a Blackhawk sitting in front of him, this Private had no concept of where the men were from, who these guys really were, or why they'd just landed smack dab in the middle of the Marine's training outpost.

"Ya gots problems with your whirly bird?" Private Purdy asked in all sincerity. A pathetic tremble in his voice betrayed his calm demeanor as Private Purdy tried desperately yet unconsciously to deflect the heat coming out of Chief's eyeballs. It was his immature, puberty cracking voice and that ignorant southern drawl that had Chief's head spinning, almost wondering if this was some sort of hidden camera reality TV show he'd been morphed into via some time warp they'd flown through. This was just unbelievable.

"Private, you go back and tell your Commanding Officer that if he's not standing in front of me in two minutes, life as he knows it will be over. Are we clear?"

Chief's patience was running thin now. They were burning daylight and losing critical flight time. There better be a damn good reason for one of these assholes to have locked on to his men and his taxi with a hot missile.

"Sure Dude. But I don't think he's gonna like it."

Gunny cut in on the comms link.

"I'll go with Chief. I think this asshole needs a wake up call."

"Roger. Just don't take all day. We got things to do, places to go" Chief warned. "Mean time, I'll get the bird fired back up and ready to roll."

Gunny was gone less than ten minutes and returned with a scrawny butter bar Lieutenant in tow.

"Hey Man. What's up. Purdy Junior tells me you guys got problems with your helicopter. That true?"

The LT was trying to cover his ass, knowing whomever had just dropped out of the sky probably outranked him by multiple levels, and according to the warning from Purdy, was obviously pretty pissed. Gunny introduced himself as the Master Gunnery Sergeant he was to this first year butter bar LT. And then Gunny gave him some very good career advice.

"I would highly recommend you come see this Team Commander on this Blackhawk. Cause if you keep fucking around and make him come find you, you're gonna be cleaning latrines at Ft. Livingroom faster than you can imagine. Copy?"

That was all Gunny said. His body language along with his lack of standard Marine Corps issue uniform and equipment told this idiot LT that these men were not the average kind of guys he'd been accustomed to dealing with in his short military career. Nor the kind of guys he really wanted to piss off. The LT's brain was locked up. And he instinctively knew he was about to get his ass handed to him.

"Which one of you goat fuckers locked onto my aircraft with a hot missile?" came the hostile tone from Chief as he seared a laser hole into the LT's eyeballs. Chief was not fucking around, and it was paramount this LT figure that out from the git go.

"Oh that! We was just training. No offense. I got some new guys and they just needed to get current on the shoulder-fired systems. So we saw you flying, didn't think you'd get all heated up or nothing. We knew it was one of ours. He wasn't going to fire at you or nothing. Trust me. He ain't that stupid".

This Lt didn't have a fuckin' clue. He'd just engaged a U.S. Combat aircraft, sent out a threat radar signature that compromised his location and could have set off the Blackhawk's automated return response fire control system had Kennedy not left it in the standby mode. Had they been on another type of mission with a different flight profile, the system would have been "ON", meaning Hellfires would have launched in response to the lock on, followed by 30 mm Gatling gun cannon fire and thousands of rounds from the mini guns mounted in the doorways, resulting in total annihilation to everyone in the grid square.

"Follow me Lt." Chief said sternly, walking off into the desert. The Lt followed behind, head down, trotting like he had a load in his drawers. Chief led him twenty meters into the distance far enough that their conversation would be private and could not be overheard by the U.S Marines gathering around the aircraft. Ten more minutes transpired and Chief reappeared at the door of the Blackhawk without warning. The Lt was no longer with him and nowhere to be seen.

"Get this thing airborne Tom" Chief spoke into his radio.

" I wanna get the fuck out of here as soon as possible."

Kennedy didn't respond. He just flipped the switch to activate the starter, and waited for Chief to get back into the aircraft. The rest of the Team recovered from their designated positions on perimeter security and hopped one by one back into the bird, covering each other's backs as if everyone in the area were hostiles. They all recognized that everyone in the area were U.S. Marines, but they responded the way they did for a reason. Imprinting muscle memory was paramount. It was a training opportunity and they did what they always did, acted in training as they would in combat.

Kennedy hit the starter and the turbine engines fired up. But, then immediately died. A warning lamp lit up on the dashboard. "Engine Failure" flashed in bright white letters on the red L.E.D screen. He tried it again. The whine of the electric over hydraulics could be heard again. But the engines again failed to fire.

" FUCK" came the loud cursing, guttural sound from Tom's throat. He knew he'd screwed up.

"Never, ever shut down unless you absolutely have to!" he reminded himself again, pissed off beyond words at himself for the error in judgment. He knew better. Not ever out here in this fucking desert.

There was a minor design flaw in the early years of Blackhawk's deployment, which had not yet been fully addressed by the contractor. Excessive temperatures, especially in the hostile desert environments had a tendency to vapor lock the fuel lines that followed the spine of the aircraft overhead position. If the lines got too hot, the fuel would expand and vaporize, causing an air lock, preventing liquid fuel from being pumped by the on board electric fuel pumps feeding the turbines. Fuel starvation prevented them from firing. The only way to get around it was to have the crew chief manually pump the fuel with a hand pump, prime the engines and break the vapor lock in the lines. Instinctively, the crew chief broke out the long, steel handle that resembled a tire iron and proceeded to climb over all the gear to get to the manual port in the upper ceiling at the rear of the aircraft.

"We're gonna have to manually pump this thing up Chief. The lines are locked. I need your guys to bail so I can get to the rear hatch again.," said the crew chief with a sense of urgency that got everyone's attention.

"Fall out. Perimeter 360 by five meters." With that simple order, the Team was outside the aircraft and had taken up positions in less than ten seconds. The U.S. Marines watching intently were impressed, all though highly confused as well.

"Thought you guys was leavin'," Private Purdy inquired as he walked up to the perimeter line. "What's up?"

"Well, we got a little problem." Kennedy said leaning out the window of the cockpit. "It won't start young man," Kennedy smiled, trying to relieve some of the tension in the air that had obviously become a major part of the otherwise unusually calm morning.

"Lts gone back to his hooch. I can gits him again if y'all wants me tah. Don' t know what that guy said to him, but he's got a case of the Red Ass now. I ain't never seen him that mad afore now. I'm betting he's on the radio contacting HQ. Guess they's pretty upset bout now too."

"Naw. Just let him go. We're used to this. Shouldn't take but a minute." Kennedy tried to reassure the young soldier.

"Hey, ya think if we git your blades spinnin' fast enough ya could pop the clutch and jump start this thang?" Private Purdy continued on, telling Kennedy he'd had similar success with his daddy's old truck. Hell, if it worked on his old Ford, it might work here. Not being one to ever let an opportunity for a practical joke pass, Kennedy leaned to his co-pilot and said,

"Watch this. It's gonna be precious".

"Well, Hell yeah! That might just work son. But it's gonna take a lot of you guys to get in on this to get those blades spinning fast enough. What you got in mind?"

"Just leave it to me. I'll hannell it," the young Private smirked as his face betrayed the instant increase in enthusiasm. In a shot, he was running around to every position the Marines had staked out, getting every man to come out of the foxhole position they had dug into and up to the Blackhawk. Chief sat down in the back of the aircraft, shaking his head in total disbelief.

"What the fuck are you cooking up now Tom," he asked over the intercom.

"Oh, just having a little fun with Gomer Pile is all. CHILL," Kennedy told him, covering his mouth as he spoke into the microphone. He didn't want anyone catching on to is plan, so he spoke softly and hid the wide grin developing on his face as he watched the now hyperactive Marine Private.

The crew chief was busy in the back opening the access panel doors, locking in the pump handle, and pumping away with the four foot long steel rod. He worked feverishly to break the vapor lock and push pressurized liquid fuel to the engine. It was going to take some doing. He'd done it on several other occasions, but that was all in training on a runway at Ft. Rucker, Alabama at the basic course. It was hot down there but probably fifty degrees cooler than what he was dealing with today.

Chief was getting impatient. He didn't like fucking around when they were supposed to be somewhere. They'd already lost critical flight time getting to the drop off LZ. Now this. For a day that had started out savoring the simple pleasures in life, it was turning sour pretty damn fast. Chief wasn't superstitious, but he was beginning to see a pattern. Any time he got any enjoyment out of anything, it usually would end up costing him later on.

* * * * *

In another minute, Chief was chuckling to himself and to the rest of the crew who had headsets locked into the intercom system. There were now no less than ten U.S. Marines lined up in a row at the nose of the aircraft. All of them had taken their belts off, hooked several of them together, and were attempting to lasso the rotor blade that drooped towards the ground in front of the aircraft. Once they looped the belt over the blade, they took off running in a clockwise direction, pulling as hard as they could to get the rotor blade to spin. When they got to the tail of the aircraft, they ducked under the boom, grabbed the belt again on the other side and continued to run as fast as they could in the deep desert sand, spinning the rotor blades. When they got to the front of the aircraft again, they passed the belt off to the next Marine in line, who would grab the linked belts and take off running. Within a few minutes, the rotors were spinning, tongues were hanging out, and several of the good Samaritans were lying on the ground face to the sky panting their guts out.

"Give it a try," shouted Private Purdy to the pilot from less than 3 meters distance, cupping his hands around his mouth as if yelling to someone a mile away. With that command, Kennedy stuck his hand out the window with a thumbs up. With a huge grin, he hit the electric over hydraulic starter switch. A loud whine emanated from inside the engine cover. A sudden new found energy invigorated the Marines as they jumped to their feet rooting like cheer leaders for the aircraft to start. Kennedy shut the switch off and the gentle whining noise faded to nothing. Despondence took over. Many of the energetic men simply fell back on the ground, while others, exhausted, over heated and out of breath leaned forward and held themselves by the knees, panting in total exhaustion.

"I think you guys almost got it. Maybe just a touch faster and it will take!" Kennedy prompted them to go on.

"Ok. We'll give er a shot," Purdy yelled back into the cockpit. "Just let us know when ya think it's ready so we can git out of the way in time."

Kennedy snickered knowing full well the Private to be the only one not expending any energy.

"Will do. Just keep your eye on me. I'll give you the signal," he snickered into his mic.

"These guys are fucking whack jobs." he said softly into the intercom, making sure his lips didn't move.

He called into the intercom to his crew chief.

"What ya think back there? Got that vapor lock broken yet? My gauge is reading 150 psi."

"Yeah, I think we're pretty close. Pressure is up back here too. Another few seconds and she's gonna fire. I'm pretty sure fuel is up to the engine now."

"Ok. Stand by for ignition" Kennedy said into the intercom.

Outside the Blackhawk, two of the Marines had taken up position as cheerleaders and were yelling at everyone else who was trying to spin the rotors.

"COME ON YOU MAGGOTS!" screamed Private Purdy, completely forgetting he was the lowest ranking Marine in the unit.

"We gotta get this thing flying. Put your guts into it."

Several of the Marines were totally spent, heaving on the ground in total exhaustion. Kennedy leaned out the window, gave a thumbs up, and the remainder of the Marines flopped to the side and ran out of the way of the rotors. With that, Kennedy hit the ignition switch and fired up the starter. A huge sense of urgency resumed as the rotors picked up speed and swirled sand and dust into the faces of the exhausted Marines. They jumped to their feet and began to back away from the aircraft. The co-pilot spoke into the microphone re-assuring the pilot and crew chief that fuel pressure was optimal and engine temps were rising rapidly. The turbines fired and in a matter of seconds, dirt and dust flew into the air from rotor wash. Chief called over his radio, "Load up Team. Let's get outta here!"

In unison, the Team re-entered the belly of the Blackhawk in the same efficient manner they'd practiced so often. As soon as they were all loaded, Kennedy ratcheted up the collective, increased engine speed and lifted off the desert floor in one smooth movement. As the pilot lowered the nose of the aircraft and picked up speed, the elevation gave everyone on board a new perspective. Looking down towards the ground, the Marines were dancing in excitement, eating dirt, covering their eyes, coughing and high fiveing each other like crazy. Kennedy laughed his ass off into the intercom and everyone on the aircraft chuckled for the first time in longer than anyone could remember. The U.S. Marines celebrated the fact they had Kick started a Blackhawk, a total impossibility. They didn't seem to know, nor care, that the helicopter didn't have a clutch. So no one on the bird was going to tell them. After all, they were happy. So was Chief again. At least he looked that way now. He grinned from ear to ear, shaking his head as they nosed down and picked up speed.

"Fucking idiots" Kennedy howled into the intercom.

"At least they know better than to lock on to their own aircraft now. Unbelievable we gotta TELL them that."

"Yeah, but I imagine some of those guys will tell their grandkids how they saved a Blackhawk by kick starting it".

The next half hour was consumed with chuckles and laughs. Not something that happened very often. Chief was thankful for the inconvenience even if it had taken nearly an hour and a half out of their day. It was worth it to see his men laughing for the first time, in a very long time. They needed more of that. This wasn't the kind of job that you got to laugh about very often. It was a precious moment in time with images of his men he hoped to preserve and sear into his memory, cracking up with genuine belly laughter. No harm, no foul. Just a joke. A damn good joke!

HVT AMA

"Sometimes, your worst problems are of your own making!"

Life Lesson Nr 7

The reward for working with US intelligence during the Russian occupation of Afghanistan was an opportunity for Abdullah Mohammed Abdullah to get a free education. AMA as he was known to US Intelligence Operatives, came originally from Yemen and was courted simply because he spoke both English and Pashto, the native language of Afghanistan near the Pakistan border. Like most students of Islam coming from high-level families within the Yemeni Government, Abdullah went to Pakistan to study in a Madrassa run by Sheik Kaleed Rhyme, a highly respected Imam who focused on Sharia Law and fundamentalism. To the rest of society in Yemen, AMA's presence there was the equivalent of someone in America sending their son to Harvard or Princeton. His family's place inside Yemen's ruling class was secured by his attendance. All he had to do was study and keep his head down.

But that was not to be. The Russian invasion of Afghanistan led AMA to join the Mujahideen, where he crossed the border along with every other male child aged 10 to 21 years old, into Afghanistan to help his Muslim brothers. The pro-communist government of Afghanistan in 1979 was supported wholly by the Russians. So America decided to support the Mujahideen to topple the rising communist threat. AMA excelled in both perfecting his English and using American technology to blow Russian aircraft out of the sky with Stinger missiles. He earned his nickname, "The

Archer" by dropping over a dozen Soviet aircraft from the sky. And then he earned his PhD in Psychology several years after the war. He continued on with his studies, and moved his family to America where he changed up and went to medical school to become a Cardiac Surgeon. He stayed in America for a very long time past the expiration date on his student visa, but then so did everyone else from the Yemen who came to America.

As he aged, living in America's great Central Valley of California, it bothered him more and more how many supposedly self-professed strict practitioners of the Muslim faith, were really nothing more than Americans with all the dirty, nasty consumption addictions included. He was mad as hell at the Imam at his local Mosque in Fresno, who professed to be a true Muslim, entertained whores at his home, drank alcohol and had the biggest collection of child pornography he'd ever seen in his life.

Abdullah eventually could not hide the disgust he felt, nor the contempt he had for this life in America and those around him. Something had to change. The rage was about to boil over. The self-loathing he maintained within him came to a boil. He couldn't continue to just accept what was going on around him. He had to do something. Allah demanded it.

At age 52 Abdullah decided to go back to the only place he ever really felt at home, Afghanistan. A place where a man could be proud and most Muslims, depending on their tribe, were real practitioners of true Islam. America incubated the Taliban and now Sharia Law was on the rise. Most of his friends and colleagues in America considered his views "radicalized" and slowly shied away from him socially. But to AMA, Sharia Law was the only true Law, sent directly from Allah to the Prophet Mohammed. And his intention was to get back to the true basics of Islam.

His wife and children rallied against him. Sharia threatened them, scared them into a submissive state they knew would terminate the comfort and freedom they were accustomed to living so freely and loved so much in America. So after a very short, hostile discussion with their father, Azza, the mother of Batrisyia, (Arabic for "the intelligent one") and Zarena, (Arabic for the wise princess) decided they wanted to stay in America, to live as they were without reverting back to such a harsh version of Islam they lived under before. Contrary to anything Sharia dictated when it came to women's rights and speaking out against the head of the house, they told AMA what they thought. They knew he was not happy with their perspectives, nor the decision they came to jointly. They thought there was strength and safety in their numbers. But they prayed to Allah with all their might that Abdullah would at least hear them out, listen to their opinions and eventually heed their wishes. For Allah was truly merciful, the most benevolent, the most beneficent.

Little did they know or suspect just how deeply AMA was morally injured, disgusted, angered beyond words by their actions, which he perceived as misconduct. This one, ten-minute conversation, as the women tried in vain to get him to understand their wishes, cast the entire family into turmoil. Not much was said from that day forward. But everyone could tell AMA was not the same from that day on. They all knew a storm was brewing. But not one of them knew how bad this storm was going to be.

Since it was against Allah and the Holy Koran for a woman to decide anything in the Islamic culture, AMA's fury was well founded in his own mind. His own wife and his own two daughters committed the ultimate sin when they embarrassed him in front of other men and the entire Muslim community by opening their mouths and espousing their opinions. The arranged marriage lasted nearly twenty years, simply because she came from a good Muslim family and knew how to keep her mouth shut. But now, after so many years in America, her conduct was despicable. She took on too many Western behaviors and infuriated him for passing it on as "acceptable behavior" to his children. The longer they stayed in America, the further away Sharia seemed to be in their lives.

For the longest time, every member of the family was a strict practitioner of Islam. But as the years passed, the indicators became numerous and AMA was truly troubled by their conduct and lack of moral compass. On more than one occasion, his daughters "missed" the call to prayer, making stupid excuses like their battery died on their phone and they didn't know what time it was, or they didn't realize how late it was. In reality, peer pressure from their friends was the hindrance. They'd come within an inch of having the life beaten out of them for their insubordination and blasphemy. Only their mother stood between the wild eyed AMA and a thrashing with a large leather belt. AMA was coming unhinged the longer their behavior went unchecked. He knew what he needed. It was time to go back to the old ways of Sharia within his household and all of them would pay dearly for their transgressions against Allah.

Abdullah could not find in the Koran, that which exonerated him from guilt for the actions he was about to commit. He searched for Allah's permission, instructions and support for his planned honor killings. He was not going to spend his afterlife in eternal hell because his wife and children allowed themselves to succumb to the wicked ways of an Infidel culture. He was sickened by the instant gratification and consumption that was American society. His own wife and children brought shame upon him and the family name. This had to be remedied. If they refused to follow the leader of the family and the Quran didn't give him the tools he needed to remedy the situation, then he knew Sharia Law would give him the tools he needed for absolution of their sins. The only thing he needed was a Fatwa from the Imam and a few witnesses. Getting a Fatwa would be easy enough since Abdullah knew the Imam was scared to death of AMA.

Imam Ali, a very well known and respected Imam in Central California, remembered very well the night he came home to find AMA in his house, rummaging through his office and personal effects. Ali turned ashen with fear and anxiety that night when AMA threw VHS tapes at him, shrieking at the top of his lungs about the bottles of alcohol and pornography stashed in his office closet. From then on, AMA was blackmailing and threatening him on a routine basis. He was genuinely afraid of who Abdullah knew and who he was connected to within US Intelligence and the great Satan, the Central Intelligence Agency. No one knew for sure if he really was connected with the CIA. But no one was willing to take that risk and cross Abdullah either.

In a fit of rage, Abdullah Muhammed Abdullah did what any good, true Sharia conforming Muslim would do. He restored the family honor by whacking his wife and children in their sleep with a machete. Instant death. "One blow to the neck" as Sharia instructed was the proper method. The aftermath looked like a cheap Hollywood freak show, but it left the intended message for every single Muslim in America he was disgusted with. Follow Sharia and Allah's word, or suffer the consequences.

Within minutes of the multiple murders, AMA was at Yosemite International Airport outside Fresno, California. He boarded the plane to LA and took his seat in first class, pulling his cell phone from a jacket pocket. As he fumbled with the seat belt, he covertly tried to open the SIM card compartment on the side of his smart phone in an effort to change it. He was going to miss technology. After all, he was a well-respected heart surgeon now. And with that job came access to all sorts of technology and communications. Somewhere in the Quran, he assured himself, were words that he knew would exonerate him for utilizing Western Technology, excusing him for using Satan's tools. Anything and everything was excusable if you looked hard enough and truly believed in your heart that you were simply violating God's law in an effort to trick the Infidels.

With all his experience in the every changing world of technology, Abdullah knew very little of military or law enforcement capabilities. He would regret that later in life.

He placed a new SIM card into his phone, and dialed 9-1-1 from his first class seat and in a muffled voice he answered the operator's inquiry.

"911, what is your emergency?"

"There's been a murder at 1701 Hill Top Terrace. Please hurry. Send an ambulance. There is blood everywhere" then hung up before the woman on the other end could ask another question. He hoped he cut the call short enough that it would not be traced, showing his ignorance of Cellular communications. Then he took out the SIM card, went to the rest room and tossed it into the vacuum with blue toilet chemicals, never to be seen again he hoped. He was leaving way too many loose ends. Loose ends that would lead the FEDs directly to him, his travel plans, and ultimately to his demise.

Within 24 hours, the Feds issued a warrant for his arrest. Three counts of premeditated homicide, as well as other charges including acts of terrorism under the Patriot Act. But AMA was one step ahead of Law Enforcement. He had one connecting flight to catch at LAX on his way to Afghanistan, another "Blip" on the Fed's radar.

Those in the Intelligence Community knew AMA as a sleeper. His time with the Mujahideen is where Chief first met him. No one outside the CIA knew AMA as the spineless puke he really was. Everyone in the Muslim world thought he was anointed by Allah himself, having served with Usama Bin Laden and Kaleed Sheik Mohammed. How else could he have survived two major air strikes? But the questions inside the CIA remained: was he careless and didn't get out fast enough? Or could it have been that the CIA controller moved up the strike timetable? Either way, it didn't really matter or change the fact this AMA guy was out for his own benefit. Fuck the rest of the world. He used people consistently and casually. And those that ended up working with him, ended up dead.

AMA was *the* key insurgent leader the U.S. and coalition forces were after now. The never ending turf wars between the CIA, the FBI and Military Intelligence allowed him to slip back into the United States and live unhindered in the quiet foothill community of Central California. He outlived his usefulness as an informant to U.S. Intelligence, was caught in one too many lies and now it was time to bring him in for debriefing and retirement. Especially now that he was on the "Most Wanted List" for murder. Agency personnel were convinced he would use his Intelligence information and connections as leverage to get out of trouble with the Law. And they were right. So they had to get to him before anyone else did. Or so went the back brief Chief attended.

Some how, after murdering his entire family, Abdullah slipped through the system once again and disappeared from the US before anyone could talk to him. Something was up. Chief had a sneaky feeling someone else was involved. Someone else, high up the food chain in the Intelligence world, was helping him. None of the good guys knew where his loyalties really were. Financially, he ripped off the U.S. government one too many times. He survived long enough that he rose through the power structure of Islamic Fundamentalists till he was near the top. If anyone outside the Joint Counter Terrorism Task Force (JCTTF) knew AMA was working as a double agent, he would have had his head cut off on YouTube for the whole world to witness. So Abdullah enjoyed a form of protection from the US Government most humans didn't get. But he was just slippery enough that no one could catch him either. This was becoming problematic.

Abdullah had all the specialized, specific intelligence the U.S. and it Allies needed to shut down Al Qaeda's leadership. He knew the organization; the central nodes of power and control, the players were his personal friends, all of who called him by name. He knew where they lived. He knew the financing. What money was coming from where, and what it was being spent on? Al Qaeda was famous for using "Cells" to keep compromise down to a minimum. But someone had to know. Someone had to be the hub of it all to keep things running. And Abdullah was it. He was "the hub" He moved quickly up the chain of command and had been involved in planning some of the most horrific terrorist attacks on targets in North Africa and Europe.

It took more than a little effort for US Intel organizations to keep him out of custody in several other countries in the past, when he worked for US intelligence, simply because he couldn't keep from bragging about his involvement in the bombings in Spain, France, Germany and England. Everyone in Europe wanted this guy dead. While everyone else was pissed that he had gotten away with murder, he enjoyed the protection provided by US Intelligence and he wasn't afraid to use that connection to piss off his local captors. Policemen all over Europe, convinced they had their guy, had to eat crow as he laughed in their faces as he while being escorted by some guys in suits, right out the front door. That made him all the more hated. But now, most concerning was his participation in planning operations that targeted U.S. Special Forces in Afghanistan and against the United States Homeland.

After several years of Abdullah missing from the radar, he finally popped up again. This time it was in Afghanistan, deep within the Hindu Kush mountain area north east of Kabul. Surveillance by Global Hawk and confirmation by a local elder set off a whirlwind of Intelligence activity. And Chief's Team was tapped for the take down mission. Someone higher up the food chain of U.S. Intelligence wanted his ass. And they wanted it bad enough to send in the best Tier One Team America had. The briefing went off as usual. And just as usual, Chief had a feeling things were about to go sideways. He couldn't put his finger on what exactly was wrong, but something was hinkey.

* * * * *

As Team Leader and Officer in Charge, Chief double-checked any new soldiers on the team. But in this case, all but one had been with him damn near 9 years consecutively. That was unheard of in Special Operations. Most guys didn't stay in service nine years, never mind stay on one Team that long. Men were usually physically and mentally consumed by the time they hit their fifth or sixth year, most of which was training and prep time. Actual mission time and real world operations came after the fifth year. Except now, everything was expedited due to the Global War on Terror. Usually, by the time men got done with school and specialty training, the attrition from basic courses, Ranger School, Under Water Demolition School, as well as the other "Weed out" training had consumed nearly 90 percent of the applicants. IF they got through that, they still had to get through another four years of specialized training in everything from weapons to communications to medical to language school. When they were finally transitioned to "Tier One" status, they were no longer anything close to a human and were completely and utterly dedicated to these concepts: to win at any cost, to accomplish the impossible, and to never, ever quit.

The guys on Chief's Team were different. Every man had gone through the normal training cycle and accomplished a minimum of twenty real world ops. Their heads were on straight. They had the experience of at least ten years in service, some more than ten, and they all had the 1000 yard stare of a seasoned combat veteran. But they were also smart. There was little bullshit when the game time whistle blew. These guys were literally the best of the very best America had to offer. No social problems, other than the normal "Not fitting in" and multiple divorces. No mental problems, other than they were "All crazy!" No physical problems, other than every single one of them was beat to shit and nursing some injury, constantly sucking down handfuls of "Ranger Candy", Motrin and pain killers swallowed with Mylanta or Maalox.

Chronic boredom was a big problem, but they all shared it, fought it and came up with some ingenious things to keep them from going nuts. They were a well-oiled terrorist take down machine, every man a ghost, highly efficient, and lethal.

* * * * *

"Operation Hook Up is a GO!" came the message over the C17's C3R, the combat control coordination radio. As the electric motors in the tail of the aircraft whined, pumping hydraulic fluid through the veins of the aircrafts aft compartment, the Operators waddled like overweight ducks toward the tailgate ramp in the back of bird. This was a picture of why so many men ended up with back injuries and bad knees. Each man carried in excess of 120 lbs. of extra equipment on top of the body armor, weapons and parachutes necessary to survive leaving the aircraft and getting to the target.

As the locking mechanism clicked into place, overhead lighting switched from white light to red, standard operations procedure to avoid compromise of secret missions. As their eyes attempted to adjust to the red light, every man was keenly aware how eerily quiet the aircraft suddenly was. Almost a foreshadowing of the dangerous events to come, Chief counted heads as each man checked the gear of another man. Another entire level of anxiety rushed through each man's veins, causing them to inhale, exhale, function check their weapons and concentrate on anything other than the cold blackness waiting to consume them just outside the tailgate.

"Embrace the fear, embrace the suck. Destiny awaits. See you in Valhalla!" someone chanted over the hum of the aircraft. Everyone's mental attitude was dead on target now. This was what they ALL lived for. Leaving the aircraft, gaining terminal velocity and swooping in to fuck up someone's day. There was nothing more fulfilling than to watch a Billy Bad Ass piss his pants in fear, knowing suddenly there was no escape. Every man had their own story, but for Chief, this was about righting so many wrongs. This was about fixing a problem. This was about snatching a man he once respected, who turned to the dark side, and now thought he was Teflon.

A gapping black hole in the back of the aircraft leading to nothingness threatened to suck the seven-man team off balance and launch them into oblivion. The rush of cold air came into the cavernous aluminum fuselage followed by the pungent smell of JP4 jet fuel and engine exhaust reminding every man on deck they were about to leave the safety and security of "home" and dive into black, unknown, hostile territory.

"DeJaVu" thought Chief. "I should have been a cook."

He hated that thick, rancid, oil and diesel kind of smell that immediately penetrated his nostrils, esophagus and stomach, making him want to vomit. The uncontrollable instinctive, human gag reflex triggered everyone else on the plane to do the same. In this case, the Team was about to go on Oxygen with the recently fielded, new F16 fighter pilot type helmets. In unison, each man lowered the windscreen, locking out the fumes and turned on the oxygen mix control valve at the tank they carried on their back.

"Turn on the God Light" Chief said into the headset strapped to his shoulder harness. And with that command, his voice traveled out of his helmet, into the C17 Combat Control radio, across the vast open sky to communication satellites dedicated to Special Operations missions. From there, the voice command relayed all the way back to China Lake Station, somewhere in the desert of Nevada, back in the United States. A console operator, sitting in a dark shipping container conversion SCIF watching flat screen panels above his desk reached over to flip the switch in compliance with Chief's order. This console operator, charged with controlling the multi-million dollar MQ-9 Reaper Unmanned Aerial Vehicle, flipped a switch resulting in an electronic command traveling the entire distance back to Afghanistan to a UAV flying overhead in support of Chief and Operation Hook Up. Flying at nearly 15,000 feet, a high intensity, focused, Infrared Light Emitting Diode or L.E.D. in the nose of the Reaper turned on and illuminated the valley floor below. No one in the target zone could see the light. But to Chief and his Team with their night vision helmets, the IR light illuminated the target area below as if it were Monday night at an NFL Football stadium.

In mere seconds, all seven men waddled forward and did a little hop maneuver they practiced so many times in training. This small hop launched the Team irrevocably into space. The jet blast helped suck them into the darkness and every man instinctively arched his back trying to gain control over the sudden impact of the gravity forced wind that slammed into their chests. Each man fought for immediate control, as their body and the weight of a full combat load torqued their spines into unforgiving and painful contortions. There was a severe penalty if they didn't win immediate control and stay within range of the rest of the Team. Within seconds, an Operator could end up going into a spin. Physiologically, centrifugal force takes over, spinning the blood up against the side walls of their veins and into one half of their heart and one side of their brains resulting in a near immediate state of unconsciousness, followed by uncontrollable flight, tumbling and eventually death. The Air Force called these men "Dirt Darts" for a reason.

Chief and Gunny were the first two out the door. Followed by the four Enforcers, perimeter security guys with sniper experience. Directly behind them came the Medic and the Interpreter. These new suits were so much fun it was like flying wings with a man in the middle. After all the hours spent in the Dragon's Breath Tower at the Special Operations Center on Pope Air Force Base N.C., these Operators were experts in body manipulation and knew precisely what moves could affect flight, speed and landing tactics. Each man had hundreds of hours of real altitude flight time and knew what could get them into trouble and what could save their teammates from serious or fatal injuries.

"Dammit! Where are they? They should have been here by now" Chief said into his intercom as the Team trailed in the sky behind him.

"This fucking Intel better be good!" Chief said, knowing full well the man and the unit that put the reports together. It wasn't that he didn't trust the Intel. But he didn't necessarily want to put his life on the line, nor that of his men when he didn't know the source of the Intelligence

"Chill Chief. It's good. They're down there. We're just a little too high to see them right now. Lets lose some altitude." Gunny said, hoping he wasn't lying. Things would get REAL ugly if they made it all the way to the ground and no one was there. Chief would really end up eating someone's lunch having spent all this time, money and effort to insert into a place and not have a target when he got there.

"You fuckin- A better be right Gunny" Chief said as he closed his legs and pulled his arms into his body. Exponentially, his speed increased and Chief flew off into the darkness. Gunny followed suit, tucking his chin tight to his chest, pulling his arms closer to his sides and dipping his body with a motion that was barely visible. Immediately thereafter as if choreographed, the rest of the team did likewise. Their speed picked up quickly and in a mere matter of seconds the entire Team was at terminal velocity, headed towards the earthen floor of Afghanistan's Miser al Sharif valley below. Mountain peaks from 15,000 to 24,000 feet in elevation surrounded the drop zone. Chief and the Team were headed into a bowl, circumvented by snow capped death traps. If they overshot the target, they very well could end up in "Stan Land", the nickname they gave the surrounding regions instead of trying to pronounce Turkmenistan, Uzbekistan and Kyrgyzstan.

"We better slow down and get the suit working before we end up too low and off target Chief" Gunny said into the intercom. "We're moving pretty fast!"

They just traveled nearly five thousand feet in a matter of a minute. Close to eighty-four feet per second, the human body wasn't made for dropping elevation changes that fast and there was a real risk of physical damage at those speeds and "G" forces. More than one operator had died from stroke, some suffered from collapsed sinuses and done real permanent damage to organs just from free falling from too high and opening too low. Each member had to consciously work on muscle control to keep blood in the brain and critical muscle groups, similar to what jet fighter pilots had to practice. There was a critical fault to operations simply as a result of being human. Pressure suits were not practical while free falling from those altitudes. Nothing could be done about it. But practice could mitigate some of the bad outcomes.

Gunny was Chief's number two and a critical part of the Team. He was the eyes and ears of the inner circle, and there was no doubt from any one that he had Chief's six. As they descended towards the valley, now illuminated by the bright green light of night vision devices, it crossed his mind that maybe the Intel was wrong but only for a fleeting second. Three other Ops in this part of the world went bad because the Intel was either bullshit or the "Host Government" was informed prior to mission start through the State Department. Bin Laden disappeared on seven separate occasions. Pablo Escobar even more. Noriega knew way too much, way too many times. When Chief and his guys got there, on more than one occasion, the targets each were gone. Thermal optics verified they were mere minutes late. On several occasions the carpet Bin Laden was sitting on was still warm, that's how close they'd come. But just like Pablo Escobar and a few other missions, most targets had enough money they could buy just about anything to keep from being captured. Including buying governments. Eventually, all of them were brought to justice. But on this night, it was too soon to tell if anyone was even on the drop zone.

In this case, Gunny knew who did the pre-mission Intelligence. Since Chief was an Intelligence Officer himself and leader of the Team, whatever was sent to him had better be good. Things were checked and rechecked for accuracy. More than once Chief had eaten someone a new ass for sending bullshit Intel and expecting Chief to put his Team in danger based on half-assed bogus Intel. Gunny knew the Intel was good. It had to be. This was his final mission with Spec Ops, something he still hadn't told Chief yet. A civilian company offered Gunny a job that would keep him closer to home with somewhat regular hours at three times the pay he was getting from Uncle Sam. He planned on telling Chief and the Team as soon as he made the decision to leave the military but the timing was all bad. They hadn't even recovered from one mission when they were out the door for the next. Timing was everything with Chief. Now was positively NOT right the time. Gunny forced it from his mind and focused on the rapidly approaching bright green earth below.

"Bingo!" came Chief's voice over the wireless radio embedded in his helmet. "Lets get em!" came an anxious voice.

"Fuckin- A, that's what we came for" came a reply.

As if choreographed, every operator folded up into a ball in unison to obtain maximum flight velocity. Every move was muscle memory now as the focus increased and adrenaline crept in.

As Chief and his Team flew deeper into denied territory, altitude warnings began flashing on the helmet screen in front of Chief's eyeballs. The Team was now a full 15,000 feet lower than when they jumped and streaked towards the valley floor below at an astounding rate. When the red light blinked rapidly on his face screen, Chief would pay more attention. For now, it was just another annoyance to be ignored. A female digital voice, tied to the altimeter, would interrupt at 1500 feet. Then, if he didn't take action, it was very possible that digital voice would be the last voice Chief would ever hear.

The automated altimeters were tied in to automatically deploy the reserve chute, in the event an operator blacked out during free fall. The digital voice was added simply because it was very easy to lose urgency and end up mis-calculating altitude on the way down. This new digital voice device wasn't fool proof, but it already had a proven track record of saving lives in the short time the prototype was fielded. So many physiological things change in the human body during the high stress situation of HALO. After all, humans were not meant to fly to begin with. But to fly at those heights, at those speeds, descending to those depths including sub-atmospheres during operations that required water landing, was truly against everything God intended the human body to do.

Right now, Chief was looking for the HVT, playing the scenario over and again in his head as he always did. Startled by a familiar voice in his headphones, Chief took in a deep breath as he answered the intercom. Gunny was calling him.

"Chief, three targets at Nine O'clock, five hundred meters".

As he swiveled his head off to the left, Chief found what he was looking for. They were there. The bastards were actually there this time. And they were never going to forget this evening. Chief was going to make certain of that!

Operation Hooked Up

"Often times you can use the enemy's ignorance to your own advantage!"

Life Lesson Nr 8

As Chief and the Team descended at terminal velocity, the altitude warning began blinking rapidly on the windscreen of his helmet. Excitement built among the Team members. They were really looking forward to some action, the kind that made "Good Guys" cheer at the sight of "Bad Guys" eating some humble pie.

Everyone knew that didn't happen very often. They didn't often get to see these terrible humans, designated as Tier One High Value Targets, meet their maker. More times than not, the bad guys lawyered up and were given all the safety and protections of the US Constitution, afforded to a US Citizen, something that really did not sit well with anyone in the Counter Intelligence and Counter Terrorism arena. There was hardly ever any satisfaction to capturing these guys. Just the opposite actually. Almost 100% of the time, Chief lost complete respect for the enemy he swore to take down. They were simply bullies. Vile souls with an agenda. Not warriors, or people Chief could respect for conviction to their beliefs. But every once in a while, things came together and they *did* get to smile, just a little bit. That is when everyone got to celebrate.

Chief was inside his head again, enjoying the ride and thinking of the last time he'd seen Abdullah in Afghanistan.

"Must have been 1979 or 80" Chief thought to himself, remembering the night he was told to load up and take Stinger Missiles and bring them to a location by mule and donkey teams. He didn't know whom exactly he was supposed to meet. All he was told was that he was to deliver the highly secret cargo and the classified trigger mechanisms to the Mujahideen high in the Hindu Kush Mountains. At first, Chief was really taken aback, shocked and perversely disgusted beyond reason. He refused to go, refused to accept what he deemed to be an "unlawful order" and really got himself spun up at what obviously was a very covert, very politically sensitive mission. Getting that hot under the collar could have ended his very promising career right then and there. But Navy Captain Holloway, a mentor Chief really respected who was on his way to being a full blown Admiral, pulled Chief aside and told him what was really going on. The Russians were wreaking havoc with their MI-8 Hind Helicopters. The Afghans didn't have a chance with their WW I era weaponry, against what was deemed a flying tank. So the U.S. intended to put a stop to the Russian massacre of Afghani villages. And Chief was tapped to pull off a mission, that if compromised could have unspeakable consequences to the U.S. Government in the aftermath of such a scandal. Chief signed up and was given a photo of the Afghani contacts. Abdullah Muhammed Abdullah and his close associate Usama Bin Laden, leader of the Mujahideen. Otherwise interpreted as "those engaged in Jihad".

As the Team dropped altitude, enjoying the flight on this moonless night, things were starting to bother Chief. He had a lot on his mind. The mission wasn't just about AMA, or getting intelligence. This was personal. Chief and his men were free falling into a foreign country, having fun doing it, to go after a man he knew personally. That changed everything at the emotional level, but Chief needed to keep things on target to keep from mixing his own emotions with his professional duty. A lot was going right, yet Chief was the only one thinking about all of the "awe shits" that could happen. Extraction was scheduled for hours later. He had no way of knowing what they might run up against while on the ground, or worse, hanging in the air on their way to the drop zone. What Chief did know, was that not all missions were "Zeus". Some really bad things happened in Special Operations history. Like what happened to Mark Weisenburg, a Chief Warrant that Chief had known for years. Mark told him about covering HVTs heads to make them talk more. Many years later, Chief was still using the technique. Wiesenburg was not. He took an Iraqi General Officer into custody and was interrogating him with a sleeping bag over the Generals head. Somewhere in the mix, while Wiesenburg was sitting on the General's chest quietly asking simple questions, the General died of a heart attack. Post mortem autopsy revealed massive artery disease, serious cholesterol impaction and heart damage from diabetes and vascular disease. Every vein in the man's body was on the verge of collapse or plugged completely.

The fact that the General died was merely coincidental to Mark sitting on his chest and calmly asking questions. All that mattered after that was the Courts Martial that convicted Chief's friend of First Degree Murder.

No one back home wanted to know the real story. The US Military Command just wanted to satisfy a fledgling Iraqi government full of Insurgents. The Iraqi political machine wanted their pound of flesh. Whatever leverage they could impose on the US only made them look better in the face of the Iraqi civilian population, those "victims" of American intervention that forever leveraged the new government and embarrassed them. They wanted substance. They wanted results. They wanted someone to pay for their frustration. And the U.S. Government gave satisfaction to them in the form of Chief Warrant Officer Mark Weisenburg. The punishment was way overboard as well. Immediate dismissal from the military, forfeiture of all pay and benefits, a Dishonorable

Discharge and a Felony conviction on his record for the rest of his life. It's like they always said,

"One awe shit wipes out an entire lifetime of Attaboys."

Chief was completely disgusted by the leadership and the political agenda over this incident. The General Officers in charge of the legal proceedings had something other than justice on their minds. Everyone was reeling from photos released about American soldiers acting badly at the Abu Ghraib prison. The whole world was outraged, especially those in uniform. But their opinions didn't count. A major campaign was afoot to convict every single person in uniform; all lumped together and painted with the same brush. US Soldiers were no longer seen as "Liberators" of an oppressed Iraqi people. Now they were seen as the reason for their anxiety, the reason for their frustration, the reason for their turmoil and unsatisfied bloodlust. The timing couldn't have been worse for Mark. But at least the U.S. had not turned him over to the Iraqis for prosecution under Iraqi law. Mark would have been beheaded or hung.

Chief was not going down that way. Mark's bad luck was a lesson Chief learned and took to heart. Abdullah better be there and he'd better survive the hook up operation. If not, they would dump his body at 30,000 feet somewhere over the ocean, never to be seen again. Not a bad idea anyway.

* * * * *

The sudden realization that there was an alarm sound going off in his ears snapped Chief back to reality. With his body traveling at 56 meters every second, a mere 120 mph, the digital woman's voice told Chief he was closing in on fifteen hundred feet altitude really fast. The rest of the team already deployed their chutes in relative silence after conducting a swoop maneuver with their squirrel suits to scrub off speed. By popping their chutes at the apex of the maneuver, the stall point as their bodies barely climbed in altitude for mere seconds, they avoided the enormous rush of air and the loud report those square chutes made when opening while traveling 120 mph towards the ground. Beside the noise, the tremendous physical strain was also avoided, making for a quiet, if not pleasant ride to the drop zone. This maneuver contributed greatly to their stealthy arrival. Combined with a moonless night, the God Light and the night vision equipment, Chief and the Team could arrive almost completely un-noticed and un-announced, a great advantage in the game of silence and surprise during covert operations.

At just under 2000 feet, the Team had enough room to maneuver, re-orient in flight and still fly silently into the target zone. Chief did not. He was too low, but he was right on target. The God Light illuminated the valley floor so well, it looked like noon instead of 3 am on this moonless night.

Chief could see the grain in the rocks as he flew past. He was still traveling way too fast, and way too low when his chute fully opened to envelope the cold night air. This was part of the fun in Chief's mind. In a matter of seconds Chief's body was racked with burning muscle spasms as his body harness cut into him, fighting against the enormous centrifugal force developed during deceleration. This was the brutal part of the ride. Instructors likened it to childbirth. Every muscle, tendon and connective tissue was tested to its limits, straining and stretching to the point of breaking. The large flat mattress chute opened with a loud report stretching the riser rope and straining the fabric as Chief neared the ground at well over 100 miles per hour. Decelerating so quickly his eyes felt like they were leaving his skull.

And then suddenly, complete relief was followed by a very nice, quiet ride through the air. That is what Chief was looking for. Endorphin overload. Peace. Quiet. Calm, all in preparation for a ferocious attack once they hit the ground. The peaceful and quiet part of the parachute decent was short lived in a HALO jump. After all, the objective was to get on the ground as quickly as possible. Not to hang in the air and enjoy the ride.

As the velocity decreased to a subtle 35 miles per hour, Chief and his team flew through the cold night air in complete silence as the targets came closer into view. There were three of them and in minutes Chief would know for certain if the High Value Target, Abdullah Mohammed Abdullah was really there. These bastards were sitting around a fire burning goat manure to heat water in a tin can to make tea. And they were about to have uninvited guests!

Chief lifted his face shield to orient himself and check the landing area. He found himself within one hundred meters of the target now. The sudden rancid smell of goat shit tainted his nostrils and Chief felt that tinge in his guts that told him adrenaline was about to strike his blood system and his brain. Anger flared rapidly within his chest. After so many missions in the Middle East, the smell of goats brought back primal memories, violence and instantaneous rage reactions.

"And they wonder why everything smells like goat shit around here?" An uninvited voice broke in on the intercom frequency. The interruption broke Chief's focus and intensity. Something he would not tolerate.

The HVTs had their backs to Chief as he pulled on the riser ropes flaring his chute to a near standstill. His feet touched the ground a mere four feet behind the HVT he'd been hunting for nearly 18 months. Abdullah Mohammed Abdullah was shocked beyond words as he turned away from his comrades, intending to walk away from the fire and go relieve himself in the distance. The large glassy eyes of something he didn't really comprehend suddenly confronted him. He was literally speechless as he stared into the face mask of what looked to be a fighter pilot's helmet appearing out of nowhere directly in front of him in the pitch black darkness of night. The other two Afghanis were startled even worse, jumping to their feet and immediately urinating in their pants. Within seconds of Chief landing, the rest of the team arrived and touched down in a similarly efficient and frightening instant. The Team stripped the three Afghanis of their weapons simultaneously, just as silently as they had arrived. Three AK-47s and an RPG were thrown into a pile a few meters away.

Every one of the team members kept their visor helmets on, breathing from oxygen tanks. The flex hose assembly wrapped around their torso, secured to the belt line, continued behind them to the tanks they carried on their backs. Their breathing sounded more like Darth Vader than humans further spooking the HVTs into shock.

The men in the black squirrel suits adjusted their bodies to gravity, twisting their legs and spreading their arms as they adjusted the panels to the windless environment. The Afghanis eyes widened in disbelief at the demonstration designed merely to re-arrange the suit's material so the men could walk. To the Afghanis however, these "things" were nothing close to human forms. They had dragon skin between their limbs. Webbing! Involuntarily and in unison, all three devout Muslims fell on their faces to recite from the Quran, asking Allah for protection from these obviously other worldly Satanic Jins, these evil spirits from hell.

With their night vision visors still in the down position in the pitch black of night, the HVTs could not see that there were real humans inside. What stood before them without warning, dropping silently from the dark night sky, had them so frantic, so surprised, so shaken they could barely control themselves.

They were looking at Aliens!

Chief and his men were not from another planet, but they might just as well have been. The HVTs had never seen such a thing in their lives. Snorkels for noses, large glassy covered eyes, muted mouths with noises emanating that didn't sound anything at all like human language. At least not any language they'd ever heard before. And the bodies before them, well, no one had *ever* seen such a display with dragon skin webbing between their legs and under their arms. Whatever these things were, to these illiterate Afghani Taliban fighters, they certainly were not human.

Chief couldn't help but chuckle as he saw the effects of adrenaline and "fight or flight" syndrome take over the HVT's demeanor. He knew what they were feeling because he felt the same spontaneous effect numerous times before. Only now it was humorous to watch it happen to someone else. There was no real danger to life at the moment. But the perception they had was real.

Watching these guys was like watching a horse get spooked. They were terrified. Chief laughed quietly at the thought that these "Billy badass" terrorists had no idea what was going on. Only a few moments prior, these Pakistani invaders, these Taliban monsters, were at the top of the food chain having no mercy on naive, innocent men, women and children in the outpost villages throughout Afghanistan. All that changed when Chief and his Team arrived. Now they were babbling little boys, pissing their drawers.

It was impossible for these young Arab men to understand what they were seeing. A lifetime of strict schooling in fundamentalist Islamic schools kept them from knowing or understanding anything except what they had been told and what was written in the holy Quran. There was no need to know anything else. No other books were read. No other subjects studied. Radios were forbidden, since in their world, any electronic device was a tool of Satan. Television was too expensive, but it was banned also. Their culture kept them ignorant of anything else from the outside world in total contrast to that which embodied the great Islamic Persian Empire of centuries before.

But in this day and age, if it was not within a 5-kilometer radius of where they were born, these men most likely never would hear anything about it. All these poor fucks knew now was how to kill people. The only thing they were taught was hatred for anyone and anything that wasn't under their control. Everything outside their world was considered the land of the Infidels. That is all they knew and all they cared to know. That made the technology gap unspeakably huge, an advantage Chief would exploit to the max.

Folklore in these parts talked of alien beings, "Jin's" as all evil beings were called. Legends talked of them coming down out of the sky at night, kidnapping children to take back to the evil underworld, even eating the children who tried to run away. It did wonders for keeping kids from walking off too far. Every generation embellished it more, until it was "fact" in their minds.

"Greetings!" Chief chuckled as he watched the Jihadis stand in complete fear, knees of all three men locked as their bodies shivered. Their body language changed drastically, dancing on their tiptoes, shivering as their voices pitched higher and higher with incomprehensible jabber and shrieks. Chief began to chuckle again as a voice came over the intercom in his earpiece.

"They sound like the Three Stooges Chief!"

Chief knew exactly what the look on their face was all about. They were losing it. What the Afghanis didn't know was Chief could see them a hell of a lot better looking through the night vision visor and the God Light than they could see him by the light of the burning goat manure. Chief clicked the mic in his hand opening a communication channel with the aircraft above as well as with higher Headquarters somewhere back in the U.S. Video feed to the rear element was established and Chief knew that whatever happened in the next few minutes would be recorded.

Abdullah understood English very well. But this was far from any English he'd ever heard.

"Arch Angel Six, Golf Tango Golf" a short, quiet beep signal faded into the background as he released the transmitter button sending his call sign and the coded message to the pilot inbound nearly 40 thousand feet up and ten miles out. The simultaneous signal went through the "UAV" overhead and back to the ground station, relayed to the Situation Room back at home.

Golf Tango Golf was military phonetics to limit the time spent transmitting over the air. G. T. G. "Good to Go!" The shorter the message, the less chance someone could locate their position through Direction Finding techniques. The last thing Chief wanted was mortar fire raining down on their heads. It was hard telling who was supporting the insurgent forces this week. Iranians for sure were helping them out. But who knew if the Russians were involved again as well. They were under suspicion lately for several attacks on U.S. Forces in the area, breaking encryption and allowing "External Signal Parametrics" to target the friendlies. After all, it was payback time for the Americans. Many Russians had a vindictive streak and it was time to pay back in spades what the Americans had done with the Mujahideen against Russian soldiers a short couple of decades prior.

"Hotel Victor Tango Alpha One!" came the next transmission. They had confirmed the identity of High Value Target number one on the "Most Wanted" list. Chief confirmed the HVT in custody was actually Abdullah Mohammed Abdullah. Things were going as planned, so far.

"Hook up in Five Mikes, Over," came a response from Stateside through the Team headsets, completely unknown to the HVTs standing just a few feet away.

One man from the team, the "Bag Man", disengaged and walked off into the darkness as if on cue. It was happening again.

No one had to be told what to do. The well-oiled machine Chief was so proud of was again in efficient motion, thinking in unison, anticipating Chief's orders and executing a response to those requirements before he could even formulate the words.

The "Bag Man" was on his first real world mission with Chief. He had with him what looked like a duffle bag. But instead of cargo and uniforms that one would normally expect to find inside a duffle bag, was a balloon of sorts. It had a series of tightly woven thin parachute cords attached to it, strapped with what appeared to be seat belt material, and over stitched a number of times. The entire mass of rope and stitching was covered with highly reflective silver tape. Attached to this over sized, vinyl clad balloon was a valve system made of high impact plastic, operated by hand to insert helium gas. The bag also contained lightweight fiberglass and Kevlar woven air tanks with a high-pressure mixture of helium gas and carbon dioxide. Lighter than air, the gas injected into the balloon from the tanks, sent it up into the higher levels of the atmosphere, dragging behind it a long, woven bungee cord attached to a parachute harness. All the while, the "Snatch Aircraft" was in a downward spiral, losing altitude so they could catch the balloon and bring the package up into the belly of the bird.

The "Bag Man" worked quickly, but efficiently. Attention to detail was not a lost concept on this man. Being his first real world mission, his entire career depended on the outcome of this mission. And he wasn't going to fuck it up. Not when Chief was leading the team. That would end his career for certain. With only eleven years in service, five of which was training and the mandatory three year probation period, he was coming up on the juncture of re-enlisting or getting out. This may very well be his one and only shot at a real world mission and he wanted it to go off without a hitch. When it came to this HVT Abdullah guy, nothing was left to chance. Every single detail was practiced until reflexive muscle memory was perfectly executed. Chief and his team were going to *"Hook him up"* in a big way and everything had to go perfectly.

"Tell us who you are! What do you want with us?" came a cry for help in perfect English from the Taliban Commander.

"We don't have any money.," squealed the second HVT, whining as if the more timid, the more pitiful he sounded the less chance Chief and the Aliens would hurt him. The thought that these idiots might consider they were being robbed was hilarious to most of the men in suits and helmets. Everyone broke out laughing softly, looking at each other in the total bright green light of night vision. Hearing their own giggles and chuckles through the snorkel tubing made the symphony of clamor even more ridiculous and the Team laughed even harder and louder, bringing Chief's unwanted attention. The Team was here to take something, but it wasn't money. And they damn sure weren't robbers.

"Hey Chief, they think we're thieves and robbers or something!" spoke one of the suited men. He spread his arms to his sides, flapped the wings of his suit and howled like a wolf. The noise sounded more like a hideous squeal from outside the mask.

"Knock it off." Chief was just not in the mood.

"Listen up you Haji mother fuckers. Which one of you is Abdullah?"

Chief was using another lead in tactic to find out if the Hajis were going to lie to him or not.

He already knew the answer. He recognized AMA from the second he landed, fighting the urge to disclose who he was and ask him "why?" Abdullah was a friend of sorts. He taught Chief the Muslim prayer, taught him the ceremonies of prayer, five times each day. He taught Chief the true meaning of Islam at a time Chief was completely conflicted with his Catholic upbringing. Why after all he and Chief had been through, why had Abdullah given in and gone to the dark side? What changed? Why had a once righteous man fighting to kick the Russians out of his country, fighting for his religion, his God, decided it was OK to blow up innocent civilians? For *money*!

As the interpreter translated Chief's words into a dialect that Chief didn't understand, two of the Arabs looked at each other. Then both pointed directly at Abdullah.

Bingo. Secondary confirmation. The unspoken rule of Intelligence Collection. "Always have second and third party confirmation, preferably from different Intel "Ints" such as Signals Intelligence (SIGINT), or Human Intelligence (HUMINT), or Imagery Intelligence (IMINT) Sources, before you get egg on your face."

"You better tell me the truth!" came the admonishment from the only member of the suited men who spoke any Arabic. He repeated the warning. The two Arabs with the extended fingers pointing to Abdullah, started to dance up and down in frustration and fear.

"On all things holy, it's him. It's him."

Abdullah was sick to his stomach. It was always sickening when he found out how quickly these "Martyrs" turned to chickens, trying to save their own necks. The dancing idiots were far more than Chief wanted to deal with at the moment. Time was short. So it was time to turn up the heat and get some results.

"Zip these assholes" Chief said.

Instinctively the four suits standing behind the two Arabs reached into the thigh pockets of their suits and withdrew large black plastic straps. Walking up behind the twins, the Operators kicked the targets behind the knees, buckling their legs. As they fell to their knees, one Operator zipped their ankles together. The other man pulled their hands behind their backs and zipped their wrists together. In one smooth move they were zip tied like rodeo steers. Hand to hand, and hands to ankles. Hog-tying was what they called it back home, but no one really knew why. Two men walked over behind Abdullah and zip tied his hands in front of his body. He was tied much more carefully since he was about to take a ride!

"If you lie to me, we're going to make one of you disappear!" Chief barked again.

"We are not lying. On all that is holy!" The twins were still dancing, only not on their feet. They were rolling from side to side out of pure anxiety face down in the dirt. They were scared beyond anything they had ever experienced before.

"You nasty fucking Haji bastards!" came the uncontrolled response from the translator. There were other tribes within his country that despised these men in front of him, rolling on the ground whining. They were called the "men in baggy pants" because they didn't wear the traditional Afghani perahan tunban or "man dress" as U.S. soldiers called them. These men were hated simply because of the smell emanating from their modified garb. The tribal custom of defecating into their baggy pants was centuries old. No one could explain why they did it, but the translator was from a rival tribe. And he hated these "men of poop" simply because of this custom.

"We need to just shoot these sick bastards Chief!"

"Shut the fuck up. I'm not in the mood for your personal bullshit. Keep focus. Mission first." came the only words Chief would speak to anyone on the team through the remainder of the mission.

Chief suspected that all three of these captives knew something valuable that the U.S. Government wanted to exploit. He was there to find out what that was.

"This is the last time I'm going to say this. Tell me the truth. Which one of you is Abdullah?" Chief poured on the pressure even harder.

The twins were really upset now and the inflection of their voices rose to a pitch so high they sounded like little girls crying in the dark. Chief had their full attention. All they knew was that Abdullah had been dragged away into the darkness behind them. He tried to say something, but he was gagged. Chief knew that 99% of whatever came out of Abdullah's mouth would be a lie anyway. The rest would just piss him off and he didn't want to hear it. He would rather concentrate on getting the info he didn't already know. Abdullah was not the one that was going to give that to him. Chief knew that. But if Abdullah disappeared, the other two would dump their guts.

Two of the Aliens worked quickly to get Abdullah into the harness. They latched the seat belt material behind Abdullah's back so he couldn't loosen it or take it off. In a few moments, his life would depend on those latches.

"I swear to Allah, we are telling you the truth. *HE* is the Abdullah you are looking for. Not us. Please. Just let us go. We are poor goat herders. We don't want any trouble.," they pleaded.

"Poor goat herders huh?" Same shit they all claimed when they were caught. Chief would have at least respected them a little more if they just admitted who they were and that they were proud to be Taliban. At least then these men would be an honorable enemy worth fighting.

"Poor goat herders my ass. We'll see about that." Chief said out loud as he took digital photos, blinding them with the high intensity LED, starting another hyperactive session as the Afghans tried to figure out what happened. As they argued between themselves about the Flash, yelling to each other that the bright light must have been the devil stealing their souls, Chief pressed a transmit button.

Within seconds the digital images jumped via satellite to D.C. for comparison on a Quantico, Virginia Intelligence database. Facial recognition software, still in its infancy, had come a long way in recent years. But it still wasn't fool proof. Chief wanted to know exactly who he was dealing with. AMA was already in the bag, confirmed with preliminary DNA swabs, blood work and digital photos. But the rest of these Hajis were still cloudy. Everyone had lingering thoughts of September 11th, when known terrorists were allowed into the country by mistake. Chief wanted to know precisely who these guys were. And if the database didn't have them, it soon would. If they were high-level Taliban leaders, as Chief had been told, then Chief would find out. They might be invisible to U.S. Intelligence up to this point. Chief would make sure in just a matter of minutes that these bastards had nowhere to hide, ever again.

"You are Commanders of evil men. You go to villages and kill your own people. Women and children hate you. Your own mothers despise you and pray to Allah for your eternal life in hell! You expect me to listen to your lies all night?"

The interpreter was having a hard time keeping up the translation as Chief accelerated the pressure.

"Ok. You asked for it." Chief turned to see that Abdullah was in the harness. He gave the thumbs up and the "Bag Man" pushed a quick release valve with his foot. The large balloon inflated towards the sky within seconds.

The noise from the rushing air startled even the men in squirrel suits. A sudden rush of heat flashed through their bodies responding to an overload of adrenaline. The noise instigated them to scan the surrounding terrain for bad guys alerted by the rushing sound of Helium and CO_2 into the enormous balloon. High above in the moonless night, the Reaper UAV had their backs, scanning the surrounding area with thermal imaging technology. There were no thermal targets in the vicinity, but instincts were instincts and the men reacted accordingly. Training and muscle memory were still a big part of this mission.

Time seemed to stand still as the Team waited for Chief's orders. In thirty seconds the balloon was nearly full and headed toward the sky. The twins squirmed on their bellies, wrenching their necks to try and see what was going on.

"I told you guys that if you lied to me, I was gonna make one of you disappear!" Chief's mood was starting to change. This was going to be fun. He looked at the balloon overhead, keyed the mike and waited for the incoming bird to respond.

A strobe light, attached to the ballon, flashed above the balloon marking the location for the incoming pilots. At that elevation, the pilots could see the strobe for miles. A quick flash of the landing lights in the nose of the aircraft illuminated the bright silver reflector tape on the balloon. For a few seconds, the balloon could be seen from the ground, for miles in any direction. And the Haji captives responded at the sight of what obviously, to them, was a UFO. The massive balloon hovered in total silence. The pattern of the straps made it look like it was constructed of some sort of bright silver alloy metal. The flashing strobe lights looked like some sort of pulsating propulsion system. And just as quickly, the incoming bird shut down the lights and the strobes disappeared. The sky was completely black again.

The two Arabs couldn't comprehend what they had just seen. Their imaginations reeled, trying to understand. This was something they'd never experienced and had nothing to relate it to. They had never seen a balloon before, never mind one in pitch-blackness with strobe lights attached. This was all VooDoo to them. These men in the dark suits with dragon skins had to be Satan. No other evil spirits had powers like this. Only Satan himself. Chief had been called worse.

As the balloon continued to ascend into the sky, the bungee cord continued to unravel out of the bag and string it's way up into the nite. Abdullah, sitting on the ground in his harness, was the anchor. He felt the cord tug as it reached the end. Seconds away from the fastest ride in his life, Abdullah started to scream too. He had no idea what was to come, but whatever it was, it scared the living hell out of him.

The urine smell came again. Only a few more seconds and this bastard would be on his way to another world.

"This is your last chance you two. Tell me where your units are. Tell me who is in charge. I want to know everything there is to know. What weapons do you have? Where are they? How much food do you have? Where is it?"

Chief was laying it on thick and fast, cranking up the pressure until the Afghans couldn't think straight, all the while, Chief was reading the digits on the corner of his visor telling him where the aircraft was and how long it would take to get there. An Air Force black ops C17 Modified was in bound to his specific GPS coordinates. They had a bead on the balloon and knew precisely what was waiting on the ground to be hauled into the back of the aircraft.

The wonderful thing about technology was that Chief didn't have to do a damn thing. Just push a button. He didn't have to talk, just watch and make sure everything was synchronized. The bright flashing strobe guided the pilot perfectly into position. The plane descended in altitude as the pilot leaned back on the throttles.

"Arch Angel Six, We have hook-up in sight. ETA one mike." came a professional voice over Chief's earpiece.

The pilot pulled back on the throttle gently a little more and the engine noise reduced to resemble a hum. The plane was nearly silent as it approached the balloon in a glide pattern. At the right altitude with the throttles back, the bird would fly just ahead of stall speed, almost completely silent even in the cockpit.

This was the newest of the U.S. Air Force's cargo planes and it was as stealthy as any other in the U.S. inventory. The capabilities were astounding. It was kind of overkill for a mission like snatching one man off the ground. But what the hell. Better than having to truck this guy out by himself over miles of inhospitable Afghani terrain.

Chief keyed the mike one time to break squelch. Acknowledgment. At the nose of the bird, two long poles extended out past the fuselage on both sides of the cockpit. The pilot flew into the bungee cord beneath the balloon. The two poles collapsed toward each other like a large pair of scissors, caught the bungee cord, cut the balloon loose, and latched the bungee cord into a reel system. The cord went under the aircraft and continued to the back tailgate. Two more of the aircrew in the back watched to make sure the cable was lined up correctly. If it failed to slide into the recovery system, they would push a button and the bird would release the bungee cord. If everything went correctly, whatever was on the ground at the end of that bungee would come whipping up off the ground at nearly 160 mph.

There were times the system didn't work right, but tonight was not going to be a failure. The cord ran straight into the pulley. A crewman ran down the ramp to catch the cord with his ten-foot long aluminum hook. He pulled as hard as he could and engaged the cord into the pulley retrieval system inside the aircraft. He hustled back into the belly of the bird and wrapped the bungee into a recovery wheel.

"Arch Angel Six we are go for hook up!" came the radio message into Chief's ear. He leaned over and spoke softly into AMA's ear.

"This is for Azza, Batrisya and Zarena you bastard!" and then he turned to the two crying men.

"Ok you guys, I gave you all the time in the world. You LIED to me!" Chief bellowed at the screaming Afghans with exaggerated anger in his voice. The translator kept up with everything Chief yelled. And then embellished it for good measure.

"Say good bye to your little friend!" Chief mocked in the Cuban voice of Tony Montana.

Chief's timing was perfect. The bungee had stretched to its full length. As the two Arabs looked up, still on their bellies pleading for their lives and squealing like little girls, Abdullah disappeared into the black of night. He just plain flew into the air as if by magic. As the bungee retracted, the speed with which Abdullah accelerated into the air increased. In a matter of two or three seconds, he went from zero to 160mph and disappeared into the sky. The twins were screaming, scared out of their minds, unable to comprehend what they had just witnessed.

"How do they have these powers?" their brains were struggling to understand. "This must really be the devil himself!"

Over the next hour, they spilled their guts, coughing and gagging over their own saliva and the desert sand that had gotten into their mouths and noses from so much struggling. They tried to speak over their own fear with complete lack of composure. Chief recorded every word.

* * * * *

In less than 20 minutes, Chief found out where the caves were that held the largest group of insurgents in the entirety of Afghanistan. There was a major operational push about to develop, and several hundred U.S. Special Forces soldiers were about to get their asses handed to them by a fully rested, rearmed, refitted

Taliban force of several thousand. D.C. Intelligence estimates reported less than a thousand Taliban remained, most of who were "on the run". But the reality Chief just uncovered was that the very same force actually spent the last seven months re-grouping, obtaining new weapons and ammunition and had grown from a few hundred men, to a nearly three and a half thousand wintered in the higher elevations in Tora Bora, a complex system of caves near the Pakistani border near the Cyber Pass. Ninety percent of Taliban fighters that the US forces were facing were in fact Saudi Arabian and Arab insurgents of Imam Mohammed Omar. Within a few days, they were headed down the slopes to ambush the American forces. The US Special Operations Forces were walking into a massacre like no one had ever seen. And Chief, by pure coincidence, now knew just how bad it could be. So he did precisely what he knew to do. He radioed in the appropriate "Force Multipliers", reported all the new Intelligence and then had his Team dig in for the long haul. And life changed again in thirty seconds.

Within 48 hours, a wing of B-52s would be over them dropping 2000 pound bombs known as the GBU Bunker busters, capable of eliminating Taliban safe havens, tunnels and sanctuary zones. Two or three of these dropped side by side simultaneously was equivalent to several nukes, without any radiation. The concussive force crushed the tunnel systems. Devoid of oxygen, nothing within the grid square could survive. Chief would sleep well tonight. There was a special place in hell for those ignorant bastards.

In less than two additional days, recon elements of the U.S. Marines climbed up into the very same hills and tunnel complexes to conduct battle damage assessment and complete mop up operations. Their mission was to move to contact, finish off whatever Taliban might be left alive in the area, determine resistance, report back, and collect any and all intelligence they could find. The Marines didn't take long. Everything was demolished. Hard drives were collected and a few laptops and documents were bagged and tagged for evacuation to higher echelon. The intelligence they contained would devastate not only the Taliban in Afghanistan, but the entire Al-Qaeda network around the world as well.

The only thing left was a set of charcoal wall drawings inside one of the caves. Four aliens with squirrel suites, dragon skin between their legs and under their arms like webbing, huge dark eyes, and an elephant type trunk going to tanks on their backs. There was an Arab man with a turban on his head flying up through the air on a beam of light to a flying saucer.

Precious.

The marines snapped a few photos and headed back to Sanctuary Base. Chief and his team were immortalized.

Water Pig

*"One decision can mean the difference between life
and death, who goes home alive and who does not!
But you don't get to know before you decide..."*

Life Lesson Nr 9

"Hey Chief! Drink up. You're two gallons behind everyone else!" Doc said in that calm, respectful tone of his.

With nearly sixteen years of active duty, half of which was in Special Operations, Doc knew Chief was the boss, a legend he proudly and confidently followed into harms way on more than one occasion. But he also knew that *he* was the Team Doctor, whose primary responsibility was the medical health of every Team Member. His primary task now however, especially while deployed on a desert operation in Iraq, was to ensure every man's water intake was sufficient. Hydration was a critical node to be watched, monitored and rectified on a daily basis. Especially out here, because every aspect of life, from decision making, to efficiency and survival depended on water intake.

Doc kept track like a worried wet hen. And it was a sure bet he was correct. Chief was at least two gallons or more behind everyone else. That was a perpetual state of affairs. Chief was always the last one to eat, last one to sleep, first one to wake up, last one off the drop zone and first one out the door. And when it came to water, he always made sure the Team was fully hydrated first. No one else really understood it. But that's how Chief was. It carried over from his childhood. With six children in the family and very little food, he always waited until last for everything. To him, it was a matter of not participating in the primal behavior he so despised. He hated when the family argued over food instead of sharing. So now, it was just part of his long practiced behavior as a leader. Take care of the men first and they will take care of the mission.

"Dammit Doc. Not now. We're wheels up in less than thirty mikes. If I drink all that now, I'll only have to piss like a race horse when we get on the bird."

Chief suddenly realized how tired he was. No one knew they were leaving yet. He just slipped up by suggesting to Doc that birds and evacuation were in the near future. Subconsciously he reminded himself to work on keeping calm. He never lied to the Team. But going home wasn't a sure thing yet either. They'd been gone way too long and the news would be met with excitement, drawing focus away from what they should be doing.

What started out to be a seventy-two hour mission had morphed into twenty-six months in this God forsaken land of dirt and heat. The SCIF was deployed into "no man's land" with the latest technology called the Low Altitude, parachute extraction system or LAPES. The tow vehicle, a U.S. Army issued Mercedes Benz diesel truck with an 18 speed pneumatic over hydraulic manual transmission, was heavy dropped from 1500 feet in the middle of a moonless night, followed by Chief and the Team doing HALO jump, landing in the same grid square. It looked a lot easier than it actually was. But the repetitious training and real world ops all came together for a perfectly smooth operation.

Once the Team pulled everything off the cardboard impact absorbing pallets and set up the perimeter with REMBASS sensors and multi-spectral laser "wire", they wasted no time getting the inflatable tennis court tent system up. They picked the perfect location. By sunrise, Sanctuary Base was established and Chief was busy inside the SCIF sending initial reports and downloading

SATCOM traffic with mission specifics. From wheels up to mission start, barely seven hours transpired.

By using the Mercedes Engineer truck's equipment, with all of the detachable excavation tools, they were able to cover the tent with sand, hiding the 50-foot trailer inside. From any direction, the compound looked like a sand dune among the other sand dunes invisible even from the air. With the exception of the antennae pole, but that was intended to deploy and retract, leaving the covert intelligence sight completely unseen. But not everything went as planned. Now the antenna was stuck in the "UP" Position. And Chief had a case of the "red ass" over it.

Doc was persistent. He'd worked with Chief long enough to know where the boundaries were. There had been some hard lessons finding the edges in the past. Push too hard and you get your head handed to you. Don't push hard enough and you've not done your best nor your job. It was a tough thing to get a bead on Chief in those early years. Doc jokingly referred to them as his "spatial acuity deprivation days". His "SAD" days, when he was a "wannabe" trying to gain favor with Chief. Kind of like situational awareness…but different. Doc was well aware of the situation, but had no idea how to engage Chief.

"Come On Chief. We got a ton of water here. We're not humpin it out, we're not giving it away to the Hajis and I'll be damned if I'm gonna dump it all on the ground out here."

"Here!" Doc said handing a water jug to Chief. "Suck the sides in on this water pig and I'll quit buggin ya."

Doc handed the square gallon plastic water jug to Chief making sure everyone within ear shot heard what he was saying. Earlier on in the mission cycle, someone used a Sharpie permanent marker and drew a curly tail, pointy ears, a hog nose and beady eyes onto the jug. Every time someone started sucking down water, the vacuum made a squealing noise everyone could hear. At one point in time, a man was sucking so hard from being two days without water that the noise the jug made sounded just like a huge pig. As he pulled the jug away from his face, after sucking for nearly a minute in desperation, a huge snorting sound came popping out of the jug. It was a freak occurrence and a one-time deal, but everyone heard it and cracked up laughing. At that precise moment, the Water Pig was born.

Within the hour, every jug in the vicinity had the same graphics drawn on it. Whenever anyone got a drink, someone was there to urge them on.

"Wa-ter-Pig, Wa-ter-Pig" came the low rumbling chant.

"Yo Man. Go for it. Make that piggy squeal!"

"Get hydrated. Suck the sides in on that water hog and make him grunt!"

Nine times out of ten, the drinker would flush his own sinuses with water trying not to laugh, blowing fluid out his nose. The humor usually struck in mid swallow and was more than anyone could handle. Every one on the Team had a turn, falling into submissive laughter while trying to get a drink.

This event, the daily ritual of hydrating, turned into something that everyone looked forward to. It wasn't just about getting re-hydrated, even though Doc made it a mandatory part of the day, keeping records on every single man. The ritual was part of breaking the monotony of endless hours of Intelligence collection boredom. Days on end of absolutely nothing but heat, sand, intense sunlight and absolutely black moonless nights preceded by torturous insertions into denied territory and equally torturous egress back to Sanctuary Base making certain no one saw them or followed them out.

Chief took the gallon jug from Doc and raised it to his mouth. It was amazing to remember when they first arrived in the desert how hard it was to force a *quart* of water down their gullets. And they had to pee constantly too. Twenty-six months later, a gallon went down like nothing. And no one had to pee very much. It was so hot all the time, the sweat evaporated so quickly, it was easy to miss the fact their bodies were dehydrating at an astounding rate. Even Doc had to wrap his brain around that at first. He'd trained hard to keep track, using charts, temperature readings, checking evaporation rates with a stopwatch. A lot of guys argued at first. Some went into painful cramps from salt and mineral deprivation before they would listen to Doc with full confidence. Eventually, everyone took Doc for granted and just did whatever he said.

As Chief finished his gallon with the obligatory suction noise and squeal, men on the team held up small pieces of paper with numbers written on them as if scoring an Olympic event. Chief received fours and fives out of possible nines. There were no tens. "No one was perfect", another inside joke that glued their camaraderie together at the shoulder.

"Man. That tasted like...." Chief started to say.

"Yeah. Like another one" Doc cut in. "Here" Doc said handing Chief another gallon pig.

"Later" Chief protested again. "Right now we got shit to do. Like one of you assholes is gonna shimmy up that pole and un-fuck the SATCOM... AGAIN! How many times have I told you knuckleheads? You *cannot* keep spinning that pole around in circles looking for the bird and expecting that cable to stay intact! It *always* pulls the cable off the antennae! You people *know* that! "

Every man on the team looked at each other waiting for someone else to make a move to the rear of the rig. Chief's patience was wearing thin. They could tell by his body language and his tone. A pneumatic over hydraulic pump was used to force the 75-foot fiberglass mast up into the air with SATCOM antennae at the top. This contraption tied the SCIF, deployed somewhere in the desert of Iraq, to all of the Intel consumers Chief and his Team fed intelligence to. Some contractor sourced the apparatus from a manufacturer that constructed mobile TV trucks with the exact same electric over hydraulic system that extended the antennae pole configuration for news networks to use "at the scene", to transmit their coverage back to their station. So if it worked for them, Chief assumed it would work for what he needed to do. So they took some black budget money, went shopping and came back with a one of a kind prototype, blended with "off the shelf" equipment that was already available. Being assigned as the "Civilian Liaison Group" military attache' had perks. Not the least of which was getting to see all the cool stuff people were building in the "Beltway Bandit" world. The antennae system worked flawlessly when the vehicle was parked on flat concrete and asphalt. Straight up, straight down. With very little noise. But it was not made for tactical environments. Especially the desert. The baby powder sand filling the pneumatic seals, packed in like cement, preventing the pole from retracting into the "parked" position. To make matters worse, after 26 months on site, the master vehicle sunk into the sand canting it just enough off perfect level that it prevented the pole from retracting under it's own weight. It was designed to retract autonomously, in the case power might be lost, so the TV crews could return to their stations. But the slight angle Chief observed was just enough to prevent a smooth recovery. The dirt made everything worse. The pole was stuck now, compromising their otherwise perfectly stealthy desert location. And it was NOT coming down any time soon.

Everyone knew it. They'd dealt with the exact same problem for months now. Up and down was a problem, but you could still rotate the pole left and right to acquire the satellite. Except that no one ever knew where the satellite was. Every time there was an Intelligence Data Dump required, the "BIRD" had to be re-acquired. The only way to find it was to rotate the pole until it locked on the beacon signal coming from the overhead satellite. And routinely, the operators inside the 46-foot long semi-trailer shelter refused to stick their heads out from the comfort of the A/C inside the SCIF to count the revolutions that the pole spun. Eventually... POP! The cable got so tight, wrapping around the pole as it revolved looking for the "bird", that the cable pulled off the antennae and comms were lost. Since the pole would not retract, the only option to fix it was to shimmy up the pole and re-connect the cable to the antennae.

Chief was annoyed again, doing his best to maintain his own temper. He complained to the contractors when the system was first fielded and told them there was an unsatisfactory condition with SATCOM acquisition that needed immediate attention. The formal written report went out four hours before the beeper went off and the system was deployed to Iraq before anyone could address the problem. In a garrison peacetime training environment, this problem wasn't a big deal. But in a real world deployment, these little things could pile up, cause problems and undermine an otherwise perfectly good mission. There was no fixing the fault before deployment. Over two years later, they were still dealing with the same issue. When were they ever going to learn?

"Hey Chief! We lost SATCOM again!" came a voice from the doorway of the air-conditioned semi-trailer. Everyone rolled their eyes and braced for what was sure to come next. Everyone's eyes were glued to Chief's face, waiting for that look. And just as Chief was about to go off, the voice continued.

"Oh Yeah. And the Helos are early. Fifteen minutes out!"

"God Dammit" Chief bellowed out loud. Cover blown. Everyone locked onto Chief's face, looking for confirmation the info was true.

The head ducked back into the trailer, the door slammed and the "L" shaped latch rotated into the locked position. The door was locked with "most haste", knowing full well they just fucked up and Chief was about to blow his stack.

Chief was *so ready* to get the hell out of there. Everyone was!

"All right. Fuck it. I'm going up the pole. You guys get to do the heavy lifting since it's so damn hot out here. Get all this shit ready to upload on pallets for transfer to the Helos when they get here."

Chief watched the body language of his men. They were all like coiled springs, waiting to bounce. In one second, the image of his men with anticipation and joy on their faces burned into his memory. He was so proud of them.

"We ordered two 47s and a Cobra gunship for air cover. Everything not on the pallets goes inside the trailer and we blow it in place. Ordinance! Set the Thermites. We'll blow this popsicle stand when we're wheels up!" Chief yelled over his shoulder as he walked to the rear of the shelter, prepping himself for the ascension up the pole.

"Be ready for wheels up in ten minutes! I am going to fix this cable for the last fucking time. We absolutely must get this last Intel dump to the consumers. There is a war coming gentlemen. No matter how much we tried to tell them there was another option, the powers that be have spoken. We gotta get this intelligence back to the big house so there is a historical record of what we knew and when. Get moving. Those birds are NOT going to wait on us. Remember gentlemen, we're in denied territory and there are Indians in them hills."

A sudden and new sense of urgency overwhelmed every man on the Team.

"Fuckin Whoah!"

"I'll be Got-dammed! We're finally getting out of this hell hole!"

Chief reached the rear of the shelter and swung himself up onto the back of the trailer. He grabbed onto the fiberglass pole and hoisted himself up. Years of pull-ups and pushups made the task look simple as his bulging biceps betrayed his age, a full ten years older than most men on the team. A sense of joy and motivation had overtaken every single man, including Chief. It was finally time to go home.

"Wow! Not bad for an old timer" someone snorted.

"Fukin "A". Let's get outta here" came another voice over the laughter.

God damn these young pups, Chief thought.

"I should have been a cook!" Chief said under his breath, tired to the bone and dreading the climb ahead of him. At least it was the last time anyone would have to climb this damn thing. A sudden sense of calm overcame Chief as he let his mind wander to the reality that they were finally leaving this God forsaken desert. No more sand, no more goat shit, no more six-hour travel through hostile desert to get into position for a shift of 24 hours of surveillance. The thought of a cold beer made his skin pucker like goose flesh. That was an indicator that it was time to shut down the emotions and focus.

"Hey. Knock off the chatter gentlemen and lets get rockin! Time's a wastin'," Gunny chastised.

"Hey Chief? Can you see the Helos from up there?" someone mocked. Everyone chuckled, yet some of the men cracked up harder as they knew Chief was pissed having to climb that pole yet again. But everyone also knew that Chief had a sense of humor and that he would be able to tell when they were teasing respectfully. No one ever thought of being disrespectful to Chief. It had been a long hard and demanding mission. They all needed a good laugh. Chief might be a little upset, but every single man on the Team knew he was up there doing something every single one of them had done in the past, several times each. Chief never made anyone do anything that he wouldn't do himself. He was *that* kind of a leader. And they all respected him fully because of it. Getting the last Intelligence Dump to the White House Situation room was top priority. Chief was all about mission accomplishment. Having the younger guys do all the heavy lifting while he ensured the Intelligence got back to higher echelon was a simple decision. A decision that would make all the difference in the world when it came to survival.

As Chief wrapped his legs around the pole, focused on the cable strands, trying to reconnect the wires to the antennae, his "Spidy Hairs" began to tingle. The hair rose on the back of his neck and for some reason, he looked up towards the horizon. What he saw horrified him. A smoke trail headed straight for him.

In a split second, everything changed.

KABOOM!

Just over the hill, nearly six kilometers away, an Arkansas National Guard Unit was tooling around the desert in a hard-shelled Hummer. On the top of the vehicle was the new, up-to-date, most highly advanced version of the Tube Launched, Optically, Wire Guided Missile or T.O.W. that the Army had in its inventory. The four man team consisting of a driver, a Commander, usually a Lieutenant, a gunner and a targeting specialist, were charged with protecting Infantry soldiers from enemy tank and armored vehicles. The heat seeker head was engineered to lock onto a target and accelerate to Mach 2, two times the speed of sound. A 2 inch diameter depleted uranium rod would puncture the enemy armor like an ancient Roman spear through a shield. Compounded Phosphorus followed the spear through the hole, detonating inside the tank or armored personnel carrier. The follow on fire from the white phosphorus incinerated the resistant armor and anyone inside, detonating any on board munitions and exploding everything from the inside out. The concept was ingenious. Because of the kinetic energy, traveling so fast, because of the phosphorus on board, and because of the internal fire, a huge missile with a monstrous warhead was no longer needed. Nor was the entire ancillary equipment and transporters required for the much larger offensive systems and missiles of the past decades. This was a versatile, expedient, violently lethal weapon of the future. And the Arkansas National Guard was so very lucky to own it.

This Reserve unit trained one weekend a month and two weeks out of every year so they could back up the Active Duty Military. At a cost of nearly one million dollars each, no one in the unit ever saw a real live T.O.W. Missile before their deployment to the Middle East. All their training was done at the local high school gymnasium, using computer simulators and canvas screens with laser pointers. Their training was just a very rudimentary video game. Now that they deployed, they were issued real live missiles and couldn't wait to see what it would do. They just HAD TO go blow something up.

So, without Command Authority, without targeting input, without weapon's release authority, the young Pharmacy worker, now Butter-bar Lt. took his crew into the desert to blow some shit up. The only problem he had? There wasn't anything out there but dirt and pipelines. Had they targeted a pipeline like Sgt. Beumont wanted, they'd really have their ass in a sling. Someone would notice the fireball and the resulting explosion. So they decided to drive further and further looking for a camel, or some Hajis to fuck with. What they thought were Hajis turned out to be Chief and his Team. They never, ever suspected they would find Americans out there in this uninhabitable land of Sand Niggers, goats and sheep.

Although the missile was intended to defeat armor on tanks and infantry fighting vehicles, Chief and his Team didn't have any armor protection. They didn't have a tank. They had a mobile SCIF made from an 18 wheeler trailer. The electronics inside were worth hundreds of millions of dollars and the Intelligence it collected, analyzed and sent back to Decision Makers was priceless. But all this T.O.W. crew saw was a target. In the vast, open space of the Saudi/Iraqi border area, there was only one thing they saw that was worth blowing up. Sand Niggers. They'd seen a few goats, a couple guys on camels and a few tents. *But this*, this unidentified tan painted box had to be some Iraqi military assholes out doing something they shouldn't be doing. Had to be.

As the targeting specialist verified the missile was hot, he told the LT and waited for the order. The gunner was giddy as he watched men on the ground uncover a huge tan box, hidden below the sand. Through the scope he watched a man on the antennae pole.

The excitement grew as he awaiting the order to fire.

"Light em up" the LT said as if rehearsed from one of the "Call of Duty" video games he was so used to playing. And with that command, the trigger was pulled.

They heard a pop as the initial ignition system went off, then a whizz as the projectile left the tube. Copper wire began to unspool from behind the missile and the targeting specialist moved the joystick left and right, watching the missile respond to his commands as it flew over and around the sand dunes, headed for the SCIF.

The secondary ignition system initiated and the rocket motor ignited, sending flames out behind the missile, accelerating to Mach 2 in the blink of an eye. The whole thing took less than ten seconds, and what used to be a target, was suddenly nothing more than a burning pile of phosphorus and metal.

"Hot DAMN! Did you see that? Those fuckin' Hajis is *HISTORY…. DOG!*"

They could hardly contain their giddiness as they celebrated the secondary explosions, ammunition cooking off and some sort of thermite grenades that contributed immensely to the fireball rising into the sky. The sinister laugh coming out of their mouths was even more grotesque because of the deep southern Arkansas drawl. Their belly laughs curled into their guttural throats making them sound more like hyenas than humans. They were genuinely proud of themselves and couldn't wait to get back and tell everyone else that they'd saved Americans from a certain devastating Iraqi attack.

What they never understood was that what they saw, was Chief silhouetted against the skyline, not Iraqi forces. They targeted the semi-trailer under him. The men on the ground outside were also U.S. Soldiers of the highest caliber who served above and beyond the call of duty for over 26 months in the most inhospitable territory known to man. They were hustling around the distinctively unfamiliar trailer and truck assembly, loading equipment and making ready to leave not because they were going to attack Americans but because they were finally going home to their loved ones. Even though those men were not the intended target, the blast radius and the phosphorus was sure to get them.

Friendly Fire Isn't

"Friendly Fire Isn't... Friendly. The pain and recovery is still the same, no matter who shoots you!"

Life Lesson Nr 10

The first conscious notion Chief had was a sick feeling in his stomach that something was wrong. Terribly wrong. He'd been in bad situations before, but this was way over the top. He had an overwhelming feeling of weakness and total incapacitation. That feeling was so foreign, so unacceptable to a man so strong and so determined. He was an elite warrior that knew what fight meant. But now, he could barely breathe, couldn't hear anything but his own heart beating in his ears and his own breath entering and leaving his lungs. There was a sense of vulnerability on a scale he'd never known and his body was completely unable to move.

As Chief's brain slowly came into full consciousness, he instinctively began to fight. Adrenaline rushed through his blood stream and a weird feeling overtook his entire body. He was suddenly aware of grit in his mouth, the familiar taste of dirt he remembered well from being caught in desert sand storms and rotor blade wash on so many previous missions. His nostrils, packed with that same dirt, kept him from getting the oxygen his body so desperately required. Chief was slowly suffocating and his heart was trying frantically to pump fresh oxygen and blood to his brain. But the oxygen wasn't getting in.

Chief tried desperately to lift his hands and wipe his mouth, blow the sand from his nose and clear away the grit tearing his eyeballs apart. It felt like sandpaper grinding into the tender cornea. But his arms and hands felt extremely heavy, yet missing from his internal conscious inventory. They just wouldn't respond, as if they were gone.

His eyes were full of mud, a result of bleeding mixing with the dirt that was blown into his face by the incoming missile impact. Blood poured from his ears, mouth and nose as well, but he couldn't feel it yet. Everything was numb and tingling, blocking most of the pain that would make him unconscious.

As Chief tried with all his might to lift his torso, pull his arms into shape to prop himself up on his elbows, he realized nothing was working. So strange. He suddenly felt something he never felt before. A deep sense of concern, a sort of self-pity mixed with anger that his body was severely injured. There was a feeling right next to being deeply offended that he just didn't understand. Never before had he felt that his body was separate from himself. But it was now. His brain was in overdrive as he tried without success to get his muscles to respond. Every command his brain ordered went unheard by his body. Slowly Chief realized that all the body functions he took for granted on a daily basis were no longer there. And it tore through his soul with fear and anxiety. For the first time in his life, he was truly scared.

He tried to will his legs to move but they didn't respond either. His brain was telling him that all of his appendages were still there, but he couldn't move his head to look and he couldn't feel them. He wrestled with the idea and forced his mind to settle.

Chief realized he was getting way too emotional. He forced his mind into idle mode and talked to himself with that deep inner voice again.

"No sense in getting all worked up about something as silly as missing limbs. They had to be there somewhere. Where would they be otherwise?" he chastised himself.

As he drifted off into unconsciousness again, his body felt like a truck had him pinned to the hot desert sand. The unexplainable combination of weakness, numbness and pain kept his brain wrestling with way too much incorrect input. Nothing added up. He had no idea what was going on, or why he wasn't still doing the last thing he was doing before he woke up... whatever that was.

"Woke up?"

Now that was an indicator!

Everything in his mind was pushed to the outer edges and became impertinent as panic set in and Chief suddenly recognized his rapid heart rate. The speed of his beating heart was the only thing he could hear, muffled by a high-pitched ringing in his ears. His breathing ceased. His body was telling him to breathe, but his chest collapsed, his diaphragm paralyzed and refused to cooperate.

Chief suddenly realized what the oncoming panic was telling him. He was dying, and he knew it. He felt nauseated all of a sudden. Finally realizing he was laying face down in the dirt, Chief willed his head to rise, arched his back and somehow got his head to move. The motion was more of a spasm than anything controlled or intended. He craned his neck and forced his face to one side. Blackout was coming fast. His heart pounded like a drum in his ears. Death danced in celebration mere seconds away and Chief could feel his brain starting to dismiss everything he concerned himself with. Nothing was important anymore. He was out of "fight". He resigned himself involuntarily to the inevitable. He was really going to miss his two sons. He felt the sinking heart and pain in his son's hearts when someone told them their dad was dead. It hurt Chief worse than the physical pain he currently endured. For whatever reason, that thought was the motivation he needed.

Through the dream-like state, Chief suddenly felt one last huge wave of strength, surging to give everything left in his body enough energy to try one more time. Adrenaline spiked and his body responded.

As he struggled to inhale, the dirt packed tighter into his nostrils and throat. Primal instinct took over and his body arched, retched, strained and ejected the precious water Doc made him force down his gut, what seemed to have been just minutes prior. The fluid flushed out his throat and spewed against the roof of his mouth, into his sinus cavity and out his nose. A strange mix of blood, dirt and water cascaded out of his head and into the sand in front of him leaving behind a moist, open airway to his lungs. Instinctively, he inhaled hugely, exhaled and began to cough. Chief's airway was suddenly clear and the huge volume of air rushing into his lungs made him cough harder, making his eyes hurt and his head thump. More of the fine dirt got sucked into his throat and lungs by the vacuum of his diaphragm finally coming back to life. A few more gulps of air and the coughing increased. His body was now on overload, trying to get oxygen to his brain while simultaneously dealing with the environmental hazards of sand, dirt, blood, water and smoke.

Barely able to see and completely unable to distinguish color, Chief realized briefly that his eyeballs were full of blood and refused to focus. They were more like dark purple grapes now than eyeballs. He wasn't really sure he wanted to see what was going on. That gallon of water he was so resistant to take from Doc had just opened his nose and mouth, saving his life. In one fleeting second, he reminded himself to thank Doc later. And then the thought was gone.

The rancid smoke filled the air tasting like tar and burning rubber. But there was something else mixed in with it. Something Chief could not comprehend right now. It didn't really matter. He just needed more air. It annoyed Chief to no end that the air sucking into his body tasted that bad. But he soon pushed the thought aside during this primal dance of survival.

Blood poured from his mouth and he was aware of the bloody mist being inhaled back into his lungs. He could taste his own blood over the dirt and Chief's brain was starting to register the implausible fact that he was severely injured. He instinctively knew it was bad simply because there was no pain whatsoever. He'd been injured before and was amazed at how the human subconscious could withstand broken bones, bullet holes, and blast injuries and never register any pain. He watched his own men in Mogadishu, taking round after round, but continuing to fight on without much concern or showing any pain. Shock could be a wonderful thing. But then again, Chief knew it could kill him too!

He was exhausted now. He knew something serious happened, but it didn't make sense that he was so tired. Oxygen was a wonderful thing when you had it. But life really sucked when it wasn't available. The clarity of his mind depended solely on how much oxygen was present as his body struggled to get more into his blood stream. Over the next several minutes, all Chief could do was breathe. He'd come so very close to checking out and he somehow processed that fact. It made him get serious and focus. The longer he breathed, the sharper his conscious thoughts became. He had to figure out what was wrong with his body and fix it. Was there something on top of him? Obviously the vehicles were in pieces. Maybe this heavy feeling, this incapacitation had something to do with vehicle parts on top of his body. But it made no sense. How could the vehicles be in pieces? As time went by, Chief assembled facts and came up with answers. It was a slow process and that really pissed him off. He needed to know what was going on and he was not willing to wait much longer.

The last thing he remembered, way out on the periphery of his memory were the words, "Going home." Damn it. He knew better than to get his hopes up. Time and time again, he and his crew learned the painful lesson of celebrating too soon. More than once they'd been enjoying the thoughts of going home, getting back to their wives, girlfriends or loved ones, only to have the aircraft diverted to some other "Important mission." More than once it was a "Hurry up and wait" mission where National Leadership, namely the President decided to give diplomacy a chance at the last minute, forcing Chief and his Team back in to the painful idle mode after being ramped up on the razor's edge. Such had been the case in Haiti during the six or seven military coupes over a five-year period. It really sucked to be coming off a mission, hoping to be making love in a few hours and end up in some aircraft hangar somewhere bored out of their skulls waiting, sometimes for days on end, "Giving diplomacy a chance to work." It never worked. But no one was going to listen to Chief until it was too late.

As the daylight inevitably came yet again, dread overtook Chief as he realized he was still face down in the sand, knowing it was going to be another long, hot, dry day in the Iraqi desert. Not a whole lot of Americans got to know this feeling. Most of the U.S. troops were yet to be deployed, and damn few people even knew Chief and his Team were deployed to "no man's land" out there in the middle of absolutely nowhere. Actually, other than a very select few at the White House and the Pentagon, no one in the military nor the American public knew that there were soldiers in this part of the world. Nothing unusual for Chief and his Team. That's what they did. They went places and did things and got back without telling anyone where they'd been, or that they were even gone to begin with.

Chief was awake now. Somehow he'd fallen asleep and stayed asleep for the duration of the entire night. He never slept all night.

The indicators were stacking up in his peripheral mind. What got his attention immediately was the temperature rising into the 100s again. That meant he must have slept eight hours, maybe more. Time didn't matter at the moment, nor did he know what time it was when he fell asleep. Things were really starting to get hot when Chief's consciousness came to full peak.

"Ughhhhh" he instinctively groaned as he rolled over onto his back. The sunlight pierced his vision and made his brain hurt on a scale he never anticipated, nearly making him vomit from the stabbing pain.

"What the fuck" his voice drifted off into space realizing his throat was toast. The gritty sand damaged his larynx. It was just better not to talk, he realized as he tried to swallow. What Chief thought was his tongue, swollen and bleeding at the edges where his teeth punctured it, felt more like a dead cat and did little to assist the swallow attempt. He had no saliva and apparently his tongue had actually been removed, replaced by an old, dry boot.

"Maybe the cat was living in the boot" he thought to himself. And then he wondered what the hell he was thinking and why he was thinking of that?

His front teeth were knocked inward, leaning up against the roof of his mouth. Several other teeth were completely shattered from the impact. Others were just gone from his mouth entirely. Every time he inhaled, the nerve pain from exposed nerve roots shot to his brain. Instinctively he closed his mouth and tried breathing through his broken nose and swollen sinuses. Chief was dealing with more sensory overload than he'd ever experienced in his entire lifetime, all the while trying to make sense of what happened.

Training kicked in. Subconsciously he was taking inventory of what hurt, what didn't, what was important. What no longer was important. Just like he always did after a mission when things went sideways. Chief's "inner self" was alive and well, an unexpected comfort when he finally realized it through the multi-front struggle.

Some level of strength was returning to his body, as pitiful as it was. Apparently the initial impact gelled his nervous system and forced his body into primal survival mode. He didn't remember falling to the earth. Just the concussive force blowing him through the air like a rag doll. But he was far enough away from the burn radius that his trip up the antennae pole must be the only reason he was still alive.

The numbness was wearing off now. A full twelve hours transpired, completely unaccounted for. Time was irrelevant right now. Pain was slowly creeping back in, and there was plenty of pain to go around for sure. The primal dance in his head between pain and blacking out was about to go into high gear.

As the hours went by, Chief started to piece things together. He vaguely remembered telling his Team to get things ready to pack up and get out of Dodge.

Anger crept into his mind as he remembered telling his guys over and over to watch what the hell they were doing so they would NOT get the antennae cable into a bind around the pole and tear it off completely like had happened so many times before.

It slowly sunk into Chief's head, that the single decision he'd made to go up the pole is what probably saved his life. But to the contrary, that decision also killed the rest of his men. Instead of making someone on the Team shimmy up the pole to fix it, Chief decided to fix it himself. His priority, regardless of how infuriated he was, was to get the Intel Report back to the consumers. Period. He was too pissed off over having to discuss the antennae cable yet again, knowing full well he would lose his temper if he had to watch the dumb looks on everyone's faces as they pointed fingers at each other claiming no responsibility. The Team consisted of outstanding professionals, but they were also like a bunch of kids at times like this. No one ever did anything wrong, it was always the other guy!

Chief's brain was primal now, unable to grasp the concept that he just survived a missile strike. Slowly he pieced together the fact that there was an explosion. The explosion had to be pretty big. The vehicle was gone. The trailer was in pieces and most of the metal was burning. A really sick feeling came over Chief, punching him in his guts as his brain pieced together what might have gone on. He vaguely remembered telling his Ordnance man to ready the thermite grenades. For security reasons, he personally mounted thermite grenades inside the classified shelter and instructed everyone on the Team how to detonate them. If enemy forces found their hide position, all anyone had to do was pull one trip wire and the entire Top Secret, Compartmented SCI system would melt down in minutes. Preventing the enemy from obtaining the hard drives, the crypto and satellite communications gear was top priority. Chief knew how sensitive this entire prototype operation was. And he was willing to put his life on the line to protect what was inside this innocuous box on wheels. Assuming the explosion must have come from inside the semi-trailer, the realization that the explosion was his responsibility shook him to the core. Then it hit him.

Where the hell was everybody?

All he knew now was that his team was missing. Now he was fighting for more than just survival. This feeling of being held to the ground was more than he could take.

However intolerable, this "problem" had complete control over Chief's life at the moment. He couldn't walk. He couldn't stand up or even sit up. He couldn't get to his knees. But after going through the internal inventory of what worked and what didn't, he somehow managed to get his arms to work so he could crawl. The bitter realization that his spine was shattered slowly sunk into the outer region of Chief's mind. That was unacceptable. So he shoved it to the far reaches and focused on what "GOOD" he could find.

Slowly he made his way on his belly, across the sand, towards what was left of the trailer. The concussive forces and kinetic energy of the explosion must have blown his body away from the carnage, to a distance outside the blast radius. Otherwise, how could he still be here? Pieces of the trailer were still burning and the smell of thermite and melting aluminum was making him sick. Rancid smoke wafted over him as he crawled through the dirt, looking for any remaining "Water Pigs". He needed to intake fluids. Maybe that way he could swallow and rid his mouth of the nasty taste and grit. Time to focus on five meter targets.

Chief was weak, only able to pull his body a few meters at a time before having to stop and rest. It took every ounce of determination he had in his soul to accomplish the most minimal of tasks. The frustration was building into rage. And that was exactly what Chief needed more than anything, motivation to keep going.

He had to find his men. They had to be here somewhere. God help them if they were out fucking off. That concept caught Chief by surprise. He knew they weren't. Why would he think something like that at a time like this? A psychological defense mechanism keeping him from admitting the fact that they were all probably dead? He had to have hope. Had to find something to hold onto, just to keep the panic at bay.

Every once in a while, Chief awoke to find himself in nearly the same position. This was such bullshit. He fought hard to overcome the human survival instinct of blacking out. He was losing strength, losing focus, losing the battle he was fighting so desperately. He needed someone to come help. But there was no one. He called out, only to find his voice escaped him. It was too hard to talk, and nearly impossible to yell. Breathing was much more important than talking. So he forced himself to concentrate on the five meter targets.

At a very young age, Chief learned in training, while submerged in twenty feet of water, hands and feet tied behind his back, to concentrate on the tasks that meant the most to his survival and prioritize where he was going to expend his energy. It was a pretty basic thought process. It made sense. Nature did it all the time instinctively, so it wasn't too hard to learn. Cutting out all the man made bullshit and drama was the hardest part. But once he'd done it the first time and knew what it felt like, it was easy to repeat.

All he knew at the moment was *everything* was wrong. The ringing in his ears, the smells of burning metal, human flesh, human hair. Then it hit him. The smells mixed in with the smoke and the dirt when he was trying to breathe....

"Oh...... my......God....". There was human flesh and hair......burning!

That meant someone was dead. His body quit on him, and his brain fought harder to stay in control. He really wanted to just stop, to rest, to just drift off to sleep. But the smell created another incendiary level in his soul, providing huge motivation by kicking his fight or flight system into high gear. A primal instinct to find his men came over him with vengeance. Fighting was part of his DNA. To fight to the death with everything he had inside him. And if he had to die, he would do so with honor.

He had to fight, to win, to never succumb. But as much as he refused to admit it, Chief was human. And the human body had primal defense mechanisms. Like black outs. Protecting the brain, making the heart return to near normal, sustaining life through the autonomic nervous system, controlling the neuro-chemical dumps. Black out the brain and recognition goes away, allowing everything to return to somewhat normal, or at least survivable tolerances.

The fight Chief engaged in now, was inside. At that place where the bullshit stops, and a warrior is born. Anyone can physically develop into an intimidating image. To lift weights, run, be a competitor. Like putting vinyl siding on a house, anyone can dress things up to look good. Inside is where it counted. Inside, where the real definition of "tough" comes from. That is where a soldier is most vulnerable. Special Operations was full of guys who could pass the test. Full of men who could get through the training. And there was a pretty good chance that if they made it through all of that, there would be a real warrior inside. That wasn't something you could teach anyone. The warrior had to be there at birth. The training scenarios just made it visible to everyone else that mattered! Training was designed with a singular purpose. To find out which ones had *it*. Then polish that warrior into a powerful elite weapon. They had to own the primal fight deep down inside. To sort out which men would find it on their own and which ones would quit and walk the other way, able to justify their actions in their own minds. Many of the men who finished BUDs, the Q course and Ranger Indoctrination Program, would go on to be great soldiers. True Warriors. But the ones who had the brains, the fight and the determination to be separate from the herd, were the ones who made it into Chief's world. That was Tier One territory. And there were very, very few who made it there. The rest of the herd would forever be, "Wannabe" soldiers.

Chief had been there a few times in his own lifetime, brushing right up against the boundary of tolerance, succumbing to his own demons.

"I don't need this bullshit" was his most likely terminology when he was at the end of his rope and couldn't find a reason to go on. That was all back in earlier days when he trained with soldiers half his age, suffering along with the rest for their innocent stupidity and baffling decisions. But right at the end, when Chief was ready to quit and walk away, something always happened. That's when he got pissed. That's when he said, "fuck you. Make me quit!"

No one ever knew until tested in battle what they really would do. Everyone hoped they would stand up to the stress of combat and do the right thing. But no one ever really knew. Not until they were there. Some men ended up very surprised that they got through. Some died trying. And more than a few recognized after a very long fight, that they were just as human as the next guy. On more than one occasion Chief was surprised by what he'd seen in his men. Very few times did he have to cut anyone loose. They all had "it".

Now once again Chief was being tested. At a primal level. He had to find strength. Some way, no matter how injured he was, no matter how much it hurt, he had to press on regardless. He had to find his men. That was the only thing to consider now. Focus. Breathe, crawl, focus....

What seemed like minutes, in reality was several more hours transitioning into late evening. Feelings were changing again. The fight was softening, turning to acceptance, resistance faltering, turning to weakness. Chief was losing and he knew it. He struggled hard again to find the fight. Whatever this feeling was that was holding him down, it was winning. And for a split second, Chief realized he was getting comfortable. Comfort was an indicator for a Tier One Operator. Warning bells went off in his head. He knew that comfort was the wrong thing to be feeling right now. Even though the human condition sought out comfort, every living thing automatically sought out comfort, tranquility, peace, he knew he had to find something inside to resist. Peace and comfort were the things a Tier One Warrior trained himself to deny. Refusing to accept comfort kept them sharp, on the edge. Ready.

* * * * *

Another complete day was gone and Chief awoke shuddering from the cold of night. Temperatures dropped twenty to thirty degrees routinely when the sun went down. In the outer reaches of his conscious mind, Chief could hear screams. Or was it? He couldn't be sure. He was blacking out again. But from what? He still had not realized how seriously injured he really was. If he was in trouble, or injured, he would hurt, right? His brain wrestled hard with making sense of it all. As Chief lost consciousness and drifted off into that peaceful, quiet state of sleep, he vaguely wondered if he was dying. The screams were annoying, taunting his brain, reminding him of Bosnia. Those damn screams......

Zeus

"It pays to have friends in your life who are really worth a shit!"

Life Lesson Nr 11

Time was a ghost without consequence or meaning now. It came and went without restraint, without any mechanical mechanism to keep track. Time was suspended while Chief's brain struggled with basic life support tasks associated with the human body.

It was impossible to determine how long he'd been unconscious. All he knew was that the sun was gone again. Unable to move from the freezing cold desert night, his body was stiff from both the cold and the apparent nerve damage to his spinal cord.

Pain woke him yet again, and Chief found his body imprisoned in a perpetual state of misery. Only this time, the pain was compounded by the full body shakes he experienced. Dehydration was setting in and the loss of blood made him weak contributing to the shaking as well.

Those God forsaken screams that brought him to consciousness so many times before were gone for the moment. Chief felt a deep sense of dread creep into his heart as he realized he was alone and really, really in trouble. He thought of his two boys, of the lake behind his house, then chastised himself for losing focus, succumbing to the denial his brain so desperately needed.

"Pussy" he thought to himself. "Time to suck it up and be the warrior you're supposed to be. The one you've been advertising for so long." He felt like such a fraud now. Whatever was going on, this was NOT the warrior Chief he knew himself to be.

For the first time since he was a young boy, fear crept into his mind, so unfamiliar, so foreign and dreaded. Fear was something he had no experience with controlling. He forced himself to control the panic, control his breathing and prepare to report his condition to himself. An internal inventory was underway again. Everything from his diaphragm down was missing. He could move his head, but barely. When he tried, the sickening sound of bone grinding made him limit his attempts. He could move his arms, but only from the chest to his waist. Anything higher seemed impossible, and lateral movement just didn't work. That meant something was seriously wrong with his spine at the cervical level. The rest was probably just pulled muscles. There wasn't any arterial bleeding he could see, so that was a good thing to hold onto. But there also didn't seem to be anything he could do about his legs, or his pelvis. Everything from the chest down seemed to be excess luggage at the moment. And that seriously concerned him.

What used to be his Top Secret Intelligence, SCI Compartmented prototype, was now spread over the desert floor in a wide debris field. Some parts still burned bright light from the phosphorus, other parts simply smoldered rancid smoke in the deep dark cold of night. The motivation Chief needed now came from a thought creeping into the outer reaches of his subconscious. Two boys were waiting for Daddy to come home. And come hell or high water, he was going home to them.

As Chief contemplated that thought, the sick feeling in his guts returned. Maybe he was already dead. This living hell he was experiencing, blacking out, waking up, being so hot from the desert sun during the day, then freezing throughout the night could all be his eternal hell. What if that's all he had to look forward to forever more? What if this was his "living hell" for eternity?

Chief shook his head, inflicting more pain in an attempt to push the thoughts from his mind, cursing himself for even considering such stupidity. He had a mission. He had to find his men. No sooner had his focus returned to the Team, when the blood curdling screams started again.

"God Dammit!" he thought out loud.

"Where the hell is that coming from? I'm about sick of this bullshit," he said to himself as he dragged his heavy legs and body over the rear axle housing of the trailer. As Chief proceeded to crawl through the debris towards the inhuman sounds of screams that motivated him into action, he modulated his actions with caution. There was a pattern developing here. Strength seemed to leave him at an alarming rate every time he tried to crawl, followed by immense pain, unconsciousness and then more pain awakening him.

The obstacles seemed to be enormous and everywhere as Chief traversed the sand on his elbows, searching deeper and deeper within to find the strength and motivation to pull his body across the desert floor. Pieces of tires, a door panel, huge chunks of metal substructure from the trailer, hydraulic pumps, one of two large air conditioners used to cool the enormous 46 foot long shelter made up the obstacle course he found himself crawling through. The last six feet of the trailer held the air conditioning units, taking up more space than some people had as an apartment. The two huge devices were jettisoned many yards away into the desert. He tried to avoid other large burning pieces, but his body was so badly damaged and he was so exhausted, there was only so much he could do to detour through the mess. Pain was driving his train. His first taste of disability was overwhelming him, while his damaged and bleeding brain kept him from processing medical facts. His situation was dire. He just didn't now that yet. And since no one told him that, he assumed his normal state: fight mode.

The night air was cold. Probably only in the low fifties. But after an entire day lying in the direct sun up to 130 degrees, half buried in sand and dirt that crept nearer to 160 degrees, the night air was downright frigid. A full 90 to 100 degrees difference.

The heat from burning aluminum, steel, bearing grease, oil and rubber was a double edged sword. The warmth was a welcomed comfort as Chief low-crawled across the sand. But the phosphorus fires burned at over 3000 degrees Fahrenheit and there was no way to modulate the intensity. He didn't have much choice of where he could crawl either. So the fires kept licking at Chief's open wounds and sores, keeping him warm as he crawled, but also burning his flesh and choking his throat and lungs from the rancid smoke.

As he crawled forward, moving chunks of debris to the side, he focused his mind on the one task that kept him awake and alive. He had to find the source of the screams. Someone had to be making them. It had to be one of his guys. Had to be. Or was there someone else out there? Chief wasn't really sure of anything anymore. His brain wasn't working right. And somehow he processed that fact. The impact from hitting the ground snapped his neck and fractured three cervical vertebrae, he pounded his temple against the hard earth causing a brain bleed on his left temporal lobe, which rendered him unconscious for a very long time.

His brain continued to bleed over several days as he crawled, causing the pressure to build until he blacked out. Cranial fluid and blood seeped from his nose and sinuses as he lay face down in the dirt, eventually relieving enough pressure to bring him back to consciousness. He seemed to be in a perpetual dream state, keeping him from any real, forward locomotion. There seemed to be no urgency in his actions anymore. No real motivation to do anything. But the screams had an amazing impact on him. Something deep in his soul was driving him forward to find the source of what sounded like wounded dogs howling into the night sky. For now, they were just primal noises that really bothered Chief. He tried to dismiss the sounds, to ignore them. After all, they were just noises. But then, *one word* changed everything.

"Chief!"

His attention was peaked and changed the dynamics of the entire situation. His eyes snapped open and in seconds, his stomach wretched and he spewed bile and blood onto the sand. A sudden surge of adrenaline shocked his body into motion and motivated him into action.

"God Dammit where are YOU?" came a voice so high pitched, so evil sounding it was barely intelligible. His hair stood on end as Chief tried to conjure an image, trying to figure out who was making the noise, tried to recognize, to legitimize and reconcile such a heinous scenario.

"Aghghghghg! Get this shit off me! Someone help ME!"

And then there was nothing more intelligible, just screaming. Banshee, soul shattering screaming. Chief didn't recognize the voice because it really wasn't a voice at all. His hearing was so damaged, the ringing so loud, how could he be sure of anything he heard? The sounds were nothing even close to human. But Chief heard his name as clearly as anything else he could hear over the ringing. That one word motivated him to crawl faster, further, to move over more obstacles than he'd done since he first woke up... however long ago that was. He had no idea how many times he'd blacked out, or how many days had gone by, but he did know one thing. He was tired of the screams.

Another burning tire, another axle shaft, some unrecognizable chunks of metal and rubber were shoved aside as Chief continued crawling on his belly towards the source. As he reached out for another grip, something to help drag his body through the sand, he burned his hand, cursed into the dirt in frustration, then began stabbing his palm into the ground, trying to put out the burning phosphorus that stuck to his flesh.

As he grabbed onto the next obstacle, to move it out of his way, he suddenly froze in disbelief and shock. A human leg covered in bloody camouflaged pants startled him. There was no disguising the American camo pattern on the pant leg, nor the brown leather boot laced up on the foot. So many foreign countries had gotten American uniforms from the vast amounts of Chinese exports, that Special Operations made the effort and spent large sums of money to obtain and issue new uniforms with distinctive camouflage patterns, just in time for this deployment to the Iraqi desert. Distinguishing friend or foe on the battlefield was paramount and changing camouflage patterns was just one small part of the effort to limit "Friendly Fire" incidents.

The limb in Chief's hand had been ripped from the body at the hip joint. The femoral artery was apparently severed by the concussion. The impact had torn the leg loose at the groin and dumped its precious fluid into the desert sand. A beautiful polished, bright white dog bone looking ball, protruded past the red meat, encased by human flesh and fat, white tendons dangling like dental floss, all covered with burned and blackened human skin inside the camo pants. The volume of fluid that drained out of the leg ensured there was nothing left in the tissue. Now, after so much time, the leg was stiff, cold, hard and the smell transcended all the rancid smoke, burning metal and rubber. Chief's brain went primal. He was more awake now than ever. This leg was the first evidence that there were more bodies to be found.

That tinge of fear tweaked Chief in the guts again. There was no way to tell to whom this leg belonged. Regular Army and Marine soldiers put a dog tag on their boot, the last name and last four digits of their Social Security number in permanent Sharpie on their boot sole, written in the archway between the heel pad and the foot-landing pad. Everyone knew that boots survived an IED blast. But Tier One soldiers, contrary to the rest of Special Operations and Regular Military Units, never had identifying marks on them. No Tattoos, no name tags, no dog tags, nothing that the enemy could use in an interrogation session to determine who they were, or what their specialty was.

Chief didn't know who the leg belonged to, but it registered in his brain that at least one of his men must be dead. No doubt about it now. He braced himself as he reached forward in the dark, grasping at things in the sand without looking now. He didn't really want to know if there were more body parts. Chief kept going forward, shoving vehicle parts to the side making his way to the screams.

"My God. Did that leg belong to this screaming maniac? No wonder he's screaming!" Chief thought out loud. It motivated him to move faster and to fight harder. He wrestled with the idea to go back and get the leg, to drag it with him, but he just didn't have the strength or wear-with-all to think it through. The sound was getting louder, closer and it was a pretty good bet Chief was within fifty yards or so. At least that is what he told himself.

"Almost there. Keep going. Five meters at a time". His inner voice, calm, collected, kept him focused on the mundane, robotic task of slowly crawling through the sand. "Narrow the focus, concentrate on the five meter targets and eventually you'll be surprised when you get to the end. It will seem easy when you're done. The only Easy Day was Yesterday." Those simple words brought such great comfort...

"GOD DAMMIT CHIEF! Where the hell are YOU?" The screams were getting less intense now. Something was wrong. Fatigue and shock were obviously becoming factors. Whoever this was had to be one strong son-of-a-bitch to have kept up the screaming for this long.

Chief pulled himself up over a wheel hub and reflexively reeled from what he saw. The target he'd been trying so hard to get to, was nothing he expected. It didn't look like anything he recognized. Was it even human? It wasn't moving anymore. Maybe Chief was too late. Maybe God had been merciful and terminated this man's agony before Chief could get to him? The sight and the smell were revolting and Chief did everything he could do to not just quit. To crawl in the other direction and not look anymore at the huge piece of flesh that screamed him into action. If this was one of his Team, he really didn't want to see them in this condition. Something made Chief stop, drop his forehead into the sand and allowed him to just fade into unconsciousness again. Whatever this "thing" was, Chief was by no means ready to face it.

He needed a break. There wasn't much option. His body was broken, a major portion was paralyzed and the rest of him was just plain worn out from crawling. His primal brain no longer felt the motivation provided by the screams as exhaustion crept in to take over, slowing his breath, fading his brain again to complete darkness.

Chief was out of steam and drifted off into another deep sleep. The pain was enormous now. There was no comfort as he drifted off to sleep. Just another passing thought questioning, "is this the last time? Is this what death feels like?"

Another round of primal noises from human agony brought Chief back to reality. He startled awake and hurt himself more as his body jerked in response to the screams. This poor man was barely ten feet away from Chief and was screaming to the top of his lungs, his heels digging deeper and deeper holes into the sand as they thrashed about in an attempt to deal with the enormous, devastating pain. The man's face was unrecognizable, black as asphalt with large pink swaths where he'd torn off his own flesh in an attempt to extinguish the phosphorus.

His hair might have been blond before, but now it was matted down in large circular patches stuck to his flesh like melted plastic. Much of it was missing from his head, now stuck between his blackened, curled and twisted fingers. The intense heat from the phosphorus shrunk the tendons in the digits of both hands, forcing his finger joints into unspeakable geometric angles. Most of the fingernails were missing from his hands as well, from the intense pressure of trying to tear off his own flesh. Several fingers were AWOL, the rest apparently sanded to the bone in places where he'd dug into the dirt, trying in vain to control the pain. Missing flesh from his chest, legs and neck was another indicator of just how bad the pain must have been. Swaths of pink, torn through the blackened skin, exposed bone, sternum and ribs where this man writhed in excruciating pain, attempting to stop the phosphorus from consuming his soul.

Chief made his way the last few feet through the baby powder dirt and was blessed with crawling across a large lump protruding under the sand. The unmistakable squiggly tail, pointy ears and hog snout on the five gallon square plastic bottle almost made him cry. How the hell did this plastic jug survive the blast? It didn't matter. Chief tore open the top and drank what he could. Then he tried to pour some onto the man who was in and out of consciousness, screaming every time he awoke.

As Chief pulled himself up next to the creature before him, he wrestled with the automatic and overwhelming impulse to vomit from the smell of urine, feces and burning flesh and hair. This man was dying, slowly in the most painful way Chief could imagine and all Chief wanted to do at the moment was get as far away from this thing as he could.

The form lying in front of Chief was missing lips. Missing eyelids, missing ears, melted away by the intense heat and searing flames of Thermite. Chief had seen something similar a decade before at Ft. Bragg when an F-16 had a mid-flight collision with a C-130 cargo plane. 172 Paratroopers from the 82nd Airborne Division were lined up on the tarmac at Pope Air Force Base in North Carolina preparing for a training jump. Every man on the ground was in full combat gear, parachute, reserve chute, jungle boots, Battle Dress Uniform, (BDUs) and helmets. The chutes, boots and load bearing equipment (LBE), were made from nylon for durability and weather resistance.

The two aircraft, less than one thousand feet above them, collided sending enormous amounts of JP-4 jet fuel down on top of them like a soaking rainstorm. They didn't have a chance. Within seconds, flying pieces of debris and munitions descended on the men and ignited the fuel. The C-130 landed safely, a testament to the forty-year-old bird's combat role and sturdy construction. The F-16 disintegrated in mid air and landed on the tarmac directly adjacent to the men, now victimized by the pompous Jet Jockey. Many of the men died from their burns. The nylon gear perpetuated the burns, dripping like hot wax candles as men bathed in jet fuel screamed, rolled and expired on the tarmac. Those who did survived spent years at Brooks Army Hospital Burn Center in Texas. But they looked exactly like the beast that lay before Chief now in the desert of Iraq. No lips, no ears, no eyelids, curled fingers where tendons had cooked in the heat, deeper burns where nylon gear was hooked on.

Maybe this guy would make it. Maybe not. All his limbs were there. His face was a disaster and as Chief assessed the body, he was genuinely encouraged. Yeah there were some ugly burns, much like those on the Tarmac at Bragg, but maybe, just maybe this guy was strong enough to pull through. He'd been shocked before when some of his soldiers amazed even seasoned burn doctors and pulled through. But then Chief pulled back the Iraqi garments that covered this man's torso and discovered the instigation behind the screams.

Phosphorus, the size of a grape fruit was burning a hole through this man's liver. The smell of burning organs and cooking human blood made Chief vomit. He'd seen the insides of animals before, as Chief was an avid big game hunter and taxidermist. He'd seen how clean the inside of an animal was after peeling back the hide, opening it up properly and field dressing deer, rabbits and pheasants. But he'd never seen a human's internal organs writhing in pain, burning from phosphorus.

"How the hell do you put it out? How do you keep it from burning?" Chief thought as his mind reeled from the morbid scene, fighting the smells and his unavoidable need to vomit, to expel this mess from his memory and his sinuses.

After all the times he'd blown things up with Thermite, after all the range engagements, live fire missions launching shoulder fired missiles, the thought of *stopping* the phosphorus had never come up.

Chief tried pouring water onto the wound. It sizzled, steamed and continued to burn. The worst effect was that it woke the creature and caused him to start screaming yet again. Suddenly, the hands grabbed Chief by the head, sliding down and pulling on his neck, forcing Chief's face closer to the missing lips and gnashing, exposed teeth.

"HELP ME GOD DAMMIT! You gotta do something!" the screams were indescribable. The volume, the pitch was something straight out of hell, but the bulging eyes devoid of lids really was freaking him out. This guy was in agony. And there was no one around but Chief.

"Hold On buddy. Helps on the way" he lied in a painful whisper.

Dammit! Was that all he could say at a time like this? What else could he say? Nothing really. This guy was *fucked*! In a big way. All those years of training, of rucking, of twenty mile runs every morning, of staying stronger than the next guy was all working against this guy. His strength was perpetuating the torture he now endured. Something had to be done. Chief just couldn't stand the screaming anymore. This guy was begging for relief.

"Chief, you gotta kill me. Please. God dammit. I can't do it myself. Just fucking shoot me. Please!" Then silence. Was he dead finally? Chief was not going to be that lucky. He searched the area for a weapon. Most everything was burned up, ammunition cooked off from the heat of the melting aluminum and vehicle parts. Then it all became very clear. A K-bar knife stuck out right in front of Chief's face. The standard issue weapon, so durable, so iconic, was sticking out the side of this man's boot just like Chief had found on the leg, a sure sign this was one of his guys. They all wore K-bars in the exact same place. Chief made it part of the crew drill. Everyone packed their ruck the same, wore the same gear, put a K-bar in the boot, blade next to the ankle, handle near the calf. He couldn't tell who this was exactly. That just didn't matter right now. But he knew this was one of his Team.

As the screams started again, Chief instinctively pulled the K-bar from the scabbard, forced his body onto the beast's head, covering the man's face with his torso and deftly pulled the blade across his neck. The impressively sharp steel sliced through the skin, just under the ear severing the carotid artery. The volume of dark, deep red blood caught Chief by surprise. It misted into the air as if a high-pressure brake line had been punctured, then flowed like a milkshake through a straw onto the shirt, soaking it quickly. The man inhaled reflexively, quickly, startled by the sting of the blade, relaxed briefly and then exhaled slowly with an almost calming effect, ceasing his shaking, inhaling again this time only deeper and much calmer.

And then, the final exhale, followed by an eerie silence. As the last breathe left his lungs, the words "Thank You" trailed off into the darkness.

"Tell Jenny "Big Much!" I love her so mu...." was the last thing Chief heard over the perpetual ringing in his head. And then he knew precisely who this was lying in the dirt, enveloped in his arms.

Jenny, his fiancéé was waiting at Ft. Bragg for him to come home.

As Chief rolled his body weight to the side, he exhaled from exhaustion, trying to wrap his brain around what he just learned. This was Goose.

Chief remembered going to Myrtle Beach in a Blackhawk, snatching this guy off the inner coastal waterway beach the night they deployed from Ft. Bragg some 26 months prior. Goose had gone to Myrtle Beach to marry the love of his life. At first, he thought Chief and the guys were pulling some prank, like some cheap "B" grade movie plot, coming to the beach in a Blackhawk to steal him away right before the ceremony. But it was for real. He jokingly introduced Jenny as "Plaintiff Number Three" to the Team, but introduced her photo to Chief as "the One"! Chief still hadn't met Jenny. Something on his "to do list". Goose left his beeper in the Condo and went out to enjoy the day with his wife to be, never imagining after six years without a single day off, that Chief would need him the ONE DAY he took off for some personal business.

Twenty six months later in the desert, he was telling everyone they were invited to his wedding when they all got back, laughing at how Chief and the Team had arrived with very, piss poor timing, that day at Myrtle Beach. And now he was dead. At Chief's hand. Those fucking grenades.

This was "Goose". A man Chief came to love like the brother he never had. Endeared to Chief as the older son and best friend missing from his life. Chief kept Goose at a distance at first. Gunny was his right hand man. But somehow, like a puppy dog, Goose encroached into the perimeter of Chief's hard outer shell. And Chief loved him dearly. His thick, reddish blonde beard complemented his beach blonde hair. On the aircraft en-route to the Persian Gulf via C5A Galaxy Star Lifter, Chief admonished him for not keeping his beeper with him, causing Chief to have to come find him. Secondary to that ass chewing, Chief briefed everyone on the aircraft on the possibility of chemical and biological weapons within the mission zone grid square they were about to invade. Goose had a sunburn from all his time on the beach. It didn't take long. After all, his Norwegian heritage pre-disposed him to red skin on the beach. He didn't believe in sunscreen. And his life in S. California routinely included surfing, and sunburns.

After the in-flight mission brief, he decided to take Chief's advice and shave his beard so his gas mask would seal properly to his face. When he came out of the aircraft bathroom, the white strap under his chin from ear to ear, where the beard used to be, contrasted against the sunburn. It was as plain as that on a Canadian Goose. And from that exact moment on, his nickname stuck. Every single man on the plane roared in laughter at the sight of his face. His new name was Goose. And Chief had just put him down... permanently!

As Goose exhaled the last words he would ever speak, Chief was drilled to the soul by the peace and the comfort that came over this man's face. What had been contorted into unspeakably twisted spasms of agony and pain, suddenly relaxed, softened and became almost angelic. His pupils dilated. He exhaled and is body went completely limp. Peace came over his tortured face and some sort of white, peaceful, sanitary energy released into the atmosphere around his body. Chief could feel it. He watched the life disappear from the eyes, felt the tension of the body's muscles release, heard the bladder and bowels release and watched as a human being turned into a lifeless shell in seconds. What lay before Chief was no longer a man, but an empty vessel, devoid of Warrior and soul. And it haunted Chief forever more. He wanted that peace. He wanted that comfort. His body craved relief from the shattered spine and his internal organ damage. Why couldn't he have that peace too?

His boys. That's why. And it made him nuts. Time to suck it up, drive on and get home. Back to focusing on the five meter targets. Water. Food, recon some more. There had to be someone else alive. Somewhere in this grid square. Time to go find them. Shut down the emotions, get on with the mission.

Of the seven-man team, only five bodies were recovered, none of them completely intact. The remains of two would never be recovered, instantly vaporized, atomized into oblivion by a direct hit from a missile moving two times the speed of sound. The concussive force of which exploded their bodies. The phosphorus had done the rest. Whatever was left of them was now liquid, or ash, spread to the four corners of the earth and burned up in the follow on fire.

Of those five left behind to suffer, three were seriously injured and unconscious. Just simply lying there, twisted and deformed. Limbs missing, Jell-O for brains, slowly bleeding out. God would be merciful to them. They would never regain consciousness and most likely never knew what hit them. The fourth and fifth were not so lucky. It made Chief wonder exactly how God determines who should suffer and who should pass with absolute respect and decency, instead of primal screams. Screams so piercing, so loud, one could not imagine that it was coming from a human. Goose was number four, Chief number five of the seven man Team.

Chief desperately wanted to get back into that dream state, that warm, comfortable, snuggly dream state. It was the best feeling he ever experienced. And he wanted more of it. He needed it. It was too ugly out here in reality. Better to go back inside his head, back to calm, back to peace.

When Chief woke again, he was amazed how he felt. An almost euphoric sense of giddiness overwhelmed him. He was excited to see the psychedelic colors of the rainbow as he imagined what an LSD trip of the 60s must have been like as he watched the colors change in the sunlight. He felt no pain, but knew something wasn't right. The flies had invaded his eyes, sucking the remaining blood and liquid from his eyeballs. Nature went on without the drama of a human's imagination. The flies were just doing what they were supposed to do. Fluid was life in the desert. Their DNA programmed them to mate, lay eggs and die. The fluid from Chief's eyeballs perpetuated that life cycle. Nothing more, nothing less. The sunlight danced across the insects hexagonal lenses reflecting off the iridescent multi-panels, the light show glinting into Chief's consciousness as if a prelude to his own death.

Chief couldn't comprehend how long he'd been out there, or how long he'd been unconscious. What he knew was that he was dying. As slow as it seemed to be, he knew it wouldn't be long now. He couldn't keep drinking. He was obviously dehydrating faster than he could consume whatever water was left in the one Water Pig he held so desperately to his chest. Death would come soon and the pain would finally be gone. Nothing mattered anymore. Chief drifted off one last time into oblivion. Maybe this wasn't such a bad thing after all. Kids were resilient. Maybe Chief was using his two boys for his own agenda, and his death wouldn't be that tragic to them after all. His mind was trying to justify his own humanity. He was giving up. And it didn't matter to him anymore that he was just plain out of fight.

* * * * *

"HEY! We got a LIVE ONE!" yelled a voice from outside. The Blackhawk crew chief unzipped the heavy plastic body bag and air rushed in as if someone had opened a window on a cold winter day.

Chief's hands were frantically clawing at the zipper, trying to get it opened, trying to get some oxygen. He again felt that feeling of not being strong enough, the one feeling that motivated him above all others. That feeling of being held down, unable to fight hard enough no matter how hard he fought. He was slowly running out of fight and slipping down to that comfortable place again. Out of fight, out of breath, out of ....

Chief suddenly realized he was inside a body bag. His lungs filled with fresh, artificially cold air. No sand, no smoke, no rancid smell, just lung filling orgasmic fresh air. He started coughing. It was colder than he was used to. The purity of the air confused him. Where was he? The daylight shot into his pupils and stabbed his brain with a pain so familiar, so hot, so pointed that he had to close his eyes again, groaning in pain. Deep ripples developed on his forehead as he tried to resist the pain, squinting his eyes tighter closed, forcing blood and fluid from the lower lids causing it to overflow and run down his dirty cheeks. Yet his subconscious persisted in making sense of it all. Trying to see, trying to comprehend. Somebody was kneeling next to him. The Blackhawk crewman's body provided enough cover to Chief's eyes that he could open them just enough now to see shadows and shapes of a man with a Crew Helmet on, microphone to his mouth.

"Can you hear me?" the voice came again over the loud ringing in his ears. Rotors and engine noise made it nearly impossible for Chief to understand the man.

"We're gonna get you to the docs OK?"

Through the noise of rotor blades Chief heard a voice he hadn't heard in a very long time. It was the voice of a true friend, his taxi driver. The one man in the world Chief knew, someone who'd dropped them off so many months ago to catch a bomb maker. Chief Warrant Officer Tom Kennedy, the "Taxi Driver" who had flown Chief and his men into so many of the deepest, darkest missions that Task Force 160 flew. They were known as the "Night Stalkers". A well deserved nickname for the best Aviation experts the Army had to offer. Those courageous, psycho pilots who took America's Tier

One Warriors into death defying missions, then came back to extract them from the very jaws of death. Honed on the hot drop zones of Vietnam as "Dust Off" pilots, MEDIVAC pilots who routinely flew six and seven missions into enemy fire to extract wounded soldiers, often times getting shot down more than once in a day, the pilots of the Night Stalkers were some of the best in the world. Not just for their aviation heroics, but for the heart and soul that beat within their chests. These were some of the truly unsung heroes of so many American Special Operations conflicts.

When Kennedy returned from the U.S. after going home to bury his own parents, killed in an auto accident by a drunk driver while he was deployed to the desert of Iraq, Tom was shocked to find a state of near disinterest when he got back to Sanctuary Base. After nearly two weeks stateside dealing with legal interests, inheritance of a bowling alley, family members fighting over mere financial crumbs, he couldn't take being away from the Unit anymore and came directly back to the Theater of Operations. When he arrived, the only question he had was,

"Where the hell were Chief and the Team?"

They were long over due. Most everyone at Sanctuary Base was in relaxation mode after the daily, mind numbing boredom of the past twenty six months snuck its way into their demeanor. Keeping men on the razor edge for that long was a real leadership challenge. A human deficiency that only the experienced knew how to deal with.

"Chief will call for a ride when he's ready. We're just chilling, waiting for him to call" was the nonchalant, yawning answer he got from the support personnel who were more interested in the free Kool Aid and sugar donuts than being out in the heat of the desert. That was a constant problem whenever there was A/C available in a land that routinely shot to 130 degrees in the daytime sun.

Kennedy had gotten a case of the red ass and requested permission to go look for Chief. After being denied twice by higher headquarters, he went back to the calendar and realized the Team was overdue by almost a week. Not unheard of, but in this case, highly suspect. After twenty six months in theater, Tom knew everyone was ready to go home. And being a week overdue this close to the end, just didn't fit. So Kennedy stole an aircraft, put a two-man crew together and took off looking. When they found the bombed out equipment spread over the desert sands, they naturally assumed it must be left over from some previous war or target range. They never imagined Chief and his men were in the middle of the immense carnage. But something told Kennedy, deep in his guts to go check it out. To never dismiss the smallest details. Chief had taught him that. So he landed the bird and confirmed his worst nightmare.

All Chief knew to do now was to relinquish command and control to the men in helmets that now surrounded him. His body and brain were exhausted now. Spent. Completely incapacitated after nearly six days in the desert heat and he truly needed someone to pick up the torch and carry on while he was down. As Chief slipped off into the unconscious bliss induced by knowing he was now safe, Kennedy keyed the mike and spoke the words of a Quiet Professional!

"Sanctuary Base this is Arc Angel One. *We have Arc Angel Six on board. Zeus! I say again, "ZEUS!"*

That was the last conscious thing Chief heard until he awoke at Walter Reed Army Medical Center in Washington D.C. He never could have imagined something going this far sideways. He heard those eloquent words coming from the cockpit of the Blackhawk, "Zeus". Chief was going home now. Finally, everyone was going home.

The Five Meter Targets

*"You can eat an elephant as long as you focus on
one bite at a time!"*

Life Lesson Nr 12

When Chief woke up in the ICU, he couldn't believe how cold
he was. He had absolutely no memory of going to Landstuhl
Regional Medical Center in Germany, nor anything else since the
time he gave up his soul to the Blackhawk crew that found him and
his Team. He had no idea how injured his body was, nor any way to
reconcile where he was now. There, several weeks earlier in the
heart of Germany's Rhineland Pfalz, the Neurology specialists and
the Orthopedic surgeons of the U.S. Army's Regional hospital did a
few scans and diagnosed fractures in his neck, his torso and a few
extremities. But the serious damage, the two life threatening
problems were his Lumbar Spine being severely dislocated and a
brain bleed.

The entire frontal cortex bled for several days lying out there in
the sands of the Iraqi desert. As far as anyone could tell, it was six
days from the time of the explosion until Tom Kennedy and his
crew found them. So the best anyone could extrapolate, nearly
sixteen days passed since Chief was found in the sand and got
professional medical help. The combat medic teams did what they
could do and Chief rapidly traversed the "in country" medical
echelons before he ended up on the "Mercy Ship" in the Persian
Gulf. In a matter of minutes, the Chief of Surgery closed the records,
shook his head and put out the order to have Chief transferred as

soon as possible to Landstuhl, a mere five kilometers from Ramstein Air Force base. Although the obvious fractures appearing on the X-rays would need attention, there was apparent secondary trauma from oxygen deprivation on the scans as well. But all that could wait till much later in life. Within hours of arrival at Lanstuhl, Chief was rushed into an ICU unit where he was upgraded to "critical" status. He would stay on the ward receiving round the clock specialized care until he medically stabilized and could be transported state side. At the moment, things were just too "IFFY". The trip alone might kill him. Nine full days after his arrival, Chief was taken by ambulance the 5 kilometers to the U.S. Air Force Ramstein Airbase, and flown out of Germany. 36 hours later, after multiple fuels stops in Torejone Spain, the Azore islands in the Atlantic Ocean and Goose Bay Canada, Chief arrived stateside at Reagan International in Washington D.C. From there, he transferred by ambulance to the Emergency room at Walter Reed Army Medical Center. Now, as Chief came into full consciousness in the Orthopedic Intensive Care Ward, he had no idea that he had been at Walter Reed going on nearly two months already, almost a full three months since the explosion.

As Chief awoke to the mind numbing cold of the room, he fought to control the pain, to keep his teeth from chattering together which in turn kept him from hearing anything over the loud, high-pitched tone that seemed to overshadow absolutely everything in his head. His brain hurt, fogged over from the extended days of anesthesia and pain medication being pumped into his body. So it was no surprise in retrospect why he couldn't comprehend where he was, or what had gone on. Nor did he have any idea how many days passed since last time he was conscious and functional. He damn sure didn't understand why he hurt so badly.

It took a while for him to realize he wasn't still lying on the desert floor. In the blink of a few more seconds, he was again trying to sort out why he instinctively wanted to crawl. Something deep in his mind, some sort of primal survival instinct was prompting him to find a weapon, to move, to crawl, to get away from whatever was causing so much pain to his body. Intuitively he needed to defend himself. The military leadership deep within his DNA required answers. Yet all he could do was struggle against the pain, the noise in his head and fight against the incredible cold his body rallied against.

"At least the screams were gone", he thought to himself. There were too many voices around him to still be in the desert. That he knew. The cold was that of air conditioning instead of the cold night air of the Persian Gulf. Everything smelled different, more antiseptic and chlorinated. He could tell his naked body was lying on freshly laundered sheets. That was different from the sand and the despicable smells he remembered from the last time he felt this bad. He didn't really know where he was. His primal brain relaxed a bit and the tension in his muscles slowly responded.

There were bright, piercing lights overhead this time. Cotton balls taped over his eyelids prevented him from seeing very much, intended as a kind of pressure bandage that kept the eyelids closed without the tape sticking too much and prevent his eyeballs from drying out. No one knew if Chief would ever see again. His eyeballs, severely bloodshot and damaged from the sand and sun, were left alone for the moment. The problems with his eyeballs were secondary to all the other much more critical medical problems the doctors were concerned with. His eyes would either heal, or they wouldn't. Sight was something he could live without. But he couldn't live without certain organs, or the proper nerve connections from his spinal column to keep those organs alive. So his shattered spine and head injury took priority over everything else.

The anxiety was high and Chief was fighting hard to keep calm, to analyze instead of react. As he tried to roll his head to one side, Chief felt two large, hard, plastic IV tubes stabbing him in the neck. He unconsciously reached for them as his brain interpreted the intrusion as a foreign body that needed to be removed. They were just an additional source of pain to his already overwhelmed sensory system.

As he attempted to reach up to his neck, the restraint system caught him by surprise, restricting his movement, triggering his fight systems again. The sudden resistance and additional pain inflicted by the IV needles and tubing made him realize his arms were taped to the side rails of the bed, his wrists encased in a leather strap of sorts with sheep skin lining intended to prevent further damage to his already torn, abraded and sunburned skin.

Being rag-dolled across the desert took a serious toll on his entire body, which was now covered in second-degree burns from the sun, complicated by third degree burns from the Thermite along with a huge amount of insect bites. Large areas of skin were missing, sand blasted and brush burned away by the sudden stop after his one-man flight from the top of the antennae pole. Infection was a real concern to the medical staff. But these damn plastic tubes in his neck were the only concern at the moment to Chief.

The hard plastic catheter tubes entered his arteries just under his ears and threaded their way down into his heart. It felt like someone was pinching down hard on his veins, taking his attention away from everything else at the moment. Even the smallest turn of his head made them hurt like hell. He didn't understand at the time why they were there, or what had gone on to make the surgical staff put them into his neck. There were a lot of unanswered questions. The tape holding them in place pulled on his skin. But the tubes were also sewn directly into his flesh, a tactic intended to keep them from falling out under the weight of the syringes they attached during surgery, full of anesthesia intended to go straight into his heart and knock him down quickly.

Apparently Chief woke up during this surgery, one of seven reconstruction and repair surgeries so far. The anesthesia wore off at some point, or his body became immune to the toxic mix. It didn't matter which really, the result was the same. Chief woke up in the middle of major spine surgery. That was a bad thing. More than once actually, which provided much entertainment for the students in the Amphitheater above watching anxiously in eager anticipation for that day several years down the road when *they* would be holding the scalpel, conducting the actual surgery themselves instead of just watching from above as a first year resident student. The lessons learned this day were far more than just surgical procedure. This day included a very important lesson on "*What not to do*" during a major spinal surgery and the consequences of allowing a patient to regain consciousness.

It was pretty obvious to everyone present when things started going bad, that Chief fought everyone in the room as if he were still in combat. Training and muscle memory compounded the innate human "fight or flight" syndrome. Chief instinctively felt his body under attack as the anesthesia wore too thin and he did what any normal human would do. Fight. He tried to get away from whatever it was that was causing the intense traumatic pain. He fought hard. With everything he could muster. Subconsciously, his brain was going through the survival skills he'd learned over the years from both training and real world experience. One male nurse assistant got his collarbone snapped and was removed from the operating room. Another got his nose broken pretty severely by a head butt while trying to talk to Chief and tell him everything was OK.

"OK my ass!" was all that could be discerned from the volume of grunts and groans that escaped passed the intubation tubing that had been forced down Chief's throat. The plastic tubing was intended to provide desperately needed oxygen to his lungs while under anesthesia. Chief tried to tear that out while he thrashed around on the table, fighting against the restraints and retraction tools that kept his body in position on the specialized surgical table. Every time he fought, he moved and became aware of yet something else that inflicted immeasurable pain on his brain and body.

He barely remembered any of it when questioned several weeks later. All he really remembered was waking up, hearing a pneumatic drill at full RPM and the sudden violent and severely painful vibration throughout his body as the drill cut holes into his vertebral bones making way for fixation hardware to be attached. Primal rage had taken over and Chief did everything physically possible to kill whoever was responsible.

His body was strapped to the table with all kinds of devices holding his torso and legs in position. Air bags encased his lower limbs attached to a pump that inflated and deflated the vinyl pants in an attempt to prevent blood clotting in his lower extremities. Hot water circulated through the pants while the pressure from the systematic air cycling instigated more pain, causing Chief to resist, to fight, to try and overcome the alien sensations he awoke to.

There were other devices called retractors holding the incisions open so the surgical staff could work deep inside on his spinal column. Chief's head was the only part that was relatively free, although there were all kinds of wires, sensors and probes wrapped everywhere. The big issue had been the tube in this throat. The hospital called it collateral damage. Chief called it bullshit.

The entire episode was now a permanent video record for every medical student of the Walter Reed Orthopedic curriculum.

* * * * *

Twenty eight days later on the recovery ward of the ICU, Chief was awake, realizing slowly that he was stuck inside a foreign body that felt nothing like his own anymore. The familiar strength and motivation from years of training and tactical experience was gone. God only knew how long it had been since he'd eaten. And whatever was in the IV bags was nowhere near what he was used to. There was no strength now. Only pain and tremendous body shaking from lactic acid buildup within his muscles, causing a deep fatigue. Every waking moment was a task in self-discipline and control. His brain was still fighting off the anesthesia and morphine from the pump that was now plumbed into his veins. The drugs made him even weaker. He hated that feeling and it only triggered the fight syndrome harder. Frustration was building. If he gave into the weakness from the morphine, he couldn't fight the pain. The morphine was supposed to make the pain stop, but it didn't. It only made his brain feel weaker and the pain would move off into the background. The pain was still there; his brain just didn't give a damn.

Something inside him kept him gritting his teeth, focusing on the task at hand regardless of how mundane. He was in a different world now, one that made no sense. The problems he faced were nowhere near as complex as the Intelligence and mission requirements he was used to dealing with. But the mundane daily tasks were far more difficult. The simplest tasks took much more concentration and effort now. The incredible pain and crushing weight of IV medications made absolutely everything more difficult and now took complete focus, complete determination and unspeakable fortitude to accomplish. Whether that was drinking a sip of water or just trying to sit up. He had to focus deeply on everything for anything to work the way it was supposed to.

Frustration and anger ruled every moment. He was paralyzed from the chest down, but *no one had told him that yet.* So no matter how hard he fought, he was not going to succeed. Exasperated beyond his own comprehension, Chief lashed out at anyone that came near him.

The recovery room staff was waiting to see.... Waiting to find out if something had really gone wrong during the surgery or if things just needed some more time to recover. Sometimes in the world of medicine, the answers came on their own schedule, at their own time. A hell of a lot of local anesthesia had been used to bathe the muscles and tissue surrounding his spine and it was too soon to tell what was really going on. Maybe his body just needed time to absorb all of the medication and bring the nerve function back. Trying to rush things was never a good answer when it came to errors on the surgical ward. The fact of the matter was that no matter how hard Chief tried, no matter how hard anyone wished, the paralysis was either going to resolve on it's own, or it just wouldn't. All the energy expended on the conversation in the mean time was meaningless.

After several weeks inside the Orthopedic ICU, Chief was transferred to a room on the Orthopedic Recovery Ward. He could sit up by lifting the head of the bed with an electric motor, but hadn't left that bed since he went into surgery some thirty-five days prior. The stench was starting to build up. He could smell his own gunk, and it triggered a primal roar within his chest. But the 900 lb Gorilla in the room was not addressed. Smell was a primal survival tool that went straight to the brain. With his eyes as bad as they were, his olfactory system was on overload and it made him mad.

"The doctor is on leave" was the only answer he could get out of anyone whenever he inquired about his "status".

Chief was starting to get pissed off. He wanted out. It was way past is tolerance level and he wanted to get back to his men, to the "Unit". He felt so helpless, so useless and it was slowly driving him insane. This place was all bullshit. Here was an elite soldier, used to running, ruck marching, jumping out of airplanes and being superman, stuck in a bed looking at the ceiling, being tended to by "Wannabe" soldiers. Frustration was mounting with absolutely no way to relieve it. And the madder he got, the more it showed and the less inclined anyone was to come to his aid.

Chief was used to having immediate compliance from his men. Immediate answers when he needed them. But he was no longer in Command now. He was in a different world all together. These soldiers were not what Chief was used to. They were really nothing more than civilians who had gone through basic training and were in the very basic phase of MOS school now learning their jobs. They didn't know what a real soldier was, nor how to act like one or what was expected of a real soldier. Military medicine was just another oxymoron to Chief in the world that he enjoyed.

Not that Chief expected to be treated like a celebrity or anything, but these idiots had no clue who Chief really was, what he did for a living, or how professional people in his circles were expected to perform.

Besides fighting the pain and frustration, Chief was having a very hard time understanding how every single person was accepting "substandard performance". Obviously, the bar was set way too low here. From Chief's perspective, a soldier didn't get to walk into the White House and brief the President by being a "wanna be" like he was seeing at every turn on the Orthopedic ward. In reality, none of these soldiers were ever expected to brief the President. They were students, expected to learn and become functional medical staff charged with helping wounded soldiers recover and return to their units. At this stage of their training, they were simply "Wannabes", wanting to be a nurse, or wanting to be a doctor... or whatever!

Several more months into recovery, it dawned on Chief that not a single one of these "wannabes" had any comprehension of what it felt like to be a patient.

No one had trained them, nor exposed them to the alternate perspective of a patient. Which meant that they couldn't anticipate a patient's needs. Never mind understand everything they'd been taught in school. They had chosen a path in life that required a certain degree of compassion and empathy as well as a level of intellect that would require them to understand and predict the unspoken needs of people who were incapacitated and vulnerable. Patients who were in unspeakable pain, under the influence of heavy narcotics, unable to articulate their needs while fighting for their lives. The paradox was frightening. These students were all at the very early stages of adult life, even earlier stages of medical experience. On the other hand, Chief was at the most vulnerable point of his entire life.

This reality struck hard. He wasn't in a premier care facility with world-class surgeons and top of the line equipment. Walter Reed was a teaching hospital. And that was something everyone left out of the conversation. Kind of like 82nd Airborne Division, everyone left out the most important part. It was still an Infantry Division. So likewise, Walter Reed was the premiere teaching hospital for the U.S. Army. Everyone kind of passed over the part about "making mistakes" as part of the curriculum.

The public perception, however, was a product of a long history of intended manipulation. A huge political machine had beat the drum incessantly to condition the public, and the military, into believing that Walter Reed was the premier hospital in Washington D. C. for military personnel. And it was nearly 100 years old with a prestigious history. But in reality, Walter Reed Army Medical Center was far from being what it's reputation touted. Commander after Commander had bought into the rhetoric, but no one had forced the curriculum to keep up with civilian technology or advances. The reality now was, that anyone who was anyone went to Bethesda in Maryland instead. Congressmen, their wives and children, even a lot of Officers from the Pentagon went to Bethesda. Walter Reed had a 100 year reputation of "excellence." But it also had a 100 year history of making medical mistakes and learning from them. And that was the best kept secret from the tactical military units. Apparently, as Chief was learning yet again, what you don't know *can hurt you* after all.

Not everyone could be Special Operations. Chief knew that more than anyone. Waking up in this foreign body, in a foreign environment, surrounded by foreign soldiers was really getting to him. His tolerance for bullshit was already minimal from the narcotics and was getting lower by the minute. He could feel the impending explosion coming. The morphine wasn't working anymore, so he'd pulled the Patient Controlled Anesthesia (PCA) pump out of his arm. He was feeling a hell of a lot better without it, except for the agony of his back and stomach where they'd gone in and hacked up his bones, drilled holes and inserted screws, rods and fixation devices. Damn it, that shit really hurt.

When spinal fusions are accomplished from the posterior approach only, the stomach muscles are a key component of support and recovery keeping the core torso muscles solid while the spine healed. But Chief had been rebuilt from the anterior as well as the posterior, simultaneously. That meant his stomach had been cut open from stem to stern as well as his back. His core was pretty strong from all the exercise, ruck marches, sit-ups, pushups and running he was used to doing on a daily basis. But now, everything was compromised from both the front and the back being surgically opened, so much of his spine involved in the medical malpractice and the 22 plus hours he was on the table fighting for his life.

This was bad. Much worse than what the explosion had done to his body. In a matter of 24 months since returning from the Persian Gulf, Chief had gone through a "Friendly Fire" incident, six reconstruction surgeries and now an incredible malpractice insult from people who were supposed to be helping him.

Even simple tasks were pissing him off now. Like brushing his teeth, washing, shaving. Everything was all different now and much more difficult. He could sort of sit up, but the pain made him black out. The electric bed helped him raise his head above his feet, but if he went too far, his body would slide to the bottom of the mattress. The weight of the plaster and the intense pain in his head from the halo screws gave him a headache that was severely compounded by the light and the morphine hangover.

When he slid to the bottom of the bed, it would take four people to come in and slide him back to the top. And that was like the Keystone Cops too, a gaggle of wannabe s sounding more like a flock of seagulls than a smooth, lean, mean machine of soldiers with one goal in mind. More than one attempt to reorient his body in the bed resulted in someone stepping on the catheter, damn near pulling it out through his urethra. The newbies had mistaken his screams in pain as being related to the surgical incisions instead of being related to the bladder balloon being pulled out through his penis. It was kind of like yanking a golf ball through a soda straw. And the damage to his bladder and tissue was substantial. When they saw his urine bag full of bright red blood, was when they learned another important medical lesson about patient care. The collateral damage from medical ignorance was building. And with every new insult, Chief was becoming even more hostile and socially unacceptable.

The experienced ones knew it was a bad idea for Chief to be sitting up. There were all kinds of concerns when it came to long-term patient care. Pressure sores would become an issue over time, especially inside the body cast. Sitting up would make it worse. Exponential pressure problems continued to worry the head nurse when the sheets wrinkled up underneath his buttocks and legs partially encased in blow up pants. Those small sheet wrinkles were murder on circulation and broke the skin down faster than anything.

There were wrinkles all over his body inside the cast from that cotton body sock. The pressure was cutting into his skin. Exponentially compounding the problem was the body sweat, temperature and moisture.

Shaving was of no concern to Chief at the moment. In fact, it was the last thing on his agenda. But it was "an important part of everyday life routines" as the anal retentive nurse wannabe had briefed him and therefore *must be* accomplished on a daily basis. Obviously she'd never been a patient either. The nurses were more worried about the Standard Operating Procedures on the Ward than anything else. They were all about Regulations, schedules and routines. Chief was more concerned with the fact he couldn't feel his fucking legs than the fact that he had a two day old beard growing on his face. But the hospital rules were strictly applied to everyone. They focused on the easy shit, and left the complications to sort themselves out, especially medical problems.

It had taken Chief nearly a full week to learn how to brush his teeth without inhaling toothpaste foam while lying on his back. He struggled with the glacial pace of life. Everything had to slow way down and Chief fought with his own mind, checking his progress and beating himself up for not accomplishing anything important. He needed to give himself a break, to accept his physical disabilities and accept a sort of substandard performance in his own actions. Washing, brushing his teeth, getting a drink, and using that damn breathing device to clear his lungs was part of the every day slow pace of mundane, mind numbing responsibilities he was reduced to. He'd rather watch grass grow.

Part of the problem was he couldn't really use his hands and arms anymore. They'd been seriously damaged during the 22 hour long surgery compounding the problems incurred from the explosion. The retraction frame used on his upper torso had impinged his muscles and nerves to the point that everything was numb now. His pectoral muscles were torn where they'd been stretched across the spine frame intended to keep his body taught, assisting in retracting muscles when he was cut open. All of his chest muscles were bruised, numb, and swollen to the point that the skin was cracking between the severe stretch marks he had as a result of being incapacitated on the surgical table for nearly an entire day. Every second of even the simplest tasks Chief performed while holding his breath, in an attempt at keeping the pain from making his brain blackout.

It was no longer possible to bend at the waist. Brushing teeth while lying flat on his back with numb arms was something he never thought about doing, never mind trained for. It struck him as funny that after all the training, all the missions and time he'd spent in the damnedest places on the planet, he found himself in a situation he was totally unprepared for. Imagine a $500,000.00 background investigation for a Top Secret, SCI clearance from the U.S. Government, every type of training in Survival, Escape, Resistance, Evasion, SCUBA, Airborne Operations, Green Beret, French Commando School, all kind of weapons, tactics and torture,......... yet he found himself in a situation where brushing his teeth was more complicated, took more brain power and focus than anything he had done in a very long time. This was ridiculous. He just had to get out of there before he went nuts and hurt someone.

Nearly150 lbs. of plaster and fiberglass encased his body now. After so long without a shower or any way to clean his body, things were getting pretty ripe. There were slits in the cast so the nurses could change the dressings on the surgical incisions both front and back. There was very little bleeding, but something was wrong. Chief remembered waking up in agony inside the damn thing.

Eventually, someone noticed that Chief's stomach was distended, red and weeping fluid profusely. This cast had to come

off. Somewhere in the anarchy of mandatory medical precautions
being documented, someone had screwed up and forgotten to put
Antibiotics on the IV pole hooked into Chief's arm. Saline was
running non-stop since the surgery. But that was all that was going
into his right arm. His left arm was reserved for the PCA Pump.

The surgeons and his team of five assistants had been inside
Chief's torso from his diaphragm to his groin leaving an incision
down the length of his stomach nearly twenty inches long. All of his
intestines, liver, stomach and pancreas were placed in sterile
stainless steel dishes during the surgery, allowing the five man team
access to Chief's entire spine with room for both arms up to their
elbows. This approach and procedure was totally outdated and
contrary to what the civilian world knew as acceptable. Too many
postoperative complications proved this procedure to be outdated
and obsolete. Success was accomplished by leaving the organs intact
inside the human body's natural internal sack known as the
Peritoneum. Civilian surgeons kept the Peritoneum intact and had
been doing so for over twenty years. Walter Reed just hadn't gotten
the memo yet. Walter Reed had been doing it this way for years and
was not about to change tradition based on an "unproven theory".
Just like putting screws into vertebrae, the civilian doctors would
cringe at what they knew to be archaic medical techniques.

They had a lot of work to perform, a lot of hardware to install
and it took a lot of room for the drills and fixation devices to
accomplish the task of grafting, fixating and fusing all those
vertebrae. And now the entire Anterior Approach was severely
infected, mostly because the Peritoneum was compromised. Chief
was spiking a fever and nearing death from infection.

Within the hour, a "real Doctor" arrived on the Ward. With all
the bedside manner of the Boston Strangler and the compassion of
Jack the Ripper, he grabbed two handfuls of stomach and pulled.
The incision split, staples flew and a flood of green, foul smelling

fluid rushed out onto the bed. This was bad. The infection had spread throughout Chief's torso during the previous weeks, involving his digestive tract, liver, bladder and especially the freshly fused bone grafting that was intended to hold his spine together.

Without the required bone growth, ensuring a solid fusion, it was only a matter of time before the hardware gave out. Like a coat hangar, it would only flex and bend so much before finally giving way. Neither Chief nor anyone else knew at the time was that the hardware was faulty to begin with. The government's process of buying from the lowest bidder was about to take on a whole new meaning. This hardware was used in the civilian world and damn near every set failed resulting in a huge Class Action Lawsuit against this exact civilian medical supply company. They settled out of court for $160 million. Neither Chief nor anyone else at Walter Reed knew was that the company simply changed its name and continued to sell the hardware to the military. Since Chief was technically a Federal Employee, there was absolutely no recourse for the damage from faulty hardware. Nor was there any recourse against the military surgeons. "Your ass belongs to Uncle Sam" was a phrase that came to haunt Chief. Tort Claims laws denied anyone on Active Duty from "retribution" against anyone in the Chain of Command. And technically, Chief was under the Command of the Medical Staff at Walter Reed. End of discussion. Legally, everyone was Teflon and Chief, along with all the other patients at Walter Reed Army Medical Center, were hamsters in a cage.

Chief's stomach was now opened to his spine. The daily ritual of "wet to dry" packing ensued. The intention of packing the cavity with wet gauze and sterile saline solution was to keep the wound from healing inside. Continually removing the scab, preventing the flesh from healing completely. This procedure kept the body producing fresh tissue that would eventually fill the void. When the body heat dried the gauze, the top skin tissue stuck to the cotton mesh. That's when things got really stupid. Every day, twice a day, the gauze was yanked out of the wound, tearing the scabs and healed tissue loose with it. Eventually the gaping hole would close on it's own. But there were months of this agony ahead. Chief would soon know the real meaning of self discipline, submission for a greater good and mercy. All on a level he never knew before.

The mission now was to change the body cast and get rid of the putrid smell from both Chief's own body chemistry and sweat, along with the incredible amount of infectious fluid that soaked into the plaster.

* * * * *

In the confusion of a busy surgical ward, combined with the lack of experienced and new personnel, someone forgot to submit the paperwork to have Chief's body mold made *prior* to the surgery. In the near future, he would be out of the cast and placed in a plastic "TLSO" body brace with a "hip spica" attachment, a device with a locking mechanism that kept him from flexing his hips. The plastic was much lighter, could be removed daily and once Chief healed enough, he could even wear it into the shower to bathe from a wheelchair. That was another indicator he missed. Obviously, no one told him yet that he was going to be in that chair, paralyzed, possibly forever more.

Ignoring his protests, the visiting doctor ordered a new PCA pump. This time, Demerol resided within. And that changed everything for Chief. Gone was the nausea and light headedness from Morphine, replaced by a much welcomed bliss. Little did he know there was a price to pay for comfort. He succumbed to the elixir of the demons and destined himself to the slippery slope of addiction. For now, it made life much more manageable and much more tolerable. And for the first time in a very long time, Chief actually got some sleep.

The practice of nurses covertly pushing the PCA pump button was illegal and morally wrong, but used often on the Ward. This time, when Chief woke up, he found himself suspended from two stainless steel IV poles. His wrists and hands were taped to them at the very top and the poles were extended as far as possible to give maximum lift. His belly was surgically opened on the left side from his nuts to his sternum allowing the anterior approach to his spine. The incision was enormous, now packed with wet gauze and taped shut. The back incision was just as long, closed with over 100 metal staples that looked exactly like those he'd seen on cardboard shipping boxes. The hard metal staples were neatly spaced all the way up his spine, the swollen skin and tissue protruding from in between every inch or so, reminiscent of a huge zipper.

Pain was the biggest gorilla in the room, but there were smaller gorillas he just couldn't work on yet. Like the fact that all his guys were dead. And he wasn't going to be there for the funerals, nor the celebrations, nor the memorial ceremonies. That bothered him in a big way. But those thoughts were fleeting at best through all the narcotics. He hurt like hell. He knew that for sure. But what he couldn't figure out was why they had him taped to these damn IV poles. That question quickly went away when the plaster man walked into the room and taped an Ammonia capsule under Chief's nose.

"Don't want you passing out and hitting the floor Chief!" he said with absolutely no hint of comedy or emotion.

This man was a civilian, in his late fifties at least and stood out from the crowd of twenty year old students and wannabe nurses. Chief was looking for some indication that this guy was joking, but found nothing but serious efficiency and determination on the man's face. His demeanor echoed the same.

His brain was fighting off Demerol the nurses had switched him to after bitching pretty hard that Chief had "illegally" removed the PCA pump.

"What were they gonna do? Shoot him?" Chief thought to himself as he listened to their lame attempt at chastising rhetoric. Someone needed to teach them what a real ass chewing was all about. They were amateurs at it. But it wouldn't be Chief, and it wasn't going to be today. There was too much on his plate at the moment. It just didn't make any sense that this guy was going to pile hot, wet plaster onto his torso to make a plaster cast. Especially since Chief was feeling so bad.

"That Ammonia capsule might make you a little nauseated, but I promise, you won't be able to pass out on me. We're gonna be done in about thirty minutes. So hold on. It's gonna suck!"

That was the understatement of the year.

At least this guy wasn't beating around the bush. Chief could understand that. And much preferred it to what he'd experienced so far at Walter Reed. No one ever said what they really meant around this place. Everyone was beating around the bush, sidestepping and making light of really bad medical situations.

Chief woke up back in his room not understanding how he got there, nor what transpired over the past four hours. All he felt was exasperation, fatigue and confusion. He remembered parts of the body molding process, but now he was back in his room, unable to sit up. He was in a full length body cast *again* with a steel rod between his knees. W.T.F? They'd made the first cast, a mold for the TLSO. But no one told him they were going to put him into another full length cast. He felt more and more like a horse that had been coaxed into a stall and then left for dead. Hatred began to grow in his soul. He didn't trust anyone now.

Life was even more impossible now. Chief tried to continue with the simple tasks he had mastered in recent days, small things that contributed immensely to Chief's positive mental state. For a few days, he actually felt like he was getting better, accomplishing something and beginning to get control over his life again. That simple feeling was incredibly important to his psyche. But it was stolen by the fever, the infection and the ignorance of medical staff in what seemed to be a split second. Just as life had changed so drastically, so quickly in the desert. Just being able to spit into the sink after brushing his teeth, or bend his neck, or shave was a huge accomplishment that was now impossible again. Because now a "HALO" kept his head and neck from bending, a steel rod kept his legs apart at the knees and everything else was encased in hot, steaming plaster, slow cooking his flesh.

The rage simmered just under the surface and Chief got inside his head again to try and control it. It was really getting difficult to maintain his military bearing. He was about to come unglued. What the fuck? Why should he remain calm? This was really, really getting to be bullshit. Not only was the entire process getting on his nerves, but the fact that *no one would tell him* what they were going to do to him, cranked him up past his own tolerance level. It was starting to feel like he didn't have any say in what they were doing to him. And that was going to come to a screeching halt. In a matter of one day, Chief went from injured superhero to "non-compliant asshole patient" And it reflected in how everyone treated him now.

The kitchen staff delivered food to his room and left it on the roll around table by the door. Chief was stuck in this damn torture chamber, restrained to the bed with tubes coming from every orifice of his body. An hour after delivery, the tray was removed and a note was put into his records that he refused to eat. No one seemed to connect the dots that Chief was incapacitated and couldn't get to the tray. Nor could he feed himself. So, three times a day, the grayish looking, plasma textured slime was delivered, sat for an hour exactly on a tray in the corner by the door, and then just as quickly, it was taken away.

After a week, it was obvious the lack of food was taking a toll on everything. The pain medication was not working as well, he was losing weight fast and a major indicator started to develop. No one really noticed the graph they were filling in that hung on the door of his room, nor connected the dots on just how serious his condition deteriorated. They just continued to put in values, checked the boxes and went on their way. Kind of like missing the forest for the trees, his temperature chart was looking more like the peaks of the Himalayas than a medical diagram. The infection was spreading and his fever spiked rapidly. Eventually, someone on the night shift noticed and put two and two together. Chief wasn't eating, his temperature was rising, his fluid intake was way down so his body was dehydrated and he was becoming non-responsive. Holy Shit. They were losing this patient. It may have been in slow motion, but they were losing him to medical ignorance.

* * * * *

By the time Chief was conscious and talking, moved from the ICU to a regular orthopedic ward, everyone on the ward heard the rumors. They all wanted to know who Chief was, where he worked and most of the staff was jockeying to be assigned to his personal care. Chief's new "celebrity status" was in full swing now, something Chief avoided at all cost. He was extremely uncomfortable with this new designation. His new status kind of turned things around from his reputation as being a "non-compliant asshole". The fact he was "Combat Wounded" put him in a whole new category for the brass at Walter Reed. Some idiot put Chief's room number on every VIP roster for those visitors that came to Walter Reed to see wounded soldiers. That meant Chief would have visitors every single day.

Initially he had to deal with the likes of Hollywood celebrities who thought being seen with "real soldiers" would boost their career image. And then there was the entourage of visitors from Congress who all wanted their photo taken with a real live "Wounded Warrior". There were also a few higher up dignitaries Chief had absolutely no respect for. So instead of a quiet existence, in a room where his entire life agenda revolved around "recovery", Chief was thrust into the bright lights of "camera crews" and VIP visitors. Something he had very little tolerance for.

It didn't take long for Chief to become Persona Non Grata with the Brass and VIP staff at the hospital. When he found the strength to tear off the Purple Heart from his pajamas and throw it into the garbage can in front of the TV Cameras, somebody decided maybe it wasn't a good idea to have Chief as part of the VIP tour anymore. Things got really quiet after that. Exactly the way Chief liked it. He wasn't used to the spot light, didn't want it and damn sure wasn't up to being someone's poster child. He damn sure didn't want to be at Walter Reed anymore either. He much more preferred being back with his men, no matter where that was. As he thought about his men once again, that sick, overwhelming feeling nailed him in the guts. They were all dead.

All of that was too big a monster to deal with at the moment. Somehow Chief blanked the entire ordeal from his mind. At least for now, Demerol and Morphine were the only friends he had left on the planet. The narcotic addiction crept into his life like a thief in the night. Chief was totally unaware that addiction was even a possibility. He'd led such a pristine life. Never associated with anyone doing drugs, recreational or otherwise. Addiction was something other, less honorable men ended up dealing with. So the possibility he was sliding down that drainpipe never came into his consciousness. Therefore, it was also something he was totally unprepared to fight against. For now, the Morphine, Demerol and the synthetic heroin called Oxy, kept him alive and prevented his body from going into shock from the pain and surgical mistakes. In a few months, it would help him get through some very dark days. But after a few years, the narcotics became a way of life. They made him superman. He wanted to get his boots back on and pretend he wasn't hurt. There was no training for what was to come, the unspeakably painful dance with the devil called narcotic withdrawal.

So Chief did what came natural. He did what all his years of experience and training taught him to do when things got overwhelming.

"Focus on the five meter targets."

Everything else would either become a non-event, or come into range at it's own time. Pain was at the top of the agenda right now. Or at least the eradication of it. He pressed the syringe into his hip dispensing another tube of Demerol into his muscles and drifted off into a narcotic induced sleep. His last conscious thought focused on the clock at the end of his bed and registered the time in his memory bank. Or at least he thought so. It would be years before he actually understood he no longer had a short-term memory. The impact from the missile had permanently erased that part of his storage capacity. His brain bled for days, cutting off vital oxygen supplies to various portions of his brain. There were other problems as well, not the least of which was the rage factor he experienced now, daily. Sometimes more than twice a day. The experts had assured him it would resolve by itself over time. But the memory issue was the most prominent problem that bugged the snot out of Chief at the moment. That and the fucking clock at the end of the bed.

Funny how priorities changed so quickly. No longer was he thinking of how much ammunition was left, or how much water each man consumed in a day, or keeping track of every single mission requirement. Everything, absolutely everything was bullshit now. Instead of considering, planning, contemplating and executing orders, he'd been reduced to figuring out how to lay still so as not to induce more pain from the fractures, surgical incisions and tubing that protruded from his penis, stomach, arteries and nose. This was as bad as any torture a man could be put through, yet being told it was all "a medical necessity for his body to recover from his injuries". Bullshit.

Like they said in training, "The only easy day was yesterday!"

However, this was the part no one ever talked about. "The rest of the story!" as Paul Harvey would say. The part no one wants to hear. The part that didn't sound good, or didn't show well in the movies. Funny how they always skipped to the bereaved widow and grieving children. The gravestone with the Medal of Honor attached to the solid, cold rock. The heartstring pulling music in the background.

None of the recruiters ever told prospective Soldiers, Sailors, Airmen or Marines what their bodies would have to endure if they lived through a combat injury. The agony their minds would have to fight through when life changed abruptly, drastically and permanently.

Every injury was different. Every individual was different. And besides, the recruiters were in the business of selling the Services to young people who were bullet proof. Not warning young men and women about the *real* hazards that were out there waiting to teach them such sinister, life altering lessons.

Chief was in school now. The school of life for which he would have to pay serious tuition if he wanted to graduate. There was no going back. Everything was different now. The calendar of life would forever more be depicted by "BEFORE" the explosion that nearly killed him and "AFTER" that. He was now permanently disabled for life. A concept that was absolutely foreign to every man on the planet, until they got seriously hurt. Then they were in the unalterable brotherhood of "Disabled for Life" men and women who would forever deal with the daily sacrifice of "Service Connected" injuries. Funny how 30 seconds changed everything.

The only way out of this situation was to suck it up and drive through it and get to the other end. Where ever that was. There was a long, rocky road in between. And Chief had only taken a very few first steps. There were so many obstacles to success in his pathway. This entire episode of his life was going to make him humble. Keep him humble and teach him a lesson. He would be grateful from now on for what he had, what he could do and would forever yearn for his previous life and body.

The biggest lesson in life was waiting in the corner of his room. A wheelchair. *No one had told him yet.* He assumed it was left there unintentionally by one of the staff. He never imagined it was there for him to eventually use. After all, he was on the Orthopedic Ward and there were wheelchairs everywhere. No one told him he was paralyzed. The "wait and see" was a ruse. They all knew. Yet no one had the guts to look him in the eye. They were all waiting for someone else to do it. That was a ten meter target. Chief was still working on the five meter targets.

Autopsy Anomaly

"Be careful what you promise. You may have to keep that promise some day!"

Life Lesson Nr 13

"Sir, the post combat review autopsy results shows an apparent anomaly," the young Lieutenant said as he walked into the Office of the Army Surgeon General. Of the several thousand post mortem combat loss reports they received, the Three Star General knew precisely which report the young LT was referring to. He anxiously anticipated the written report specifically because it contained information about Chief, his close and personal friend.

LT General Fred Gerber was a soldier's soldier. He knew Chief personally and instructed his office to complete the autopsy and official review of the Friendly Fire Incident expeditiously with haste. In other words, "do it right now!"

"What kind of anomaly?" General Gerber asked, one eyebrow raised, the other squinted. He really did despise the uncommon vernacular of the medical world. No one ever said what they meant. A simple question was always answered with some version of the truth while trying to sound educated. Nine times out of ten all that kind of language really did was confuse people and make them sound like aloof morons. Fred spent nearly twenty five years of his life as a soldier, in the field, with real soldiers.

This Pentagon stuff was really starting to get to him. Maybe it was time to move on, retire, and get into something he really wanted to do. But this latest twist, with all the "Special People"

involved really had his "whitey tighties" in a knot. The fact that he
knew Chief personally only added to the pressure. He was doing
everything he could do to make sure the entire process was above
board so that absolutely no illusion of impropriety could possibly be
suggested. But he and Chief had a history, one that included some
very private things Chief would take to his grave. Now that Fred
was a General Officer, he was further divorced from real soldiers.
And he missed the candor and brutal honesty Chief was famous for.

"Well Sir, there is an injury on one of the deceased that are not
consistent with an explosion", the young LT said searching for an
inoffensive explanation without looking up at the General. He knew
about the history and why the new Surgeon General was interested.

"Spit it out Lieutenant. You know I don't like double speak.
"What the hell did they find?"

"Well Sir, one of the victims had his throat cut.," he said,
locking eye to eye with his far superior Officer and Commander.
The General outranked the LT by a mere seven grades, and about
twenty three years time in service. And that was something not lost
on the young LT.

"It's pretty clear, the wound did not come from shrapnel of any
sort, it was inflicted by a K-bar knife found at the scene, and it was
done up close and personal. The length of the slice, the location and
the depth indicate it was done intentionally. This was not just a stab
wound, or some other "accident". The medical examiner checked
this three times and had four other M.E.s check it and give their
opinions as well. By the book sir. We have to open an Article 32
Investigation as soon as possible. He was probably going to die
anyway from the phosphorus burning through to his spine, but he
wasn't going to die right away." the LT explained, searching the
General's face for some sort of indicator. None was forthcoming, so
he proceeded, without emotion, to simply recite what the report
said.

"The medical examiner results prove beyond a reasonable doubt that at least this one soldier was murdered. He died of Quote ...blood loss not related to injuries from shrapnel or other explosive concussive forces or foreign object trauma. Unquote.

"Give me that report!" Lt. General Gerber snapped with any hint of humor vacant from his voice. His forehead showed extensive wrinkling as he frowned, leaning forward in his chair stubbing out a huge Cuban cigar into a makeshift ashtray standing next to his desk. As his eyes darted back and forth across the page, the General suddenly stopped reading and flipped to the attached photographs.

"You gotta be shittin me."

"What do you want me to do with this Sir?"

"Lock it in my safe. I'll be back later," the General said as he picked up his government issued cell phone and headed for the door.

"I'll be at Walter Reed. There is someone over there I gotta have a talk with. I am going to get to the bottom of this bullshit.," he said. His voice trailed off as he forced marched out of his office into the hallway at a rapid pace.

The trip across town from the Pentagon to Walter Reed Army Medical Center could have been made in a matter of minutes by helicopter. His three stars afforded him the luxury of rapid transportation. Pilots and aircraft were consistently on standby for just such an occasion. But Fred Gerber routinely drove his own car, or that provided by the U.S. Army. It kept him in touch with the soldiers, not just the brass. Besides, right now, he needed time to think and the long drive across D.C. would give him over and hour to contemplate the situation. He couldn't imagine Chief doing anything as described in the Autopsy report. The Chief he knew was compassionate, honorable, rock solid.

As he left his office, his Aide De Camp immediately picked up the phone and instructed the Surgeon General's driver to pull the car around front. As the General approached the front door, a mid 90s Pontiac Bonneville arrived. Without much flash and over 300,000 original miles on the clock, the car was old, but up to the task and about as luxurious as the Army allowed. It was better than having to travel in a Hummer, which the General preferred actually but found it to be prohibitively large traveling the streets and highways of the D.C. Beltway. The Hummer was also a target of other drivers on the freeway. Everyone he saw was either gawking at the huge green beast, or mad as hell about his presence. So he stuck to the Bonneville every chance he got.

As his driver traversed the winding, traffic infested roads and toll booths along the D.C. Beltway, Fred was lost in memories of so many missions with Chief. Spring was coming soon, obvious from the new buds on the hardwood trees that lined the Washington Parkway. The last of the snow drifts on roadside shoulders were finally melting. Months of snow removal by huge V plow trucks deposited large piles of snow, now melting as the days got warmer leaving hardened chunks of ice impregnated with cinder dust, gravel and asphalt. The pure white snow that blanketed the earth in winter months was now in transition. The pristine blankets of white, swirled by gusting winds into drifts across meadows and fields degenerated now into the dirty phase. That transition time everyone dreaded as the surrounding forests and parkways morphed into gravel encrusted icicles, just months before lush green grass and new leaves magically arrived, dotted with crocuses and tulips. Fred suddenly found himself amused by the highway hockey as he watched cars with salt dust halfway up the doors jettison ice chunks from the rear fender panels into traffic, sliding like hockey pucks from one lane to the other only to be crushed by on-coming vehicles. Aggravated by his lack of attention, the General knew what was going on in his head. He just couldn't fathom Chief killing his own Team.

"What the fuck was this all about" he thought to himself. He knew Chief. For the previous ten years, Fred was Commander of the 37th Combat Army Field Hospital in direct support of Special Operations Command. He'd met Chief in the mid 90s, when his Bonneville was brand new while prepping troops for deployment to Bosnia. He remembered how exhausted Chief looked, slumped on the floor in a corner grabbing a few moments sleep while soldiers underwent vaccinations and refresher courses on Combat Medic Technique and Training. It was useful information for any soldier to obtain. But this was the wrong time to be forcing soldiers to learn something they already knew. Some idiot in NATO Head Quarters somewhere across the pond in Belgium wanted NATO to get all the glory. To hell with FORSCOM soldiers and all those weenies stateside who were too close to the flag pole. Bosnia was going to be a European war. Something that NATO had trained over 40 years to get into. And NATO had the lead. So, with that mentality, someone at the top of the food chain decided that to keep Bragg soldiers out of the fray as long as they possibly could, NATO would require a six month medical review process be conducted and signed off on by the Surgeon Generals Office before any stateside soldiers would be allowed into the country. There was an unspoken, political turf war going on. And this was NATO's way of controlling who got invited to the party!

Fred called NATO Headquarters to inquire why this administrative detail was being throw into the mix just hours before the Teams went wheels up? The answer was not forthcoming. In fact, it was insulting to call multiple times as a full bird colonel and have some Major hang up on him. That was not going to stand. Fred restrained himself from getting on the next military hop to Brussels to have a wake up call session with the lad. But he *would remember* the man's name and ensure his medical career had some remedial training in the very near future, training that would include a refresher course in respect to a superior Officer. Fred already knew he was going to be the next Surgeon General of the Army at the time. But the Major in Belgium did not. A major miscalculation to say the least, no pun intended.

As the car drove up to the circular driveway of Walter Reed, the MP escort came to full attention and saluted the car displaying a red flag on the front bumper, all three embroidered silver stars in full view. Fred stepped out onto the curb without waiting for his driver to open the door and headed directly into the building. As Surgeon General, he'd visited Walter Reed on more than one occasion. The soldiers genuinely liked him and looked forward to his visits, as opposed to other top level Brass who consistently had a sour look on their face, forever basking in the glory, pomp and circumstance their rank afforded them.

But Lt. General Gerber was different. The soldiers all knew it. They could sense it. And when he talked to them, he had a way of putting everyone at ease so they could speak their mind freely and get their point across. But today, everything was different. His body language betrayed him in advance. Everyone noticed the grimace on his face and curt movements in stark contrast to his normal demeanor of saluting and shaking hands, engaging soldiers in small talk and banter before he left the area. Something was wrong this time. And everyone knew it.

* * * * *

"Sir. We didn't know you were coming today," squawked Janice, the secretary at the front office desk. Her job among other things was to run interference for the Hospital Commander. But Fred wasn't up to interference at the moment. It was all he could do to put in a courtesy call to the Commander letting him know he was in the building. After all, the Commander was a One Star General. And a Three Star could do whatever he wanted, whenever he wanted. The Hospital Commander answered directly to the Surgeon General's Office anyway.

"Jack, I'm headed up to your Orthopedic unit. There is a patient there I wanna see. Old friend of mine. You mind?"

"No Sir. Go right ahead" Jack answered knowing full well it didn't matter if he minded or not. Fred was already spinning on a heel headed for the elevator door as he shook hands and inquired about Jack's wife and kids.

In a matter of minutes, Lt. General Fred Gerber was scrubbing into a gown, laced up from the back by an attending nurse and fitting his face with a mask.

"How's he doing?" Fred asked impatiently making conversation with the nurse as he readied himself to enter the sterile environment of the ICU.

"Well, better than yesterday, but he's got a long way to go. The surgery was a brutal assault on his body. 22 hours and we had some pretty serious complications. Right now we're fighting a serious infection. Peritoneal Sepsis. Is there something in particular you need to know that I can help you with? You want his chart or anything?"

"No, I just need to talk to him. When was the last dose from the PCA pump?"

He didn't wait for the answer as his brain reeled, blurting out the next command that came to mind.

"I need you to discontinue the pump till we're done talking. I need him as alert as I can get him."

"He's on 30 mg Morphine every hour, but he's been pushing the button like crazy. The computer has him locked out and won't re-initiate until the timer resets back to zero. But he's pushed it probably a dozen times every half hour in between which means he's not getting any relief. We're in the process of switching him over to something stronger now. I understand you want us to wait till you're done talking to him? Are you sure that's a good idea?"

"Absolutely. I know that is gonna suck for him, but I need him awake and responsive".

"I'll make it happen Sir.," the nurse said leaving the room as she tied off the last facial mask string behind his head.

Fred stood for a second looking in the mirror over the scrub sink. The smells of disinfectant soap and sounds of the air conditioning caught him by surprise and made him stop for a second, reflecting while he watched the man in the mirror. It wasn't too long ago he himself was right here at Walter Reed cutting soldiers open, trying to fix their broken bodies.

` Fred wasn't an Ortho surgeon. His specialty was veins. He didn't cut or fix bones, but had been called in to assist on many Ortho cases that included bones that had cut through veins and arteries. He was one of the best Thoracic Emergency surgeons in the U.S. Army inventory as well. But as with all things in the military, he had to make a choice. Stay in the surgical suite and be passed over for promotion and career advancement, or go to the Command and Staff College, get his combat time with the troops and go up the food chain. To become a Four Star General, which was what he truly wanted in life, he had to make the tough decision between balancing his family life, his career and what he really loved to do. Surgically repairing the plumbing that provided vital blood to so many organs and vital parts of the human body was fascinating to him from day one. He loved it. He looked forward to every time he scrubbed up, no matter if the patient was a superhuman Spec Ops warrior, or the dependent daughter of a tank crewman. He loved the intricate work of sewing up veins.

Within a year of making the decision to leave and go to Command and Staff College, his wife filed for divorce, he was taken off surgical rotation and Fred was assigned to an Airborne Unit at Ft. Bragg N.C. That was where Fred belonged, but such an assignment was in complete contrast to the lifestyle his full bird colonel wife had grown accustomed to. She enjoyed riding in a chauffeur driven limo to Tyson's Corners in Alexandria Virginia to shop. She loved being driven to Walter Reed to meet her husband for lunch, appearing at the Officer's Wives Functions fashionably late at such locations as the Bethesda "O" Club.

Fred didn't go for that kind of bravado or celebrity status. But she damn sure did. If he was going to play solider and jump out of airplanes, she wanted nothing to do with it. The discussion about him going unaccompanied to Ft. Bragg didn't go over very well either. It wasn't until Fred took the Command position that she dropped divorce papers on him. Via fax. What the fuck was it with these women?

"Hey Chief. It's me. Fred Gerber." Fred said as he approached the bedside, intending to announce his presence from as far away as he could. Fred heard what happened during the previous 24 hours and his heart sank.

"Poor guy" he thought, quickly followed by "Fucking idiots should have known this was a warrior they were working on".

Fred was genuinely glad that no one was permanently physically damaged, but also upset at the same time that Chief had woken up during the procedure and caused so much more damage to his spine.

"How ya doing you old fart? Damn!! Your hair is almost completely white now. You getting old on me or what?" The General said, trying to lighten the mood with some humor. The stress of six or seven back to back surgeries was taking a toll on Chief's body. His dark brown hair turned almost completely white within a month or two following so many surgeries. Anyone who knew him was shocked. Chief didn't care. He had way too much else on his plate at the moment. Besides, when he got back to Bragg, he would shave his head again as usual. It was very seldom he ever had hair anyway. The places he went were usually hot, humid, full of bugs, fleas and ticks of some sort, and it damn sure was easier keeping himself clean without hair. Everyone at Bragg knew that. Some of the Rangers and 82nd guys had "Beaver tops", hair left on top as padding for the Kevlar helmets, preventing sores from developing by helmets rubbing into the scalp. The sides were "high and tight". But for Chief and his Team, bald was the routine!

A slight smile formed around Chief's lips as he struggled not to gag on the N.G. tube inserted into his nose, threaded through his sinus and deep down into his stomach. The tubing was taped to his nose full length and up to his forehead, bringing yet another frown to Fred's face.

"What's with so much tape?" he asked the attending physician and nursing staff.

"Sir, he keeps pulling the tube out. So we had to reinforce the tape to keep it from falling out again. We taped his arms to the bed to prevent him from pulling on the tubing, but he somehow keeps getting to it. His stomach was full of acid and gas............." The voice drifted off as the General raised a finger for them to shush, nodding his agreement and understanding.

"Chief, you gotta leave this tube in your nose. It goes into your stomach and pumps out all the bad attitude so you'll heal better. You got me?"

Chief nodded agreement that he understood and then tried to talk, immediately gagging and forcing his head up off the pillow, trying not to vomit again. There was nothing left in his stomach. The inflammation caused by the tubing exacerbated the gag reflex. The dry heaves were making his stomach staples pop out, opening the wound again and again. The gagging forced the hard silicon tube to move, sawing into his sinus and the back of his throat, destroying the tender mucus membranes and scarring over the Eustachian tubes. Fluid build up caused enormous pressure on his inner ears, compounding the pain from the explosion damage to his ear drums. Hearing was nearly impossible now. His epiglottis was seriously inflamed from infection now, causing more pain the longer the gagging went on.

"Get this thing out of his nose" Fred ordered. How long has this been in there anyway?" he demanded.

"Forty one days Sir. We couldn't discontinue it till the doctor signed the order, and he's on leave till the end of next month"

"You gotta be fuckin' kidding me soldier! What is the maximum time an NG Tube can be emplaced without the patient having adverse reactions and permanent damage?

Look at your protocols and tell me that. How long is this thing supposed to stay in?"

" I don't know Sir. I just do what my supervisor tells me to do".

"And if the surgeon is on leave for another two months, what were you planning to do? Leave it in till he gets back?"

"Well Sir. I guess I would bring it up at the shift change meeting...." he was cut off by the General's rigid stare and flaring nostrils.

"Get your head out of your ass. This needs to come out NOW. Get every single person on deck who has been involved in this man's care and get them here NOW!!"

With that order, the room cleared. No one wanted to argue when the elephant started stomping. After all, this elephant had three stars. With the rapid exodus complete, Fred had the perfect opportunity to talk to Chief without any unwanted ears around.

"What the fuck happened out there Chief? We got a problem with one of your men. He had his throat cut. You got any idea how that happened?"

"Yeah, Indians." Chief quipped, smiling briefly under the new Demerol drip. Didn't anyone in this fucking place understand directions? He was supposed to be off the narcotics long enough for the General to have a conversation. But it was suddenly very obvious, that was not the case. The smile on Chief's face quickly faded as his eyes locked with Fred's for the first time. Tears welled up, filled his eyes and ran down his face into his ears.

"I got tears in my ears cuz I'm laying on my back crying about YOU baby...." Chief softly sang in half coyote, half human mustering all the strength he had trying to put on a humorous face and to feign a deep southern accent as he sang. The song was an old familiar joke that Fred and he shared. It was customary during Team indoctrination for the newbies to sing in front of the instructors and permanent Team Members. The Team's job was to humiliate the newbies and howl like coyotes during their indoctrination ceremony. In the end, everyone had a good laugh. But no one was laughing now. At the end of the song, Chief quickly inhaled to regain his breath, causing yet another round of gagging and choking to ensue.

"I'm fucking serious Chief." Fred said as he leaned closer, almost whispering into Chief's ear as he stared intently into Chief's eyes. The damage to Chief's body was extensive. Fred knew from the chart things were bad. But seeing Chief in person, looking into his eyes, he knew there was a lot more going on than the chart could ever disclose.

"We got a problem and I need to know what the fuck happened out there. You could be in a damn serious pile of camel shit here."

The Demerol was finally relieving the pain and making Chief superman again. For the first time in a damn long time, nothing mattered. He was on his way to dream land and it felt awfully good. Too good. Chief would settle for that right now. Fuck this serious stuff again. Everything was serious. Hell, Chief was the only serious one on the entire ward! Maybe in the entire hospital. The rest of these wannabes were just going through the motions to get a paycheck. They weren't soldiers. They were students. And now, NOW of all times Fred wanted to be serious? Where the hell was he the last six months? When shit was super serious?

"Yeah. I know its' serious, Fred. I was there. And it was damn serious when I did it. You don't have a fucking clue how serious it got out there do you?"

"You did it? You actually did it? You, yourself? Not some mistake, not some shrapnel…You?" Fred repeated in sequence with utter disbelief, totally missing the concept. Chief was better than that. Fred's time away from the unit, away from the real soldiers, his time in the beltway had diluted something. Something no man should ever allow to get diluted. His soldier perspective was now that of "The Brass" and Fred was more concerned about the Autopsy and what that meant, than understanding just how difficult it must have gotten for Chief to have put one of his own soldiers down. The gravity of those words alone was elusive.

"Chief. I know you. You'd never do something like that." He stuttered in disbelief, looking for some hint in Chief's face that he was joking, or lying, or covering something up.

"I promised him Sir. We all promised each other way back before we even went down range. You know the deal. Haven't you ever promised someone you'd have their six no matter what?" Chief slurred as he pushed the button on the PCA pump yet again. In a matter of seconds, he drifted off into a well deserved, narcotic induced sleep.

When he awoke, the General was gone. Chief couldn't remember if he'd actually been there, or if it was some sort of hallucination from the Demerol drip. It didn't really matter. This Demerol was really doing the job. Hell, he could probably get up and walk now. That would help him recover faster and get back to Bragg quicker. So he started struggling with the restraints, getting his arms un-done, forcing himself to sit up deliberately, looking around the room for something that could assist him to get over the railing and get his feet on to the floor.

With a loud, cold slap on the concrete and tile flooring, Chief landed face first in a heap. His feet and legs were tangled in the sheets with more restraint straps attached at the ankles. The Demerol kept him from feeling too much of the pain. But he also couldn't figure out why his legs were so heavy and wouldn't respond.

"Not this bullshit again! I thought they said my legs would come back in a few hours," he screamed from under the bed as the nursing staff hustled to get him off the floor and unwind his feet and legs. Blood poured from his mouth again. The floor had dislodged his teeth again. A small stream flowed from his ear. And the ringing got much louder.

"Chief, you can't get out of bed yet. You've only been out of surgery a little while! It's gonna take a few more weeks, maybe months before we can even attempt anything close to this." The nurse frantically tried to get Chief to understand.

"Well, when the fuck was anyone going to tell ME THAT " Chief said slurring in disbelief, sounding more like a happy drunk than a patient in severe pain.

"I got shit I gotta go do!" The Demerol was working way too good now. Obviously.

As the attending nurse came around the end of the bed, she reached over and did that which was considered a cardinal sin on the Orthopedic ward. She opened the computer controller and hit the override switch, pushed the PCA pump button and watched as Chief slowly drifted off to sleep. Patient Controlled Anesthesia was strictly that, for the patient to control and NOT to be done by nursing staff as an adjunct to patient care. She'd just committed a violation she could be fired for. But she didn't care at the moment. She was more concerned that no one had told Chief his real condition. Her concerns revolved around the physical and psychological welfare of her patient. And knocking him down so they could get him back into bed was the best thing she could do for him at the moment.

The Dream

*"Betrayal from those closest to you is still betrayal.
It just feels like something else a lot worse!"*

Life Lesson Nr. 14

The sound of the C130 overhead was undeniable. Everyone knew what it was. There was no mistaking the distinctive sound of those engines in flight, one of the last propeller driven aircraft in the U.S. Air Force inventory. Anyone who'd spent anytime at Ft. Bragg, N.C., Ft. Benning, Ga., Ft. Lewis, WA, or anywhere near an American flight line over the past forty or so years, knew precisely what a C130 sounded like. But no one knew who owned this one as it flew over the triple canopy jungle of South America. Was it Colombian? American?

Regardless, Chief's only question was,

"What the hell was it doing here?"

Before he even finished the thought, the distinctive, diminishing sounds of the propellers and engines told Chief the throttles were being cut way back. It got quiet again as the aircraft overhead drifted with full flaps deployed, almost at stall speed. Then, the familiar sounds of parachutes opening in mid air echoed throughout the quiet of the night time jungle.

"What the fuck are these guys doing?" Gunny spoke softly into his headset. "Chief, you copy?"

"Yeah. I copy. Get on the Sat link and tell Higher we got company. Find out if it's ours." Chief said in nearly a whisper.

"Roger. I'm on it" was the un-necessary reply. The entire Team sat motionless, trying to blend into the surrounding jungle as the aircraft deployed paratroopers one after the other into the dense jungle below.

"They're fuckin' nuts" came another voice over the squad radio channel.

"They're gonna be cutting guys down for weeks out here. No way in hell they gonna make it to the ground. There can't be a DZ around here for twenty miles in any direction. What the FUCK are these idiots doing?" came another inquiring voice on the Team freq.

"Knock off the chatter. Focus. You should be looking at the jungle, not the skyline. Get your game face on gentlemen. This is not a drill." Chief instructed with serious stern-ness in his voice. Any time there was something this bizarre going on, the first thing anyone should assume was that it was a distraction. An attempt to pull attention in a specific direction. There was no warning, no reason for a plane full of paratroopers to be jumping into triple canopy jungle. It was beyond stupid, it was suicide.

Suddenly, a huge noise caught everyone's attention. Night vision goggles struggled with the immediate surge of light that could only be an explosion. In seconds, the entire jungle was lit up as the bowels of the C130 disgorged its fuel tanks into the air overhead, igniting into a fireball that could be seen for miles around. The huge cargo plane exploded in mid flight directly overhead from where Chief and his Team were tucked away on the jungle floor, snapping the fuselage in two, dumping the cargo plane's contents into chaotic carnage on the way to the jungle floor below.

This was bad. Someone fired a shoulder launched heat seeker right into the belly of the bird, dumping JP4 jet fuel all over the jungle. The night was pierced by the screams of men burning alive, suspended from their chutes as they impaled themselves on tree limbs as they penetrated the upper canopy of the jungle trees some

70 feet above the ground. Other paratroopers, instinctively engaging their training, ran bicycles circles in mid air, a training maneuver intended to help a man spin in the proper direction in order to untangle his riser lines and inflate his chute. Others were crashing at near terminal velocity into the trees and bounding from limb to limb as their bodies headed for the deck. A morbidly obscene vision was unfolding. Parachutes dripped liquid fire as the nylon risers and canopies burst into flames, melted and stretched towards the jungle floor in long strings of illuminating fire suspended from branches and tree limbs. Parachutes enveloped tree tops while the weight of human bodies, burdened by the weight of ruck sacks, weapons and full combat loads made them dance in the fire light like yoyos, up and down in the night. Chief took off at a full run.

"On ME!" came the instinctive command. The entire Team lifted off the ground as if in unison and raced forward following Chief's lead. Fuel rained down in sheets, vaporized, and then exploded in deadly clouds of fumes and fire. Bodies bounced in the night suspended from parachute riser lines, flexing branches that responded by springing the screaming soldiers back into the sky. Everything was a surreal setting that no man could have imagined. The smell of burning tissue, melting nylon jungle boots and web gear that each man wore brought Chief instantly back to Ft. Bragg, that terrible summer when an F16 had crashed into a landing C130. So many burned, the smell forever seared into his memory banks. The faces, the screams, the carnage.... All because of bravado and stupidity. So many good paratroopers, gone from a peace time exercise, but never forgotten.

Chief was focused on his Team now.

"Break Left. Get as far away from that fuel as you can," he ordered into the Team frequency.

"That shit will burn you alive. Rally point to be confirmed later. Keep your shit together gentlemen. This is not a drill.", Chief repeated for accentuation.

Instinctively, every man focused on finding darkness and ran full speed in that direction. They knew how to scatter, and would be able to re-convene in a different location when it became necessary. The task at hand at this particular moment was getting the hell out of Dodge. When the initial blast from the fuel was over, the jungle returned to complete blackness dotted only by the burning bodies and clothing that danced in the night.

"Start looking at survivors. First aid to those you can reach and cut down. Focus on the ones that are on fire, put it out if you can. Any question if they are going to make it or not, get Doc to take a look at them. Any of them you can't reach, leave 'em hangin' for now. We'll work on a plan later. Copy?"

Chief was in auto mode now. Then, the unexpected hit. Fuselage. Wing parts. Landing gear hit the ground with a thud so loud, so much kinetic energy it made the entire jungle shake like an earthquake. Chief was confused now. Something wasn't right. Why had it taken so long for the aircraft parts to hit the ground? His mind grappled with the physics of it all. And then he was suddenly aware of the screams again. Men burning alive. In the middle of it all, his interest was peaked by a sound he knew was not a man. It was a woman. He knew that voice. As the bodies bounced around him, some hitting the jungle floor, he was aware of the impacts and it reminded him of tossing hay bales from the top of the loft at his grandfather's dairy farm. Every night before sun down, he would climb into the top of the barn and toss down several bales for feed the following morning. He and the other boys that worked there often would play chicken with the bales, tossing them down to the guy on the ground, trying to scare the other into submission. The ground would shake, the bales would explode if they hit on the ends, breaking the wire that held them together. The bodies impacted with the same intensity.

"Chief, you better come check this out" came Gunny's voice into his earpiece. Chief caught a glimpse of a uniform, a patch, and familiar blond hair that fell from under the Kevlar of one of the bounding bodies. He climbed as high as he could into the tree, trying to catch the human limbs flapping in the air without grabbing into burning nylon, causing his own demise, irreparable burns and wounds. A sharp pain hit him in the guts. It was the unmistakable pain of sudden realization and recognition. He knew this one. The patches came from Ft. Bragg. The uniforms were U.S. What the fuck were they doing down here. None of this made sense. And then, the unimaginable. He recognized those cheeks, those lips, that long blond hair that fell out, burning in spots, leaving the distinctive aroma that burning hair and flesh leaves as it passes by, one time falling to the earth, next time recoiling towards the sky.

"Oh God NO!" Chief screamed into the darkness. How could this be? It was his wife. His Airborne wife. She too was a soldier. Or at least she thought she was. Chief tolerated her ambitions. After all, not everyone could be a warrior. The military needed support personnel as well.

* * * * *

"Now what the fuck is wrong?" came a voice from the night. It didn't make sense. As he looked into the face of a burning corps, the voice that belonged to the face was suddenly coming from behind him. The sudden shock made Chief gasp for air. He was in bed at his home in N.C. Not in the jungle of Colombia anymore.

After six major spinal reconstruction surgeries, Chief was dealing with a lot more than just the memories of the desert. Body cast after body cast, missing his two son's baseball and football games, season after season. Doing nothing but looking at the ceiling, finally getting out of the cast, going back to work and breaking screws. The docs had told him the hardware couldn't be broken. But it had. In Somalia, again in Bosnia and always at a time that was most inconvenient. Most likely, the ruck had a lot to do with it. The added weight, the limited range of motion he was dealing with, the immense pressure and exponential leverage just from the geometry alone, carrying too much weight, causing way more stress on an already compromised vertebrae stack. The pain killers were amazing, so being Superman was even more fun, and way easier. But now he was home for the first time in years, waiting to see if the surgery worked this time. The narcotics made the nightmares so much worse, so very real, so....

"God Dammit" her voice, so filled with rage and hatred shocked Chief into a completely different mindset.

"I gotta be at work in a few hours. Get the fuck out of my bedroom! " She screamed at him.

HER bedroom? The words did not even register and Chief missed the indicator as his mind grappled to make sense of it all. His heart raced to nearly 200 beats per minute. It felt like it was beating out of his chest. He grabbed himself in the armpit trying to keep the pain from tearing his arm off.

"I mean it, get the fuck out of here and close the door." she said with a venom that Chief could not even fathom came from her soul.

"I am SO sick and tired of this bullshit you keep pulling! You fucking wake me up almost every god damn night with this bullshit nightmare stuff. When are you EVER going to just suck it up and be a real man? Get the fuck out of here NOW!" she screamed at him, throwing pillows, her voice nearly unrecognizable with venom, hatred and volume.

Chief grabbed a pillow and pulled it over his sweaty face. What the fuck was wrong with her. Maybe he just gave her too much credit. His version of a Registered Nurse, something she worked to obtain, was completely different than what she was demonstrating. Of all the nurses Chief had experience in his brief time as a handicapped soldier, every one of them demonstrated some sort of empathy, understanding and compassion. But she was just being a bitch. Maybe this wasn't her calling after all. Maybe it was just another "Degree" for her "I love ME" wall, along with the five Associate degrees she possessed, mail order courses she put on her wall and fawned over. Was she really that bad? Did she have ANY clue what Chief had been through? He knew she had no comprehension of who he really was, what he really did, or where he went when she was home at night sleeping while he deployed for 90 days or more at a time.

She didn't really give a shit where he was. And it didn't take much for him to keep his "Covert Action" life compartmented. The kids asked more questions than she did. As long as the paycheck came in, she really didn't give a shit.

Breathing was nearly impossible now as Chief sucked air through the cotton casing that covered the polyester pillow in an attempt to control his anguish and get a grip on his brain, searching for some sort of self control. Rolling to one side, what little breath he could manage to get into his lungs was forcibly knocked out as his body hit the floor falling from the king sized bed. The abrupt thump on the floor shocked him into yet another reality filled with pain. It was all a dream. Nothing but a bad dream.

He struggled to make sense of it all. But now, he couldn't move. It took another few seconds for him to realize he was still in a plaster body cast. The draconian torture chamber the spinal surgeon put his body into, kept him from sitting upright and limited his movements until the massive bone grafts healed. The pain was enormous. He blacked out and fell against the floor again. The thud of his head hitting the floor woke him again in a vicious cycle, only to fight the pain that tried again to put him into unconsciousness.

"I'm Sorry. I didn't mean to wake you up", he whispered between breaths.

"I need some help. I can't move." Chief managed to spit out as he held his breath and tried to keep his composure.

"Fuck you. I want a divorce" came the voice from across the room.

"Great" Chief thought to himself. Here was the singular woman he'd dedicated his life to, been married to for 22 years plus telling him to fuck off at a time when he really needed help. Where was the empathy, the compassion? She was a Registered Nurse for God's sake. How much more bullshit was he going to have to endure simply because her comfort zone was tweaked? Or was this yet more of the same passive aggressive bullshit because he forced her to get out of the military when the boys were born?

There had been a real bru-hah-hah over that. The boys, aged 2 and 18 months were having real problems adjusting to babysitters whenever there were exercises and she deployed to the field for 90 days at a time. Chief was down range on real world operations specifically designed to coincide with Edres (Emergency deployment Readiness Exercise Scenarios) and Reforger (Return of Forces to Germany) Exercises, annual exercises that simulated returning massive combat forces to Germany every single year in. case of a Soviet invasion through the Fulda Gap. Chief and his Team took advantage of the airflow, the huge number of personnel and equipment that filled the tarmac and sky en-route to Europe. It was great cover for Special Operations. Yet she didn't see it that way. She had her own agenda that backfired on her career motivations.

She got pregnant twice in an attempt to keep Chief in her life. Things were going sour and she knew the one way to keep Chief from leaving was to hit him where it hurt. His loyalty and honor. Getting pregnant was the sure fire way to make him stop and consider both. Honor would keep him from straying, and pregnancy was a sure way to keep his loyalty as well. Both boys were born in Germany. Chief forced her to make a choice. The kids or the military. After seeing the impact the military had on the family, the time required of both of them, Chief suggested that one of them get out to ensure the boys were taken care of and knew who their parents were. She was fuming mad at that. Chief was higher rank and was making more money. But she also knew under no uncertain terms that Chief was absolutely willing to leave the service and resign his Officer status after ten years in service if it meant the boys were going to have a stable home life. That was incredibly stupid in her mind. But she wasn't willing to give up her two years active duty either.

The "forced compromise" came when Chief put his foot down and gave her an ultimatum.

"One of us is getting out. I'm NOT going to put up with coming home to two babies who are screaming all night long cause they don't know who their parents are and want the babysitter. That's just fucked up. So you make up my mind what I'm doing here."

After nearly six months of arguments, the decision finally came down to this one conversation. A conversation Chief couldn't believe was happening. What the fuck was wrong with this woman? How could ANY mother leave her babies for three months at a time, when they were so young, so vulnerable, and so impressionable and needed their mother? What Chief didn't know was that this was just another indicator of a much deeper problem that would eventually bubble to the top at a time he really couldn't wrap his brain around it. When he was in the ICU himself, extremely vulnerable and depending on her for everything he needed, medically, emotionally and financially. Just as she did with her own babies, she betrayed him, abandoned him. On every level. More than once. Just like so many times before, given enough money, enough time, she would go right back to her old self. This had to be some sort of stress indicator. What the hell was SHE stressing about? She had everything a woman could imagine! Money, a new $40,000 dollar car, a brand new house, clothes, a career. But she always wanted more.

"Give it time", Chief thought to himself as he lay on the floor. Just like always, she'd get over it.

Moral Wounding

Life changes in thirty seconds!"
Life Lesson Nr 15

As crazy as it sounded to everyone in the medical world, no one had taken the time to tell Chief he was injured. That one fact was an important part of Chief's situational understanding. He wasn't hurt until someone told him he was. To Chief, everything was about fight, recovery time and getting back on the horse that threw him so he could ride back into battle. That single concept eluded every single person charged with his medical care.

The fact that he was injured was just so obvious to everyone who saw the X-rays, read the medical charts and were charged with taking care of him as a patient. But Chief hadn't done those things. He hadn't seen the X-rays, hadn't read the reports, hadn't been there for shift change and gotten the briefing on how he was supposed to be treated, when his dressings were to be changed and how much it would take to do it. Patient and medical staff were running on two completely different time tables. Chief was in the "week at the most" phase of recovery while the medical staff was in the "we'll see, maybe never" mode. They just didn't communicate that well, assuming Chief understood.

Five years had come and gone since that terrible day in the desert. He still hadn't said "Goodbye" to his men. All the funerals, all the ceremonies were done while he was in the ICU or recovering from extended reconstructions. Chief was on surgery number seven now. The first five were catastrophic failures. He was told the hardware was unbreakable. So to him, it was just logical to suck it up and drive on. After the basic 30 day convalescent medical leave, Chief returned to full duty without restrictions. A very bad idea indeed, but the narcotics helped Chief stay in his superman mode. A deployment to Bogota damn near turned fatal simply because altitude and Demerol don't mix well with dehydration and physical exertion. Chief blew it off and the Team Medic briefed command that "Maybe he just came back a bit too soon." The screws pulled out of the bone and Chief was destined back to Walter Reed during post mission recovery time.

The surgical gerbil wheel routine was getting old. Deploy, break the hardware or break the bone grafting, go back for more surgery, deploy again, repeat. Haiti destroyed the initial bone grafting. Bosnia snapped another set of screws. Somalia put him back into the hospital for a long time. And now, he was about to hear some very, very bad news.

"Hey Doc. You finally found the room I'm in huh?"

Chief started the banter as Dr. Porley entered the room with his white medical jacket, stethoscope around his neck, beeper clipped to his belt, carrying coffee in a stainless steel travel mug emblazoned with the U.S. Army Walter Reed Medical Center logo. He wasn't in his normal "Ranger Smile" mode this time. It was much more serious and Chief picked up on it immediately.

"Someone piss in your corn flakes this morning? Or is there something you need to tell me?"

Chief looked for some indicator switching from eyeball to eyeball as Porley spun his back to Chief while trying to sit on a stool and land his coffee cup in the same motion. Eventually Porley lifted his head, raised his glasses and took in a deep breath as he wiped his brow and began polishing the lenses. A strange look came over the surgeon's face as he plucked a Kleenex from the dispenser hanging in the one man room.

"Was he about to cry?" Chief thought to himself as he watched Porley's Adam's apple bounce in his throat.

"We had a problem while we were in there Chief. I'm not here to blow smoke up your ass. I know you well enough to know some of your background and you wouldn't appreciate me covering this shit sandwich with icing and calling it your birthday cake, so here it is."

Chief was suddenly not so humorous. In fact he had that 1000 meter stare directly into the soul of this doctor sitting in front of him, looking more like he was targeting than listening. The room was vacant except for the two men.

"Your lumbar three vertebrae was removed wrongly. That was however repaired and will most likely heal by secondary intention. The discs above and below were also compromised and had to be fused. By the time we realized what was wrong, we'd already fused level three and were attempting to connect level three to level four when we discovered level four was also compromised. Level five was fractured, out of place and indeed seriously compromised with what we call a pseudo-arthrosis noted at L5 and S1. The anterior approach provided us with an opportunity to rectify the L4 breach with more bone grafting so we could extend the L3 hardware to cover the fault line." his voice drifting off as Chief motioned with his hand to stop.

"Back up Doc. You're confusing me. I thought we were doing L5 and S1, the bottom two vertebrae and just screwing in new screws and rods from behind? You know, the shit I broke down in Bogata? What the hell happened that now we're talking about two levels above with approaches from the front *and* the back?"

"That's what I'm telling you. L3 was compromised so we had to fix the vertebrae and the discs above and below that vertebrae to stabilize the injury before we could work on L4, L5 and S1."

"From the explosion? Is that what's been causing all the pain? We missed the L3 and 4 injury during the first three or four fusions and it just showed up when you were in there this time? Whatever you did while you were in there, it stopped the pain. It feels better than it ever has." Chief didn't even realize he was using that "Team Language", saying "We" this and that.

What Chief didn't know at the time was that heavy amounts of injectable anesthesia had been used inside and outside his thoracic cavity where the vertebrae were cut out and discs removed. It would be another 12 hours before the anesthesia wore off and pain would return. Boo Coo pain. Return of motor function was questionable. Permanent nerve damage wasn't even in the conversation yet. It would be months if not years before anyone would really know for sure, what was broken for good and what would come back. The combination of anesthesia with Demerol in the PCA pump made Chief feel invincible. Like the "old Chief" he knew prior to the "desert incident".

"Not a big whoopie Doc. It's gonna heal right? Then we're back to business as usual! When can I get outta here and get back to Bragg. I got shit to do!"

The doc looked away and ran a hand over his mouth. This was tough. He'd practiced over and over with the legally reviewed and approved paragraph the Chief of the hospital and OIC (Officer in Charge) of the Orthopedic ward had agreed upon. But the conversation *was not* going as planned.

Chief was doped up for certain. In fact, it was probably the first time he was completely out of pain since the explosion in the desert. But it was becoming very obvious he was not comprehending the severity of the situation. That damn warrior spirit of his was going to cause more problems. The Surgeon decided it was time to put on his Ranger face and get Chief to understand.

"Chief. We had a serious problem in there. We had to go in through your stomach and work on three levels as opposed to what we planned on. The one level fusion was not enough to fix the error. We had to fix all three levels."

The word *error* caught Chief's attention and his stare became fixed as he breathed through his mouth, jaw slightly flexed with his bottom row of teeth showing.

"What do you mean *"error"*? Chief felt that sudden burn in his stomach as adrenaline spiked and rage burned in his soul.

"I thought you were going in to fix the broken screws and do some more bone work to make the fusion stronger. What kind of "error" are we talking about here", again using the proverbial Team language of "we" and "us".

"Ok. Lets calm down and start over."

"I am calm. Tell me what the "error" is all about".

"Chief, about ten hours into the surgery, I went out into the hallway to talk with your family. Major Levine went on without me to close you up and get you into ICU. Somehow things got out of control and he cut into the wrong level, which then had to be corrected before we could get to the rest of the problem."

"What the hell do you mean "wrong level"? L3 is a hell of a long way from L5 and S1. What the hell are you telling me?"

"What I'm telling you is that you are paralyzed from your diaphragm down. You are paraplegic."

There. He finally said it. And now, there was total silence in the room.

"Yeah... I can't feel my legs right now, but that will change when the anesthesia wears off right? I mean how long is this going to last? Just a day or two like before right?"

"No. That's what I'm trying to tell you. It's permanent. You'll never walk again. The damage was too great and the error compounded things to the point we had to do a lot more reconstruction to fix everything. We depleted all the bone grafts we harvested from your pelvis, used all the autonomous transfusion blood you self donated so we had to get more bone from the bone bank and put expanders into the blood, plus use more from the blood bank. What should have been six to ten hours turned into 22 hours in the surgical suite. It was a real marathon in there. Everyone was exhausted which is why it took so long for me to come back and talk with you. I'm sorry. We did everything we could. There was way more cord damage than we could see on films. I'm sorry Chief."

And without so much as a look in the eye, the Doc left the room in a rush. What Chief didn't know was that the doc was covering his face to prevent himself from busting out crying. He was so pissed off at that junior grade surgeon for being such an asshole and cutting without his supervision. But there was absolutely nothing he could do from this point on. It was a done deal.

Chief looked at the ceiling for a long time holding his breath. He hadn't even realized he was holding it until nature took over and he expelled it from his lungs, waking him from the self induced trance he was in.

"You gotta be fucking kidding me" was all Chief said. The room was empty. Chief was in shock. And for the first time Chief realized how much he missed the silence and peace of the desert. What the hell were they doing to him. He survived the missile. He survived the first six surgeries. He'd even survived dying on the table, then waking up trying to kill everyone in the room. But what the fuck was this all about? No way in hell was this going to happen. As he reached down checking himself he realized there was a clear delineation just below his rib cage where the feeling stopped. It itched in places, making him crazy that no matter what he did, the itching would not stop. But no matter how hard he squeezed, no matter how hard he tugged and pulled at things, he couldn't feel his legs. They hurt like hell, but they weren't there. They were heavy again, just like in the desert sand when he was crawling trying to find the screaming monster...and then it hit him hard in the stomach. They were all dead. What did he have to bitch about? He was home... or at least Stateside.

"Time to wrap your Whooah brain around reality and consider that it could be a lot worse. Stay with the five meter targets. Focus on what you can influence and work on the rest when it gets to you." Chief slipped uneventfully into total denial. It was too much for his brain to take.

"So, that's why that chair has been sitting in the corner all this time?" Chief thought out loud. Suddenly, a beautiful red headed Lieutenant interrupted his privacy. She looked more like the centerfold for Playboy Magazine than a LT in the U.S. Army Nurse Corp. But she had some fire in her belly too.

"What the fuck do you want, Nurse?" Chief spit out with a venom that surprised even him.

"I am NOT a nurse. Mister Chief Warrant Officer. I might be new to the Army, but I know my job".

"Yeah, you're obviously new cause you don't use Mister and Chief Warrant Officer in the same sentence. It sounds ridiculous, but it's also incorrect. If you're going to use "Mister", then use the last name after it. If you're going to use Chief Warrant Officer, use the last name after it but only if it's serious, legal trouble, marriage or award time. Otherwise, just call me "Chief". Got it? Now, what the fuck are you doing in my room?"

"I'm LT Christine Morgan, your new Physical Therapist. I understand you've been briefed on your physical status? I'm here to make sure you understand *your limitations*, and *our expectations*."

"Holy Shit. Nothing like letting a guy wrap his brain around things for a minute. Exactly a minute! You do know the doc just walked out after dropping a bomb like that on me right?"

"Yep. We planned it that way. The red hair and the big boobs was supposed to be a distraction so you'd get your ass out of bed and stop feeling sorry for yourself."

Chief glared at the gorgeous specimen at the foot of his bed, searching her face for some indication of humor, ignorance, or teasing.... Finding none he simply rolled over on to his side using the guard rails as handles and buried his face in the pillows.

"FFFFFFFFFFFFFFFFFUUUUUUUUUUUUUUUUUUUCCCCC CCCCCCCCCCCCCCCCCKKKKKKKKKKKKKKKKKKK!" the curse could be heard down the hallway regardless of how many pillows were stacked under his chin and over his mouth!

The door to his room slid shut, carefully and slowly cutting off the light of the hallway and darkening the room where Chief laid. His breathing had ceased again, the heart rate monitor the only indicator that he was still alive pulsed rapidly to over 200 beats per minute setting off alarms, in turn causing staff to scurry to see what was wrong.

"Let the alarms go off" the red headed LT quietly told the attendants. "He's gonna need a few minutes. It's Ok. I got this", she said as she gingerly waved for the concerned respondents to "go away".

Eventually Chief resigned himself to another five meter target. Holding his breath made the pain worse. The narcotics combined with the lack of oxygen gave him an enormous headache, making his heartbeat the only sound he could hear. So he found the self discipline to breath normally and get his mind to start thinking about something other than what he had just learned. In actuality it was a form of denial, a protection mechanism he desperately needed at the moment.

How things played out from here was totally up to him. And he wasn't going for the crippled guy routine. He would get the full documented report in a few days. Until then, he really didn't understand what had happened. He was conflicted with being happy that the pain was gone, but nothing worked from his diaphragm down. Nothing. At 33 years of age, his manhood was a proud part of his body and his mental, self body image. All that was gone now. And it would take time for Chief to consume the bad news and try to adapt.

All paraplegics and amputees have body image symptoms and issues. It was a matter of how bad and how they accepted or denied them that would take the most time to sort through. What really pissed him off more than anything was this gorgeous red head standing at the end of his bed, giving him what felt like an erection from hell after being deployed for so long in a God Forsaken desert where there were no women. Yet when they did get to town, most of the women wore Burkas. He hadn't seen his wife in nearly three years, but he hadn't had sex with her either for at least another year. So here he was, four years into deployment and medical hell, horny as a felon on death row, a gorgeous red head in his private room, yet there was absolutely no response from his body. Internally everything felt like it was reacting...but nothing was in the physical realm. That was voodoo. And it sucked big time. Why the hell would they do something like that to him? The mental olympics were just beginning.

Within an hour, Chief was sitting as upright as he could in bed, still trying to feel his legs and sorting out what did work, where it stopped and what didn't work. There were two sets of nerves he was concerned about. The motor nerves that ran muscles and kept them moving, and the sympathetic nerves that transmitted pain and feeling. One could work without the other. But if *both* were gone, then all bets were off. As he studied the neurology book Lt. Morgan left with him, he was interrupted by another knock on the door. Impatient and frustrated, he flopped back on the bed, looking at the ceiling and yelled, "Now what. Come in. *Come IN!*"

"Sir. I am Captain Epstein from the Staff Judge Advocates Office here at Walter Reed Army Medical Center and this is Sheriff Deputy Michael Loftus from Silver City County Dispatch Office. The Deputy has papers for you to sign."

Chief's brain was in a whirlwind. Why was a civilian law enforcement officer inside Walter Reed with papers for him, especially being escorted by a JAG weenie? It didn't make sense. Until the Deputy started reading....

"Sir, it is my duty to inform you that legal action has been taken in Fayetteville N.C. against you in the form of Divorce.".... The words drifted off into the distance as Chief tried to collect himself and comprehend what was going on. That dream. Waking up screaming. Chief knew she was pissed about being woken up, but damn.... This was carrying things a bit too far. After all, he was seriously fucked up at the moment, was still trying to figure out why the doctors were telling him he was permanently paraplegic. What the hell was she doing?

"Hold up. Hold up. Can this wait till I get done with this medical stuff? I mean seriously. Divorce? There has to be some mistake here. Yeah, she was pissed that I woke her up, but damn.... You gotta be kidding me?"

"No sir. I'm sorry. This came over from her lawyer on the Fax machine this morning. I was sent to deliver it with proof of service by close of business today. I'm sorry sir. If there were any way around it, I would have found it. I get it. I was in Desert Storm with the First Marine Division. I heard about what happened to you and I'm still sick to my stomach they are making me do this. But I'm a civilian now and a Deputy Sheriff. I have to do my duty as it's given to me, Sir. I'm sorry. There is nothing I can do!"

A tear welled up in the Deputies eye as he squeezed his nose trying to keep it from running. The tear fell from his eye and rolled down his dark black cheek, dripping onto the clip board holding the "Notice of Service" paperwork. As he signed it, the ink blurred, mixing with the tear drops. Without so much as trying to keep it from messing up any further, the Deputy pulled the sheet from the clip board and handed it to Chief over the bed railing, then took it back and laid it on the table making a notation that personal service was impossible due to the "Defendant" being restrained to the bed rails after "serious spinal reconstructive surgery". The Deputy wrote everything he could to indicate to the Court and to the Judge that this service was complete under extreme duress. It was just un-American to do something like this to someone in the Intensive Care Ward, to a man unable to defend himself.

"Sir, this service is hereby legal and that is all I am allowed to say. But on a personal basis, if you've got a good lawyer, you need to contact him as soon as possible. There is more I cannot say, but it's extremely important you get legal assistance as soon as possible."

With that he put on his Smokey Bear hat, brought up a perfect salute, returned his straight arm immediately to his side and did a perfect "about face" maneuver, showing full well that he was still a U.S. Marine under that Deputy Sheriff uniform. He marched off smartly through the open door being held by the red headed Lt. Morgan. Tears filled her eyes as well.

"What the fuck..." came the words from her mouth as she wiped her nose and turned to see Chief still laying on the bed looking at the ceiling.

"I don't fucking get it. Hey God. What the fuck did I do to deserve *this* shit?"

"Well, it's none of my business, but I assume you've been having marital problems before now?" the LT asked. She really didn't want to get too personal. After all, she just met this guy. But some things were just too obvious.

"Yeah... big problems, like not being in the same grid square for more than ten minutes out of the year. I've been deployed constantly for two years. It's not like we had any time to start a fight or anything. She gets my full paycheck every month for whatever she wants. So what the fuck? If I was a drunk, home beating her ass every night that would be one thing. I would deserve this kind of shit. But Damn it to Hell and back. I have been down range chasing bad guys, doing hostage rescue and taking out HVTs for years on end. She knows what I do but she's pissed I don't tell her anything. She does NOT have the "Need to Know" on every mission I go on. And she has to have a little faith when I leave in the middle of the night. But whenever I get back, it's always the same story about "how hard it is", how her life sucks having to take care of the kids all the time. Those boys are the reason I come home from this psycho shit. What the hell is she thinking? Now, of all times, when I'm down this hard, this far, for this long.... *Now* she decides to dump me like a bag of rocks. What the fuck is going on with this bitch?"

It was leaking out now. This was totally out of character. Now Chief was talking like a victim. He never called her a bitch. She was the wrong one and Chief knew it from the day they got married. They were never tied to the soul. He just "settled" like so many other people did in their lives. Settled for "someone" instead of "The One" simply out of boredom, from being lonely and tired of looking. She knew what she was hooking onto and did so with all the desperation of a gambler and the leverage of a mafia bookie. She didn't need any guidance. The evil was born into her and Chief stayed 22 years with a woman he couldn't stand, simply out of loyalty to his two boys.

The double edged sword he knew so many women lived with was brutal. He never would have had those two wonderful boys if he never met her. Yet he cursed the day he met her, cursed her for all the evil she dragged into his life, constantly leaving him on guard for the next unexpected, self inflicted problem. For whatever reason, she constantly bounced checks. Somehow, she chose to flirt with the one thing she knew would end his career. The FBI did their routine investigation on her background, so she could get an interim clearance to start school. But the Feds found a lot of dirt. Very disturbing behavior and inconsistencies that put her on Security Hold. Most of the problems revolved around financial discrepancies. You don't get to buy things on credit and not pay for them, and then expect to get a Top Secret clearance. You don't get to keep a Top Secret clearance and bounce checks. Chief was warned by the FBI and the Command that her conduct would have serious consequences with his career if he didn't keep it under control. Like a good soldier and loyal husband should do, Chief bent over backwards to help rectify her negligence, pay back everything she owed to everyone she owed and professed his undying loyalty and devotion to a woman who had every excuse in the book. "Love is blind, but the neighbors ain't!"

When Chief finished language school, he was re-assigned to Germany to use the languages he learned and continue the Covert Operation missions he was used to. She was forced to stay there at Defense Language Institute/Foreign Language Center (DLI/FLC), in Monterey, California, on security hold. Within two weeks of leaving her there, Chief was back in Europe, preparing for deployment to Italy to rescue a U.S. Army General from terrorists operating with the Red Army Faction. Chief was prepping to write the "This is not working out" letter. But he got a letter in the mail before he could send his.

"I'm pregnant"

The hook was set and the loyalty of a Warrior in Special Operations Intelligence was going to keep the hook in place. A bit over a year later when things were really dicey and about to break up, the same tactic worked again. She was pregnant with Chiefs second son while he was deployed with a beautiful Female LT conducting recon missions throughout Europe. She was his "undercover wife", red headed, beautiful, fit, smart, strong, but very young and a serious liability Chief needed to keep a watch on. She could get killed due to her lack of experience, or worse, get him killed too! At home, the drama never ceased. Although Chief was more than tempted, the young, beautiful LT and he really hit up a friendship that would last a lifetime. Never once did Chief stray. But she didn't believe him. No amount of loyalty, love, endearment, proclamations of love and fidelity seemed to matter at all. The relationship with the LT, as work related as it was, was a continual source of venom and anger whenever she brought it up.

The "incident" in Italy damn near put an end to things. He was on his last nerve with her bullshit when he got called in on the carpet. She was caught stealing goose down comforters from an International Hotel while on tour with American Officer's Wives Club. That alone damn near put the nail in his coffin. He would never forget the embarrassment, nor the sting of being called before the new Commanding General and being ripped a new ass. He didn't know Chief. Nor did the new Commander know Chief's stellar reputation as an Intelligence professional. What Chief eventually came to realize, was that this incident was a demarcation line in their relationship. Nothing was the same after that.

"If you can't control your dependents, then you don't need to be an Officer and I will not have someone like that in my Command! Are we CLEAR?"

What the fuck was she thinking. This was just another version of obstacles she was throwing into his life at a time he needed it the least. "Plaintiff number Four" made so much more sense now and Chief smiled slightly as the words rushed through his head, remembering how Gunny introduced his new fiancée. The " Italy incident" was secondary only to Chief being interrogated by the Polizei as he was packing to return to CONUS and finding out she had an illegal abortion at an illegal clinic to dispose of "zwillinge", the German word for twins. Those words rang in his head and left him forever contemplating something he still couldn't understand. Abortions were illegal in this Christian country. Having one done at an illegal clinic explained where all the money went to, but left him with so many more questions he needed to answer. He was so busy dealing with terrorists, stopping the bombing of American housing areas, finding the remnants of the Red Army Faction who killed his best friends and figuring out who left the bomb in his car that was destined to kill his family, he never noticed she wasn't complaining anymore when he got home. If they were his, she aborted them without his even knowing she was pregnant. But the chances were pretty good they weren't his and she was trying to get rid of them simply from the embarrassment and the torrential storm they represented to their relationship. Either way, Chief was wounded to the soul. But she would never know that he knew the entire story. She would never know the hurt she inflicted. He just didn't say anything. He returned to the States, signed into Ft. Bragg and dove into his work.

And now, after 22 years of marriage, she was divorcing him when he had just survived a major injury, a major medical mistake during a major 22 hour surgery, and was facing a major hurdle in his life. He was paraplegic now and had no idea how he was going to get through the next day, never mind the rest of his life.

"What the hell else can happen today" was the comment barely out of Chief mouth when another knock came on the door. The buxom Lt Morgan reached to open the door just as Chief let out a loud report.

"*WHAT!*" he yelled at the top of his lungs. Chief assumed Captain Epstein forgot something when he walked back into the room. But instead, the young Captain stepped aside, stood at attention while holding the door to allow someone else to walk into the room. That "someone else" was a full bird Colonel, which meant this was a no bullshit situation. He instantly thought of his boys and wondered if he'd gotten all of the Red Army Faction. Abu Nidal was dead for sure, but Chief never could be sure someone hadn't put a contract on his family. His mind swirled with possibilities in anxious anticipation of what would come out of this guy's mouth. Maybe she was in a car wreck. Or was it something else? In another split second, all of his questions would be put to rest.

"Chief? I am Colonel Ralph Bastogne from the Pentagon's Adjutant General's Office. I'm here to read you your rights and inform you that you are being charged with Six Counts of Premeditated Homicide".

The room went completely silent as Chief's heart monitor alarm kicked on again.

"Colonel, I've had a pretty shitty day so far, so if this is some sort of a joke, it's really not appreciated. And it's damn sure not very funny either! Who set you up to this?"

"I assure you Chief, this is not a joke. In Accordance with UCMJ, a 15 dash six was conducted. I'm sure you know that is a fact finding investigation. Sufficient evidence was found to instigate you being charged under UCMJ with Article 118, with premeditation."

Chief's mind was numb, trying to figure out what this Colonel was talking about as he watched him intently focus on the clip board in front of him. As he read the mandatory paperwork, Chief just couldn't imagine what had gone so sideways.

"Any person subject to this chapter," the Colonel continued, checking boxes as he read,

"whom without justification or excuse, unlawfully kills a human being when he: -

1. Had a premeditated design to kill;

2. intends to kill or inflict great bodily harm;

3. Is engaged in an act which is inherently dangerous to others and evinces a wonton disregard for human life; or

4. Is engaged in the perpetration or attempted perpetration of burglary, sodomy, rape, robbery, or aggravated arson;

Is guilty of murder and shall suffer punishment as a court-martial may direct, except that if found guilty under clause (1) or (4), he shall suffer death or imprisonment for life as a court-martial shall direct."

"Life imprisonment or death? Wow, what an option." Chief thought out loud.

"Engaged in acts which are inherently dangerous to others? Holy shit. Not like we did that every fucking day huh?" The Demerol was over riding any "military bearing" Chief could muster. This was fucking ridiculous. And in view of what just happened within the last hour, Chief was mesmerized by numbness and denial. This couldn't be happening, not when he couldn't fight back.

"A hearing took place in absentia under Article 32 which concluded while you were here in the hospital. As a result, you are being formally charged with pre-meditated homicide. Six counts. Do you have an attorney?"

Emptiness and Betrayal

*"We are born alone, we die alone. Everything in
between is a facade!"*

Life Lesson Nr. 16

After nearly 18 months laying in Walter Reed Orthopedic
Recovery Ward, Chief was ready to go postal. As he lay in the
specialized spine bed known as a Stryker Frame, his brain yet again
went into automatic mode and started reviewing the mental
priorities he set and then began planning how to bring them to
fruition.

The never ending gerbil wheel of laying in a bed, totally
incapacitated, looking at the clock on his wall, was slowly making
him nuts. Minutes went by like hours, taunting him into disbelief
when he closed his eyes, thinking at least an hour went by to find
only a few minutes transpired. He resolved himself to counting his
breaths, concentrating on defeating the pain, and forcing himself to
think about anything but his Team and his two boys. There was
nothing else in the eight foot wide by ten foot long room accept the
huge electric bed he laid on, a roll around table that extended over
his bed so he could eat from the dining tray and the clock on the
wall. Basically, a prison cell.

Chief was resigned to living in his head now, struggling with
the fact he was no longer superman. He wrestled with his disability
and the urges to go run, ruck, jump out of airplanes, to train his
Team and deploy on missions that really mattered. The ever present
reminders of just how crippled his body was, were road blocks to
his recovery. He still hadn't made the transition from Special Ops

Superman, to that of a crippled, paralyzed, totally useless blob of flesh, lying in Walter Reed. Transition never felt like transition. It always felt like chaos, or something way worse and much more sinister. He might as well be on another planet. Because no one at Ft. Bragg knew where Walter Reed was. Nor did they want to know. To all the "high speed, low drag" soldiers of XVIII Airborne Corp, the 82nd Airborne Division's "All American, America's Guard of Honor" and Special Operations soldiers, Walter Reed was a place that meant an end to life as they knew it. That was a world of medical nightmares that no one on Active Duty wanted to participate in. Other than the obligatory visit from Commanders, everyone else pretty much stayed off the radar, using the excuse "it takes five hours to get there" to insulate themselves from any real meaningful visitation. Besides all that, Chief was one of those guys that didn't really exist. So no one came to visit. Even his wife made excuses so she didn't have to come!

The body cast, the HALO screwed to his head and the relentless depressing and obstructive visits by nurses coming to check his vitals was slowly eating away at any motivation he carried in his heart. Being a patient, being a victim, being disabled was so foreign, so un-like anything he ever lived like, that Chief caught himself with the full time task of trying to ignore just how crippled he really was. His entire life now was like watching grass grow. Instead of dealing with a multitude of missions, multi-tasking and being involved with real life or death situations and consulting with the highest levels of decision makers in the U.S. Military and the civilian oversight and leadership within the U.S. Government, Chief was now just part of the herd. Or worse! Right now, Chief was not part of anything! Just a patient lying in some secluded Orthopedic ward, off the radar, out of sight and out of mind. And naturally, he did what he normally did, what his DNA required him to do. He started planning another mission.

The first thing on his mind was getting back to Bragg to see his two sons. That was the emotional target plan that brought him the most motivation. He was sick and tired of the excuses she was giving him for not coming up to visit with his boys. So if she wouldn't bring them to Walter Reed, he was going to go home to find them. And nothing was going to get in the way of that, come hell or high water.

Secondary to that mission, finding out what the hell was going on with his wife came in a close second, followed by the Courts Martial charges. Someone at the JAG office at Ft. Bragg had to be in the middle of all of that, so as long as he was going back to Bragg, he could at least find out what was really going on. After he got answers and influenced the outcome of those three things, he would then start considering what the hell he was going to do with the rest of his life from a wheel chair. That was the 9,000 lb. Gorilla in the room he didn't want to even talk about, never mind consider accepting.

All his dreams, all his intentions during all those missions was to get to the point that he could retire, move to the mountains of Montana and build the log house he'd always dreamt of. But doing it from a wheelchair, permanently paralyzed never crossed his mind. That was a target much further away than five meters. So he shut it off for now.

The thought of laying in the damn hospital for another ten months was making him crazy. Literally. He just couldn't imagine doing the same thing he was doing, for that much more time. He knew he could do it, just lay there and heal. He could do anything if he put his mind to it. But at this point in time, Chief was so tired of life at Walter Reed, he made up his mind to just leave. To escape. To pull off a covert operation that included leaving the Ortho ward and going home. There was nothing on the books he knew of that said he *"had to"* stay there. The doctors were more interested in going on leave to play golf than doing anything to expedite his recovery, and the nurses routinely left the ward unattended whenever the ice cream truck showed up. This would be easy.

In reality, the surgeons did more damage than good. And that was something he buried so deeply he didn't even want to think about it yet. Everything he was, everything he did that made him "Chief" was stolen away because of ignorance. Just like the ignorance of Friendly Fire, the "wannabe" surgeon made a mistake Chief would spend the rest of his life paying for.

There was way too much rage attached to all of those thoughts. He tried with everything inside him to ignore the emotions and just deal with the realities he needed to deal with. The fact he couldn't feel his legs. The fact he was paralyzed from the diaphragm down. The fact he had minimal contact with his wife and zero contact with his sons. Those were real, pertinent facts he needed to deal with. The emotional shit could wait.

Chief was a Team Player. And he was searching very hard for a way to forgive the guy who'd taken away his dreams forever. Someone was going to get their head handed to them if they brought that subject up. Maybe some day he would get there, to find the forgiveness and get on with his life as a cripple. It just wasn't going to be today!

As if Chief didn't have enough on his plate, as if there weren't enough moving parts to keep him busy and stir up even more anger, Chief had recently received a legal letter in the mail disclosing a Federal Class Action Lawsuit against several manufacturers of spinal hardware called "the Pedicle Screw Litigation". Apparently, all the civilian patients in America who had spinal hardware implanted had gotten together and sued the manufacturers for faulty metal alloys. This metallurgic fault was causing the hardware to fail nearly 100% of the time. The slick willie corporation had been denied an application to market the screws and rods as "spinal fixation devices" because it wouldn't take the body weight when implanted in spines. So they'd changed the federal application to read "bone screws" and got everything approved. But the fine print stated that the hardware could *ONLY* be implanted in long bones such as legs or arms, since those extremities were supported by ancillary devices like slings and support braces, or peripheral devices like crutches and wheelchairs when the legs were involved.

But since the previous medical disapprovals for spinal implants prevented them from obtaining so much corporate profit, they simply changed the wording on the application form to "Bone Screws" and re-submitted the application to Medical Authorities for approval. The review process didn't take into account that it was the same exact manufacturer, and since it said "Bone Screws" the approving authority assumed the company would do "the right thing".

The manufacturers, as a defense in the Class Action Lawsuit, claimed that since the approval as "Bone Screws" didn't explicitly forbid in writing the use of their devices in vertebrae, which in their opinion was a bone, they felt they were authorized to market them for Vertebrae Fusion Surgeries. To them, it didn't matter that they were denied by application disapproval in the past. So the company went ahead and marketed the hardware with the caveat that they had recently been approved by the Medical Authorities. They just didn't bother to explain the fine print to anyone that bought their bogus alloy hardware.

As with most military acquisition processes, Walter Reed submitted their requirements for "Spinal hardware" through the medical supply channels. The Pentagon, going with the lowest bidder, purchased the hardware at an astounding rate and then allowed Walter Reed Army Medical Center to start slapping that hardware into soldier's spines. About twenty a year. Most of which were either Special Operations Personnel, or Airborne/Rangers who consistently fractured their spines with the excessive amount of ruck sack weight they encountered on a routine basis, compounded by the Airborne Operations they routinely experienced. After all, these soldiers were highly motivated, highly trained, in great physical shape and could be used as guinea pigs since the military doctors and hospitals were immune from prosecution or any lawsuits under Federal Law.

Using these strong young guys for medical testing already had precedence in the legal world. The Military Medical Establishment could do whatever the hell they wanted. They were immune from prosecution or any type of recourse. Especially when it came to malpractice. In turn, soldiers had absolutely no recourse if something went wrong. In reality, these men were true patriots. So the chances of these soldiers having the financial ability to hire an attorney, never mind actually filing a lawsuit against Uncle Sam, well, the chances were really slim. It was a win win for the hardware manufacturers. And the surgeons who performed these implants were on the fast track to making millions when they got out of the Military and started their own private practices. There was no oversight, no medical malpractice lawsuits to contend with or be afraid of and they could fill their resume' with hundreds of spinal fusion operations. Because no one in the civilian medical world, ever asked how many of them were actually successful. The dirty little secrets just seemed to pile up. And the catastrophic result, the disabled American Veterans, were just kicked to the curb and hidden away from public view.

As usual in the medical world, no one ever suspected anything bad was going to happen. These were upstanding Civilian Manufacturers with strong ties to the military medical world. They had a proven track record of everything from knees and hips to prosthetic limbs. Spinal hardware was just a further endeavor to help the military fix the broken bodies of war torn soldiers. The problem was, every single set snapped off within the first 90 days. And in Chief's case, three different sets broke within a year requiring more surgery, more hardware, more bone grafting and excessive damage to his spine at differing levels. Yeah, he probably should have taken a bit more time off, instead of deploying on missions, but to Chief, all this medical stuff was like dealing with the Keystone Cops.

Chief's life was permanently altered by a "wannabe surgeon" who not only put in faulty hardware for the fourth time, but had also taken out the wrong vertebrae and the wrong discs. The lawsuit paper work about faulty hardware, that came in the mail to his room at Walter Reed, was telling him he'd been rejected and removed from the class action suit simply because he was considered a "Federal Employee". His Active Duty Military Service put him in a category that insulated the perpetrators from any recourse. Fuck you very much.

The resulting 150 million dollar settlement was split between the remaining plaintiffs and their lawyers. Chief was out in the cold. Some obscure Tort Claims Doctrine from the 1950s made sure he'd stay out in the cold. There was no recourse. Period. And since Chief was being considered for Medical Retirement, there wasn't much to look forward to. Especially if convicted in this fucked up Courts Martial. They'd take away any retirement and all his benefits for certain. Felons and murderers didn't get full benefits from Uncle Sam.

Life wasn't fair. Chief knew that. He'd seen his share of unfairness. But this was just fucking ridiculous.

* * * * *

It was early April and the azalea trees in North Carolina were coming into full bloom. Chief was looking forward to seeing all the glory of Spring in the Carolinas. The bright pink, red and white blossoms stood out against the bright green background of Bermuda and Fescue grasses. Giant Dog Wood trees accented the surrounding woods made up of Persimmon trees, tall standing sugar pines and red cedars, his favorite. Thoughts of deer season, laying in the cedar deer beds brought a smile and some much needed mental relief to his brain.

Most of the yards in Chief's housing area were well groomed with pine straw covered flower beds, self timed watering systems and dozens of flower species. People really took care of their yards, a source of not only pride, but of community as well. It made him realize just how much he missed home, considering where he'd been in the stark contrast of Iraq, Afghanistan and other places in the Middle East, North Carolina was part of the American dream that so many other humans on the planet wanted to experience.

The injury, the explosion, the time way from home sincerely brought a new level of appreciation to his soul. He loved America. And he yearned to be home with his two sons. He wanted very much to take them fishing, to find out who they were now. So much time away and they'd grown so much. They turned into little human beings he didn't have any real understanding of. They grew up while he was gone. And with all his heart, all his soul, he wanted to get to know them. To bond with them. To seriously become the father they deserved, not just the absentee sperm donor he felt like. Every time he came back, they were doing something that amazed him. A vivid memory of coming off a secret mission haunted Chief. The screws broke again when he was down range and had to be repaired for the fourth time. God dammit he was getting tired of the same old routine. The damage was bad enough, but the severity of scar tissue to his cord and the rest of the vertebrae stack was getting more serious every time the bone grafting broke and the screws either pulled out or snapped. Discharged from Walter Reed after his fourth or fifth spinal surgery, Chief was on medical leave, 30 days of free time off to heal when he came back to Bragg and found them swimming at the pool on post.

"Dad! Watch this!" They said as they climbed the high diving board platform. And without so much as a blink, with zero hesitation, they dove into the water from the 30 foot platform. Chief was shocked to the soul. They were fearless. Young, tanned, beautifully innocent, having the time of their lives and dead set on impressing Dad. Something happened inside Chief's soul that day. He knew it was time to quit. Time to come back home and be a real part of their lives. The wake up call he dreaded came without any warning. And he yearned to connect with the only human beings on the planet that really meant anything to him. These two wonderful humans he called his sons.

No one in America knew the U.S. was going to war in Afghanistan in the very near future. Chief did. But that was normal. He always knew before the general population did. As he laid in bed, contemplating his predicament, Chief battled with memories of by gone days when he was an important cog in the wheel of Special Operations Intelligence. He remembered how spooky it had been that Christmas night in 1989, driving around Ft. Bragg watching soldiers non-challantly packing their rucks, jabbering about nonsense, not knowing that after they loaded into an airplane, the next time they saw daylight or smelled fresh air, they would be floating down to Panama from their parachutes. Not jumping into Holland D.Z. on Ft. Bragg.

It came with the job. Having the inside information and not letting anyone else know. It hurt Chief in a sense and made him feel like a traitor. Everyone would eventually find out in due time. When they truly "needed to know". But for Chief, knowing so far in advance was a burden he didn't relish like others in the job did.

For now, everyone was extremely content that the U.S. had whooped ass in less than 100 hours and was coming home from

Saudi Arabia. Operation Desert Storm was a huge success. At least most of them were coming home. No one really gave two shits about those who didn't come back. To the public at large, the entire war was a huge video game that didn't require real soldiers to get hurt. And no one really understood that along with all the smart bombs, cruise missiles and Stealth Fighter jets, the largest tank battle in the history of mankind had taken place in the deserts of Iraq.

The U.S. Abrams kicked ass, losing ZERO tanks to Iraq's 3000 or more losses. To Chief, the success of the U.S. tank commanders was bitter sweet, a result of intelligence collection under "Operation Elsa", something those tank commanders and crews never heard anything about. Chief had recovered a brand new T-72 tank. When it finally got shipped to the U.S. Foreign Science and Technology Center, the materials, fabrication and armor capability were precisely what the U.S. engineers needed to build the M1 Abrams tank that would defeat the T-72 so decisively. There had been just enough time in between the "purchase" of a brand new T-72 in Eastern Europe and Desert Storm to reverse engineer the Soviets' premier tank and put upgrades into the M1 Abrams to be able to defeat it.

U.S. tank engineers out gunned Iraq's Soviet T72, the primary tank Saddam had purchased by the thousands. The armor used on the U.S. M1 was a classified high grade ceramic and titanium mix, impervious to the Soviet weaponry. Field testing showed that the Abrams could take a direct hit from a hundred yards away and never even get a scratch. Crew survivability was essential and the intelligence Chief and his crew had recovered from the East Bloc was an integral part of why the engineers had been so successful in building the Abrams, making it not just superior, but completely invulnerable. The Iraqi's never had a chance.

Chief was deep in thought, contemplating the poor Iraqi bastards who positively believed they were invulnerable inside a T-

72. After all, they'd never been challenged. People saw the huge machine and ran the other way. The Iraqi tankers never had to engage enemy tanks. So they really didn't have any competition, nor any experience. Until the Abrams showed up in the desert. It was a turkey shoot for U.S. tankers. One round, one kill. The laser designation combined with thermal optics and GPS far outclassed the T-72. But the real issue was the Abrams' far superior gun, popping Iraqi tanks at over a thousand meters farther than the T-72 could even shoot. Images of thousands of burning tanks rampaged through Chief's mind.

Suddenly, the "other incident" rushed to the forefront of his mind. Friendly fire. A dead crew. Exploding ordinance. American soldiers. It all flashed into his brain with lightening speed. The bile churned in his stomach as his mind raced trying to fight, to put it all back in the box as soon as he could. They were all dead because Chief set Thermite grenades inside the trailer SCIF. Someone must have tripped the ignition wire and everything went to hell. No matter how hard Chief tried to convince himself otherwise, it was his fault. Wasn't it? Setting the Thermite was his idea. Thermite was the only option to absolutely positively ensure that none of the highly classified Intel got into enemy hands. The equipment was so sensitive, so classified, all prototype stuff that involved so much of America's future arsenal and intelligence capability that losing it to enemy hands was out of the question. Chief personally talked the brass into letting him deploy the system to such a dangerous area, convincing them he would take personal responsibility if anything went wrong. Sensitive Top Secret SCI intelligence capabilities were never deployed to hostile arenas simply because the threat of compromise was too high. But Chief assured everyone, including the head of ISA, the President, the Director of Intelligence at the Defense Intelligence Agency, the Secretary of Defense at the Pentagon as well as the civilian contractor developing the system, that nothing was going to happen to the equipment. Chief gave his personal assurances and convinced everyone this was a good idea.

Only now, it was all gone. The enemy never got any of it, but it was gone none the less. And that pissed off a boat load of people. It didn't seem to matter much that nothing was compromised. They were all pissed that the prototype was destroyed. One hundred thirty seven point seven six million dollars. Vaporized because Chief put Thermite inside. Or at least that's what everyone was saying.

The explosion from six thermite grenades was big enough, but not too big. The white phosphorus would ensure that all the prototype classified equipment and technology would be melted down beyond recognition. There was no chance of compromise, nor of recovering anything after the 3,000 degree fire. Chief carefully planned everything and placed the grenades perfectly so that critical components were the first to melt down. He studied the grenade burst radius, figured out where to set them, how many to set and tested them at the range on actual equipment prior to deployment. Chief perfected the placement and ignition plan so the Operators could escape the blast radius and leave nothing but a pile of dust and melted aluminum for the Iraqis if their position ever got over run. It was fool proof with a safety mechanism that ensured no one could inadvertently set them off. He couldn't imagine how they'd gone off without someone intentionally doing something to override the safety device and pulling the charge wire. Everyone on the Team was fully briefed and trained on the devices. Everyone knew the risks and knew how to set them off just in case.

Chief went over it in his head a million times. He knew he did exactly the same thing he did so many other times in so many other operations. Never once did any of the others grenades go off unintentionally. What the fuck happened this time? It made him crazy trying to go over it again. So he pushed it from his consciousness and tried to get on with his plans to get the hell out of Walter Reed.

Chief had already been in the exact same hospital, on the exact same ward, in the exact same room on four other occasions with at least one mission down range in between each reconstruction. Apparently, the hardware wasn't strong enough to take on a truck wreck as he was told. It obviously couldn't take the extra weight of a rucksack, nor sliding down a rope from a Helo. Each time, the fresh hardware snapped and his spine and his body was insulted. The resulting damage from broken hardware and medical malpractice was getting worse. Recovery times were taking longer. Eventually, things got so twisted, Chief could hardly remember which surgery, at which time, had resulted in what! He just took more Demerol or Morphine and insisted on going back to work. The first surgery was to fuse the fracture at L5 and attach hardware from the rear. That initial surgery was only six hours and Chief came out of it relatively unscathed. He was in serious pain, but went straight back to Bragg to work in the SCIF with the primary intention of doing post mission after action and battle damage assessment work. Finding out what happened was up to the 15-6 investigation. And he was on pins and needles waiting to get the paperwork so he could read the result. As usual, some lame ass Captain "wanna be" from the Pentagon was in charge of the investigation, trying to make a career jump instead of finding the absolute truth. Chief wasn't even deployed, staying in the rear with the gear. But no one ever came to interview him. So how the hell would this Captain conduct an investigation from a desk in the beltway and come up with any intelligent answers?

The real answer was, "He wouldn't" but Chief had no say in the matter and was told under no uncertain terms that he was not to interfere in any way with the Captain or his staff. If nothing else, Chief was a soldier and took orders pretty well.

Shortly after returning to Bragg, the first set of screws snapped. Little did Chief know the faulty hardware was the real issue. Instead, the doctors told him he was trying to do too much too soon. The bone graft failed, the screws had to come out and Chief was sent back to Walter Reed for another surgery. He missed the indicator.

The second surgery was a bit more involved because the broken hardware had caused more fractures, the holes from the self taping screws were elongated and cracked in numerous places at numerous depths. So new hardware had to be manufactured with completely new structures, rods and metal cross ties to ensure a solid foundation for all the new bone grafting being harvested from Chief's pelvis, a region called the Illiac crest along the top of his belt line. The second surgery was a bit longer, a full eight hours. But shortly after Chief awoke in the ICU he was asking how long it would be until he was allowed to leave. The doctors told him he wouldn't be leaving for another 18 months since they couldn't trust him to stay down. He'd argued successfully that the body cast would keep him from deploying and that his wife was an RN who would be more than willing to keep an eye on him and change the bandages. What he didn't tell anyone was that she was a workaholic, or so he thought, and wasn't ever home. She was never home for other reasons Chief didn't yet understand. But the ruse worked and the doctors relented. Chief was gone from the ward in under ten days.

Just shy of 90 days later, Chief was working in the SCIF leaning his 380 lb plaster cast encrusted body back in a folding chair when he heard a pop that sickened him to the core. The burning, the shooting pains down his legs and hips told him precisely what was wrong. Again. Something broke. The very hardware he was told would take a truck to snap had just severed and stabbed him in the cord. As he blacked out, he knew he was on his way back to Walter Reed.

Surgery number three was a disaster. He'd woken up from the anesthesia, tried to kill everyone in the room, and ended up doing serious soft tissue and nerve damage from the retractors that kept his body open. The broken hardware did serious injury to his cord. What he didn't know was that the tissue that made up the cord was so delicate, so fragile, so insanely complicated that once it was broken or torn, there was no recovery. Whatever damage was done to the nerve fibers by the broken hardware, was permanent. The resulting scar tissue would exponentially increase the pain level to a point Chief would permanently be on some sort of pain killers. It would be a very long time before he knew exactly what those severed fibers were connected to. Doctors were elusive at best whenever he asked them what the prognosis was.

"We won't know until we know" was the bullshit answer everyone gave as if on script. That was just unsatisfactory to Chief. So he left the hospital again, just short of a world record twelve days post op. Demerol and Morphine were a wonderful thing and Chief returned to the field environment with his Team. On a major operation to "snatch" an HVT from Afghanistan, the hardware gave way yet again and Chief could feel the bones break. The mission was a huge success, but he lost all bowel and bladder control as well, decidedly making the trip home much more miserable. For the first time, Chief was scared. And the thought that he might have done serious damage to his spinal cord shook him to his soul.

This was the fourth time the spinal fixation hardware snapped and Chief was beside himself with rage. After 22 hours on the table, he was seriously injured by some asshole student who took out the wrong disc and vertebrae. At the eight hour mark, the head surgeon went into the hallway to brief his family on progress, promising them Chief would be in recovery in a few hours. But now he was in fully incapacitated condition.

Femur bones were harvested from cadavers and many hours later, a team of exhausted surgeons left Chief in the ICU to recover. They were in "Hail Mary" mode now. There was no telling how bad this was going to be. But they all knew chances were pretty good that Chief would never walk again. How much residual nerve damage would remain was an unanswered question no one would have the answer to for many more months. The one thing Chief knew more than anything else, was he really would rather be in a fire fight.

* * * * *

As Chief climbed into the taxi cab outside of Walter Reed hospital, he couldn't help but think, " I should have been a God Damned COOK!".

With all the strength he had left, he held his breath and tucked himself into the back seat of the taxi, landing on his back, looking at the ceiling. He had no idea how the hell he was going to get into an airplane, but some how, some way, he was going to go see his two boys. Just the thought of them was motivation beyond anything he'd experienced before. Things were different since those two angels came into his life. They were everything to him now. He remembered the soul soothing peace of them falling asleep on his chest, holding their prefect fingers in his huge hands. Feeling the soft spot on the top of their heads as he kissed them goodnight. Feeling the strength of their arms and legs when they played "Karate" with him as they grew. They were the sole motivation for his surviving and coming home. And he missed them beyond words. Nearly three years transpired since he deployed, kissing them softly on the forehead as they slept so angelically before he left on a C5 A Star Lifter in the middle of the night. He cried all the way to Green Ramp, driving up the back roads of Southern Pines to the dark side gate of Pope Air Force Base on his way out of the country, as so many warriors had done before him. And now, no matter what, he was going home to see them. Or at least that was the plan.

The taxi driver grunted as he lifted the wheelchair from the trunk, metal clanging on the ground as the foot platforms of the chair hit the concrete driveway. Fayetteville was a long way from D.C. and this driver could pass for a twin brother to the one Chief dealt with a few hours prior. From a prone position on the rear bench seat of the late model Ford Crown Victoria, Chief yelled instructions to the driver. At ten o'clock at night, he didn't even realize what kind of noise they were making, nor did he care really. He was two minutes away from seeing his boys after nearly a complete day of travel.

"Just bring it over here by the door. I'll talk you through the process. It's not a big whoopie. I've done this before. As a matter of fact, we just did this in D.C. at the airport a few hours ago!"

As Chief looked up towards the ceiling, he caught the driver's expression and tried to reassure him that things were going to be fine.

"I promise. It's gonna suck, but it's gonna work. The driver up there had the exact same look on his face." Chief said, referring to the cab driver in D.C. who could have passed for this guy's twin brother.

The driver looked sheepishly down at Chief as he opened the doors on both sides of the car, resolving himself to the fact that no matter what, he needed to get this guy out of his car. Getting him into the car in this contraption was a bad idea to begin with. But that was a mute point now. Chief was laying face up with a halo screwed to his skull and a body cast from his arm pits to his knees. The body cast took up all the seat room and Chief's legs were folded at the knee, stuffed behind the driver's seat. After several minutes, they were numb from the body cast pinching off all the circulation. The steel rod between his knees assured that his hips remained static.

The hardware in his spine, pelvis and hips was intended to stabilize the fractures until the bone could heal. The entire contraption attached to Chief's body was intended to restrict body movement until the bone healed. But the draconian tactics did nothing for his muscles. At least, nothing good.

Ten hours earlier, Chief left the hospital under what was known as "AMA". Against Medical Advice. Only Walter Reed still had not figured out that Chief was no longer on the ward. He convinced the local bank to give him an advance on his American Express card, called a cab to take him to Ronald Reagan International Airport, booked a flight to Raleigh Durham with a final destination of Fayetteville, N.C., home of XVIII Airborne Corp, the 82nd Airborne Division and Special Operations. And Chief couldn't wait to get there.

As the taxi driver cautiously leaned into the car to lift Chief by the shoulder blades, he nearly vomited from the profuse smell emanating from the body cast. After nearly 18 months and being changed only once, his body was pretty ripe inside that plaster. Medical personnel knew the cast wasn't made for active people who pushed themselves till their body sweated. Chief was one of those patients that broke all the rules. Some how, he had gotten used to the smell and his reputation. Or at least he though he had. He planned on getting the damn thing cut off as soon as he could get to the garage and get his tools. But the five meter targets at the moment only included getting out of the car and into the wheelchair so he could get into the house and see his wife and two boys. It had been way too long since he'd seen them and he had a *lot* of questions about why the hell she hadn't come to Walter Reed to visit. Not even to bring the boys. That's what really pissed him off. No phone calls, no nothing. He was fighting off that feeling of being left for dead again, and it sucked.

The grunting and groaning sounded more like a wrestling match as Chief worked his way out of the car feet first. The driver was doing his best to lift Chief and push him towards the door, but the plaster cast added nearly 150 lbs to his already 220 lb body. The texture of the plaster and gauze cast caught the naugahyde seat covers and resisted any sliding maneuver. The body cast was just a touch too long, ending mid knee cap, preventing Chief from bending his legs much more than a few degrees and causing immense pain from the pressure and geometry of trying to walk. He felt like Herman Munster every time he tried to take as step. There was a serious balance loss from nerve damage to his spine, but there was also enormous pain from the surgical site, front and back that kept him humble, breathing cautiously so the stomach surgical wound didn't push too hard on the plaster. The added weight was something he fought against daily. It didn't really weigh all that much compared to what he normally carried on his back on missions. But on top of the surgical sites, the nerve damage to his spine and the inflexible harshness against his injuries, the cast tweaked his hips and made them burn to the point of muscle failure. The excessive pushed down onto his tail bone causing the pain to spike to the point of blacking out just from standing or getting upright.

The "candy stripers" assigned to the ward inadvertently left him standing by the door one morning after getting him out of bed. Their immaturity and exuberant oblivion contributed to a very important lesson about patient care. Chief blacked out from the weight of the cast pushing down onto his hips and pelvis. He woke up with his head jammed into a corner, halo hooked on a coat rack preventing him from hitting the floor. He cringed to think of what would have transpired had he actually fallen completely to the floor. His face would have taken the hit, full force and God only knows what it would have done to his neck, head and spinal fractures. The young woman left the ward in hysterics, simply because Chief told her,

"Don't ever leave a patient like that".

He wasn't mad. Just in pain. She was so very young, filled with hormones and drama and she took Chief's comments, delivered in his "Team Voice", extremely hard. She resigned, which cemented Chief's reputation as an asshole patient into perpetuity. Oh well, can't fix stupid. What Chief quickly learned was, he had to communicate with those tasked with helping him, or suffer the consequences of their ignorance. That lesson was important now. He had to communicate with the Taxi driver, or things were going to go sideways, fast.

As Chief got further and further out the door of the car, it became apparent that he was not going to be able to bend in any fashion to stand. So he instructed the driver to pull his feet out from under him, straighten his legs and let him fall onto the concrete.

"No way man. I'm gonna call someone for help. I don't want this to be on me. If you get hurt again, I'm gonna end up losing my job."

"Look, cut the bullshit and get me out of this fucking car. I'm not waiting till someone else shows up. I swear to God. I'm not going to sue you. But there is no way in hell I'm gonna be able to get out of this car unless you do what I tell you. We're almost there. Don't fucking quit on me now. God Dammit. I can't take much more of this shit. Just do what I ask.... please!"

With that, the driver rolled his eyes, took a deep breath and pulled Chief's heels out from under him, grabbed the steel rod between his knees and pulled. Like a log sliding off a river bank, Chief slid out of the car and landed on the cement driveway with a thud. The steel rods that went up from his shoulders to the halo on his head hit the concrete with a twang loud enough to echo through the neighborhood, making Chief's ears ring.

"Now, that wasn't so bad was it?" Chief said holding his breath, grinding his teeth together as the front porch light came on. Finally, he was going to see his family. He couldn't wait.

"Help me get into the chair. Quick! I gotta get off the ground before my kids see me and start freaking out"

The driver helped Chief roll over on to his front side and helped him get to his knees. As Chief attempted to pull his toes under him, alleviating the pain of his knees and the body cast cutting into the back of his legs, he started breathing heavy to keep the pain in check and grunted with all his might as he pulled himself up onto his feet. He grabbed the top window frame on the taxi cab door and pulled himself harder into an upright position.

"Quick. Get the chair," he said almost too loudly, giving away the anxiety, stress and fear in his voice. Chief had real fear of the consequences should he miss the chair and end up falling onto the concrete driveway. The driver snapped into action and hurriedly ducked under Chief's arm to grab the wheel chair, trying to position it behind Chief's butt.

"Now, lock the wheels and hold on to it so it doesn't roll backwards." Chief said, looking out the corner of his eyes, trying to estimate where the driver was and hoping the chair was located accurately behind him. In the next second, Chief let go of the car door frame and allowed his body to lean backwards and free fall. He knew it was a perfect landing when he felt the back of the chair impact the plaster cast somewhere between his shoulder blades, flipping the chair seat up into his rump as the cast bridged the gap. The inability for his hips to flex meant he was going to have to ride the chair completely stiff, bridged between the seat back and the seat.

"Whew! That's better" Chief said, releasing his breath and allowing his legs to relax. His thigh and calf muscles were burning from the pressure and pain of the cast, as his body tried supporting the additional weight.

"Now, if you look in that bag on the back floor, there is some cash in there for the ride. Take a twenty for your tip. I sincerely appreciate all your help."

The driver took the money, left the bag hanging on the back of the chair and drove away shaking his head.

"Fucking soldiers!" he thought to himself. The fifteen minute drive from the airport had resulted in absolutely no conversation, so the driver was none the wiser about who his passenger was, or what had happened to him. Although he asked several times out of curiosity, simply trying to make conversation, wondering how he had gotten injured and why he was in a body cast, the only answer he got was,

"I was riding this camel and the bastard just went nuts".

As the cab drove away, Chief sat quietly in the driveway trying to catch his breath. His head ached even worse now and the halo was starting again to push the limits of his patience. The cold night air felt incredibly good as the sweat ran down his body and out the bottom of the plaster cast onto his legs. The smell of baby powder was faintly detectable but a mix of body odors and sweat combined the powder into a putrid smelling bread dough consistency that made Chief want to vomit. It was time to get out of this fucking thing.

As he slowly rolled down the incline of the driveway, Chief did his best to reach the rubber tires on the wheels of the chair, manipulating the braking mechanisms to control his decent down the driveway towards the front porch. The last thing he needed was another near miss. He couldn't afford to run into the strange car parked in the driveway, nor run head first into the porch steps and railing. The worst thing that could have happened was missing everything, picking up speed, rolling down hill and face planting into the lake behind the house.

Two things suddenly awoke Chief's brain and made him think about something besides controlling his breathing and trying not to black out.

"She must have gotten a new car," he thought under his breath.

"Oh Shit. I never thought about the stairs!" came the next thought.

There were only two stairs. But Damned if he knew how the hell he was going to maneuver to get over them to the front door. No sooner had he figured on getting out of the chair some how and walking up the steps, when the front door opened.

"Can I help you with something" came a voice from a woman he never met before.

"Yeah. You can get my wife and kids and tell them I'm home!" Chief answered in a barely civil tone of exhaustion and frustration.

"I'm sorry. Who are you looking for?" the woman asked with a bewildered look on her face.

"Who are YOU?" Chief asked, intent on finding out who the hell was blocking his progress from final mission completion. He was now within ten feet of the door after an incredibly long day trying to get there, and now this bimbo was asking him ridiculous questions.

"Well, I live here. Who are YOU?" she responded in kind.

"Wait a minute. What the hell are you talking about? Am I at the right address? What's the address here?"

Chief's mind started to reel. He searched his brain trying to remember what had happened just a few short minutes ago in the cab. He remembered telling the cab driver the address, then remembered seeing the house and recognizing the Pompus grass by the driveway that he planted the day after they bought the house.

But the Demerol and morphine, the pain from the brutal task of getting home and the exhaustion complicated things. He wasn't really sure he was in the right place. The woman at the door repeated the address confirming Chief was positively home at last! But then she said something that really blew his circuit breakers.

"We bought this place almost a year ago. The lady we got it from had two little boys and they moved to some apartment out of state. Who are you? What are you doing on my front lawn?"

Chief couldn't answer. All he knew at the moment was that he was really getting pissed, was totally and completely out of steam and needed some time to recover.

"Can I get some water please".

"Sure. Stay right here. I'll be back in a minute."

As she opened the front door, Chief could see the hardwood floors he personally put in while home on leave a while back. He glimpsed into the front room and saw the fireplace brick surround, but the walls were painted from the dark forest green to white and the cast iron ornate fireplace insert was missing. They found it at a yard sale shortly after arriving in the Carolinas and after telling the nice old lady owner that they had just arrived, bought a new house and he was stationed at Bragg, the lady insisted they take it home for free.

"You remind me so much of me forty years ago when my husband came to Bragg with Special Forces. Please. Give this thing a new home and enjoy the warmth. We did for nearly thirty years before he passed just this last winter. I'm too old to be hauling firewood anymore. Please, take it home and enjoy it."

With the nod of a humble servant, she shook Chief's hand and then gave him a hug. "God bless you my son" were the last words she said before turning to hide a tear and walking into her garage.

As Chief peeked through the opened front door of the house, the cavernous hole where the old cast iron insert used to be was a striking vision that grabbed Chief in the gut. The missing fireplace insert epitomized the loss he felt deep in his soul. Something else was missing. Something much more than a fireplace insert. And it shook him to his soul. He couldn't look at it yet, the huge loss his life experienced in the desert. The loss of function. The loss of comfort and security. The loss of his entire Team, and now, faced with the loss of his family, those two amazing little boys he lived for!

What the hell was going on? Why did the insert represent so much more than he could reconcile? As he tried rolling closer to look further into the house, he heard the woman on the phone.

"Yes ma'am. He's out here on my sidewalk right now, in a full body cast and a wheelchair with some sort of contraption on his head. I want him out of here. Yes ma'am. I'll wait."

She came out the door carrying a small glass of water, feigning concern about Chief's condition.

"Are you ok?"

"Lady, I know you must think I'm a whack job. But I swear to you, this is MY HOUSE! That hardwood in your hallway... I put that in several years ago after I got back from Desert Storm. The living room used to be a dark forest green with white crown molding. The carpet used to be a white Berber with Oriental rugs over it in the center with pecan coffee table and two end tables. Where did all my furniture go? Where are my wife and two boys? What the FUCK is going on?"

Chief was starting to come unraveled now. He recognized it, but didn't give a shit. This was utter bullshit. And someone was going to come up with some answers, or else.

As he drank the water down, Chief realized he could hear his heartbeat again in his ears. Not a good indicator. He tried to focus, to control his temper and his breath. But his brain was fighting the spinning feeling that overcame his very thoughts of staying calm. Adrenaline coursed through his veins and he felt that need to choke the living shit out of someone. No sooner had he closed his eyes, swallowed the last of the water when headlights panned across the front yard. The front porch furniture was the same, but the house had been painted. Chief couldn't turn to see who was coming up behind him or who was in the car, another trigger to his pathetically vulnerable state. But he didn't have to when the second car arrived siren blaring and bright blue high intensity lights flickered across everything in sight. Now the adrenaline was getting worse. Fucking cops. Just what he needed. Maybe they'd actually be able to help him this time. But usually, cops ended up just pissing him off even worse.

"Sir, we're here to help you. Do you know who you are and where you are? Do you know what day it is?"

Chief's brain reeled as he rolled his eyes into his head. "I can't fucking believe this" he said to himself. Fucking rookies.

"What is this? Romper Room? Do you know who YOU ARE? Do you know where YOU ARE? Do you have any fucking clue who you are talking to?"

Out came the handcuffs.

"Oh you gotta be fucking kidding me. Like I'm not fucked up enough? You actually think I'm some sort of threat sitting here like this that you have to cuff me? Why don't you just get a Taser and a baton and beat the shit out of me too? I might resist or something".

"Sir, I need you to calm down. You've obviously scared this poor lady showing up on her porch this late at night. We're here to find out what is going on and make sure everyone is safe. Do you understand everything I've just said to you?"

Obviously this young officer was following protocol. But Chief didn't understand that at the moment. All he understood was his wife and kids were missing and some strange lady was trying to tell him she now owned his house. Nothing made sense and the longer the sirens blared, the longer the lights flashed, the worse Chief's headache became. He really wanted to kick someone's ass, but he felt vulnerable. A condition he'd never felt until he woke up in the desert, face down in the dirt. That same feeling was taking over now. And Chief was trying with all his might to fight it off.

"Someone needs to call my wife and find out what the fuck is going on. In the mean time, this lady needs to get the hell out of my way so I can go inside and lay down on my bed. It's been a hell of a day, and I just need some time to catch my breath."

With those words, the junior officer reached up, pressed the microphone hanging on his shoulder and called for backup. In another instant, he backed up, pulled his weapon from the holster and pointed it directly at Chief's head.

"Sir, if you move, or attempt to gain access into that house in any way, I will shoot you. Do you understand me? I'm serious. We're not going to have any problems here are we?"

The young woman screamed and ran into the house just as three more cruisers squealed rubber coming to a halt on the blacktop at the top of the driveway hill, followed shortly after by a large van with "Fayetteville Police Department" painted on the side. A hydraulic noise echoed across the neighborhood as a lift gate lowered from the back door onto the pavement. As if by divine intervention, a familiar voice came out of the shadows.

"Shut those fucking sirens off. Are you guys totally stupid? What the hell are you doing?"

The comfort of those words, spoken by a voice Chief knew but couldn't put a name to, took everyone by surprise. The officers complied and relative quiet ensued for the first time in nearly ten minutes. Chief felt like vomiting. There was way too much negative input for his brain to handle and the morphine was starting to kick into high gear. This day had started nearly 21 hours ago in Washington D.C. Chief was exhausted and desperately needed some fluids back in his system. His body was overheating, the pills were making his brain spin, the pain was exponentially worsened by the frustration and stupidity he was now in the middle of and it was time for him to check out and get some peace and quiet. With no warning, his body slumped in the wheelchair and his legs slacked. The halo kept his head from moving and his neck from falling backwards from the weight of his skull. The body cast kept his torso stiff and had the Police supervisor not seen Chief's eyeballs roll back into his head just prior to "lights out", no one would have suspected what was going on. Chief had just blacked out. He never got a chance to sort out who the familiar voice was. Nor would he remember it anyway.

When he awoke, he was again laying in a hospital bed in the Emergency Room of Cape Fear Memorial hospital, several miles from his house. Or whoever's house it was now. After unsuccessfully getting any information from him, a young Police woman was sent to his bedside to pull finger prints as he slept.

"Sir, you'll have to lay still so I get a good imprint from the ink. Please, just relax and let me do all the work."

In his very best attempt at humor, Chief smirked and asked the young brunette in his best Jimmy Stewart impression,

"So, where you been all my life missy? I'll lay here all night long and let you do all the work if you want me to!"

She didn't smile. Must be the body odor Chief thought.

"What the hell are you taking my prints for?"

"Well Sir, we've not been able to identify who you are, you won't cooperate, so we're going to take some prints and run you through the system so we know who we're dealing with. OK?"

"Won't do you a bit of good. I've never been arrested so I'm not on your system, and Ft. Bragg and the people I work for have done an outstanding job to make sure I stay invisible. Don't I get a phone call or something?"

"Well, if you ask nice, I might be able to arrange something like that. I know a few people like you. The guys who don't exist. I can make a phone call for you and hook you up with someone I know very well. Maybe if you help me, I'll be able to help you."

A second later the ceiling lights glinted off the brass nameplate on the young Police woman's left breast pocket. It took Chief by surprise and he started to chuckle.

"What's so funny Sir?" She asked with peaked interest.

"You married?"

"Why is that any of your concern? You already started hitting on me soon as you became conscious. What makes you think I want to discuss my personal life with an obvious carouser like you?"

"Cause I knew a guy in Special Forces who was married to a cop with the same last name that's on your chest. She was a knockout from the photos I saw and he always talked about her. I think he had brain damage of some sort. His name was Phil. Your husband's name Phil by any chance?"

She didn't have to answer. The look on her face gave everything away. The look of shock suddenly changed to anger as she looked away trying to conceal the sorrow and the heartache that had taken her so severely by surprise.

"God Damn it. Why the fuck did you have to bring that up?" she said, reaching up to hold her nose between her thumb and fore finger, using the rest of her hand to cover her mouth.

"Hey. I'm sorry. I didn't mean to upset you. I was just hunting to find out who you were and if you were any relation to the guy. We served together in Panama back during Christmas 89. What the hell got you so hostile all of a sudden? You two get into some shit and split up or something?"

It was obvious to her this guy had no clue what had happened. She tried to ignore everything and just get on with taking the prints like she was supposed to do. But the emotions were too strong, the wound too deep and the pain still too fresh.

"He's dead," she said as bluntly and plainly as she could. "He went to Iraq on the first insertion, jumped into Baghdad International with Team One and his Hummer hit an IED within the first thirty minutes of being on the ground. That was before they had the "up armored" versions. Nobody in the vehicle made it. That was four years ago. Where the hell have YOU been? It was a big deal. Everyone on Bragg knows about it. If you knew him so well, why the fuck don't YOU know about it?"

Chief sat in total silence in total disbelief. Phil was gone too? The one guy he hoped could help him out of this shit storm of continual moronic disbelief.

"What happened? No more smart remarks? No more pickup lines? You suddenly got a soul?"

"Look. It's been a bad fucking day since I woke up."

"Yeah. I gathered something happened from the looks of you. When was the last time you had a shower? You smell like a week old dead goat!" a comment that sealed Chief's suspicion.

"Phil said that all the time. He was your husband wasn't he?"

"Yeah. Who the fuck ARE you?"

"I'm Chief. He might have mentioned me once or twice. I don't know. Maybe not."

"So You're Chief? I'll be fucking damned. I never thought you were real. He always talked about you, but no one ever knew what you looked like. I was beginning to think he was delusional. Yeah. I've heard a hell of a lot about you. What the fuck happened. You've been gone for nearly four years now huh?"

"Yeah. We had a bad hair day."

"We?"

"Yeah. Me and my... fuck. Never mind. Look. It's been a long day. I need to get out of here, get some food, get some rest and then try to get hold of my unit so I can un-fuck whatever it is that's gone on the past 18 months while I was at Walter Reed."

"Oh, that answers a lot of mail. If you've been at Walter Reed, I'm pretty amazed you are still alive. Those fucks damn near killed my husband. I ended up taking him AWOL to get the out of there. They wouldn't release him, so I put him in the car and kidnapped his ass."

"Well, great minds think alike. I did the same thing this morning. I'm not even sure they know I'm gone yet, nor how long it will take them to realize I'm not there anymore. In the mean time, I got a lot of shit I need to get done before they DO figure it out. So, you gonna help me or what?"

"Listen. Why the hell would I even consider helping you? You've been an asshole all night to all my partners. They said you tried to attack them when they came on site. You got a problem with cops or something?"

"What the fuck. Are you kidding me? Those guys are such pussies they had to make up a fucking weak ass story like that? Look at me. Do you think I look like someone who can attack four guys with guns and badges? Like I don't have any fucking sense at all, right? Who is the dumbass who wrote that up? Don't tell me you believe that shit. Phil always talked about how smart his wife was.

Not just book smart, but street smart. If you ARE Renee', then I know you don't believe a fucking word of that bullshit."

She grinned from ear to ear.

"You actually ARE Chief aren't you? I can't believe this. I can't believe I actually met the infamous Chief."

Chief was starting to feel the pain again. The exhaustion was sinking in and his face lost all color as he held his breath and looked at the ceiling. Renee caught a glimpse as his facial expressions changed. Her attitude changed just as suddenly.

"Ok. I'm gonna help you. But you gotta do exactly what I tell you to do. No bullshit. It's my way, or not at all. OK? We got a deal or what?"

Chief glanced over from the corner of his eye and shook his head in agreement. He didn't have much choice at the moment. For the first time in a very long time, Chief felt a twitch in his guts that made him feel like she was in his corner. Tears started to fill his eyes as he thought of the loss she must also be dealing with. Phil was gone too. Dammit. The loss of his team, the loss of his body, the loss of his manhood and function. She was gorgeous, voluptuous, slender, and fit even under the Police uniform and bullet proof vest which concealed almost everything. For the first time in almost four years, Chief thought about how wonderful it might be to have a woman in his arms for an all nighter. Something he hadn't done since just before he'd gotten married nearly twenty years earlier. He'd dedicated his life to one woman and stuck to the marital oath just as he'd done with his Oath of Office.

"Well, I convinced them to drop charges and allow me to take you home with me tonight." Renee' said as she walked back into the room. But you gotta stay there. No more of this bullshit. I'll get you something to eat and you can sleep there for tonight. We'll figure out something in the morning. Let's just worry about the five meter targets for now."

With that statement, Chief broke down and cried. He couldn't believe how good it felt to have someone in his corner that spoke his language. And he couldn't believe yet another very good friend was dead. She must be one hell of a woman.

"Yeah. Let's do the five meter targets tonight. I'm gonna need to have my shit together when I go after the 1000 meter targets tomorrow." Chief said, showing the exhaustion of the very long day.

"Listen. I'm sorry about Phil. I had no idea. I'm sorry. Honestly, I wasn't trying to push your buttons. I'll fill you in later, but for now, suffice it to say I've been down range a lot longer than I realized. And obviously something has changed between my wife and I. It's embarrassing as hell. Sorry to put you in this situation. But I sincerely appreciate the offer. I'll try to stay off the radar and make this as painless as possible."

"Only one promise I gotta ask you for. Let them take that fucking cast off, get you cleaned up, and put another one on. The docs say that thing should have been changed months ago."

"Yeah. I'm up for that. I can't stand the smell anymore. It comes right up from the chest cavity and wafts under my nose whenever I breathe. It'll make a dog puke. How soon can we do this?

"They'll be in shortly. They're getting the cast technician out of bed. Just lay back and rest now. I got this."

And with those comforting kind words, Chief closed his eyes and fell into a deep slumber. She walked over and turned off the florescent lights, pulled the curtain and slipped out into the hallway.

" Let him sleep" she told the technician as he approached. It was nearing 1 am.

" I know they woke you up to come in and do this. Come with me for some coffee and give this guy a break. If anyone needs it, this guy does."

Renee' wrote a note with a large black marker on a sheet of paper and taped it to the door of chief's room.

"Do not disturb. Call Lt Renee Phillips before entering this room" and then she escorted the cast tech to the basement cafeteria. For the first time in a very long time, Chief slept. No dreams, no nightmares, just well deserved sleep. God only knew how bad he needed this rest. Tomorrow had some pretty ugly things in store for him. But for the next three hours, none of that mattered. He was done working on the five meter targets for now.

Blindsided

"Life is about what you do to other people"
Life Lesson Nr. 17

When Chief woke up the following morning, the pain made him wish he never had. He was running low on pain meds, a critical node he was going to have to address sooner than later. Most of his contacts with medical guys through Special Ops had dried up. There was a good chance most of them deployed to the Middle East for the upcoming missions that America was about to embark upon. Maybe he would get lucky and Renee knew someone. Regardless, he would have to deal with the issue when it became more critical. At the moment, it was time to find his wife and two sons, at least be able to talk to her and find out what the hell was going on.

"Look" Chief said speaking into the phone. "I don't know what happened while I was in the ICU up there. But I got back home to find some lady living in my house."

"It's not your house anymore in case you didn't get the memo" she snapped, chuckling under her breath.

"Who's that in the background I just heard laughing? You think this is funny?"

"Actually, it is funny. This is payback you bastard!"

"Payback? For WHAT?" Chief said incredulously.

"For all that time I stuck around waiting on you, never knowing where you were, or who you were with. I'm fucking done with this. I've been wasting the best years of my life on a guy who obviously doesn't get it."

At least he was getting to the bottom of things. He didn't understand it, but at least he was hearing the real deal straight from the horse's mouth, as enlightening and as informative as that was, it was also a completely separate reality.

"What the hell does THAT mean? You knew exactly where I was, who I was with and what I was doing! I was with the TEAM, doing MISSION! Don't you dare go down the road that I somehow betrayed you."

"Yeah, well fuck you and fuck the mission!"

Chief's mind was spinning. The pain was getting worse and he was having a very hard time concentrating.

"Listen. I can't do this right now. I'm in too much pain, it's hot as hell in this fucking body cast and I have no idea what it is you're talking about or why you're so pissed off. What I do know is that I need some money. My paycheck goes direct deposit to an account I no longer have access to. Its gonna take weeks to get that all sorted out and change it. All my investment accounts have been frozen, along with my savings and retirement accounts. I'm broke, have no place to go, I owe someone money for getting my truck out of the junk yard, and I really need a fucking break at the moment. I don't know how all this got so fucked up, but I need some money to get some food and put gas in the truck. I'm down to the basic one meter targets at the moment. Where did all the money go and why can't I get to anything?"

"Well, YOU were the one who insisted that I have a Durable Power of Attorney in case something happened."

"Yeah. We talked about that. It was the smartest thing in case something happened. You'd have access to the money and wouldn't have to wait for all the legal shit if I ended up dead or something. So why the hell am I shut out? I don't have a dime to my name, and can't get anything either!"

"Well, in case you haven't realized, something *has happened.*"

"Like what?"

"Like they told me you were dead. So I filed the paperwork for the life insurance and what kind of a surprise do you think was waiting when I got there. You weren't dead."

"And that pissed you off for some reason?"

"No, YOU pissed me off a very long time ago."

This was going nowhere in a hurry. Whatever was going on, Chief was in no position to fight. She had it all. The house, the car, the money, the kids and Chief was sitting in a body cast, halo and wheelchair trying to get her to talk to him about whatever it was that was pissing her off. This was like digging out of a sand pit. The harder and faster he dug, the deeper the hole got and the more the side walls came down on top of him. There was no telling how deep this pit was.

"Listen...." Chief started to say.

"Fuck you. You listen!" she screamed into the phone. "I am absolutely done with you. WE are over. I filed for divorce for a reason. And if you can't figure that out, then tough shit. I'm not going to waste my time trying to get you to understand. Not a single minute more. It's pretty obvious you haven't been listening for the past twenty years and nothing you are going to say right now is going to change my mind. If you want ANY more information, you can call my attorney. I'll see your ass in court!"

And with that, the phone went dead.

What the hell Chief was going to do now was way past his imagination. He'd spent the weekend at Renee's home. But his welcome was wearing thin. She had a life of her own to recover after losing her husband. And Chief's mere presence, a constant reminder of her husband before he died, was more than Chief was going to put her through. She'd been gracious enough, but just the sight of

Chief being there brought up raw emotions that she wasn't ready to deal with yet. He knew it. He could sense it every time he tried to talk to her. So the best thing he could do, the only honorable thing was to just leave. So he slipped out the back door, banged his way down the steps in his chair and headed to the nearest phone. His pickup truck was gone, so was the phone that was bolted to the console floor. He had no clothes, no food, no money, and no way to get any.

As he rolled across the street, Chief suddenly realized HE was one of those homeless Veterans he'd seen in the park so many times on his way to town. He'd often wondered how the hell a guy spent a career in the military and ended up living in the park, homeless and destitute. Now he knew. But he still had no idea how it happened.

The fact of the matter was that pure, unadulterated betrayal landed him in the situation he found himself in. She flat out didn't give a shit if he lived or died. That might not be necessarily accurate though. She did give a shit if he was dead. That was her preference, because if he died, she stood to inherit a three million dollar life insurance policy with a war clause. That meant that even if he was killed in combat, they still paid. She'd insisted on that part of the policy. It was a lot more expensive, but would pay out big time. In an instant, Chief realized just how badly he was fucking up. Indicator Analysis and 20/20 Hind Sight were joining forces to punch him solidly in the stomach, knocking the wind out of him and getting his full attention! The abortion in Germany, the war clause, the voice in the background...did Chief *even know* who the hell the woman was he called his wife?

As Chief sat in the sunshine, he fought off sleep. The pain killers were working overtime combined with the humidity of the Carolina springtime, the heat from the sun and the radiant heat coming from the body cast. His head hurt from the halo, his spine was thumping like a big dog too. But now, the pain from his heart and his gut over rode all the other pain his body fought with. How the hell could she do this? He took a lot of time and put in a lot of effort to ensure that his family was taken care of in the event he didn't come home. It was the honorable thing to do. It wasn't about the money. He just wanted to make sure she and the kids were taken care of for life.

Before Chief had even gotten to Washington D.C. and checked into the hospital, she'd taken the Durable Power of Attorney and withdrawn the $480,000 dollars, the result of Chief's investments over his 30 year career. It was gone in a day. Along with every dream he had for post retirement times. Transferred to some account owned by a guy he'd never met. Someone she knew from work. Another used car salesman who touted himself as a "day trader". She never connected the dots that a CNA working at a nursing home, claiming to know everything there was about the Stock Market, was a major indicator.

The money was put into ENRON a month before the major scam artists collapsed and took half the nations retirements with them. They were crooks. Yet no one knew it until the bubble burst. The $480,000 invested into the energy giant would have brought in over $60 million in just five years. But they didn't even last five months. What took Chief 30 years to grow, was gone in a matter of minutes after he signed over his faith and trust to the wife he married. The mother of his two sons. What the hell had happened while he was gone? And who the hell was this "guy"?

The short answer was, the guy she was fucking. Along with five or six others. This was the baseball coach, a former solider turned Certified Nursing assistant and pharmaceutical salesman. A "get rich quick" puke that left his own wife with six daughters to raise on her own by having an affair with one of his own soldiers. It was bad enough he'd picked a young and inexperienced woman who looked up to him simply because he had a Beret on his head.

But she was in his Chain of Command. A subordinate. That was a Cardinal Sin that no one could over look and he was Court-martialed and kicked out of the service. This was the asshole Chief's youngest son was enthralled with. The guy who was teaching his son, mentoring him to become a major league baseball star while Chief was in surgery and recovery! Why wasn't she protecting his son from assholes like that? Why would she even let this asshole into the same grid square as the family? At ten years old, Chief's youngest son was good. Very good. And this guy had stepped up to the plate, another Chief Warrant Officer from Special Forces at Ft. Bragg, to teach and help inspire the boy while Chief was down range fighting bad guys. That's what soldiers did for each other. They backed each other up, took care of family, went over and mowed their yards, helped to fix the family car if it broke down, delivered groceries or even baby sat children if needed.

However, there was a more sinister side to the FSG program too. The bastards who never deployed were like seething little weasels. Vultures. Varmints. Evil little bastards that were disloyal, dishonorable with opportunistic tendencies. If Chief had his way, they all would be exterminated, not just discharged, to prevent the Earth from being over populated by oxygen thieves. They often hit up on lonely wives who had no idea when their husbands were coming back from long deployments during exercises, or extended combat tours of duty in places no one ever talked about. Some of the dependent wives were so unfaithful, they couldn't WAIT for an exercise so they could go out on the town and pick up GIs that didn't deploy. It was a huge issue. The divorce rate had skyrocketed to nearly 45% during Desert Storm. Some units like the 82nd Airborne and 7th Special Forces Command had divorce rates nearing 70%.

A lot depended on what Battalion a guy was assigned to. But overall, infidelity was a major issue that affected other statistics as well. Like the crime rate. Within 30 days of units returning to Ft. Bragg after deployments, the assault, battery, attempted murder and murder rates went off the charts. Husbands found out their wives were pregnant, or had been cheating and all hell broke loose.

The only saving grace at the moment was Jeff's Auto Salvage and Towing company. Chief had done a lot of business with the owner over the years buying, selling and swapping parts as he rebuilt Corvettes in his spare time. Jeff had seen Chief's custom Dodge Pickup on many occasions and knew who it belonged to when he got a call to come pick it up out of a driveway. The lady said it was broken down and was going to cost too much to repair it. She just wanted it out of the driveway. Jeff had paid her $200 bucks for the $25,000 dollar Custom. She snatched the cash from his hand as fast as a crack whore. Jeff started the truck and drove it around the block before putting it on the flatbed tow truck. He went back to tell the lady that there was nothing wrong with the truck, offered her more money, but never mention that he knew Chief or that he knew the truck was Chief's prized possession. When he found out she was having a yard sale the next day, Jeff offered more money for the stand alone air compressor and full auto body painting system and tools. She let everything go for less than a thousand dollars. Jeff couldn't figure out what was going on at the time. There was nearly $50,000 in tools, enough to outfit a highly professional automotive painting facility. Maybe Chief had been killed overseas. Maybe he wasn't ever coming back and she just wanted to rid herself of bad memories. Whatever the case, Jeff was going to buy whatever he could and hold onto it until he knew for certain what happened.

Shortly after Chief got home, he sorted out what had happened to all his stuff during a brief conversation with a neighbor, a nurse working at Cape Fear Regional Hospital. She had seen the yard sale on her way to work and wondered as well what had happened to Chief. They knew each other, but barely. Chief had helped with an out of control teenage son acting out while dad was deployed. A common problem Chief was more than willing to help out with. When she saw Chief getting out of the cab in a body cast, she instantly knew something serious was going on. She slipped her card to the EMTs that responded to Chief blacking out in the chair and hoped to hear from Chief in the next few months. And when she finally got the call, she was mortified to find out what REALLY transpired. The bitch lied to every single person in the housing area. And every single family in the housing area was mad as hell now. They'd all fallen for her bullshit story and been snookered into feeling sorry for her. Now they knew her real story.

The Real Estate neighbor told Chief that Jeff's Towing Company had taken his truck. Chief borrowed the $200 from the neighbor lady to get his truck back, a third of what Jeff normally charged other customers. At least Chief had a place to live now. In the bed of the truck. The tow hitch held the wheelchair lift, the bed was big enough for him to lay flat in the body cast, and at least he had wheels to get around now. But living in the truck, parking in the County Park was not something he'd planned on doing when he got back. In a matter of two days after leaving the ICU at Walter Reed, Chief had gone from the senior Intelligence Officer to a homeless guy living in the park. In the far reaches of his mind, Chief felt the rage start to boil. This was bullshit. It was time to dig down deep, find the strength and start fighting back. It was time to find an attorney who could help him. Come hell or high water, he was going to find the money and make this happen.

Honor On Trial

"Sometimes the deck is stacked, long before you enter the game!"

Life Lesson Nr. 18

"Your Honor, my client has recently undergone very serious medical trauma. If it please the court, we'd like a 30 minute recess."

"Denied Counselor. I'm sure whatever the problem is can wait until we're done here. This is not going to take long. I'm not too pleased with the fact this hearing was granted to begin with. I was on vacation and the visiting Judge allowed this on the calendar. I made my ruling last month on this case. What exactly are we doing back here today?"

"Well, your Honor, my client has been in the Intensive Care Ward for the past 18 months. All the previous proceedings were done without his knowledge. We're here today to request the order of this court be set aside and allow my client some redress of the complaint. I think it's in the best interest...."

"Counselor, I'm not going to sit here and allow you to make a mockery of my Court. I'm well aware of the complaint, the request by opposing counsel to expedite the dissolution of this marriage and I've already made my ruling. Your client had plenty of time to address the court, and decidedly refused to even respond to ANY of the Courts attempts to notify. I understand he's recently had some surgical procedure. But appearing in this court room in that condition is nothing more than pure theatrics. And I am not falling for it."

Theatrics? Chief was unable to comprehend the words coming from the female Judge. He had a lot of respect for Judges and the sacrifices they endured. Especially in small town America where a neighbor, or someone they'd grown up with could be a defendant they had to rule on, or jail. But the fact Chief was in a body cast, halo and wheelchair had absolutely nothing to do with "Theatrics". In reality, he would give anything to be back in a highly starched uniform, beret and jump boots. The fact the Judge assumed he was trying to play a sympathy card was an indicator that was not lost on Chief. But he had no idea why the Judge would think something like that. Obviously, Chief had been living in a very small bubble, where honor and integrity were a way of life. He had no idea the depths to which dirt bags would go to "use the system". It would take a few more years for him to wrap his brain around the civilian world and the complete lack of self discipline and honor.

"Opposing Counsel, do you have anything you want to say?"

"Yes your honor. If it pleases the Court, we request the previous order stand. The defendant refused all offers of mitigation and court scheduled sessions prior to the final Divorce filing. Obviously he didn't care enough to attend, didn't respond to any of the certified mail we sent and is here now because he's mad that he lost his precious Corvette. When in fact your Honor, he forfeited his rights to the family home and all the assets as soon as he filed the Durable Power of Attorney for his wife. Now he wants a "DO OVER" simply because he didn't like the outcome."

Forfeiture? Chief was simply trying to do the right thing for HER and the boys. How could his kindness, his honorable code of ethics, his good will, and intentions be twisted so wrongly into something it wasn't? Something evil. Twisted by an Officer of the Court who was supposedly upholding Truth and Honor in the Court system? As Chief shot a look of total disbelief at his own attorney, he wondered why the man was sitting silently, watching as if he had a front row seat. A small note slid across the desktop to Chief, confusing him even more.

" I strongly urge your Honor to uphold the Court's original order and be done with this case. This is a waste of your Honor's time, the Courts time and my client's time. She has a very busy nursing schedule with real patients that need her Home Health Care nursing skills."

"Wait a fucking minute. Real Patients? What the hell is *that* supposed to mean?" The words blurted out at a volume that shocked even Chief.

"Counselor, if you can't keep your client under control, I'm going to find you *both* in contempt and fine you. Do I make myself clear?"

"Hey, wait a fucking minute. When is the actual truth going to get addressed here? I've been locked in the ICU for over a year because the doctors did a hatchet job on my spine and all this legal stuff was going on behind my back. What notifications are you talking about? My attorney tells me you imposed some sort of sanctions against him and he's not even allowed to discuss this case or say anything on my behalf? What kind of half baked bullshit is this anyway? I thought we were in America for God's Sake"

"Counselor, I'm warning you. One more word and I'll put your client in jail. I'm not kidding. I've given my decision. I see absolutely no reason to re-open the case or change my order. We're done here."

"Wait a damn minute. What about the fact that every "notification letter" was sent to HER. Then it ended up in a 90 day U.S. Mail System loop to forwarding addresses because she kept moving with her boyfriend and the letters all ended up in a dead letter box instead of being delivered to me? I'm sure there is a General Delivery for the homeless Veterans at the park downtown. It's not like no one knew where I was when I got out of the hospital. Oh yeah. I forgot. It couldn't wait till I was conscious. There was some sort of an "emergency" filed? No one has the common courtesy God gave a goat to actually talk to me and tell me anything. At least they could have sent the documents to Walter Reed. Eventually I would have gotten *something*! Instead, everything was done behind closed doors.

"Counselor. If you don't control your client..."

"Yeah. We already heard that threat three times."

There was that Team language again. It was lost on the Judge, but not Chief's attorney. He didn't want to go to jail, so the "WE" part didn't really compute!

"Go ahead and put US in jail. I could use the food and a shower. It would be a step up from living in my damn pickup truck out there in the heat. Do you have any fucking idea what it's like living in this body casts and wheel chair? Any idea what happens to a body in a cast when it's 100 degrees with 90% humidity? What the hell is your problem Judge? All I'm asking for is ten minutes of justice here. I spent the last six hours sitting in the damn hallway waiting to get in here. Now my attorney tells me he's not allowed to even talk and you're not going to even listen to anything I have to say?"

"Bailiff, roll him out of my Court Room. Obviously Counselor, you need to inform your client who runs this place. One more word and you BOTH are going to lockup."

"Chief. Just shut the fuck up will you. Give me a few minutes and let me try and talk to the Judge. The more you interrupt, the madder she is going to get. Don't make it any worse than it is. I promise. I'll do everything I can. But you gotta shut up. Go out in the hallway before we both end up in jail."

"In jail for *what*? Speaking? You gotta be fucking kidding me." The morphine was kicking in and Chief's judgment and military bearing was out the window.

"Yeah! Actually, exactly that. She can put us in jail for "speaking". You don't know a damn thing about civilian law do you?" The Attorney turned his attention back to the Judge, hoping Chief was just going to shut up and listen for once.

"Your Honor, my client is under a great deal of stress and is taking medication that is obviously impairing his judgment." the Attorney interjected trying to smooth over some feathers with the obviously pissed off Judge.

"Please, can we have a ten minute recess so I can talk to my client. Please your honor."

"We're done here Counselor. Get your client out of my Court Room. The Court is in recess until 1pm."

"ALL RISE" the Bailiff interjected. The clerk was looking out the corner of her eye, watching intently as the Bailiff rolled Chief out the side door of the Court Room. A strange look on her face made Chief realize she was waiting for something bad to happen. Perhaps an explosion maybe?

The Judge left via the rear door and proceeded to Chambers. Chief was pissed. And his now "EX" wife and her current boy toy huddled in the corner with their attorney, snickering, shaking their heads and acting like a bunch of teenaged assholes who had just gotten away with something really sinister. In this case, that's exactly what transpired. Chief had been blindsided by a freight train. The entire divorce, the flat out deceit, robbery and active participation by an Officer of the Court was despicable.

Chief suddenly found himself surrounded by the same sub-species of humans he spent his entire career intentionally disassociated with. These were the same kind of people who rose to power to become bad guys that he would spend so much time bringing to justice. Only now, they were running his life. Chief had often wondered why people hated him so much in different parts of the world. Was it because he thought he was fighting for righteousness and good? They hated him because he usually won. Was this pay back by the evil forces of the universe? One for the bad guys?

"What the fuck was that all about?" Chief said to his lawyer. As he walked into the hallway looking down at the broken warrior in a wheel chair, he couldn't help but feel infuriated and extremely sorry for the man who'd given so much to an ungrateful nation. It hurt him deeply that he wasn't getting anywhere with a Judge who obviously had no idea what she was doing, and frankly, just didn't care. This was a pretty simple case. Chief was incapacitated, unable to defend himself and his "wife" had taken advantage of the fact Chief was on so many pain killers, was going through so much with surgery and recovery and obviously had serious brain damage from the explosion. But no one gave a shit. It was business as usual. Not even the Judge, who made a very serious mistake, really cared what her decision would do to Chief. She was more concerned about her trial schedule than anything else. This wasn't a Judge who took things very seriously. It was more about her prestige and position in life, on the ladder to becoming the next Attorney General, a woman in a very southern, very male environment. This case was just another obstacle in her way. The sooner she disposed of this nonsense, the sooner she could involve herself with things that really mattered to her. Like the political dinner and TV spot she was about to film. She was the primary reason Chief was living in the County Park as a homeless Veteran. This was not only unjust, it was unspeakably cruel.

Turning to the Sheriff Deputy standing just within arms length, Chief looked up past the bars of the halo and said,

"Look, I know you have your orders. And you look like a pretty nice guy, even though your badge and your brass could use some polish. But this is private stuff I need to discuss with my Attorney. So if you could possibly back up, or better yet just go back to the Judge so she can put her leash back on you, that would really be appreciated."

"Chief. You gotta knock this shit off. This judge is gonna put you in the slammer if you don't shut up! I swear to God. You are making it impossible for me to represent you! Do you *really* want charges added to this mess on top of all the other shit we have to deal with?"

Without even realizing it, the Attorney was speaking that Team language.

"Look, you obviously don't get it either. Going to jail is a major step up in my life right now. You have no fucking idea how miserable this is. I have to stop the pain killers to be able to drive and sit here all day long, alternating between sweating my ass off with water running down the back of my ass, to freezing from the air conditioning, falling asleep and waking up with shivers and unspeakable pain, and smelling like a dead goat as I was told. We've been through four continuances making it even more miserable, cause I end up wasting entire days trying to get a word in edgeways with a Judge who obviously has already chosen sides or at least has a contrary agenda to fairness, impartiality and justice! Represent ME? You didn't say a damn word in there. What the hell are we actually here for? You told me we were finally going to have a hearing. You said we were going to get the Judge to lift the order..."

"Chief. I told you I would TRY! That's it. Try."

"And I had to find $5,000 dollars so you could "TRY", but there were sanctions in place before we even got here, so you weren't allowed to even *speak*? What kind of bullshit is that? Tell me what the fuck we just did besides pay you $5 grand for nothing to happen. I could give a shit less if I end up in jail. What the fuck do you think I have to lose? I already lost it all. When the hell do I get a say in seeing my kids? When is the judge going to un-fuck herself and recuse herself from this case? It's pretty obvious to me she's a man hater. Yeah, she's prior military, but this is just blatant bullshit. I can't fucking believe what I just saw!"

"Maybe you don't give a shit about going to Jail Chief. But I do. Just please try to...."

The Court room door swung open and Chief's now ex-wife paraded through holding onto the arm of the traitor. With a smile from ear to ear, sauntering as if on a major fashion show runway, she flipped her hips from side to side imagining she was a major celebrity of some sort. Chief hardly recognized her after the boob job, the fat injections into her lips and the dip dyed hair. But there was no hiding that huge wide ass. It was an obvious identifying characteristic that had grown out of proportion during the third pregnancy she aborted.

The sauntering circus act coming out the door of the Court was a pathetic epitaph to a relationship that had worn Chief down to the soul. He tried. Really tried to make her happy, to give her everything she wanted. But it was never, ever enough. Coming home from psychotic missions that beat his body to a pulp, tore his heart out of his chest seeing women and children buried alive, coming home and swallowing the bile in his throat, perpetuated by the evil he witnessed humans do to each other. Refusing to say a word so as not to ever perpetuate the evil he experienced, he continually packed the emotion down in a box in his psyche, over and over again only to come back and be deluged with the infantile minutia of her self inflicted boredom, misery and over inflated, selfish consumption. She was turning into everything he hated about America. And she was oblivious to his pain, his disability, and his life changing circumstances. To her, it was all about her. All he wanted was to see his two boys. To hold them close. To tell them he loved them. Instead, he was consumed by pain and the circus of divorce court.

Most of the time he was ashamed to be associated with her. She was not a kind person. She constantly talked bad about and mocked people in restaurants, on buses, in public arenas. It was pretty obvious now that she was relishing the misery of Chief's predicament. And in a moment frozen in time, Chief finally understood what made her tick, what was so elusive to making her happy. *THIS* was making her happy. He'd never seen her so happy. Some deep seeded, dark vengeance that drove her to being an absolute bitch. Power. Control, and the realization she could make people's lives a living hell. That is what her soul needed to be happy? No wonder he never allowed himself to love her. Contrary to all the jubilation flowing around her and her new fuck friend on her elbow like a trained puppy dog, her attorney had a much more serious look on her face, scowling as she glanced over at Chief, looking from head to toe at the halo and wheelchair.

"You enjoying this as much as that bitch is?" Chief spouted off without warning. The walking penis stopped, turned and started towards Chief. As he opened his mouth to speak, Chief rolled the chair towards him with hostility boiling out of his eyeballs. He was ready to fight. Even from the vulnerable position of a wheelchair. The rage boiling in his soul, the muscle memory instinctively rising to the occasion fed the adrenaline dumping into Chief's bloodstream. He would chew this guy to pieces with his teeth if he had to. And win.

"Come on baby. He's not worth it," she said as she grabbed his elbow and pulled the worthless coyote towards the exit.

"Counselor, you need to get your client some anger management classes," her attorney spouted. "He's a danger to society".

With that, Chief almost came unglued.

"You have no idea how dangerous I am you bitch! This ain't over you cunt! I promise you that!"

"Is that a threat Sir? I could have you arrested, you know that?"

Chief's Attorney stepped in between them.

"Look, just get the hell out of here and leave this man alone. Can't you see he's had enough today? Do you really want this to escalate into something serious? Does someone have to die before you get it? Just leave him alone. God Damn. What is wrong with you people? You already gutted him while he was down, now you want to make this into an even bigger circus? Does he really have anything else to give? I mean seriously. What the fuck do you people want? Is it EVER enough?"

With that, the plaintiffs walked out the exit and got into the brand new emerald green Chrysler Chief was still paying for. Chief sat there in total silence as his Attorney started talking. He was asking some sort of questions, but Chief couldn't hear him. He was gone at the moment. Somewhere inside his head, he was reliving all those terrible moments in the desert. There was no rhyme or reason to why whenever the stress got to him, his brain went back to that place. His ears were ringing, his eyeballs tearing up, his heart rate increased but his breathing slowed to a whisper.

It was only when his chest heaved and he took in a long breath that his trance like state was broken. They called it a flashback, but to Chief is was more than that. It was an escape triggered by rage. He was pissed beyond words, transformed into an almost manic state. But in the overall scheme of things, he realized he was the luckiest man on the planet. He really didn't give a shit that she was screwing someone. Somewhere around day three of the marriage, when they'd returned home and found all that mail from the FBI doing her background clearance, all the unpaid bills, all the collection agency mail, Chief instinctively knew he'd made a huge mistake. That was over twenty years ago. And this day, this terrible, miserable day proved that he was right. There was a reason he never let her near his heart. He just didn't trust her. Now he knew, he really never did love her either.

Through the tears, Chief tried to tell his attorney that losing all the "stuff" didn't matter to him at all. He really just wanted to see his two sons. To talk to the two boys left in his life that meant everything to him. And she obviously knew it. She made it a point to sabotage that first and foremost. Now he was alone. His boys wouldn't talk to him. He didn't even know where they were. They were gone, just like his Team.

Chief sat in total silence, total numbness as his lawyer babbled on about North Carolina custody laws, until the Attorney reached over and took his shoulder.

"Look. I gotta go. Call my office when you're feeling better. I have a deposition I have to go to. I'm sorry. We'll talk more later. Take care of yourself."

"Me too." was all Chief could muster. "See yah later."

"What do you mean "ME TOO?" the Attorney inquired. You got some other legal stuff to worry about?"

"Nothing you can help me with." Chief said confidently, then reconsidered.

"You sure? I'm more than willing to look into it if you trust me enough"

"Buy me a burger!" Chief said, "We'll talk on the way to Bragg".

* * * * *

Two hours after leaving Divorce Court in down town Fayetteville, Chief reported to the Headquarters Building on Ft. Bragg, Attorney in tow. He sat motionless in the only clothes he had left that were anywhere near clean, a pair of highly modified Walter Reed medical pajamas with Velcro closures that barely covered

Chief's naked hiney, exposed from the back below the plaster body cast. He was ashamed to be there. But the humiliation about his appearance was over cast by the profuse disbelief that he was fighting for his own life now. Again. Only instead of fighting to survive the hostile desert after being seriously injured, he was now fighting a much more hostile environment and an enemy he didn't yet understand. There was only so much he could do in this condition on his own. His Attorney was in total disbelief after reading the Article15-6 Investigation and charge sheet as a result of the Article 32 hearing that happened without Chief being present. Nothing made sense. But in a few more seconds, the proceedings were going forward whether he was ready or not.

"How does the Defendant Plea?" asked the Three Star General seated at the center position of the long bench table. A panel of seven people was assembled directly in front of Chief as he sat in his wheelchair staring at the floor.

"Sir. With all due respect, my client pleads "Not Guilty". As a matter of order, we request all charges be dismissed and the Defendant be re-instated to full active duty."

"Denied. Counselor, did you not read the charges? There are SIX counts of pre-meditated homicide against your client. Is there something I missed? Why would you ever imagine that I would dismiss the charges?"

"Your Honor. The prosecution doesn't have a case. They have absolutely no evidence this man is guilty of anything. The *only* thing they have is a 15-6 Investigation, which is obviously seriously flawed and an Article 32 Hearing in Absentia that is seriously compromised, all of which were apparently done from a desk in the D.C. beltway. There is an Autopsy report that speculates with no solid basis for the conclusions that my client had *anything* at all to do with the death of the soldiers under his Command, and frankly, as non-substantive as that report is, I can't imagine why the prosecution has even filed any charges against my client. So my asking for the charges to be dismissed is simply a matter of good order and conscience in an attempt to prevent the subsequent embarrassment of this Court and the United States Government should you deny my request and insist that we proceed with this fiasco."

"Watch yourself Counselor. I would highly recommend you take heed and mind your manners!"

"Sir, am I to take that as a threat? Because I am here with the sole intention of protecting and defending my client against these malicious charges. Not to consider my future promotions or demotions. I'm a civilian. And that rank is about as high as I'm ever going to get! "

"He can still put you in jail!" Chief whispered.

"Oh. Ok. Let him." came the unexpected response from the Defense counselor.

And with that statement, Chief knew he had the right guy sitting to his right at the Defendant's table. For the first time in a very long time, Chief breathed a sigh of relief and relaxed a bit. The deep impressions in Chief's forehead and temples were covered with band aids now. Chief removed the halo from his head a week earlier in the men's room of the County Park and the skin was healing well. But the impressions were deep and Chief caught himself subconsciously picking at the calluses and scabs left behind. As Chief looked up, he realized the General was about to read the charge sheet and attempted to stand at the position of Attention.

"Counselor, please have your client remain seated as I read the charge sheet." The General said indicating to Chief's attorney the deviation from normal procedure. He totally missed the cue as he looked at Chief with a confused look on his face.

"Chief Warrant Officer Samuel Hill. I have reviewed the file, and I want to personally extend my congratulations and thanks for an outstanding career to date. Your years of service and your stellar reputation precede you. However, there are some serious allegations pending against you. My only question is why did you not participate in the 15-6 Investigation and the Article 32 Preliminary Hearing? We could have avoided this entire proceeding had you participated and given your version of events!"

" Sir, permission to speak freely?"

"Granted!"

"With all due respect Sir, the Captain who conducted the 15-6 Interview was an hour into the interview process when I woke up. He was talking to the guy in the bed across from me. He had no idea the man he was talking to was brain dead. When I woke up, I asked him who he was and what he was doing and he told me it was none of my business. He claimed the man was "unresponsive to his questions", asked me to sign some paperwork to that effect as a witness, proving that the respondent was "unresponsive and obstructive". But he left the room when I refused. It wasn't until I was formally charged and read the Investigation report that I put two and two together and figured out just how fucking stupid this guy was. I assumed everyone else knew as well, so I didn't think I had anything to worry about."

The court room broke out in laughter.

"Order. Gentlemen, you better find your military bearing, because if you think I'm going to spend my time baby sitting you men, you have another thing coming. You will conduct yourselves in a highly professional manner or you will be removed from this case. Do I make myself clear?"

A round of "yes sir" could be heard as each individual responded one at a time as the General engaged them eyeball to eyeball. Suddenly, everyone was aware of just how serious this judge was, and just how serious these charges were, regardless of how ridiculous Chief made them out to be. As a Lieutenant General, everyone knew he was tapped to be the next Chairman of the Joint Chiefs of Staff. And everyone was trying to strap hang on him to improve their own career and climb the ladder of success. Everyone but Chief and his Attorney. They were the only two men in the room with a dog in this fight. And the General was well aware of that.

"Chief. I'm not sure where you are going with this, or why you think that statement will hold any weight in these proceedings. You do know that Captain Smart is going to testify to his findings?"

"Yes Sir. I look forward to that time as well. I'm sure my esteemed Counsel will be more than adept at getting to the truth."

"Are you saying that the Captain is lying about something?"

"No Sir. I'm just saying that if the same man that was talking to a brain dead soldier in Walter Reed is the same man who wrote the report that caused me to be charged with six counts of murdering my own men, then there is a serious problem here which is much more important than any other problem I've had in my life prior to this. It's just absurd to think I had anything to do with killing my men."

With that, his Attorney cut in.

"Your Honor, at this point I would instruct my client not to make any further statements that could be construed as a spontaneous utterance, and respectfully submit that the time for these questions and answers is somewhere during the follow on proceedings. We're here today to simply enter a plea of "Not Guilty". That's it. So if there are no further questions, if it please the Court, could we please refrain from doing so in open session and reserve any further comments for the Classified portion of this process?"

With a stern look from the General, the gavel struck the pedestal and Court was adjourned. A mere ten minutes transpired, but it was the most important ten minutes of Chief's entire career. He was now officially under Courts Martial and all the rules were different now. It was imperative not to discuss anything with anyone. It was even more important that he stay on post, and keep contact with his Attorney. No more living in the park. No more looking like a homeless puke. It was time to get back into some semblance of uniform and start acting like the professional soldier he was. No more excuses. He had to cut way back on the narcotics. Above all, he needed his brain back. There was a lot of legal maneuvering about to happen, for which Chief had full confidence in an Attorney he barely knew. Some serious questions were going to be asked about how Chief conducted operations. All of which would be answered by one simple phrase.

"With all due respect Sir, you don't have a need to know."

At which time an objection would be raised by the prosecution. To which the Defense Counsel would respond,

"I'm sorry Sir, but no one here is cleared to that level. Any answer responded to the question would undermine National Security and bring great risk to the United States Government."

The plan was solid. But it went against the very fabric of Chief's conscience. He wanted to take the gloves off, to fight, to stand up for himself and his Team. The realization that he was on trial for murdering his own men was something Chief just could *not* wrap his brain around. He kept thinking there had to be some mistake. It was impossible for someone to be this sinister, this incredibly stupid and vindictive and be in the same Military Service to the Nation as he was. But then, he never imagined the woman he called "wife" could possibly turn into what she was demonstrating now either! What the hell happened to America while he was gone? Or was this some weird psychological readjustment affecting his brain from the explosion. He wasn't really sure what was going on. What he did know was that he didn't like it. It was painful. In the matter of one year's time, he'd gone from being a highly respected, highly sought after Intelligence professional to a homeless Veteran. In one smooth easy 15-6 investigation and one Article 32 hearing, Chief went from superhero to suspect, to defendant. Trusted confidant to possible murderer. Good hearted mentor, to "back stabber". And the very thought shook him to his soul and made him want to vomit.

How the hell could they stand him up like a pop up target? What had he done to deserve all this? The confluence of two distinctly impossible, simultaneous situations had Chief's mind warped. Divorce and Courts Martial. What a concept!

Chief was on the verge of a total mental melt down. Way too many surgical procedures, way too many spinal fusion failures, way too many narcotics, sleep agents and pain medications were having a resounding affect even before this insidious treason occurred.

A sudden spiritual resolve came over him. He didn't like what was going on with the divorce, nor the Courts Martial. He damn sure didn't like what the Divorce Attorney said, no matter how untrue it all was. Nor did he like what the Courts Martial Judge was saying, with all the negative connotations and implications. It didn't matter what they thought. Chief knew he could look in the mirror in BOTH cases. And that is what mattered. In the midst of the worst chapter of his life, Chief found faith and hope. A most unexpected turn of events. Now he had to strengthen his resolve, strengthen his faith and resilience and drive on until TRUTH and Honor were restored.

Honor was silenced by both situations. Truth was muted. But both could and would be restored. Or Chief was not worth the oxygen he was stealing from good soldiers. It was his choice.

Everything was up to him. He could quit, or he could pull himself up by his nickers and get on with it.

He felt so alone. He had a few neighbors that were willing to help. But he also knew there was a limit to their kindness. They weren't "his type of people". They had a comfort zone that was more important to them than anything Chief was going through. He had an Attorney that was worth a shit. But the same went for him. He was there to do one thing, earn his money, get the charges dropped, or at least mitigate the damage. Not help him survive or move Chief into his house. Everything was coming together in a manner Chief never expected. His entire life, his career, his very being was challenged, brought into question and looked at under a microscope. Chief wasn't going to just lay down and die. He had a lot of fight left in him. Yet the motivation to fight was difficult to find in the presence of such horrendous physical injuries and such emotional trauma. All Chief know how to do was focus on the five meter targets. What he knew now, was a wide spread agenda was already presented. And he had to play catch up in order to influence the outcome. Something was wrong. The fact he was fighting for his life in a Military Courts Martial was one thing. Doing it while simultaneously fighting in Divorce Court was just a twisted chain of events that made everything more difficult. Especially while he was trying to recover from a botched Spinal Fusion surgery, sitting in a wheel chair.

The more alone Chief felt, the more he wished he had died over in the sand pile. After being told so many times how lucky he was to have survived, how terrible it was that all those men died, Chief wasn't sure they didn't have it backwards. Tears filled his eyes as he remembered watching Goose fade away. That amazing relaxation he saw, the dilation of his pupils and that wonderful, intense glow of energy, the contentment that replaced the agony on his face. And he yearned for that more than ever now. Why the fuck had God done this to him? Why did he live through all that, come home to see his two beloved sons, only to have them snatched away. What a cruel joke this was. What a miserable, sinister, evil turn of events. The moral wounding was horrific. And now he was on trial. But to Chief, it wasn't just him that was on trial. Honor itself was on trial. And he had to have faith that his conduct, that miserable day in the desert that changed everything in Chief's life, would be seen as Honorable. Not criminal. Honor had to win. Or life on this planet just wasn't worth living. He didn't want to live on a planet where Honor didn't exist. Did no one understand what a promise meant? How bad thing were that day, for the previous five days? Six days of listening, hearing this man scream in agony was all he could take so very long ago in the desert of Iraq? He did something he never wanted to do. He killed his best friend, his brother, and his Team mate. And he did it because he wanted to relieve that man, that brother from having to suffer any more than he already did. Yet no one seemed to understand that. Come hell or high water, he had to fight. For himself, and for every other soldier who died for Honor!

"The Fed"

"Karma returns to our lives when we least expect it!"

Life Lesson Nr. 19

Special Agent Thomas E. Bone was on his seventeenth year with the FBI. As he made his way through the rural Virginia traffic, he couldn't help but obsess over why the Director wanted him to run the gauntlet of D.C. Beltway commuters so he could personally come to the office instead of talking to him via electronics of some sort. There were encrypted "video conferencing" devices so that meetings could take place without worry that classified information would be leaked. There were a number of other methods including the third generation Secure Telephone Units or STU III.

Being called directly to the "Big Dog's Office" was unusual to say the least and it bothered "T-bone" deeply that not even the subject matter would be discussed prior to him getting there. Now *that* was an indicator.

The only time prior to this that he'd been summoned to the "head shed" was immediately after the Oklahoma City Bombing. T-bone was still considered a "Rookie" back in those days and he'd stuck his head out way too far, way too soon. Everything he was telling the brass about the explosion at the Federal Building went against the grain, against the speculation, against everything everyone in his Chain of Command wanted to hear. He was the only voice of dissent, which, combined with the relative few years in service he had, made T-bone a target of both ridicule and disrespect.

Ridicule because he was new and didn't have a stellar reputation. Disrespect, because he was going against the prevailing opinions set in motion by those with years on the job, some coming to the end of their careers with as many as 30 years in Federal Forensic Recovery work. Yet he proved beyond anyone's imagination that the smallest of details in forensic work was the difference between positively identifying the perpetrator, and speculating at best. To him, the job was all about what would stand up to defense counsel scrutiny in court. And that, well that was what he lived for.

With all the death and destruction of Oklahoma City, all the speculation of foreign terrorist involvement, came a LOT of emotional responses that turned into political pressure. Those in charge of the investigation knew everyone else in the building. Some of them had children at the daycare center, which was under rubble. Everyone on duty that grim morning had lost a comrade. Many of them lost multiple friends, co-workers and some lost everyone they ever loved or cared for, in a mere thirty seconds. The emotional responses were considerable, yet understandable. Agents, secretaries, cafeteria workers they'd lived and worked with for twenty plus years were now stacked as corpses on the concrete, at the casualty collection point just outside the blast zone, wrapped in body bags, headed for a refrigerator truck on the way to the morgue. When T-Bone walked onto the scene, it was pretty clear emotions were running high, polluting the science. No one in the "food chain" really wanted to listen to the proposition that real live Americans had done such a horrible thing. For whatever reason, everyone was pushing the "Foreign Arab Terrorist" program. T-bone was the first one out of the box to argue against the prevailing hype, the enormous pressure that some foreign Muslim entity was responsible. He was the very first one with scientific proof that unequivocally proved he knew what he was talking about. That neither Muslims, nor Arabs, nor any foreign entity had anything to do with this heinous act of violence against a "soft target" of Federal employees. This wasn't some random act played out by Al-Qaeda. Nor a response for some U.S. Foreign debacle like so many times in the past. T-Bone had scientific evidence and complete faith in the fool proof method he'd learned from some of the best in the business, the old timers who had done forensic bomb recovery for a lifetime.

"You have to be completely emotionally detached if you want to be the best in this business," they told him early on in his training.

"Find the science and follow it, not the other way around."

T-Bone took those words to heart and eventually, those words paid off big time. So many in Law Enforcement had fallen into emotional traps. They let their prejudice get in the way, came to the conclusions first, and then tried to find evidence to support "their Truth". In the long run, it was much more efficient, much more timely, much more accurate and rewarding to look at the science first and allow "it" to lead the way to a conclusion. Not vice versa. Since that fateful day in Oklahoma City, T-bone rose from the lower ranks of a Rookie, into the line of sight of the big brass at the highest levels of the FBI, the White House and the Department of Homeland Security.

At first, he was in a very uncomfortable position with the weight of the entire Oklahoma City investigation on his shoulders. The longer it went on, the more he was suspected and the more the World Media cranked up the heat. When all was said and done, T-bone was right and the brass took notice. Not only of his scientific work, his stellar procedure and bulldog attitude, they took note of his demeanor. He was absolutely cast iron, rock solid and completely unflappable.

From that point on, Special Agent Thomas E. Bone was watched, mentored and groomed to become someone in the upper echelons of the FBI. But, no one asked him what he wanted. A desk in some office in the Beltway was the furthest thing from happiness T-Bone could imagine. He loved the field. The hard science, the smell, the taste, the cold night air of winter and the humid warm nights of spring and summer. Working around the clock is what he did best, providing the continuity, chain of custody and forensic science is what made him tick. It took dedication. It took time away from his family and it took part of his soul. But that is what T-bone signed up for and that is what made him the professional that everyone respected.

As he made his way through traffic, the ring tone on his personal cell phone told him that his ten year old daughter Susanne was calling. She was the center of his life now. He was often amazed how much she had changed his life. The Bureau was no longer the center of his universe. The were relegated to second place when this green eyed, red haired beauty entered his life that breezy fall day in September, 2000. A year before America changed forever, he now knew what "precious" really meant. Like so many other Intelligence professionals, T-Bone struggled with the choices of being a father, and being the "GO TO" guy when it came to bombs.

As he changed lanes, heading for the exit out of Dulles International Airport, he breathed a sigh of resignation that yet another two hours or more of his life was about to be consumed by the never ending highways and traffic of Washington D.C. Every once in a while, he glimpsed back and realized how much the "beltway" changed over the years, literally right before his own eyes. What used to be hardwoods and corn fields were now strip malls and buildings. McClean and Herndon, Virginia used to be a bedroom community, now a massive expanse of "Beltway Bandits" supporting the incredible tech industry of the United States Intelligence Services.

"Hi baby. How was school today?" he asked, tilting his chin up slightly. The "hands free" microphone of his 2017 Z06 Corvette was just above his eyesight on the "A" pillar of the windshield. Even though the sensitivity of the microphone could pick up even the slightest voices from anywhere in the car, it was purely habit to speak louder and tilt his chin up as if talking into the microphone. Shaking his head as he caught a glimpse of himself in the rear view mirror, knowing full well it was muscle memory. He tried to focus on what Susie was telling him over the phone.

"Tommy got sick in class today".

The words just didn't sink in. Somehow, the intensity in her voice, the sincerity, Susanne's perspective on how serious this problem was, just didn't click. He heard what she said, but he was so twisted up about the meeting he was late for, that he did what he normally did.

"Uh huh! And what else happened today?"

The sigh from the other end of the line brought him back to reality and left him with a heavy feeling in his stomach that told him he just messed up again. Being a "daddy" was much harder than being a Special Agent. A lesson he would re-learn over and again the older Susie got.

"I'm sorry baby. I just have a lot on my mind right now. I didn't mean that."

"That's what you always say Daddy. I'll talk to you when you get home. Bye" and the phone went dead. Half way through redial, he put the phone down and breathed deeply. It could wait. Obviously the damage was already done. His wife Jackie warned him about his daughter getting teenaged hormones. But he just didn't "get it". Susie probably wouldn't pick up anyway, even if he did call back. T-Bone was learning the lesson so many dedicated professionals before him had learned. He was coming upon a time when he was going to have to make a decision. Or at least find a balance between what he loved to do and the daughter and family he truly loved as well.

Things were changing. Faster than he could even comprehend. He didn't want to make the mistake he'd seen so many others make, picking career over family. The consequences of making that mistake meant losing his baby girl and most likely his wife and the relationship they had. The job sucked the life out of him at times. Something he continually buried and drove on through to excel in his profession. A profession very few would ever enjoy as he did! Someone needed to write a book to tell men that life wasn't fair. That if they really wanted anything to do with their children, to affect their growth and be part of their lives, they better be involved at an early age and be there continuously until their child reached ten or twelve years old. Because what T-Bone was learning, upset him beyond words. By the time Suzanne was twelve, she was already her own woman, with her own life and her own friends. Trying to be a "daddy" at that age, was counter intuitive. And he was learning the bitter sweet lesson his wife already instinctively knew. At age 12, she was already half way out the door. And T-Bone was screwing up by the numbers trying to reel her back into his version of what she should be doing.

As Special Agent Bone approached the Director's office door, after enduring a full two hours of brutal traffic, followed by a full thirty minutes getting through the security gauntlet, fatigue was setting in. He really didn't need the additional stress of not knowing what the Director wanted. He just wanted this to be over, whatever " it" was, so he could get back to more important things. Like talking with his daughter.

"I know you're wondering why I called you here today" began the Director, knowing full well that T-bone didn't have a clue.

"What I'm about to disclose to you is above Top Secret. This is compartmented information that would cause irreparable harm to the United States government if it were disclosed outside channels. Do you understand that?" the Director said leaning forward in his chair, elbows on the desk top. The Director's eyes were focused directly on the center of T-bone's eyeballs. The pucker factor went up as T-bone cleared his mind and focused intensely on what was being said. Obviously, this meeting was much more serious than he'd anticipated.

"Yes Sir. I'm cleared to Top Secret and compartmentalization as you already know."

"Yeah, I do know that. But what I am telling you goes way beyond your clearance level. This is "Must Know" only information. Not just anyone gets to hear this, simply because they are cleared for a particular classification level. This is mission essential knowledge and only those involved in this particular mission will be allowed to know anything about it. That means Congress doesn't have a "need to know". There is no oversight on this program. It's strictly blacked out. Do I make myself clear?"

"Absolutely Sir. I understand."

"You will be required to sign a Non-Disclosure agreement that specifically prohibits you from speaking with any other person other than your direct first line supervisor, which is ME, and those under your command. Do you understand that as well?"

"Yes Sir."

Bone was starting to wonder if he really wanted to hear this. Obviously, something was going on of which he had no idea. So it must be highly political, or way above his pay grade. Whatever "IT" was, Bone was intrigued now and was more interested in finding out what it had to do with him. For the moment, his daughter faded off into the tree line.

"Sir, May I ask what this is all about?"

"You, Agent Bone, have been selected to supervise an Operational Field Unit. It's a classified mission for which I am personally responsible. You, my Deputy Director for Operations, and whomever you select as team members are the ONLY people authorized to know what this operation is, the only people authorized to discuss it, and *YOU* will report directly to *ME and ME alone* on an "as needed" basis. All communications will go through "Special Intelligence" communications channels via the Special Security Office network. Any and all hard copy files will be returned to this office via Special Access Courier and any and all electronic files will be encrypted before leaving your custody. You will be fully briefed on the specifics of this mission in a few days. I just wanted to bring you here and speak with you face to face, so that there are no questions in your mind about how serious this is. Do we understand each other?"

As Bone opened his mouth to respond, his peripheral vision caught a glimpse of something on the corner of the Director's desk. A red flashing light on the side of a digital recording device indicated that everything T-bone said, indeed his every move was most likely being recorded. Probably since he drove into the parking lot. A flash of heat erupted from his stomach and escaped from around the collar of his white shirt and dark navy blue tie.

"Sir, I've been with the FBI for over a decade now. I know how to handle classified information. I completely understand the communications process and want you to know you can depend on me. But in order for me to agree with whatever it is you want me to do, I have to know what it is you have planned. I know that sounds like an oxymoron, but."

The Director cut him off.

"Ok, Agent Bone. America has a problem. The rest of the world has no idea what technological leaps and bounds have occurred over the past ten years. As you know very well, the FBI is strictly a "Domestic Only" Law Enforcement Agency whose primary task and jurisdiction pertains to crimes within the boundaries of the Continental United States. However, since the signing of the Patriot

Act in recent years, world events have dictated that the FBI
Forensics Unit get involved in a "support" role *outside* of the U.S.
Specifically, the bombings of the Embassies in Kenya, Nigeria and
other places like Khobar Towers in Saudi Arabia. The State
Department has personnel in the Embassy. The CIA has a station
chief. But they are all forced to rely on local Law Enforcement most
of the time when it comes to crimes. The past few bombings were
botched so badly by the local police, that we have absolutely no way
to forensically tie the bombings unequivocally to a specific group or
individual."

Bones knew all of this, but his head was spinning trying to
figure out just how the Director's plan could possibly be legal.

"With that said, the impressive knowledge base and tactical
collection capability of the FBI, the prowess of the FBI might I say,
has been disregarded. Until now. The President has directed that a
small contingent of Federal Officers be deployed to specific Middle
Eastern partner countries in order to train them on some of the more
basic tactics of collecting forensic evidence. I hope you understand
the sensitivity of this program. There are those in Congress, the
press and indeed the American Public that just wouldn't see the
benefits of something this important. They would get all tripped up
and wrapped around the axle on the FBI's intended mission of
"Domestic Only" jurisdiction and make a political football out of
this operation. As it is now, we're getting quite a bit of flack from the
Central Intelligence weenies. We believe we can support the
Intelligence Community in a very unique way by supplying our
personnel, our technological advancements and our expertise to
those Agencies who need it the most, the U.S. personnel attached to
our Embassies around the world and the local law enforcement they
depend on. Do you think you can handle this?"

The enormity of the task was starting to sink in. Balancing the
political sensitivity of what was being suggested was pretty mind

boggling. Never mind the security aspects of such an operation. There was much to be considered. Cultural differences, language barriers, the illiteracy rates among foreign police agencies.

As Special Agent Thomas Bone got deeper and deeper into his own head considering all the tributaries of this proposal, the Director's voice broke the silence.

"Is there a problem Agent Bone?"

"No Sir," came the response before he even knew he was speaking. A problem? What kind of problem could he possibly be referring to? This was no problem. This proposal was professional and personal suicide.

"I hope I don't have to remind you that this is highly classified.," the Director said, searching T-bone's face trying to get some sort of reaction.

"Sir, can I have a few days to consider this before I give you my answer?"

"I don't think you understand. I'm not asking if you'll command this unit. If I didn't think you were up to the task, you still wouldn't know a damn thing about this. Was I miss-informed about your professionalism and abilities? Or what?" the Director said leaning back in his chair, lighting a huge green Cuban cigar.

"Sir, the implications of what you are telling me are... well, what I mean to say Sir, is that this decision is not to be taken lightly. I mean..."

"Just shut the fuck up and say Yes dummy", T-bone thought to himself. But Susie kept creeping into his brain. This means travel to foreign countries, limited communications with his family, little or no contact with his kids again, no phone calls whatsoever, and his wife and the rest of those he loved would never know where he was, what he was doing, or when and if he was ever going to coming back. DeJaVu of his military days.

"Yes Sir. I would be honored Sir. Thank You Sir".

Before he even knew what was happening, he was being escorted out of the Director's Office side door into a hallway. A secretary took him in tow and led him through a doorway to yet another corridor with a staircase at the end of it. Scanners in the doorjambs and walls swept his body for electronic devices, wires, bugs, recording equipment, and weapons as he walked. As he descended the metal spiral staircase, he realized he was headed into a basement SCIF. The huge metal doorway reminded him of the meat lockers he'd worked in while he was Active Duty at Ft. Bragg so many years ago. The cypher locks were much more up to date, augmented with retinal scanners, finger print recognition and thermal imaging scanners. Someone inside the SCIF knew he was coming and watched his every move. As the secretary approached the metal door, the latch suddenly clicked and a voice came from the upper left corner of the hallway.

"Come on in Agent Bone. Take a seat and we'll be with you in a moment."

As Bone entered the SCIF, the air conditioned office struck him as being overly cold and out of place. It was unusually cold. That could only mean one thing. There were computers in here somewhere. Sensitive computers that needed external temperatures to be well below normal cooling parameters to keep the hard drives from crashing.

"Hello Senior Special Agent Bone." a young woman said as she entered the room. The lack of reciprocal introduction struck T-bone as hard as the air conditioning had. She had a name, but even if he were introduced in the socially acceptable manner, she would most likely give a false name. After all, it didn't really matter what her name was. They were never going to see each other again. That was a given.

"Please read this and sign your name at the bottom.," she said as she prepared the raised stamp similar to a Notary kit. She would sign this document as a witness, stamp it with the raised seal and take physical custody of the document, treating it as if it were evidence, preserving the chain of custody until it reached it's final destination in some four drawer safe somewhere within the Special Security Office SCIF. T-bone chuckled a bit under his breath. This was pretty ridiculous. After all, he *was* cleared for this stuff. It's not like he was a rookie or anything. The entire afternoon, including the meeting with the Director was a bit overboard even for him.

"Agent Bones, I'm required to inform you that by disclosing this classified information to you, you are now subject to the Espionage laws of the United States of America and can be fined or incarcerated or both. This non-disclosure agreement will not expire until 2087. By signing this document, you relinquish your rights as an American Citizen and are bound by the Laws and Articles stated in the fine print at the bottom. Do you understand? Do you have any questions?"

"Yes and no".

The young woman looked up somewhat perplexed. T-bone smiled sheepishly and said, "Yes I understand. No I don't have any questions".

Without missing a beat, the "witness" signed, stamped and dated the document, then deftly put it into a folder, rose to her feet and walked out of the room. The silence was deafening.

"What the hell did I just get myself into?" T-bone thought to himself as he fumbled with the door knob trying to exit the room. Suddenly, a very bored, very tired voice interrupted his task.

"Turn the small knob on the upper lock to the left while simultaneously turning the large knob on the door handle to the right." a digital sounding human said from nowhere. The tone and boredom reflecting just how often the voice had to repeat the instructions. Someone was watching him still.

"Thank You!" Bone said, catching himself again as he slanted his chin towards the ceiling, speaking louder than usual. The act mimicked what he had done in the Corvette just hours earlier and Susie suddenly rushed back into his mind.

"What was he going to tell her now?" he thought to himself as he walked down the hallway towards the staircase to the upper levels. This was going to be tough.

"Jordan: A Land of Mystery"

Jordan was a very strange country indeed. T-bone and his team were in country ten days already and had yet to go any further than the airfield they'd arrived at. They were picked up in the middle of the night and scurried to a housing complex surrounded by a ten foot tall brick wall, complete with guard towers and roving dog patrols. This was not what he expected at all.

Jordanian Special Forces escorted him and his team of three forensic recovery experts in bomb and bullet proof vehicles in a convoy similar to what the President of the United States and his entourage used. Six armored General Motors Suburban SUVs lined the highway with blacked out windows, no chrome whatsoever and a bevy of heavily armed body guards standing on the side rails, ready to off load in seconds to conduct perimeter security detail. The rear hatch was loaded with machine guns and rocket launchers capable of taking down helicopters. According to standard procedure for close quarter security and VIP protocol, all four FBI Agents were constantly kept together in close proximity traveling from the airfield to their quarters, a high end apartment complex with polished marble floors and a staff of personal servants trained to five star hotel level.

Although everyone they encountered since their arrival was extremely gracious, the unmistakable rift between the Agents and the locals was palpable. They weren't from around these parts. And everyone knew it. They were welcome because they were guests of the King. But there should be no mistake made they were Infidels in a Muslim land, tolerated simply because they were told to tolerate their presence.

The tension was obvious from the second they arrived in country. Although there was a degree of professional courtesy, neither side knew the other and natural suspicions seemed to dictate every aspect of the encounter between them. Niceties were exchanged inside the large aircraft hangar, but things went south rapidly when Special Agent Bone protested leaving his expensive and vast array of specialized forensic equipment at the hangar. The head of Jordanian Special Forces assured him that no one would touch the equipment and that the entire hangar would be treated as Sovereign United States territory, just as if it were located in an Embassy compound. The assurances didn't sit well with T-Bone. This wasn't his first rodeo, but it was his first Jordanian encounter. He knew being an American in a foreign country would have its problems that he needed to overcome. But he also knew that he didn't have much choice in this matter. This wasn't how they did things in the FBI. Protocol and procedures were established over decades of FBI field duty with rules set in stone for a reason. But everything since their arrival in Jordan was outside the boundaries of proven protocol. After all, his ass was on the line. In any case, T-bones didn't know this man, so how could he trust him. An obvious Americanism, directly contrary to the Muslim belief that every man is treated as honest and honorable until he proves himself otherwise, for which there were extremely severe penalties. That was a lesson T-bone had yet to learn. In the mean time, since he couldn't set up cameras and didn't have enough people to leave behind as guards, he did what he had to do to make himself feel better. When everyone else was pre-occupied, he reached into his bag of tricks, pressed his thumb into a fine white powder and placed his thumb onto the handle of one of the large green equipment containers. He picked the heaviest one, knowing full well if anyone wanted to move it, or look inside, they would have to touch the handle. The powder residue left behind was invisible to the naked human eye.

He chuckled to himself as he left the building.

"We'll see. We'll see" T-Bone chuckled to himself. He'd been around the barn a few times. So, regardless of the Muslim customs, they had to prove they were worthy of his trust.

Mid week of the third week in country, the head of security notified T-bone that he and his team would be guests at a dinner where they would be introduced to the King of Jordan and the Royal Family. Before he could even process what he'd just been told, he was taken a bit by surprise again when asked, " Are your accommodations to your liking?"

"Absolutely. But I would like to get to work in the very near future." T-bone replied with just a hint of aggravation.

Those words took his sponsor by surprise.

"We thought you might need a week or so to acclimatize yourself to our country, customs and the desert environment. I'm certain once you meet with the King, you'll be allowed to begin your work teaching our Special Forces units on whatever the task is that is your specialty." the sponsor said revealing the compartmental mentality of everyone the FBI team seemed to encounter. No one seemed to know why the Americans were there. Nor did they ask any questions. They all just sort of knew this was a "must know" classified situation. And to T-bone, that was just hinky. What he didn't know was the Jordanian culture. No one asked questions. They just took orders and did what they were told to do. End of discussion.

"Until that time, you are the King's guest. Please make yourselves comfortable."

This was going to be harder than he'd imagined. The fact that the head of Security had no idea why T-bone and his team were there was a major indicator of just how compartmented this operation was. But it also told T-bone just how short the Chain of Command within Jordan was as well. On one hand, he was "in charge" of the U.S. Contingent. On the other hand, they were on foreign soil as "a guest" in a very Muslim country run by a King. In other words, held hostage by the whims of a man he'd never met, who was a significant and strategic ally to the U.S. Government.

This guy, this King, was no dummy. His wife was American. Something that didn't sit well with the locals, especially for his political sustenance. Gorgeous too. The conflict was not lost on anyone. Here was a King who could have anything he wanted who chose an American woman, a graduate of UCLA with honors and a PHD in Psychology and Middle Eastern Culture, living in a Muslim country that enjoyed extremely hostile neighbors on three borders in a region besieged with unrest and turmoil. No matter how T-Bone tried to justify his being there, 99% of the country was offended at his mere presence. There was a reason their activities and travels were restricted, no matter how inconvenient it was to his intended mission.

"So, is there some place around here that we can take a look and figure out where to train your guys? I mean, we can do it in a classroom, and show your men how to go through the motions, but if you really want them to know what they are doing, we need a bomb site of some sort. Maybe a practice range?" His sponsor dually noted the obvious stress in his voice.

"I'm sure that once you meet with the King, Special Agent Bone, and get approval for whatever activities you are here for, we can accommodate your every desire." came the pretentious, condescending tone T-Bone would experience on more than one occasion. There was however, no offense intended. Even as his sponsor tried to hide the boredom of having to deal with yet another "Cowboy" American. And with that conversation obviously concluded, the sponsor bowed, turned and walked away, closing the apartment door behind him. Within an hour, T-bone and his crew were being fitted for black formal tuxedos in anticipation of the upcoming dinner with the Royal Family. Something he'd never worn before.

The one female on the team, Angelina Alyruk-Nevets, was decidedly a problem. The one problem T-bone anticipated and the one person he fought hard to keep on the team. She was the best recovery specialist he had ever worked with. But she also had a history of Military Intelligence and could connect the dots on so many other levels. She was invaluable to the team. Regardless of being a woman. T-bone damn near dumped the entire mission after an argument with the Director himself. To T-bone, she was the expert he needed. As with most things in T-Bone's life, gender didn't count. Her conduct did. To the Director, she was "just a girl" taking up space that a real man should be sitting in. Everyone from the President down was spooked about sending a woman to the Middle East. Everyone except T-bone. Her contributions would far outweigh the perceived problems, and T-Bone knew that in his gut. He decided fight, to never relent and to keep her on the Team. What he didn't know is that Angelina would provide an opening T-Bone needed in the near future. Even with as little knowledge as he had about the Jordanian Queen, Angelina's presence on the Team would provide serious opportunity and good will. The dress code was the least of his worries. But he also had no idea how important the dress code was when it came to women in a decidedly Muslim culture.

Evening gowns were not allowed, nor was Burqa the recommended attire. So in normal Jordanian fashion, Angelina was supplied with an elegant, conservative dress fit for a queen. In fact it was sent by the queen herself from her personal wardrobe. That was an indicator of the respect the Queen had for this female Agent. The tension on the Team was mounting and everyone could feel it.

* * * * *

Within 24 hours of meeting the King, his wife, the royal entourage and being humbly welcomed into the Kingdom, T-bone and his crew were given the "all clear" to commence training operations. Everything T-bone needed or wanted was at his personal disposal. And he was reassured during the pomp and circumstance of full diplomatic reception, that if any requirement were not met, he had a direct line to the King himself. Everyone in Jordan already knew T-bone and the FBI team were the King's personal guests, so they were treated accordingly. The reception only stood to reinforce the concept so no one had an excuse for screwing up. Disrespect or personal opinions were not tolerated.

When the FBI Forensic Team arrived back at the aircraft hangar, again under control of Special Security convoy procedures, T-bone pulled a flashlight from his pocket. With the flick of his wrist, the LED changed from bright white to purple and red. As he shined it on the handle of a large green equipment container, he was pleasantly surprised to find his thumb print, glowing in bright purple-blue where he left it. The IR, black light sensitive dust was his backup plan. He really wanted to check all the Jordanian's palms and fingers for residue. That would have proved his instinct to be correct. But only if the same bluish purple light reflected off their skin somewhere. Otherwise, that would have set off a whirl wind of problems. Instead, T-Bone's suspicions were put to rest. It was obvious that absolutely nothing was touched since their departure, exactly as their sponsor had promised, and his Team busied themselves with the task of unpacking equipment and setting it up on the folding tables their sponsors provided. Everything so far, was precisely organized as T-bone requested.

Ten minutes later, an American made UH60 Blackhawk landed, tail to the hangar on the tarmac and twelve soldiers disembarked. They formed into columns of two and marched 90 degrees away from the bird, executed another perfect 90 degree turn and marched directly into the hangar. In silent cadence, as if to announce their professionalism and dedication to perfection, they broke ranks and came to parade rest positions in a lateral line formation, awaiting further instructions. Their drill and ceremony was perfection. Everything about Jordan so far impressed the Americans. These men were here to learn. And their demeanor telegraphed their intentions, professionalism and loyalty to the King.

During the next thirty days, T-bone and his team took turns teaching from a podium in the hangar, reviewing Forensic Recovery Technology 101. Every man on the Jordanian Special Forces team understood English perfectly and asked pertinent questions. The soldiers engaged the curriculum with an appetite seldom seen in American classrooms. They came to class every day with the same fervor and desire to ingest and assimilate the information into their professionalism. Small labs were set up to experiment with the detection chemicals, equipment and techniques of recovering bomb related evidence and materials. And at the end of the second month, they were all ready for field trials to begin.

"Any word on a location we can use to do some real life Forensic Recovery?" T-bone asked, expecting to be put off yet again.

"Special Agent Bone, we do have a place. There is a large caravan of Bedouin herders that use the ancient trails across the desert. They've told us of a place many miles from here where they say American soldiers were killed in a bomb blast of some sort. One of the elders talks about a fire arrow that streaked across the desert and caused an enormous explosion. We found that place. We'll take you there by helicopter. If it suits your requirements, you may use it for your training needs. But you'll have to talk with the King personally. It's in a very sensitive area and we're going to need permission from the tribal leader."

"Permission? I thought your King owned everything?"

"Contrary to American customs, the King still affords the respect of the tribal leaders, just as he in return expects them to respect him. It's a matter of honor to inform the tribal leaders of the King's intentions, even if it does seem a bit unorthodox. What you don't know because of your own lifestyle and culture is that everyone in the desert depends on everyone else at some point in their life cycle. Keeping things on good terms is always of utmost importance. You never know when you'll need reciprocation. No sense in making enemies when you don't have to."

"Smart!" T-bone thought to himself as he chuckled under his breath. Too bad he didn't learn that himself before he came over here to Jordan. Maybe those words could have saved him some heartache.

There were so many unspoken rules, regulations and customs that a man could live a lifetime in this part of the world and not understand it all. Perhaps, he too could learn something from being here.

* * * * *

As the elite Special Forces team arrived at the desert location, they did what any good team would do. They approached the site as if on a real world mission. As T-bone and his crew watched from higher elevation, the Blackhawk filled with Jordanian Special Operators flared to a hover over the site, leveled off several dozen meters above the ground as ropes were released over the side. The eight man team plunged to the earth using American derived "fast roping" techniques. In less than three seconds, all eight men were on the ground, dispersed to all four corners of the compass to set up a secure LZ for the next Blackhawk to land. Agent Bone and his team watched and once again were impressed with the accuracy, speed and lethality these men represented. In a matter of minutes, they too were on the ground, equipment unloaded and stacked while shade tents were deployed and set up by the Jordanian men. Within the hour, everything was ready for collection to commence. The FBI team again stood in awe, impressed with this Team's professionalism and teamwork.

The site was out of a movie. Burned parts from some sort of vehicle were everywhere within the perimeter, but there was actually nothing useable left in the desert sand. Several large axles remained, but after extensive searching in the hopes of finding and identifying the vehicle by serial number, it was quite apparent there was nothing useful left. Bone simply wrote the story off as just another Bedouin legend. After so many years, there was no way of knowing where the story originated, or how it transmitted over the years through a bunch of camel jockeys. T-bone wasn't even sure he had first hand, eye witness testimony. It was hard telling what really happened out here, or how the Bedouins actually came across what was left. His heart sank when he finally resigned himself to the realization of just how much time they were wasting.

He was hoping for some bomb fragments, some gunpowder residue, something to show the trainees how to chemically test and use a spectrometer to identify compounds used in explosives. Way too much time elapsed at this site for any residue to exist now. He brought along numerous samples and he could teach them everything they needed to know. But his preferred method, what had proven a most valuable teaching method over the years, was testing samples the students collected in the field. Things really connected in their head when students were looking at samples they knew to be the ones they collected from the field, following strict chain of custody protocols and laboratory investigative techniques. If the samples were faulty, that was even better. Students learned from their mistakes.

Everything used for identification was burned beyond recognition. There were no part numbers and no serial numbers, which in itself was an indicator. T-bone just hadn't thought about it long enough. By the end of the day, all that would change and the realization these remains belonged to a United States Covert Special Operations unit would give him goose flesh and curl the hair on his neck.

The day was coming to a close and sunset was nearing the horizon when one of the Jordanian students asked a very significant and intriguing question.

"Why isn't there any paint left on anything?"

That was the motivation T-bone needed to stimulate his brain into action. There had to be a reason. After all, he and his team were supposed to be forensic analysts. The very best in the entire world. It didn't really matter how much time transpired since the explosion. What mattered was what they could find forensically. What mattered was teaching these guys to follow protocol and procedure in collecting evidence, preserving the chain of custody until laboratories could analyze the recovered samples. T-bone suddenly realized how distracted the Team was by all the stories, legend and lack of apparent evidence at the location. It was time for him to turn on the afterburners and go into action doing what he did best.

"Break out the kits and lets start collecting evidence.," he told his Team.

"Get these students into full forensic protection gear and monitor collection. There has to be something out here we can use."

T-bone barked, trying to shake off the frustration. Everyone on site jumped into action with a new found sense of motivation.

After a few hours of monitoring the students performing the collection process, T-bone had over 200 vials of sand along with samples of rust from the numerous vehicle parts collected tagged and put into the chain of custody. Procedure was the primary teaching task at the moment. Not forensic laboratory results to prove or disprove anything. Darkness would be upon them within the hour and recovery training would go on through the night. Continuity was important. Something T-bone had learned during the Oklahoma City Bombing. So it was very important to teach the locals the same lesson. Work didn't stop just because the sun went down. Lights were set up, generators fired up and the process continued until nearly dawn. Working under lights brought another entirely new perspective to the collection tasks. Fatigue, cold and darkness were key components to training as well.

Another top priority at this point in training was the preliminary reporting process used to guide an investigation. Preliminary confirmation of samples was critical in the initial reporting process. So the next step in teaching these students was showing them how to do preliminary analysis pending laboratory confirmation. They needed to know that experts in the lab must confirm whatever they did in the field. They needed to learn how important it was that their initial results and reporting were to leading and focusing the investigation based on the science, not what they thought or felt.

Several of the specimens and samples recovered by the students were set aside so T-bone could spend a few hours in the makeshift desert laboratory looking through a microscope at what they recovered. Boredom was setting in. He'd much rather be on a real bombsite, doing real recovery. But if he could effect the future by teaching these student, well, he had to find a way to overcome.

As T-bone pulled yet another glass tube from the rack to load into microscope slides, he saw something glittering that made the sample different from the rest of the samples taken in the same area. The color was different. After reviewing the paperwork that accompanied the sample, he determined that this sample was taken from *under* one of the large steel tire rims that remained. Although most of the rubber was incinerated, there was still something under the large metal rim that would give him some sort of hope. One of the Jordanian students correctly deduced that the tire and rim were blown off the axle during the explosion and landed on top of whatever else was burning. Hopefully, the weight of the rim preserved whatever was in the sand underneath, protecting the evidence from years of wind and sand degradation. And he was right!

As T-bone loaded the sample onto a microscope slide, most of the students gathered near a large flat screen computer display panel with eager anticipation. As T-bone focused the microscope, he plugged a cable into the USB port and watched the image instantly light up on the big screen. The attachment allowed everyone inside the tent to observe simultaneously, that which T-bone viewed through the microscope. And with the twist of a knob, a small black chip came into focus. An audible gasp came from the students as a chip with micro print laser engraved numbers on it came into view. As T-bone switched between numerous amplifications available on the computer controlled microscope, seconds later it was very obvious there were hundreds of these small black chips in the sand samples, all of which had the exact same serial number imprinted on them.

The students were flabbergasted at what they were seeing. But T-bone knew instantly that he was looking at Microchips routinely embedded into combat military warheads. They were looking at proof positive that a missile strike of some sort occurred at this location. Exactly what kind of missile and who it belonged to was a fact hidden within the serial number. One phone call to Quantico, Virginia or to White Sands Missile Range in New Mexico and T-bone would know the precise answer he sought. But a sudden tight, sick feeling in his gut reminded him of the conversation with the red flashing recording device. The *only* link he was allowed to contact was the Director of the FBI himself.

T-bone had a lot of thinking to do now and some serious decisions to make. The conflict between the scientist within him and the loyalty he felt as a Special Agent of the FBI was tearing him apart. On one hand, he not only promised the Director that he would honor the Chain of Command, from him to the Director to the President, he also signed the Non-disclosure agreement. That agreement didn't cover the investigative process. Indeed, there was nothing in the Non-disclosure agreement that even came close to saying anything about finding microchips in the desert sand. So if he did call someone to verify the serial numbers, T-bone could easily tell them it was classified and not get into why he needed the information. Since there was no oversight, no one else in the food chain, he could keep his cards pretty close to his chest. He knew who he wanted to call, and he knew he could trust them with his life. Yet he also knew that if he wanted results he could depend on, he had to call colleagues and friends that were completely outside the Chain of Command.

Over and over T-bone reminded himself that the *only* thing he was there to do was to train the host nation specialists in Forensic Recovery Procedure. Nothing else, just procedure. The fact they discovered microchips at an explosion site so far removed from any combat operation locations was inconsequential, no matter how much it intrigued everyone. He knew that. But in reality, he also knew he could not ignore what was staring him in the face. And that was the rub. If he acted on the science and did what he normally did, with the same ferocity, professionalism and integrity, he would positively get to the bottom of this, which put him way off the reservation. The common sense side of him kept telling him to

"Stick with the program. Just train the soldiers on procedure. Nothing else!"

The pit bull in his soul mandated he find out everything he could. But if he ignored these microchips and just stuck with the program, there was no way he could live with himself. The conflict was making him nuts. Question after question came into his mind and the pressure was getting to him. After all, what exactly would the Director say to him if he called and reported what they found? T-bone knew the operation would get shut down, instantly. But he would also be told to ignore any and all further anomalies and just do his freaking job, "train on procedure." Nothing more, nothing less. Never mind being removed from the Operation, if the Director knew the entire story, T-bone knew he would lose his job, his clearance and possibly his career. And then he might never know what really happened out there in that remote area of the desert.

What the students didn't know, but T-bone did, was that microchips were only installed in high end warheads intended to be deployed to foreign countries. Those missiles used at the firing ranges within the Continental United States, didn't have chips. And only certain military units got those types of weapons, totally unaware that chips were embedded. That was still classified and T-bone had no intention of telling the students. There was a very good reason behind the idea. To keep anyone from knowing there was a forensic trail that would hold up in a Court of Law. Strictly intended to be a safety net in case one of the missiles were stolen or fell into enemy hands, the microchips were a sort of trail of bread crumbs that could be followed. The idea had already saved the U.S. taxpayers a lot of money in investigation fees. More than one criminal was caught and the microchips were instrumental in putting them away forever.

After chemically testing each sample and running it through the Gas Chromatographic Spectrometer and an electron microscope, T-bone could unequivocally say that the area was contaminated with White Phosphorus, confirming witness accounts that "A flaming arrow" had indeed impacted the site. The fact that Thermite, a compound of White Phosphorus was part of the warhead, combined with the microchips narrowed the suspected weaponry down considerably from the arsenal of missiles in the U.S. inventory. Now he had to call in some favors from his military contacts. And it was time to sit down with some Camel Jockeys and find out what else they could tell him. Something was bugging him about this story and the pit bull within him was re-awakened.

$$* \; * \; * \; * \; *$$

For the first time since his arrival, T-bone decided to use the power of his position and call the King personally. After explaining what they uncovered out in the desert at the training sight, T-bone requested permission to speak with the wandering Bedouin herdsmen who provided the information. The King was impressed that T-bone had the integrity and honor to acknowledge protocol and offered nothing but encouragement. Within 30 minutes of hanging up with the King, the head of Jordanian Security called T-bone at the desert training site and informed him of a meeting with the Tribal leader. Shocked that things happened so quickly, T-bone was in the middle of expressing his gratitude when his sponsor cut him off with more shocking news. The Tribal Leader would arrive by camel the following evening to meet with T-bone at the training site. Someone would contact him this very evening to disclose what was expected at the meeting complete with a welcoming ceremony and customary Tea celebration. T-bone was in for another immersion in Middle Eastern culture that would change his perspectives and his mind about who these Camel Jockeys really were. He just didn't know it yet.

* * * * *

The enormity of what Special Agent Bone didn't know about Bedouins was embarrassing to say the least. He felt so very out of place, but even more so like an idiot after spending nearly four hours in a tent that looked more like the Taj Mahal than a tent. His interpreter took great pains to impress upon T-bone that this Tribal Leader was a very important and well respected man. The interpreter continued through the night to provide a crash course in Bedouin traditions and customs. For the first time T-bone heard of the importance of verbal tradition and that honor was everything next to hierarchy in this culture. The Bedouins were a respected culture going back to the very beginning of time and they conducted international commerce on a cash only and bartering basis. Everything about this visit ranked right up there with a United Nation summit. Attention to detail, perfection and honored tradition and cultural history was apparent from everything he looked at. The tent, hand woven from camel and goat hair, was adorned with hand stitched gold and silver threads. The poles were hundreds of years old and hand carved with intricate designs from ancient Acacia trees which no longer existed in the Arabian desert.

Every item they used to exist in the harsh desert environment had been passed down from generation to generation with all of its' luxury, colors and hand tied adornments. The floor of the tent was covered with hand made rugs, mostly woven from goat hair dyed by the harem that followed, fully dressed in traditional Burqa garb, sandals and prayer beads. Incense burned in hand pounded brass urns at all four corners of the tent. Upon final erection and completion of the posh desert accommodations, blessings were bestowed upon its interior ornamentation and occupants in a prayer ceremony. Food, wine, water and a large selection of fruits, nuts and dried dates were presented in the finest handmade trays woven from desert grasses with gold and silver threads inlaid throughout. Not a thing they owned was mass produced and absolutely everything in sight was steeped in centuries of history and tradition. Respect was beginning to blossom within Special Agent Bone with a reverence he felt for very few things on planet earth.

As T-bone entered the tent, he was taken by the elbows from both sides by women fully cloaked from head to toe in soft, brightly covered scarves, leading him to a plush stool upon which to sit, to have his feet washed. The honored tradition of foot washing was an experience that would change T-bone's perspective completely. He'd read about Jesus, with Mary Magdalene washing his feet, drying them with her hair. But the act itself was much more exotic, much more personal and much better understood and received when it was experienced in person. The difference between Western footwear and wearing sandals in the 130 degree heat wasn't lost on him either. T-bone was starting to understand something about these people of the desert. There was no fluff to them. Everything they did, said and respected spoke directly to their heart through their heritage. T-bones realized just how ignorant he was to life in other places on the planet. And it would haunt him from this day forward.

At the end of what T-bone thought to be an elaborate ceremony, the Tribal Leader gestured slightly, revealing just how much power he wielded in his hand alone. Every human within the tent vacated immediately. It was time to get down to the serious business of why the Tribal Leader had come so far to meet an American FBI Agent.

After another hour plus of interpreter history lessons and explanations of Bedouin customs and honor, T-bone better understood that the story he was about to hear of what happened so far out there in the desert nearly five years prior was based in facts and would be passed on for generations to come as a verbal history that everyone's honor depended on. The Bedouin Leader talked about a group of seven men who had come to this area and lived for more than 25 moon cycles, the only relational experience they had to a calendar. On the last day, a U.S. Humvee appeared with four men who were acting completely different than the seven man team acted. They were wild and rebellious, not reserved and quiet as the seven men had been the entire time. The Bedouins kept their distance and refused to interact with any of the foreigners, keeping out of sight as they recorded every action, watched and analyzed their every move as if they too were covert operatives. Only theirs was not for political reason, but survival techniques passed down through centuries by Bedouins whose very survival depended on their stealth and accuracy.

For what appeared to be no reason, the four men in the truck launched a "Fire Arrow" from atop the vehicle at the seven man team resulting in an enormous explosion that knocked everyone to their knees and made their camels run away in a stampede. The aged leader complained of how long it took them all to recover the animals and what problems they had with their ears ringing from the explosion for months later. What was cemented into their ancient traditions and tribal minds was that their fear of foreigners was completely justified. Foreigners were dangerous and not to be trusted. Especially Americans who were ignorant of Arabic rituals and traditions, where anyone met in the desert was treated with respect and dignity. Instead, the Americans killed or destroyed everything in their path. To the Bedouins, Americans were animals and word quickly spread that no quarter would be given to them.

As the story went on, the tribal leader spoke of helicopters arriving many days after the explosion to recover the dead. There had been very little movement after the explosion as the fires continued into the following nights for almost a week. When the fires extinguished themselves, helicopters arrived and took away the corpses. The camel herders had not witnessed much more as they continued to recuperate and recover their camels from miles around.

The fact the Bedouin leader decided to even meet with the American FBI Agent was purely out of respect for the King. The King sent a personal envoy to request this meeting take place. And now T-bone fully understood the impact of the King's earlier statement. Everyone depended on everyone out here in the desert. A lesson the rest of humanity could benefit from. Regardless of the environment, the concept of respect was a good thing to understand.

At the end of the meeting, T-bone thanked the Tribal Leader and asked his interpreter what he should do to show his respect and thanks to the leader.

"Just go away and leave them alone as soon as you can" was the response. As T-bone had learned so early in life, the prejudices he experienced belonged not to him, but to those who had come before him. He continually struggled with modifying his own conduct, because of the actions of the others who came before him, acting a fool. Americans were hated in this part of the country for a reason. And T-bone marked his memory with the intention to thank the Jordanian King profusely. It was time to get to his satellite phone and make a call to Quantico. How to do it without leaving a trail was the next problem. A problem he knew could be fixed by a King. It was time to come clean and tell the man what was up. The shock and surprise coming to T-bone from the conversation with the King was unprecedented. And what he just found out burned him to the soul.

After making a clandestine call from the palace office, T-bone transferred the serial number data to his friend and colleague at Quantico. He trusted Charlie with his life and had since their time together in High School. Charlie was now part of Quantico's inner circle. They jokingly called themselves "the Gate Keepers" because they had the key to super technology and science that answered everyone's mail. Charlie was Asian. And they often joked about his Asian background being a key component of being so smart; rising to the level he got to. Charlie countered with smart remarks about T-Bone being black. It was all in good humor. They were brothers at the soul. And T-Bone was counting on that relationship to not only give him the answers he needed, but to keep it completely off the record as well.

The answer came almost immediately and confirmed the microchip T-bone and the students recovered was from a U.S. made Tube Launched, Optically Wire Guided missile the Army called a T.O.W. The rest of the data told him that the missile in question was built by a well known U.S. Arms manufacturer and deployed to Kuwait City during the Coalition buildup to go after Saddam Hussein and his henchmen. Who actually got the missile was anyone's guess. But the fact T-bone had recovered microchips with those serial numbers proved beyond any reasonable doubt the missile destroyed a target of some sort.

When T-bone hung up the phone, his stomach was in a knot. The look on his face of total disbelief and mystery was the key to what happened next. He was escorted by a Jordanian staffer to a lavish office and offered the customary tea and a glass of crystal clear, cool water, which he graciously accepted. He needed time to wrap his brain around what he just learned. But that time was not forthcoming. The shock of his lifetime was about to come to fruition.

As T-bone finished the water and sat the empty glass back down on a glass topped table to his left, he nearly choked as he swallowed, looking up to see the King himself walking into the room. The Special Agent was caught completely off guard and jumped to his feet, nearly knocking over the table in the process. The

King approached with someone to his left, walking precisely one step to the rear. Colonel Abu Mumani, Commander of Jordanian Special Operations Intelligence and special envoy to the King. Cordially and in perfect English T-bone was introduced to the head of Jordanian Intelligence, a middle aged man with perfectly manicured nails, trimmed salt and pepper hair and beard. He spoke perfect English just about as well as the King did, but with a slight British accent.

"Special Agent Bone, may we have a frank conversation?" was all T-bone remembered at the start. What transpired after that was something he never expected to hear in a million years. The Jordanian Intelligence services monitored the desert location for nearly two years and watched the United States covert operation inside the borders of Iraq almost from day one. The Bedouins had complained to the King, of the foreigners trespassing on their sacred travel routes nearly seven years ago to the day. Jordanian Intelligence kept the secret and knew more than they were telling T-bone about the operation. After all, Jordan was now in a very delicate situation. The less they said, the better. But T-bone needed more answers.

What T-bone wanted to know had nothing to do with the obvious Covert Intelligence operation that went on for so long in the desert. The Jordanians knew the U.S. soldiers were targeting Saddam, so they monitored them to ensure no danger would come to the King or his Royal family and allowed the Operation to go on uninterrupted. The friendly fire incident was also monitored. A strict hands off policy was adhered to simply because they didn't want any further violence to come to their own forces, nor to the Bedouin friends they cherished so much. Whoever the soldiers were in the Hummer, they could not be trusted. So the sooner they left, the better everyone else would feel. And without a word, the Jordanian Intelligence Chief handed T-bone a small piece of paper upon which was written the vehicle bumper number and unit designation.

"ANG/HQ-03", Arkansas National Guard, Alpha Company Headquarters vehicle nr 03. In military jargon, this was the platoon leader of a T.O.W. missile field artillery unit.

The puzzle was solved. But not all the answers were in. That would come in the next hour long discussion between Special Agent Bone of the FBI and Colonel Mumani.

"Look, Col Mumani, I was born at night, but it wasn't last night. It's hard for me to believe that a King would be so involved in another man's fate when that man has nothing to do with Jordan. He's just a foreign soldier to you guys. Why did the King intervene?

"The King must not be seen interfering in your country's politics, never mind it's military."

"So why is he so interested in this one man?"

"That man saved his son's life."

"What?"

"Special Agent Bone, sometimes there are things that happen in a man's family that he is not proud of. The King is not immune from such things. He cannot control everything, even though he is King. His son went to Kuwait to visit a distant relative, a sister. She took him, unknown to the family, to Baghdad where she attempted to martyr him through Jihad. The King obviously was furious. So he sent a special security team to relieve the team charged with protecting his son and bring the boy home. A special group of Americans called the Civilian Liaison Group told us what happened and that your "Chief" had saved the young boy's life. They called him a Chihuahua for some reason, a rather disrespectful term in our culture. However, the King is forever indebted. Call it what you will, but the King cannot repay the favor as he would like, simply because he is the King."

T-bone was rattled to the soul. The dots were getting connected and he suddenly realized everything was not as it seemed in this mysterious land. The Bedouins, the explosion site, the training mission all were just gentle nudges in the right direction so T-bone and his team would find what they needed, on their own, and the rest was up to him. The King knew of T-bone's reputation, the pit bull in his soul. And the King was more than grateful that things went the way they did. He could wash his hands and be satisfied that justice would prevail. Allah would truly be happy.

As T-bone returned to the field site, he had more questions than answers. How much of this he could tell his own FBI team was another consideration he needed to contemplate deeply. Immediately upon arrival, T-bone gave the order to tear down the site and prepare to return to the hangar. Everyone looked shocked, but T-bone took no notice. They were all taken just a bit by surprise at the completely detached demeanor of their leader. The Jordanian Special Forces took no note whatsoever of the difference in T-bone's attitude and proceeded to tear down and pack equipment. The sun would be up soon and that meant the heat was coming on. Time to get a move on. Within the hour, everything was loaded onto the UH-60s and everyone was strapped in.

T-bone rode in silence, reviewing in his mind everything Colonel Mumani told him at the palace office. A survivor was on trial at Ft. Bragg, charged with six counts of homicide for which he was completely innocent. It was only the right thing to do giving T-Bone the Intel. Everything was completely up to T-bone now, and the pit bull in his stomach was becoming even more restless and predictable. Why did he feel like he'd just been used? Was the site simply a convenient location? Or was he led down the rose garden path by Jordanian Intelligence? He could bet his life on the Bedouin story being not only true, but highly accurate. Just as accurate as any written history of any other culture. That was not the problem. The problem now was, how to get to Ft. Bragg and stop the trial. A huge injustice was about to occur. He needed time. Time to think. Time to sort things out, and time to act. But time was a luxury he just didn't have.

A phone call to the Director confirmed the training to Jordanian Special Forces was complete and the Forensic Recovery Team was returning to American soil. A request for two weeks personal recovery leave time for his entire team was granted without even a blink from the Director. After congratulations were laid upon the entire team, T-bone contemplated the route he would drive to Fayetteville, the home of XVIII Airborne Corp, the 82nd Airborne Division and Special Operations. He would sort out the rest when he got there back to D.C. For now, he was on a Covert mission not even the Director of the FBI was in on. And that was dangerous.

"Exoneration without Redemption"

"Sometimes, doing the honorable thing doesn't feel honorable"

Life Lesson Nr. 21

"Special Agent Bone, do you have some sort of death wish? Or do you just intend to spend the rest of your life in prison? Cause that's where you are headed with this mess. You know that, don't you?"

The Director didn't have to tell anyone he was pissed off. T-Bone knew he would be even before he made the call. And now he was seriously wondering if he'd made the right choice in deciding to tell the Director he intended to testify for the Defense at the Ft. Bragg Courts Martial.

"Sir, I told you. This man doesn't have a chance in hell of defending himself. All of his men are dead. The only witnesses are Bedouin Herdsmen which I seriously doubt this Chief Warrant Officer even knows about. I didn't even know about them until the head of Jordanian Intelligence told me. And he wouldn't have told me either if this guy hadn't saved the King's son during some bomb lab raid outside of Baghdad. The kid was five years old. I'm pretty sure this Army guy had no freaking idea the kid he almost killed was part of the Jordanian Royal family. Hell, no one knew. But instead of cutting the kid's throat, he saved his life and now the kid is back at home with his family. That tells me something. This guy is worth a shit."

T-bone ignored the silence on the line. He knew the Director was mad. But that just didn't matter at the moment. The Director needed to listen to what T-bone had to say. So in the face of more silence, he pressed on.

"The Bedouins were watching out there in the desert the entire time and figured out what was what. They told me. And they are the only ones who know what happened out there. Which means I am probably the only one on the planet who knows the entire story. How the hell would this guy even contact them as witnesses, or figure out how to bring them in to testify on his behalf? This is a very serious, no shit situation Sir. I verified everything through my own sources in the Middle East, Quantico and at Bragg. There's very few of my military contacts left since I was in, and this is a very hush, hush Courts Martial. But this "Chief" guy has been charged with six counts of homicide, any one of which would put him on death row if he's convicted. At a minimum, he's looking at life in prison. Just on the extemporaneous charges they tacked on. Conduct Unbecoming a Military Officer alone carries a 25 year sentence. The military still does execute people. You know that right? "

The tension in the Director's voice became very obvious.

"I don't give a flying fuck. He's not one of ours. It's not our problem. You sound like this is one of your own men! Do you know this guy or something? Or did you just flip your lid and decide to countermand every single order I gave you when I called you into my office? There is a reason for military 15-6 Investigations and Article 32 Hearings! Obviously they found something in that investigation, or he wouldn't be standing trial. Which part of our conversation about "non-disclosure" and reporting directly to ME, and me alone didn't you understand Agent Bone? Is your memory defective? Or are you just pulling my crank for the fun of it?"

T-Bone now knew the Director knew a lot more than he was telling him. The 15-6 was supposed to be classified. Or at least that's what T-Bone's contact told him. The fact it went to a Article 32 was something not many people knew. But somehow, the Director knew.

"Sir, I can promise you, this has absolutely nothing to do with you. This isn't about pulling cranks, or any other agenda besides doing the right thing for an innocent man who's been wrongly accused. I found evidence that will set the record straight and exonerate him. I can't look in the mirror for the rest of my life knowing I had the information in my hands that would save an innocent man's life and didn't have the balls to bring it to the authorities that needed it."

"I don't give a DAMN about your mirror, or your balls, or any of the rest of the stuff you are spouting out. You were given a direct order. By me! And you violated my trust and the trust of this Agency. Was I wrong about you? Was everyone wrong when they told me you were a man of honor and that I could trust you?"

"Sir that's the point exactly. I am a man of honor. I'm on leave. Leave that *you* approved after spending all that time doing what *you* wanted me to do in Jordan."

Things were starting to leak out now. T-bone could feel it creeping up on him. That sick feeling got hotter in his stomach as his temper rose and he neared that boundary of disrespect and contempt for the Director. Neither of them ever discussed how the Director used T-bone's forensic abilities to gain respect and rise to the top of the Chain of Command. T-bone didn't care at the time. He was more interested in the science than the politics. But as the years wore on, that tiny annoyance became even more unbearable as the politics became more and more back stabbing.

"Now, I'm not spending Agency time, there is no Agency money involved, and as far as anyone else is concerned, the information I am giving the Defense Counsel will be limited to the facts and not be exposed to any back story about me, the Agency, or anything else that will compromise the mission or the sensitivity thereof. My conscience tells me this is the right thing to do. Just like the Oklahoma City Bombing when everyone said it was foreign terrorists and Muslims, *I saved your ass* by telling you my gut reaction, then proved it with the science that could not be refuted. It stood up in court, it stood up to scrutiny, and in the long run, fertilized your career. You would not be the Director if it weren't for me and you know that."

That blew the lid completely off the conversation.

"Listen you pompous little ass. Don't you dare bring up Oklahoma. That has nothing to do with what we're talking about now. I don't know who you think you are dealing with. But this is *way* out of the box, even for you. I'm giving you a direct order... again. You will return to this office *IMMEDIATELY*. You will NOT go to any Courts Martial to testify, and you will turn over any and all evidence in your possession to the proper Chain of Custody within the Agency, or I swear I will make it my life's mission to see you are prosecuted to the maximum extent of the law. Do I make myself clear?"

"Are you still there sir? Sir? My cell phone is going dead, or the signal is breaking up... can you hear me?"

And with those words, Special Agent Thomas E. Bone hung up the phone, turned left onto I-95 South where a sign greeted him saying it was a mere 198 miles to Rocky Mount, North Carolina. From there, another two hours would put him at Fayetteville, N.C. Fayette-nam as it was known to so many soldiers! In six hours, he would be there. But with the new 2017 Z06 Corvette under his butt, at least that seat time would be pleasant. As he headed down the ramp, shifting late in the power curve, he pushed the stereo button and leaned back into the seat, listening to "Five Finger Death Punch" on the surround sound stereo.

".... arms wide open, I stand alone... I'm no hero and I'm not made of stone. Right or wrong, I can hardly tell. I'm on the wrong side of Heaven and the Righteous side of Hell!"

He had a lot of thinking to do, with even more critical assessments to make when it came to the evidence and how he was going to present it to the Courts Martial Convening Board, yet still maintain security. He believed in the process. He believed in the non-disclosures. But he also believed in his gut. There was the rub. Straddling the confidentiality of his work and the orders he took, with the reality that one man would forever be labeled a criminal and possibly be put to death. And he alone had the information to exonerate the potential victim. A man already victimized. It took T-bone no less than two weeks to put the original story together, to find the Defense Attorney representing Chief and to confirm the Jordanian Intelligence story.

The simple fact remained; there was no treaty, no agreement and no law that said Jordanian Intelligence had to tell him a single thing. There was no law that mandated doing the right thing. Pointing T-Bone in the right direction, allowing him to come to his own conclusion and encouraging him to follow the science was nothing more than an act of pure honor and Karma payback for Chief saving the life of a five year old, who just happened to be related to the King of Jordan. T-Bone wished for Karma in the past. Some of it bad Karma, some of it good Karma. But what he witnessed, what he was now involved with at the moment, felt more like destiny than Karma. And he knew in his soul what he had to do. To him, this was a matter of honor. He resigned himself to the fact he would lose the 19 years and 8 months he spent serving as a Special Agent with the FBI. But if that was the sacrifice he had to make in order to do the right thing, so be it. At the end of the day, this was a simple choice.

* * * * *

Chief entered the court room in a wheelchair, body cast and halo, eyes fixed on the ten feet of floor in front of him as he motored through the doorway, intent on keeping his exposed feet and legs from being impaled on obstructions. Several historical incidents in a parking lot showed him just how close to the edge his pain level already was, routinely throughout the day. Getting hit by a car bumper, or having his legs rammed into a door casing, or his toes slammed into a door was not something he wanted to do again on this day. Life in a wheelchair was completely different, exhausting, frustrating, and feeding the demonic rage just under the surface in Chief's mind. People were like a herd of cattle anyway. But things were much worse when he was sitting in a chair, no longer a human in their eyes, just another obstacle to their comfort zone.

Chief looked as if he were in a drug induced stupor. He was way overdue on the pain meds, intentionally so. He decided to limit how much he took before court so he could comprehend what was about to happen in the court room. But the Demerol, combined with muscle relaxers, anti-depressants and sleep medication put Chief into a non-reactive mode just shy of full incapacitation, Chief was, in fact, on way too much medication. Period. The multiple meds and high dose affected his brain, his respiration rate and inflicting more collateral damage on a body already ravaged with scar tissue, nerve and bone damage. The medications just complicated everything.

To Chief, every time he tried to reconcile where he was in the recovery process, there was a weird mix of medical text book terminology and distance. Distance between the doctors and reality. After all, there wasn't a single doctor in Chief's life that had ever had multiple spinal fusions, not a single one that had ever endured the pain a dozen plus failed fusions with snapped hardware, nor of trying to recover from all of that collateral damage. Never mind the simultaneous emotional pain and suffering of losing absolutely everything in his life that meant anything. In a medical world that Chief formerly respected, the reality of how much the doctors *didn't* know was shocking.

"That's why they call it 'practicing medicine ,'" he said to himself. The doctors prescribed medications based on what the was the preferred dose as dictated by the pharmacies. That was usually based on how long it took for the liver to metabolize the specific meds to get a beneficial level of the active ingredient into the blood system. But not everyone was the same. So the generic pharmacy template that dictated how much Chief was taking resulted in taking way too much. The result of the side effects alone, never mind how many other meds were prescribed to counter those side effects, combined to make Chief feel less than human. In fact, he just didn't give a shit anymore. About anything really.

Living in the park was actually the only solace he had left in life. The house was gone, but that didn't even come on his radar until it came time to us the bathroom, something exponentially difficult in a body cast, with a halo screwed to his head. What hit him the hardest was that his two boys were gone. They were coming into their teenaged years now. And their life was busy with sports, girls and anything else mom could get them involved in so they wouldn't have time for dad. The two things that got him through the toughest incident in his life, his two boys, were no longer there. And his soul ached for them. His Team was gone. In the blink of an eye, vaporized! At least part of the Team was. He spent every single waking moment stuffing the emotional costs into a box, and burying that box deep in a closet. The drugs helped him stay in denial. Stay in control. Yet the narcotics also made him defenseless. Things that his attorney worried about didn't even come close to the level of concern Chief had about finding some flat place on the ground he could lay on to get some sleep, finding clean water, or finding someone to help him wipe his own ass. He needed help. Help that was not forthcoming. The pain meds made him forget it all. And as he entered the court room, it was obvious Chief had abandoned the fight. He was resigned to the fact that his life was over. Everything he endured in the desert had been a mistake. Coming home was just the mere consequence of his primal self survival instinct. Nothing more.

His Attorney was frustrated. Not only was his client medically incapacitated, but he didn't have a place to live either. He didn't have a phone or any way to communicate with his client other than driving to the local park to find him among the homeless. Most times he would find Chief slumped in the bed of his pickup truck, sweating from the 90 degree humidity and flinching from the neuro-toxicity the meds inflicted upon his body along with the muscle spasms and the nightmares. The image made him sick to his stomach, this once pristine Officer of Special Operations, now slumped in a truck bed, constricted by his disabilities, the body cast and a Halo bolted to his forehead. He just could not wrap his brain around how this could happen. The surreal punishment inflicted upon a man of such history, such honor. How could a Warrior Hero end up this far down the drain pipe? Were the rest of the homeless Veterans this unfortunate as well? No one ever asked how they came to be in the park. Everyone assumed it was drug abuse, or dishonor, or mental weakness and the frailties related to combat. These obviously were the ones who "couldn't hack it" and ended up living a lifestyle that relinquished their honor, their dreams, their integrity and forced them into a lifestyle of begging, living off panhandling. But how the hell did Chief end up here? He wasn't like them. Or was he? Whatever was going on, he felt it his moral duty to be involved and try to turn this train around. For whatever reason, he needed to do something to help Chief.

This man, this warrior, this hero of numerous unspoken missions and unseen, unheard of operations, a guardian of the unspoken tuition so many men and women had expended, was headed for prison. Or worse. And he was doing everything in his power as an Attorney to defend a broken soldier he knew only as Chief. A client he had no concept of how to defend simply because he had no idea what had actually happened "over there". The fact was, he didn't have a clue who Chief really was. He suspected things, but just couldn't fathom a man that deeply embedded in the "inner circle" of the Intelligence world, now living as a homeless Veteran in the County Park outside Ft. Bragg, N.C.

He wanted to know, genuinely needed to know simply because he wanted to do his very best as an Attorney for a client he somehow had a genuine regard for. But there just wasn't anything there to defend him with. The charges were serious. He knew that. The consequences of losing this case were astronomical. This man, this soldier, this warrior of freedom and peace, could end up being executed. But every time he tried to find out something from Chief that would help this case, would help HIM try to defend against the prosecution, the only answer he ever got was the same.

"You don't have a need to know".

How the fuck was he supposed to help a man who wouldn't let his own Attorney help him in return? The military wouldn't do the honorable thing, the socially acceptable thing like civilians did. There was no lethal injection. There were only two methods by which anyone was executed at Ft. Leavenworth, Kansas, the only place Chief would end up going. Firing squad, or death by hanging.

"Fuck it. Let them kill me." is all Chief would say when the Attorney tried to engage him, tried to motivate Chief to help in the defense strategy. The Attorney wasn't cleared, for any level of classified information. And Chief did what he normally did whenever questions were asked about where they had been, what they'd been doing, why the mission went so very badly wrong. He responded with the robotic statement he always answered with the exact same rhetoric, as if he were trying to get himself killed.

"You don't have a need to know."

After hearing that so many times, he was seriously tired of it and the consequences of caring so much for a man who didn't care about anything, was building to a point he was ready to just walk away and quit. He seriously considered forfeiting the case and letting some other poor asshole take over. He didn't need this. He damn sure didn't need the pressure, or the consequences. And he didn't really need a client that was less than forthcoming, distant and uninterested in his own fate. It was time to re-evaluate, reconsider and figure out if there were some other strategy to defend Chief. Chief wouldn't even consider any kind of psychological plea. Insanity was off the table, yet if there were any client he'd ever known and represented before now, Chief was the one client most likely to be on the verge of insanity. The real issue at hand was that this Attorney was hog tied by the Military version of law. UCMJ, the Uniformed Code of Military Justice. It was similar to civilian law, but different enough in important ways that it made negotiating the red tape and ceremonial bullshit extremely painstaking. One slip, one "assumption" and his client could be in serious jeopardy.

"Chief! Good to see you. I need to talk to you before we get started. I got some good news late last night. Let's go out into the hallway and have a talk before the judge gets here."

"Good news huh? They're just gonna shoot me here and now instead of waiting forty years on death row?" Chief said as he rolled out into the hallway.

"Come on man, you know it's not that bad. I had a phone call from an FBI Agent who seems to think he has a lot of information we can use for your defense. Do you know who I'm talking about?"

"No. I don't know any Feds." is all Chief could muster in a thinly veiled lie.

"Well, he seems to know an awful lot about you, and apparently knows all about what happened over there in the desert."

"Bullshit. No one was there but me and my Team."

"Well, I set up an appointment to talk with the man. He's supposed to be in town around noon today. Driving in from D.C. and he's been on the road all night. I'm going to ask for an adjournment until I get a chance to talk to him and find out if he has anything we can use. You do understand that up to now, we don't have a thing on our side we can use for a defense, right?"

"I didn't do anything wrong. How's that for a defense. The charges are all bullshit. How's that for a defense."

The anger was starting to bubble up to the surface, and the Attorney knew it. Time to disengage and regroup.

"His name is Special Agent Thomas E. Bone and he's a Forensic Bomb Recovery Technician and Senior Investigator with the FBI. I think it's going to be worth our while just to meet with him and see what he has to say."

"You got me all the way down here to tell me we're not going to get anything accomplished today?"

"Chief, just trust me on this one. I have a feeling he might have something we need to hear. Will you meet with him?"

"What the fuck for? You meet with him. That's why I hired you. Just tell me if I have to stay in this monkey suit all day, or if I can go back to my truck and get some sleep. It's fucking hot out there and this body cast is killing me."

"Go. I'll come find you later on tonight. Just go get some rest and if this guy has anything worth hearing, I'll let you know. Just stay in the same place so I don't have to keep running in circles looking for you. Or at least get a phone or something so I can call you."

By the time the Attorney even had the words out of his mouth, Chief had turned his wheelchair around and was half way out the doorway. There was no talking to him. There was no getting him to respond. He just looked like hell. And he smelled even worse. Something had to give. Somewhere, some how this man needed some intervention that would turn him around and give him a better outlook in life. Watching this man, in this condition, with all of this hanging over his head was more than he could take. He needed a miracle for this defense case. And that miracle came by the name of T-bone.

* * * * *

Half way through the conversation in the Attorney's office, Special Agent Thomas E. Bone stopped in mid sentence.

"What do you mean you don't know what your client was doing over there? How can you defend him if you don't know what happened. My God. It took me forever to get all the information, check it against the evidence and to find you and him. Do you have any idea what the hell is going on? Do you have any clue how serious this is and how deep this goes? We're talking National Security at the highest levels here. Holy Martha. Who is this guy?"

"Precisely Sir. That's been the problem from day one. Chief won't talk to me. He won't tell me what they were doing, or what happened. All he ever tells me is,

'You don't have the need to know' and that's it. No details. Nothing. All I have is the charge sheet that says there was an anomaly on the autopsy from one of the injured men, and they extrapolated evidently to assume that Chief killed that man, and then killed the rest of the Team. The charges don't even speculate on a motive. It's easy enough to defend him on lack of evidence, but the fact they even decided to charge him is beyond my comprehension. It's just nuts. I haven't been able to get a THING out of Chief."

"Well, I'm not at liberty to discuss any details. Nor am I even allowed to tell you how I know what I do know. What I am here to tell you is that Chief didn't blow those men up. There is absolute scientific proof that will stand up in court beyond any reasonable doubt. And more forensic proof that the White Phosphorus that killed those men might have been from the security melt down system, specifically the grenades, but they didn't go off by themselves nor where they detonated from the primary ignition system."

"Phosphorus? What are you talking about? Explosion? I wish you would tell me what is going on. I need to know everything you know. Cause this is the first time I've heard anything at all about phosphorus or an explosion."

"An Anti-Tank missile hit that trailer. The grenades were a secondary detonation from the missile. I know this is hard for you, but I can't give you anything else. Just the facts. I'm going to invoke my 5th Amendment rights, and classify my testimony under the National Security act and tell you that everything I have to say cannot be used in open court. I don't know how you want to run this show, cause it *IS your show.* But the information I have is absolutely protected and must stay classified. It literally is a matter of National Security."

"Well, I don't know what else I can do but request an in chambers meeting with the Judge. Once he hears what you have to say, we'll see what happens. But if what you have to say honestly does exonerate my client, then we need to get this done as soon as possible. How do you know Chief?"

"I don't." was the curt answer provided.

"Then how the hell did you find him and decide to come testify on his behalf?"

"I can't tell you that."

"Ok, I get it…. Need to know and all that huh?"

"But I can tell you this. I don't have a thing to do with Chief. Nor do I know what he was doing over there in the desert. What I do know is everything I have to tell the Judge is highly classified and my involvement is going to cost me my career."

"Are you sure you want to do this?"

"Absolutely."

"Then lets get on with it. Can you meet with the judge this afternoon if I can arrange it? Are you up for that? "

"Positively. I'm ready now."

Within the hour, T-bone was in chambers telling the Three Star General precisely what he knew, where he found the micro-chips, how he verified the Bedouin story and verified where the TOW Missile had come from. He didn't answer any other questions. All he could tell them was "You don't have a need to know, nor am I authorized to disclose that information". The Judge authenticated who Special Agent Bone was and shook his head in total disbelief. How the hell did things get this out of hand and this far from reality? Somewhere in the mix, the new generation of soldier had lost sight of just how serious it was to press charges on an Officer. Especially charges that would bring a man's integrity and career into question and possibly put him on Death Row!

In the Generals mind, after reading the charge sheet and seeing the evidence, there was only one item that brought up any question in his mind. A wound on a dead soldier. Exactly how that was extrapolated into six counts of homicide was way beyond his imagination. Even without the Special Agent's testimony, he was hard pressed to see how the Prosecution was going to prove its case.

There were no witnesses, no testimony, nothing but an autopsy report, a 15-6 Investigation, and an Article 32 Preliminary Hearing conducted by this young Captain.

At the end of the conversation, the Attorney sat motionless watching as the General, the Prosecutor and Agent Bone shook hands and disengaged. The Captain sat motionless in a corner listening to every word. Suddenly, the content look on his face was replaced with a pasty white, pale look and it was noticeably difficult for him to swallow with the dry mouth and swollen tongue he now possessed. He'd gambled on making a name for himself. But he had not counted on that name being written in mud and disgrace!

"Counselor, we'll reconvene at 1300 on Tuesday next week. Have your client here in full military uniform. I'll make my decision then.," the General said with his characteristic curt and professional snappiness.

"You, Captain, should consult your own attorney. This isn't over. You don't get to do this without good cause. And in my humble estimation, you've committed an egregious violation completely outside the purview of your authority, which obviously betrays your true intentions, and a total lack of honor. To file additional charges of "Conduct Unbecoming a Military Officer" on a man of this caliber, with the military record he has albeit as classified as it is, you could have gotten a one time read on and been privy to that information as you were the Article 32 Investigating Officer. But instead, you went on a witch hunt. You made up evidence and you impugned the honor of this Intelligence Officer beyond anything I could have imagined. You, Sir, will be charged as soon as I can get a clerk to type up the JAG sheet." And with that, the General left the room.

By 17:40, Chief's Attorney was walking through the park looking for the highly modified Dodge Ram pickup truck. He really didn't know what he was going to say, but he had to talk with Chief, because NOW, he *DID* have a need to know. He needed to know what the hell he had gotten himself into. He needed to know a lot more than Chief was telling him. He needed to know the entire story so he could plan a strategy for next Tuesday's court date. He needed a lot more information if he was going to predict, understand and be prepared to counter whatever it was the General had in mind. And come hell or high water, he was going to find out.

* * * * *

After twenty minutes of walking around in the County Park, looking for Chief, the Attorney found him laying in the grass under a Dog Wood tree, blankly staring at the sky as if he were in some Huck Finn novel, chewing on a blade of grass without a care in the world. As he sat down next to Chief, the words came out as if pre-recorded, deeply contemplated, and simply delivered without emotion.

"Let me ask you something. You're an Attorney right?"

"Yep. Have been for the past twenty five years."

"How many cases you ever lost?"

"Not many."

"Did you see it coming?"

"You mean the loss? Yeah, in retrospect I knew they were weak cases and I didn't have much of a defense. Some of them could have gone either way, but it's never a slam dunk when it comes to juries and the law."

"How many of those cases were bullshit charges?"

"Well, you never know what someone is going to get themselves into."

"That's not what I asked." Chief abruptly interrupted. "The question was, how many of those cases you lost were bullshit charges you KNEW would never stand up in court?"

"None. All the cases that had weak charges ended up getting pled down to lesser charges, or dismissed completely."

"Then tell me why *this case* is any different?"

That was a cold shower. The immediate impact of Chief's statement took him by the nutz and froze him in time.

"Let's face it," Chief continued in that slow, instructor voice he often used when he was mentoring his Team, "these are bullshit charges based on one Captain "wannabe" who's spent his entire career to date, all five years of it, in the RESERVES working at a civilian job all week long, then doing one weekend a month, and two weeks out of the year in a uniform working as an administrative assistant in the Pentagon. Somehow he ended up as a glorified secretary at the JAG office simply because he wanted to be a lawyer some day. He doesn't have any legal background. He doesn't have any Intelligence background, nor does he know how to run an investigation. Suddenly, a war breaks out and this guy gets popped up to active duty and becomes a HERO by picking out one case in a how many thousands of fatality and incident reports? He keys on one word, "Special Operations", highlights it, gets a woody and then decides that's his ticket to becoming a General Officer one day. A real legend in his own mind. Do you have any concept of how ludicrous it is that they even filed these charges? Did anyone do their homework to determine who I really am? Did anyone do any research to find out if I would actually kill my own men? The men I lived with, ate with, and prayed with! My BROTHERS! I trained these men to be lethal, compassionate, highly professional and efficient and then we were all baptized in the fires of hell together! Does any of that matter? Or is this just another case of a bunch of Pentagon Wannabe idiots who never do anything REAL in their lifetime, then set themselves up to be judge and jury so they feel like they did something important? Something special?"

The anger was obvious. But underneath it all, Chief had a real point. A point the Attorney hadn't even considered yet. He obviously gave the prosecution way too much credit. He assumed the Pentagon was professional and efficient and extrapolated from there that the Prosecution had some sort of case.

For whatever reason, the reality hadn't struck him in the heart yet. Now it was obvious his civilian training as an Attorney did absolutely nothing to prepare him for this kind of a case. He had no business representing Chief. This was a world he didn't understand. A world he was never going to be a part of. A world of brotherhood, honor, integrity and hard core soul searching work that others would shy away from. This wasn't a job for just anyone. And it was more apparent now than ever before that the circumstances of whatever had happened over there in the desert had nothing to do with the actual charges. It was clear now. The charges should be dismissed on face value alone. There was no evidence Chief had done anything to any of his men, had no motivation to kill the men he loved, the men he honored and had worked so hard with to take out the garbage no one else would dare to do.

"Chief, tell me how you know anything about this Captain. I haven't been able to get a thing out of anyone. The Pentagon still hasn't answered any of my legal interrogatives and I'm still waiting on the Freedom of Information Act requests from four months ago."

"Save your breath, and don't waste any more of your time. They are never going to answer you. You are an outsider. Period. This entire subject is about saving face and making the Department of Defense look good. I've got sources you'll never have. Let me know what it is you want and I'll get it for you. In the mean time, try to answer at least ONE of the questions I just asked you."

It was late in the game, but at least Chief was starting to sound like he wanted to work on his own defense. The hard part was going to be sorting out what the General was going to say on Tuesday.

"Do you have a clue what kind of betrayal I'm feeling right now?" Chief asked rhetorically.

"My wife is gone, fucking God knows how many other assholes who don't have a shattered spine. Do you have any clue what she said to me? 'If your dick still worked, maybe I wouldn't be looking for someone else!' Some Baptist Minister came to find me, asking for forgiveness cause he says he didn't know she was married. But HE was. I asked him why he wasn't apologizing to his own wife? He wouldn't answer me. Then some Doctor came to do the same thing! What is it with these assholes? They didn't have a conscience when they were fucking her, then they find out I'm a cripple and come to ask ME to forgive them. Do they not realize they are doing this for their own benefit? Like I wanna know they were fucking my wife! God Dammit. "

Things were starting to unravel and the Attorney wasn't sure he really wanted to be involved in this conversation. But then again, who else would listen? He decided it was just better to sit quietly and listen, then to try to intervene. The longer he sat, the more seemed to boil out of Chief's memory, spewing onto the ground in front of him like molten volcanic lava flows.

"My two sons, the only thing I lived for, the only reason I came home, are so wound up in a psychological war with her and her new fuck buddy, that I can't even talk with them. All I ever hear is how "AFRAID" they are to be around me, and God Damn it, I just don't fucking get that. We were so close before I left this last time. They were my entire world. They were the only motivation I had for coming home. That fucking bitch!"

Obviously, the Attorney should be used to surprises by now, but he didn't have a clue that Chief was going through a divorce at the exact same time he was on trial for his life. The pieces were starting to fit together and he was beginning to realize just how "civilianized" his life really was in comparison. Filing a compassionate motion to delay the trial would only play into the Prosecutor's hand and he dismissed it knowing Chief wouldn't go for it anyway. But he needed more time. Time to sort things out. Time to verify what he'd heard in Chambers with the General, T-Bone and the Prosecuting Attorney. His thoughts were interrupted as Chief continued his rant.

"Then some asshole from the Pentagon shows up while I'm in the ICU fighting for my life, right after they tell me I'm gonna be in this chair for the rest of my life and tells me I'm being charged with murdering my own Team. Are you fucking kidding me?"

The Attorney was watching Chief closely, observing the color shift in his face from pale white to crimson red. In a matter of minutes he'd seen the subtle arrival of huge night crawler worms, morphing up his neck from being barely visible to large pulsating living organisms on the sides of Chief's neck as he talked. The blue/black tributaries snaked up to his temples betraying the incredible increase in blood pressure and heart rate. The pin pointed pupils guarded Chief's soul, refusing access by the Attorney and restricting any light from the sun as well. Chief was pissed. Pumped up like a peacock, muscles hard, jaw clenched in between words, temples pulsating with his heart rate. With the exception of his speech, Chief looked more like an ax murderer waiting to happen than a vulnerable homeless Veteran.

"Do you have any clue how stupid this entire thing is? Does anyone really understand who I am, and what I stand for? Or am I just relegated to the junk pile of assholes in the world? Is that the civilian standard? To pass judgment without anyone knowing what I really do? My own wife, parents, hell my own two sons don't have a clue what I do or where I go when they go to sleep at night. Because in my world, the less they know, the better things will be. Hell, most of America has no idea what really goes on in the shadows at night because they are busy sleeping their way deeper and deeper into their own comfort zone. And when they wake up, they get to be judgmental about that which they have no fucking clue, instead of thanking those who protect them while they enjoy slumber in peace and sanctuary!"

Chief was venting now. The Attorney knew that. It was about time. With all the things going on simultaneously, it's amazing Chief hadn't just gone postal and become another statistic. Another police casualty. Another whacked out "combat veteran" that just couldn't fit back into society and gone rogue.

"We don't do the shit we do so other people can fawn over us, give us medals and awards for an "I LOVE ME" wall. We are those silent professionals who go into the night and kill the miserable assholes of the world, the ones who plot to take away our sanctity, our tranquility! We go after the ones who hate us simply because Americans have the freedom to do whatever it is we want to do. We have a choice. They don't have the same code of conduct nor the rules of law that govern our great nation that allow it to become even greater. They don't have the mentality it takes to adapt, respond and overcome like America does. And America wouldn't be able to do what it does best without men like me, without men like those on my Team that gave their lives in a very dangerous, very hostile environment where they would be tortured to death on YouTube simply because they were American soldiers.

"Don't you fucking get this? Or do I have an Attorney who has no fucking clue what's really going on. This isn't about me. This isn't about my men being dead. No one could really give a shit less what happened to them over there anyway! That became very obvious when I got out of Walter Reed and talked to the families. Every one of them got a letter, signed by a machine at the Pentagon with a signature from the Secretary of Defense, on a letter that he probably never saw that said their sons, their fathers, their husbands and loved ones were killed in a 'Non-Combat Automotive accident.'

So, there is the reality. The children, the wives, the families don't get shit. No college fund, no benefits, no insurance money simply because some dickhead in the Pentagon decides this was a black op and they could save money here. The legalese language alone proves they contemplated this action. Honor and loyalty doesn't automatically come to a soldier simply by putting on a uniform. It can't be taught. It's either there, or it's not. And Special Operations people are not immune from having the exact same problem as the rest of the world. We have our own empire building wheenies who stay in sanctuary, pad their records with schools, patches and badges and never ever go down range to do the hard shit. The stuff no one wants to talk about. Prosecuting America's foreign policy with extreme vengeance. You know all those stories they write about? All the "Black Ops Warriors" they make movies about? Have you ever met one of them? And would you ever know when you did meet one?"

What started out to be venting was now becoming insulting. An entirely new perspective began to crystalize in the Lawyer's mind as he contemplated life from Chief's shoes. But that didn't mean he had to take the ridicule and rhetoric either.

"How bout giving me a break. Do you have any idea how hard this has been for me?"

"Oh, yeah. Pardon me all to hell. The twenty grand I had to borrow to retain you didn't do enough to salve the wounds? Now you are going to tell me how hard this has been for YOU?"

"Stop. That's not what I meant. You see! This is what I've been talking about. How the fuck do I represent you when I have no idea what you were doing over there. No idea who you really are. No way to verify any of the facts you might have let slip. Because honestly, there is no way to defend you until I wrap my own brain and my own heart and soul around what it is that I'm fighting here. Because for the most part, it feels like I am fighting *you* more than I am fighting the prosecution. *You* are my worst problem when it comes to winning this case. So, if you're not going to help me, how the hell do you expect me to help you?"

"Well, that counselor is the easy part. You're not fighting me. *You're fighting a mentality* that persists within the great walls of a five sided building inside the Beltway of Washington D.C. You are fighting a syndrome of power mongers. Not the Commanders of outstanding soldiers, but the giant turds who float to the top, just like a septic tank. If they stick around long enough, just like a tick, they can hold on long enough, eventually when a board of review looks at the records and compares it to a guy who doesn't have any school time, no awards or recommendations. Who do you think is going to get promoted? Because the absence of "I Love me" shit in a soldiers records never equates in the minds of the board members that maybe, just maybe this guy doesn't have any of that bravado bullshit simply because he was too fucking busy going down range, too damn busy being deployed to some foreign country to have any time to go to school. Way too many irons in the fire loading, unloading and sitting in a spider hole doing surveillance for 90 days at a pop to be doing mail order college courses. A few too many missions pulling innocent civilians and dependent children out of Embassy compounds being over run by the local militia and insurgents to "check the blocks" and get more paperwork stuffed into his record telling the Board of Review they are "worth a shit"."

"The one thing you have to realize, after you comprehend how ignorant these charges are, is that this JAG Captain didn't get this far by himself. Someone had to approve this going forward from the 15-6 Investigation. Someone had to believe his bullshit to instigate an Article 32 Hearing. You do know what that is don't you? A preliminary hearing? The one that took place in absentia? The one that went sideways while I was in the ICU at Walter Reed? You do know what I'm talking about, correct?

As much "artistic license" as was used to write that 15-6 Summary Report, the fact is that no one checked the facts. No one verified his investigation conclusions. Somehow, the entire time I've spent, nearly 30 years deploying around the world to places that are not even on the map, the problem in the Pentagon has been allowed to fester, swell and turn into a cancer. Someone once told me that the Pentagon and its make up of military forces, directly reflects the fabric of the Society it represents. If that is a fact, we're in serious trouble. Because the America I knew, the one that was founded on strength, honor, grit, loyalty and concern for your fellow man, is gone now. It's been replaced with a society of people more worried about their own comfort zone, their own possessions and status in life than they are about the rest of the planet. They never have to make hard choices in their lives. They never end up in a situation like I found myself in the desert. I don't mind being held accountable for my actions. But to allow some asshole with cubicle disease to deem those actions criminal, is just unacceptable. Goose was going to die a very slow, very painful, agonizing death. A dishonorable death. And because I kept a promise, a promise we all made to each other as brothers, some weekend warrior gets to call me a murderer? Are you fucking kidding me? Tell me, what would you do? What would the outcome be if it were your best friend, if it were your brother lying there screaming his guts out? Fuck all of them. I can look in the mirror. You seriously think I just decided out of a clear blue sky to terminate my entire team just because I didn't have anything better to do? Do you have any idea how many days went by with nothing but screaming and Goose begging for me to put him down? Do you have any idea how hard that was?"

Chief was choking up now. The steel within his resolve rose to the surface as he gritted his teeth, swallowed hard and wiped away water from his eyes. His breath had ceased to exist for a moment. His chest heaved heavily as he absorbed more air into his lungs, and then slowly exhaled through his nose. Instinctively, he closed his eyes for a moment. The throbbing night crawlers of his neck seemed to calm, as did Chief's voice suddenly.

"Do they? Or how much I fought myself, back and forth, hoping for something different, for someone to come help? Even after five or six years, do you think I can sleep at night and not wonder, 'What if I waited'? What if the choppers came, what if they could have saved him? Then what? What would his life have been like? Would Jenny still want him? Would *he* want to live a life of God knows what kind of dysfunction and disability?"

It was all leaking out. The Attorney had no idea what actually happened over there, but he was starting to become conscious of the fact that it wasn't a simple case of killing a soldier. Or of an explosion. There was a very convoluted mess of combat fatigue, confusion, misunderstandings and mistaken identities. The small bits and pieces that T-Bone had disclosed were starting to make sense now. These charges really did have a defense. And it was as simple as Chief had stated to begin this very conversation. He hadn't done anything wrong. In fact, he'd done one of the most heroic, most horrific things any man could do for a fellow brother in arms. He kept a promise. And the reality soon sunk in just how putrid, how incredibly unfair this Courts Martial was. The only question that remained was how was the judge going to view it. If the ass chewing he'd witnessed on the Captain were any indicator at all, it was a fair bet to say Chief didn't have a whole lot more to worry about. The General had reached the identical conclusion a full ten hours ahead of him. It all made sense now. But he still needed to be ready just in case.

For the rest of the night, into the sunrise of the next morning, he sat intently listening to Chief talk, slowly uncovering the details of what he knew, what he could remember and listened over and over to the words, "I just can't remember". The drugs were taking their toll, but it became very obvious that Chief had suffered some real injuries to his brain, his memory and to the rest of his nervous system. The explosion must have been enormous. The only mercy was the total blackout Chief had suffered and the primal response to massive trauma that kept him from seeing, hearing and feeling much more than numbness, a piercing ring in his ears and the blindness of having his eyeballs crushed by the concussive force of the TOW Missile. He didn't have to do much more research to put this story into context. Humans were not made to withstand such forces, forces specifically engineered to destroy armored vehicles and tanks.

* * * * *

Shortly after sunup, Chief was suspiciously surprised to watch a U.S. Army van pull up to the park. The driver got out and made his way to the passenger side rear sliding door, revealing a wheelchair ramp. He was there to pick up Chief and take him to Ft. Bragg. A lot of time had passed since Chief had a driver. And he couldn't help but wonder if this was out of respect, or just making sure he wasn't going to skip town. The young Specialist had a brand new Uniform for Chief, encased in plastic from the dry cleaners, with all of the appropriate patches, badges and medals Chief was authorized to wear. It caught Chief off guard, but he was pleasantly surprised when the young soldier saluted and presented the uniform to him just outside the concrete men's urinal at the County Park. Chief rolled himself inside, washed and shaved as best he could and put the uniform on. The Specialist was not only helpful, but highly inquisitive about not only the task he was ordered to undertake, but also very interested in Chief and how he came to be in the Park. Chief took pity on the young soldier and refrained from his standard "You don't have a need to know" answer, giving a little and telling the soldier bits and pieces of how he came to be a homeless guy in the park, as screwed up medically as he was. The conversation continue as the van left the park and traveled up All American Freeway, past the new civilian manned Check Points and onto Ft. Bragg's Gruber Road, home of the 82nd Airborne Division. As they passed 82nd HQ, and traveled further down to Long Road, Chief recognized the WWII white buildings where the Courts Martial was going to proceed. And as the van pulled into the parking lot, his demeanor and conversation changed completely as struck Chief deeply that the parking lot was nearly full. As he made his way up the ramp to the front door, he was again shocked beyond words as he noticed the entire front foyer filled with people to standing room only. Tears came to his eyes as he realized most of the men, women and children standing in the hallway were the family members of his fallen men. They were either here to watch him hang, or they were here to demonstrate a united front. But then again, maybe they were here to listen and find out what really had happened to their loved ones. Chief didn't really understand what they were doing there until one by one they reached out and touched him with almost reverent gestures, taking care not to make his pain any worse.

The somber, criminal, suspicious nature of the Court Room's occupants was noticeably different when Chief and his Defense Attorney walked in, replaced by an almost irreverent tone reserved for a celebratory occasion. When Chief and the Attorney entered the room, they both were shocked that every single person, jury and all were prematurely seated and came to their feet at the position of attention when Chief came into the room. The shock on their faces reciprocated when they saw Chief standing upright, in full military Class A uniform, a chest full of medals and awards, crimson Beret and highly polished jump boots hobbling on Canadian crutches with large aluminum clamps that circumvented his forearms. Chief had spent several hours in the park with a small pocket knife the previous night, cutting away at the fiberglass body cast that encased him. It needed changing anyway, but Chief was more concerned with the putrid smell emanating from within, even more so about the condition of his skin after finally releasing himself from what he could only describe as a mobile coffin. The sweat, baby powder and gallons of aftershave that had been poured into the cast for some ten preceding months had rotted the inner cotton body sock to a point that everything was doing more harm than good. And Chief was just begging for a reason to get it off of his body. So he did. After which he took a much needed bath in the local park fountain, scrubbing with a bar of deodorant soap, spending much needed time peeling dead skin and cotton material from his wrinkled, prune like pasty skin. As Chief slowly dragged a leg behind him, an obvious result of nerve impingement, he grimaced and held his breath, working hard not to let the discomfort show. The look of wonderment and disbelief on the General's face prompted Chief to speak out of turn.

"You told my Attorney 'full military uniform' did you not General?"

The General nodded concession, looking at the desk top and shaking his head with a "I should have known" look on his face. As Chief came to the defense counsel's table, he stopped and stood at Attention as the rest of the room took their seats. He wasn't sure what this was all about, but he knew in a very few moments he was either going to prison, or he was going home.

"Counselor, in light of your clients injuries and subsequent medical status, would you please have him take a seat for the rest of these proceedings?"

"I'd rather just stand sir. It sucks getting back up." Chief cut in between his Attorney and the Presiding Judge. Defiance was the order of the day, and Chief had already made the decision that if they were going to imprison him, or kill him, he was going to accept the sentence on his feet. Even if *that* killed him. This was a matter of Honor!

"Suit yourself. I'll try to make this as brief as possible." The General said, and then he began to read the Verdict disposition form aloud to the entire court room. The Court Recorder typed frantically as the General's words filled the room.

"It is hereby the decision of this Court, based on new evidence and testimony brought forward by the Defense Counsel that I accepted in closed session in my chambers with the Prosecution, the Investigating Officer and Defense Counsel present, that this Courts Martial Convening Board be dissolved and all charges against the Defendant be expunged from the record. In accordance with the authority vested in me I pronounce this man exonerated and returned to full active duty with all the appropriate rank, pay, benefits and honors commensurate with his outstanding career to date. It will be the recommendation of this Board that this Chief Warrant Officer be considered for the Congressional Medal of Honor, the Silver Star and the Purple Heart for action in enemy controlled territory while conducting Intelligence Operations in support of U.S. Military Joint Special Operations Command for the appropriate period to be designated by an administrative authority. Further investigation into this matter is closed. These proceedings and all records pertaining thereto will be permanently closed and all copies, statements and administrative records will be classified Top Secret with a declassification review date of no less than 85 years from this date. Counselor, do you have anything to add to this statement for the record?" the General asked looking directly at the Prosecuting Attorney.

"No your honor, I think your words reflect the sentiment of every man in this room"

"I would like to say something your honor," Chief cut in, " if it please the Court" he added, looking accusingly at his Attorney, who beamed with pride knowing full well Chief was at least learning something from HIM!

Chief stared at the floor in front of him, fighting off the urge to pass out as the General nodded consent and waited for Chief to speak.

"I would kindly ask the Court to rescind any and all recommendations for honor or recognition on my behalf and instead, make sure that the men who didn't come home are honored. Their families deserve to know their loved ones did not die in a 'non-combat automotive accident' as the machine prepped letter from the Pentagon so rudely and dishonorably dictated the scenario to these families! Even though this entire mission will remain classified, they deserve to know the truth. Or as much as we can provide to them. The only thing I personally wish for is that they know their loved ones didn't die because their Commander was a dirt bag who would murder them. It's an insult to their memory to bestow any privilege upon me, without any acknowledgement of their service and actions that went way beyond the call of duty Sir."

"How did I know you would say something like that Chief? I'll take your request under advisement. Now, unless anyone else has something to say, this Courts Martial is adjourned."

The room erupted in applause and cheers, and a sudden feeling of energy flooded Chief's heart and soul making him fight for his own composure for the first time in a very long time. He felt the flood of emotion purge from his stomach into his throat, headed for expulsion into the room in the form of something very unprofessional. So he choked it down as best he could and tried to focus on the five meter target. For the first time in a very long time, he felt like he had something resembling a family standing there in the room. As the investigative Captain, the sole source of this fiasco walked forward, hand outstretched to shake Chief's hand, he was met with a glare from Chief that would stop anyone in their tracks.

"Captain, I am not here to make you feel better by shaking your hand and saying, 'don't worry about it'. In fact, if you take one step closer to me, I promise you that you'll regret it for the rest of your life. Now turn your ass around and walk away. Just fucking walk away."

Chief wasn't kidding. The Captain knew it. The Defense Attorney knew it and the Prosecuting Attorney motioned to the M. P. guarding the door to come escort the young Captain out of the room. The lead prosecutor was on Chief's shit list too, and everyone knew it. After all, he was prosecuting Chief on behalf of the entire U.S. Government. And in this case, he had been on the wrong side. He was half tempted to talk to Chief, apologize to him and tell him how glad he was of the outcome. But he knew that would also be the wrong thing to do. Better if he just walked away too and left Chief alone. He had a lot of thinking to do. Now that he knew the real story, he needed to figure out why the checks and balances hadn't worked, what was wrong with the system that something this enormous could have gotten this far out of whack. And after he figured that out, he would need to spend a lot more time looking in the mirror at his own motivations.

It was too easy to be satisfied with the outcome and claim no harm no foul. There actually had been a lot of harm. And the foul was against the honor of good men and women who often spent entire careers doing Intelligence work for which there was hardly any thanks, any recognition and very seldom any redemption.

Diagnosis PTSD

"Fight or flight is hard wired into humans. Deal with it!"

Life Lesson Nr. 22

It had been one of those days. Chief was exhausted again, still, going on 72 hours without checking his eyelids for holes. Old habits were hard to break. But the fact was, every time he laid down to sleep, something in his adrenal system kicked him in the ass and he was up. As tired and exhausted as he felt, his inner self fought sleep. And that didn't make any sense whatsoever.

The front brakes on his 1970 Corvette were making some sort of noise requiring another 26 mile trip down the mountain to town. There was a Catch 22 going on. If he ordered things off the Internet, they had to be delivered to his house. Which meant another round of cameras and alarms going off, the gate being broken, the dog doing his barking thing going apeshit. Which all happened right in the middle of when Chief was trying to sleep, between 10 a.m. and Noon. It didn't matter how much he pre-coordinated. The delivery company changed truck drivers so frequently it was impossible to get any routine, or common sense. He'd spent an inordinate amount of time trying to be nice, trying to get them to understand that he didn't sleep at night, and that they just needed to text him and just leave the package at the gate. But it never failed. Most of the drivers were on way too much adrenaline, caffeine and energy drinks with "big brother" watching their every move to have time for any common sense. Their job was to deliver as many packages to as many addresses without damaging the truck. Period. And to them,

Chief was just being an obstacle to that agenda. Scanning bar codes and jumping to the next deliver was an art form, keeping them all moving at the brink of insanity. So courtesy and common sense were out the window for sure.

The follow on PTSD episodes, instigated by the rudeness and lack of any kind of insight or manners were just too much negative input for Chief to take. It seemed like every single time Chief dosed off to get any kind of quality sleep, the dog went nuts barking at some delivery idiot that didn't read the "Do not Enter" signs, jumped the locked gate and decided it was "OK" to just come to the house and beat on the door. The tree whackers were even worse. Never mind the convoy of Jehovah's Witnesses and frozen steak salesmen and people lost, looking for Vacation Rental homes after following their fraudulent GPS systems. No matter how many times Chief told them how the mountains blocked four of the six satellites, they insisted they were in the right place because their car told them they were. The fucking herd!

So Chief just quit ordering anything, including car parts and went to town to deal with things on his own terms. His time line. "They" got to order the parts, add their middle man dollars and make his life exponentially more miserable. Most of the time the parts that came were the wrong parts. Other times, they just didn't order the right thing to begin with. Evidently, "customer service" was one of those things that must have died while Chief was deployed, and he was seriously getting fed up with the civilian lifestyle, apathy, total lack of motivation or concern and ridiculous glacial pace at which everyone moved. He felt so much like a square peg in a round hole. He didn't have any friends, not even after ten years being out. And that made him feel like a Martian in his own home town.

As he pulled into NAPA, Mike, standing by the door smoking a cigarette had the perfect opportunity to throw yet another cutting comment Chief's way. Chief didn't know Mike all that well, but underneath all the inappropriate banter, he suspected not everything was as it seemed on the surface. Mike always watched Chief get in and out of the car, grimacing in pain, sometimes on crutches, other times not. As confusing as it was, Mike sensed there was a mushroom cloud waiting underneath it all. He had no idea his cigarette smoke had anything to do with Chief's change in demeanor. Neither did Chief. But it was plain as sunshine, when Chief got a whiff, there was an instant and drastic difference in body language and facial expression. So Mike preferred to just keep things humorous and taunt Chief from a distance, but not dig too deeply. He wasn't sure if Chief just didn't like him or what was going on. So he kept his distance and just stayed out of Chief's grid square.

Chief had that look on his face again today. His jaw was locked, his body seemed to be stiff and he was breathing heavily at times. Everyone could tell when he was fighting the pain. There were intermittent interruptions holding his breath, sometimes lasting minutes in duration. That's what he did when he was up and active. He held his breath and raged internally against the disabilities, the fatigue and the pain. The veins at his temples pulsed, as Chief tried in vain to disguise the impact four sleepless nights had on his body. He was inside his head, trying to get through the day, totally ignoring Mike's jabs partly because he couldn't really hear what the man said over the ringing in his ears, partly because he just couldn't fake it today, and partly because he really didn't want to deal with any more bullshit, from anybody.

The word was out. Chief was a hero of some sort. No one knew exactly why, they just knew the stories they heard, the ones that Chief would never hear. Rumors were rampant that he was a SEAL, one of those badass boys that did America proud. Others knew he was more than that. Driving a Corvette like that meant he was a drug dealer with Cartel connections that not even Law Enforcement would fuck with. Others knew the dirty little secret, that he was blackmailing his poor wife, a Veterinarian that worked her ass off and bought him the car to keep him satisfied so he wouldn't sue her for divorce. And then there were the ones who had part of the story right. He was an Officer. And everyone knew SEALS were never Officers. Some knew his wife, simply because she worked on their animals. But they didn't really know her. They told everyone else they knew the "real story" though they were never willing to tell exactly what that story was. Chief knew better. She never told anyone anything. Just maybe that he had a bad back, and maybe some found out he was retired military but nothing more. What everyone could agree upon was that Chief had that "thing" when he walked into the room. A presence. An aura. Kind of like E.F. Hutton. The room went silent and every one seemed to gravitate towards him. It bugged him beyond words. But he ignored it as much as he could and just acknowledged their presence by saying "Hey, how yah doing" to everyone he met.

You just had to be perceptive and wait for the right time to approach him, lest you get your head handed to you. Everyone heard something, from some one in this one horse town and knew that this guy in the red Corvette was a Hero. So they just wanted to reach out to him, talk to him, test the water and maybe eventually get up the nerve to ask him the burning questions they reserved deep in their heart. More times than not, they were disappointed when Chief told them "I was just a cook". Because when he told them that, the questions were over. Everyone knew what a cook did, even if they didn't really know. So when he told them that, Chief would physically watch the air blow out of their sails and they walked away with that look on their face like they just discovered there was no Santa Claus. If he told them he was an Intelligence Officer, he would field questions for the next hour about everything from aliens to Satellite capabilities that could listen to you in your bedroom, through the roofing on your house from twenty five miles into space. They knew what they were talking about. And no matter what Chief tried to teach them, they already knew. It must be a civilian thing. So many of them did it. They asked a question not to find the answer, but to tell whoever they asked precisely what they knew to be the answer. So, he got used to telling people he was just a cook. Well, he should have been....

As he scanned the shelves looking for the silicone brake backing gel, a familiar rant ran through his mind. Not the one about being a cook, but the one Goose always referred to. The closer he got to "Alive Day" every year, the more it seemed to pop up.

"Only in America". Dammit. Why was Goose still in his memories at times like this, completely irrelevant, unintended, unwanted.

There were so many similar products, from so many different companies in differing packages and colors, mostly from China and Indonesia, all intended to do the exact same thing. Sorting through them all was just part of the routine that civilians were accustomed to. Like the one hundred boxes of breakfast cereal on the grocery store shelves, or the bazillion types of tooth paste, razor blades and hair products. The insanity was beyond words. It was hard enough for Chief to stand in the grocery store, looking at the million different types of canned tomatoes, when all he wanted was just plain tomatoes. There were stewed tomatoes, with hundreds of subcategorized varieties of the exact same thing, by nearly as many differing producers and canners. Diced tomatoes, petite diced tomatoes, regular original recipe, Italian recipe, "choice" as opposed to "prime", ready cut, and chopped tomatoes. It was no different in the pasta isle. God forbid Americans have to suffer through only five dozen choices of pasta. They might have a fit and revolt or something.

For a guy like Chief, after being gone for so long and living in so many different third world countries from the East Bloc to Central and South America and the Middle East, it was mind boggling to think that Americans had so many choices when other places didn't even have a grocery store. So it was more than ridiculous to him that he should have to sort through another five or ten dozen types of adhesives at the part store, just to find something that would fix the squealing brake pads that made him crazy. A good piece of duct tape would to the trick. But there were several hundred types of tape too! Of course the packaging and the astounding price gouging was another entire rant he just didn't want to get into. Standing there having to read the packaging on every selection just added to the hip, leg and spinal pain he endured on a daily basis. The enormity of what happened to America while he was gone was truly staggering. He remembered listening to a taped version of President George Bush Senior talking about a "New World Order" and "A thousand points of light". But dammit, this was out of control. Corporate greed was rampant and something he really preferred to just ignore. He couldn't go choke the living shit out of some asshole that really deserved it. And nine times out of ten, Chief found himself wanting to throw furniture at the TV. Whatever happened to America while he was gone, needed to get fixed. But that was nearly impossible in the environment he found himself dealing with. At times it was just annoying. Other times, just plain infuriating. But it was their own fault. The American people allowed this to happen and then were consumed by their own apathy, the result of which was Corporate Greed and the never ending consumer products intended to keep them all in their numb little comfort zones, feeling all safe and secure in their entitlements, ready to scream at a moment's notice if their comfort zone got wrinkled.

Chief reached over, just above shoulder height, to pull yet another package off the long metal peg, to begin reading the back panel instructions when everything went black. Like a sniper in the night, adrenaline spiked instantly into his brain. Muscle memory kicked in as he grabbed the threat around the neck and the head, forcing his elbow deeper against the critical wind pipe and arteries. He pushed his wrist with the opposite hand, closing the gap, making it nearly impossible for the threat element to breathe, yet still shutting down blood flow to the brain. As he felt bone popping, intending to make the threat submit, the carotid arteries in the neck collapsed and he felt that tell tale sign of resistance melting, conforming involuntarily to his will. Chief felt the threat's muscles relenting, the resistance fading. Either this target would submit, or he would force it to go unconscious and drop to the floor. Maybe even kill it. Muscle memory took over and Chief breathed in the unsuspecting victory of compliance. The age old tactic was battle proven, and muscle memory in this case was a wonderful thing. Chief didn't really have to think at all. Just react. By forcing his hips to twist, his own body weight exponentially added to the pressure and the target, the threat, was on its way out in a matter of seconds. However, in this particular instance, an old woman in her eighties had deftly and quietly, in all his deafness and disability, breached a secure zone from behind and walked up behind Chief and slipped between him and the shelf. She merely wanted to bypass the obstacle he was to her, walking under his armpit as she headed to checkout. After all, at five foot one inch and barely one hundred ten pounds, she was hardly any threat. At six foot three and over two fifty, Chief was a refrigerator in her way. The sudden movement from behind startled him. His peripheral vision instigated a torrential flood of adrenaline, epinephrine, cortisol and corticosteroids that flooded his brain and blood system. It didn't make any sense. But in an instant, he reacted. She was a threat, sneaking up behind him. What the hell was she thinking?

Suddenly, his sight came back and he realized he had this poor, tiny, innocent woman by the neck, about to lift her from the floor, forcing his weight into a geometric configuration he learned from Krav Maga that would ensure snapping critical vertebrae that kept her head in place. His heart was pounding, breathing deeply trying to contain the huge growl developing within his chest.

"What the FUCK!" Chief roared as he released the woman, catching himself an instant before it was too late.

"My God lady, what are you doing?" he blurted loud enough that everyone in the store heard the commotion.

Her eyes were as big as saucers, her face pale with fear, mouth agape, pupils pinpointed and scared. After a few seconds, they both regained their composure enough to speak.

"It's OK sonny." She said in a tone reminiscent of his grandmother from so many years ago.

"I'm sorry. I'm so sorry. You scared the hell outta me. I didn't hear you, and I damn sure didn't see you. You're too short for me to see coming from behind. And my hearing is so bad, I don't know that I would have heard...." he struggled for words, his brain swirling in confusion and embarrassment. What the hell just happened? The smell of her sickening sweet perfume insulted his nostrils, made him nauseated, reeling with disgust and anger.

She cut him off, tapping him gently on the shoulder as he collapsed to one knee. His hand was over his mouth now, helping him to filter the smell and to hold his breath. His heart pounded in his ears again, making it more difficult to hear. His muscles burned as he tried to clear his vision with the forefinger and thumb of his other hand, leaning on his knee as he tried desperately to control the shaking rage that attempted to take over his entire being. Even on his knees, she barely came up to eye level.

"I told you, it's OK Sonny. My husband used to wake up like that all the time. I bet you were in the service weren't you?" She said in a sweet, chipmunk, angelic voice that grabbed Chief by the heart and made his anger and genuine embarrassment even worse.

The sudden recognition caught Chief by surprise and a large lump developed in his throat. He couldn't talk now. Tears welled up in his eyes. Layers of embarrassment caught him off guard as customers peaked around the end of the aisle, looking to see what the commotion was all about. The immense "Fight or Flight" syndrome he experienced forced him into action. He had to get out of there. Chief apologized one more time and made a hasty exit to his car, fired up the 454 engine, nailed the gas pedal and burned rubber leaving the parking lot.

"What the fuck was that all about?" Chief thought to himself, watching his own eyes from the rear view mirror. They were red, dilated, spooky dark and his chest was heaving hard as he tried to retain the contents of his stomach. He drove for nearly an hour before that huge sigh of relief allowed him to think again. Nose breathing was way different than the past hour of mouth breathing. The stress, pain and tightness of his chest finally relaxed as Chief inhaled deeply, and contemplated what he'd just done. She could have torn his life apart. Law Enforcement involvement would have gone really badly. As he imagined the charge sheet including terrorist threats, assault on an old lady, the very real possibility of civil complaint and lawsuit made him shudder. Confused and bewildered, Chief crawled out of the car and forced his mind to shut off the pain. Maybe there was something to this PTSD thing after all? Whatever just happened at the NAPA store just wasn't right. There was no reason for him to react that way. She was just an old lady, not some HVT. Nothing was going on for him to have responded that way, with such ferocity and intensity. It bothered him on a level he didn't even understand. Maybe it was time to do some homework and figure out exactly what PTSD was and if the doctors were correct in diagnosing him. He didn't believe it. But now, after this incident, he still wasn't sure they were right, but he knew damn well, not everything was "OK" either.

Post Mission Review

"Transition never feels like transition. It somehow always feels like anarchy!"

Life Lesson Nr. 25

As Chief sat in the cool night air high in the Sierra Mountains of Central California, his mind slipped back into old habits of introspection, reflection and self evaluation. Much time transpired from his time in the Deserts of the Middle East, seventeen reconstruction surgeries so far with no end in sight, a divorce and the loss of his two sons. The sudden realization that he never had a chance to say "Goodbye" to his Team struck him pretty hard in the heart as well. A lot of things seemed to be coming back to bite him in the ass from that box in the closet, buried so deeply within his primal psyche. He missed all of the funerals and the memorial ceremonies. He'd been stuck in the ICU at Walter Reed while everyone else mourned the passing of their Warriors, their loved ones, their husbands, Dads, sons. Life went on without him regardless of his condition or how bad he wanted to be there. There was no closure in his life yet, no grieving process, nothing but the cold hard reality of surgery, recovery, divorce, the Courts Martial and now, above and beyond everything else, there was this disability thing he had to deal with every waking moment of his life.

He was back on his feet now, out of the wheelchair after five long years thanks to an amazing doctor near San Francisco. New technology finally caught up and a "Dorsal Column Stimulator" implanted directly onto his spinal cord kept his leg muscles alive long enough to get the bone work done by someone who knew what they were doing. It was not an easy task after seven other surgeons were in there. The scar tissue was immense. But the mistakes were astronomical and complicated his medical status on a level that was nearly incomprehensible. But the new computer system worked and he was walking on his own two feet again. Not everyone got that chance. And Chief knew just how lucky he was. A millimeter higher, or deeper and his cord would be severed. One more screw up by surgeons and the screws could have cut his descending Aorta and bled him out in seconds. So much of the previous damage was permanent. Yet it was not intended to prevent him from coming back, for whatever reason, it was bad, but not bad in the right places to stop Chief from recovering most of this life again.

But now he was beginning a new life, with a new wife and three new step children, having moved completely across the country to a quiet place in the Sierra foothills where no one knew who he was, nor the history behind his injuries. She was pregnant with his child, an absolute miracle baby girl.

The thought boggled Chief's mind that he'd come so far, been through so much, came out so fucked up and met the woman he was always destined to meet. She didn't care that he was in a wheelchair when they met. That was a huge indicator in itself. Either she had that big a heart, or she was that desperate. A small chuckled filled Chief's chest as he remembered telling her that. The response was nothing he expected. She smacked him in the chest and called him an asshole. Fully deserved.

As Chief sat in the cool night air, leaning on a rock that emanated heat from a long day in the California sun, he tried to figure out what it was that bothered him so much. As he struggled with the turmoil within his soul, it suddenly dawned on him that everything had to be the way it was in order for him to be where he was now. The bigger task was learning from it, understanding it all and figuring out how to get through the rest of Life!

The soft wind hushed through pine needles, swirling through the 100 foot tall pine trees just outside Yosemite National Park. The sweet smell of Lilacs struck him as he watched bees gather nectar, seeming to appear from nowhere, returning to a phantom place of sanctuary. Much like his Team, appearing, doing their mission and then disappearing again. Darkness would come soon. Chief drifted off into a slumber, instinctively absorbing the peace and serenity of the mountain air.

As shadows from the full moon danced on Manzanita leaves and buck brush undergrowth, huge California Great Gray Owls taunted each other in the primal dance of mating season. The dry night air swirled through the rocks and caverns of the Merced River canyon, wafting up the scent of sage grass, mixing with the distinctive smell of Sugar Pine tree sap, lupines, and tar weed. The mental post mission review was in full swing.

What had all of this been about? Why had he lived, yet so many didn't? What made him so special? Or was it the other way around? Maybe the special ones were those who got to go on to the euphoric pleasantness he'd experienced that day in the desert with Goose and that day on the table when he died at Walter Reed, only to be deprived of that ecstasy he yearned so desperately for? What was the lesson he was supposed to learn? There absolutely had to be a reason he'd gone through all of the turmoil, heartache, trauma, betrayal and agony. Because if there were no reason... well, that would be just too much to take. Thirty two men and women died on his watch. Some were close personal friends. Others mere acquaintances. But all of them were Active Duty military personnel directly under his Command. There was no way to count the civilians who died helping him. He'd done enough of his own betrayal, coaxing people into helping him, only to then leave the country and abandon them. It shamed him. But he also knew that every single person that signed up for the job knew they were expendable. These were the unsung Heroes of Intelligence who did the hard jobs, never looking for recognition or awards, giving their very lives if required. Those where the ones Chief missed the most. Because that work ethic, that character trait was found so few and far between in American society. It was tearing Chief apart inside. The longer he was confronted with the American population of consumer oriented gluttony, the harder it was for him to reconcile the loss of so many good men and women.

In the far reaches of his mind, Chief looked at his life and realized how much it resembled the making of a Samurai sword. Repetitive cycles of heating between forging hammer strikes kept the steel malleable without cracking, a centuries old secret shared between the Masters of the craft, those who had a "Need to know". There was a technique to forging a Samurai sword. There were lessons learned over centuries of paying attention to the smallest details, experimenting with how much to heat the steel, when to strike, how many times to fold it over and blend it again and again with hammer strikes and more heat. Most of this knowledge was unwritten, passed on from Master to Student through many generations of humble instruction. Only the true Masters were revered, spoken of in sincere reverence and appreciation for the dedication they showed to the craft they pursued. It was the same in Special Operations. The key to a hard blade, one that could survive the rigors of combat, was the careful attention to quenching. A white hot ingot heated in a coal forge, then folded and pounded so many hundreds of times, reheated again and again to keep the blade from cracking while mandating structural changes to the steel on a molecular level. And when the blade was finally drawn into it's final shape, red hot from the flames, it was quenched in an oil bath forcing the steel into a hardened weapon. The trick was to produce a weapon harder than the original steel, with a change to its molecular structure that didn't crack on quenching nor warp with the sudden excruciating temperature change. So had it gone with Chief's life. He was wholly a different human being than the seventeen year old young man who'd signed the contract with Uncle Sam some thirty years prior.

Chief was now part of a similar cycle within the Tier One Warrior community. Just as the pounding forge hammer would form stronger and stronger strands deep within the blade making a pseudo composite metal that would withstand the most brutal combat, so had Chief's life sustained the brutal blows under extreme pressure and stress. His entire life had been forged through the alcohol induced beatings of his father, his military life on exercises, training and all of the real mission cycles. Forged just as the repeated hammer strikes had shaped the Samurai Sword.

The incredible pressure at such a young age, the enormous responsibility placed upon him, the constant stress of operations, training and keeping it all wrapped up inside, compartmented so that no one could see it, was the heat that kept him malleable. Kept him from cracking from the torturous physical pain and emotional suffering. The hammer blows of death, betrayal, surgery and recovery could have cracked and fractured him all the way through to his soul. Whatever it was he had, it kept him alive. Intact. Molded into something different than the rest of the herd. Chief felt like he was a specialized weapon now. A tool that had been tested and come out the other end a bit dinged up, but much wiser and more committed than ever. And now, it was time to figure out what he was supposed to do from here on out. *Was it all for nothing?* Or was this trial and vast winding trail of tribulations a test. The consequences of which would divulge a goal worth pursuing?

The lifetime of selfless service, professional dedication and sacrifice that he, his men, and so many others before him endured for the cause of freedom in America, seemed to be lost on the very people he'd sworn to protect and defend. Such a paradox existed between the bumper stickers, the flag waving patriotism and the left over damage and suffering so many Veterans were dealing with.

When Chief got to the bottom of the subject, past the smoke and mirrors, past the slogans and the ad campaigns, the same cold hard questions remained.

"What the hell did we actually accomplish over there? Was it worth it all? Did it matter? Or was it just a diversion to keep the American people in their comfort zone?" The burning question became almost obsessive the longer Chief was home, exposed to the civilian world so lacking in honor and integrity. There didn't seem to be any personal responsibility left in American society. No more self discipline or professional ethics no matter where he looked.

"That's just normal" was the answer he got when he asked questions from those who'd been civilians all their lives. He just needed to understand if the people he engaged on a daily basis worth the loss of so many honorable men who gave everything? Was the personal sacrifice of such honorable soldiers even understood by those who benefited the most? Such thoughts were hard to reconcile as he tried to re-assimilate into a society he no longer knew anything about, and no longer felt a part of!

Chief, like so many other career soldiers, had given up all of his own rights when he joined the service. That was the personal cost of being allowed to defend everyone else. At age 17, he was really too young to comprehend what those freedoms meant. He had to travel the world and see what he had seen in order to even ask the questions he now needed answers to! The "catch 22" was obvious now. They hadn't seen what Chief saw, hadn't been where Chief had been. So how could they understand what he was asking them? They all had their own reality. Their own comfort zone. All most of the civilians knew was they were supposed to say "Something" to

Veterans. And someone came up with "Thank You for your Service". To every soldier Chief knew, that was the most offensive thing they could say. They didn't ever ask questions. They didn't want to know. So the very sanitary, very safe, "keep your distance" phrase had a way of disturbing Veterans.

"Why not just say "Welcome Home" or even "Fuck You" instead of something that insulting?"

How could they thank Veterans for something they had no idea about? How could they thank them for what they did over there, when they didn't want to know? And for those coming home, swallowing the fur ball on a daily basis, being thanked for what they now locked deep within their heart was insulting. Better to just not say anything and walk away!

That was an indicator. Not everything inside was as calm as what was going on inside. The rage simmered. Even after all this time. Chief went from a high speed, low drag, superman to a loaf of shit on the couch in a body cast in a mere matter of a few months. Now, so many years later, he missed his men. He missed the mission. And the daily struggle of finding something worth while to do, to be a part of, was just as fleeting as smoke on river water. Grab too hard at it, and it just goes away.

As Chief sat on the mountain side, he questioned everything he believed in. Everything he was. The America he knew, the one he truly believed in and fought for, was no where to be found. What Chief witnessed now made his stomach churn. Had it always been this way? Or had something drastically changed while he was gone.

Corporate America, adults who never served America, never knew what sacrifice was, were capitalizing on the death and destruction caused by war. Something mankind has done since war began centuries ago. But things were way more twisted now. Bygone Generations knew what they were fighting for, and everyone either supported them or fought against them. There were sides. Black and white sides. Now, everything seemed to be so much more complicated. There was no white and black. There was only grey! Most of the U.S. population was detached, disinterested, simply changing channels when it came time to be involved and make a choice, or to make a difference.

When Chief was young, everyone served in World War Two. Or knew someone who did. Then there was Vietnam and things got confusing. Panama, Zaire, Rwanda, Bosnia and Desert Storm were all TV wars. No one really knew what the conflicts were about. And it was "entertainment" for the moment, wars with no real meaning and no consequences. No one really knew the largest tank battle in the history of mankind took place in the desert of Iraq, or that the U.S. Abrams decimated over 12,000 Iraqi tankers. All they knew were the images on CNN of bombs going down air shafts in buildings and windows being blown out. The "Video" war of 1990 was nothing more than a blip in their subconscious.

Now, there were those who fought the wars and those who didn't. A very small percentage of the population joined the "all volunteer force", for a myriad of reasons. But, not everyone had a dog in the fight. And that was dangerous. There were those who profited from war too and didn't lift a finger for the common cause. And that was making Chief sick to his stomach. After 30 years of fighting evil, it appeared to be more widespread than ever before.

Fifteen years in Iraq and Afghanistan and what was the outcome? Six trillion dollars spent, thousands of U.S. Soldiers lives lost, uncountable numbers of Iraqi and Afghan civilians lost to "collateral damage". The birth of ISIS, comprised mostly of the very Iraqi Army that had kept peace in the Middle East under Saddam Hussein for nearly forty years, now the strongest, most fanatically insane Army on the planet, owning all of the best equipment American taxpayers bought and given to the Iraqi Security Forces, only to have them walk away and abandon the equipment for ISIS to pick up and use against them! And no one saw that coming? Everyone in the Intelligence world saw it coming. And they were told again to shut up and sit down. 9/11 had come full circle. And once again, Chief's lips didn't work.

The final outcome was that America now knew retreat in the face of victory. Withdrawal from a two front war based on arbitrary calendar dates, not mission successes or failures. Fabricated intelligence to support an agenda, not real Intelligence that would support victory and an honorable return home.

But the most sickening part was that the American people were none the wiser. Nor did they care. They simply went with whatever their elected officials decided. And that was that. Less than 2% of the population was serving to protect the nation. America was becoming a government no longer "Of the people, By the people. Or for the people." It was about Corporate greed. What the hell had happened while he was gone?

"I should have been a cook!" Chief thought out loud. He could feel the frustration building, anger beginning to boil. Sitting in such a peaceful place, watching nature doing its natural thing, he struggled to find and maintain his inner peace. His brain was swirling and he didn't yet have the tools to control it.

Chief was still having difficulties with his brain. The explosion, exponentially worsened by the narcotics he was forced to take every four to six hours for pain, detrimentally affected his memory. Publicly he joked about the Morphine, methadone, Oxycodone and Fentanyl as "The breakfast of champions." But he hated the drugs. He struggled immensely, every single day with the dread and depression the narcotics brought to his brain. His personality was different now. He could feel it. It seemed like forever since he knew what a laugh felt like, or what humor was. He was completely different from the happy, funny, romantic person he knew himself to be years ago. How could it be anything but? How could anyone survive what he'd been through and be blamed for "not being the man she married?"

His body was rebuilt in some of the most serious and sensitive areas of the spinal cord. His face, rebuilt from extensive fractures and injuries, was filled with prosthesis. Almost all of the dental work in his mouth was artificial now with studs, crowns, caps and implants. Daily bowel and bladder pain and dysfunction, muscle fatigue, spinal cord pain, scar tissue tearing constantly, new fractures in old bone grafts...all that alphabet soup of pain constantly assaulted his brain and made his soul curse his very existence.

Although he was thankful for his new life, the underlying medical problems were a constant reminder that he really didn't have too much longer on this planet. That thought taunted him constantly. He fought so hard that day in the desert to survive, to come home, and to live. Yet now, he wished for death so often. The eternal paradox of selfless service, against his primal need for peace was tearing at his soul.

Now his daughter came into the mix. How could he tear her life apart and destroy her innocence by being selfish, by "checking out?" The innocence of his daughter's heart, the love and the dedication of his wife kept him alive now. And it made him wonder how he could espouse honor and integrity, yet be filled with such shame at the thought of ever inflicting such pain onto all of them now. This was the double edged sword of love! She was the one and only woman who taught him what "Love" really felt like. And now that his daughter was getting older, "I Love you Daddy" took on a whole new meaning.

Chief struggled deeply and secretively with a new concept that now defined his life. He was no longer expendable. He'd spent an entire lifetime being expendable, with a woman who preferred he didn't come home. He spent a lifetime dealing with a family devoid of empathy or caring. It was just normal. But it also made life easy for Chief. He could deploy without anyone caring where he was, do the mission and come home to people who didn't care he was gone too long, nor ask questions about where he'd been. So it sort of suited him, kept him from having to deal with inquisitive people who cared. He lived an entire lifetime, in the fast lane, never expecting to live long enough to retire. But now, for the very first time ever in his life, he allowed himself to need. To reach out and ask for something he needed, love, compassion, comfort and companionship. All those things he knew on a different level. All those things meant he was human, so they stayed in a box and Chief kept himself from partaking. Love and compassion would make him weak. They took away his warrior mode and made him yearn to be home safe in a bed with someone he loved. She wasn't that person. And he wasn't really sure if there was a person like that for him until he'd met his new wife. His self inflicted, self denial helped him surf the top of the insane mission tempo. Those who knew him as Chief provided the empathy he required. But a woman's touch, delivered by one who genuinely cared, brought a whole new dimension to Chief's experience. He yearned for her. He dreaded every second they were apart. On a conscious and scientific level he understood it all. But on the emotional level, he was far from comprehending anything. This must be where the story of Sampson came from. A woman's touch that could relieve him of his immense warrior capability. She had her own baggage, her own history. And she was the most highly compartmented person he'd ever met. Quiet, secretive, professional yet the master of understatement.

Chief genuinely yearned for that final peace. Maybe they would understand some day. That was something he just couldn't deal with at the moment. There was too much on his plate. The underlying status of being diagnosed with diabetes exacerbated every aspect of his other serious medical conditions. The pain was worse because of it. The never ending throbbing of scar tissue, nerve damage, and now diabetic neuropathy kept him in a perpetual state of "FIGHT". He fought sleep. He fought exhaustion. He fought pain. He fought the narcotic drudge that kept him forever sullen and miserable. PTSD was constantly mere seconds away from ruining his life and scaring the living hell out of everyone who loved him.

As Chief struggled with his own worth, self survival instincts crept into his mind as he sorted out lessons he learned, valuable perspectives and insights that he knew were important to pass on. But there were not a lot of people listening, or willing to hear what Chief had to say. A whole new perspective of being in the civilian world was a challenge Chief was not ready for. So he kept to himself most of the time.

Most nights when he couldn't sleep, he strapped his damaged body into his Z06 Corvette and drove the winding roads of Paradox County, high in the hills of Central California's Sierra mountains. The 780 horse power motor, six speed transmission and 14 inch wide rear tires were so well suited to the roads, it was hard to believe General Motors hadn't specifically designed this car with Yosemite in mind. The cool night air ingested into the massive 7.8 liter motor gave Chief a noticeable increase in torque and thrust as he cut through canyon roads, climbed past the five thousand foot altitudes, shifting into fourth and fifth gears with the windows down, while "*In the Air Tonight*" *by Phil Collins* played on the Bose stereo system. It was Chief's favorite "psyche therapy" CD, played so many times on the aircraft during so many previous night time operations.

"I was there and I saw what you did, I saw it with my own two eyes. So you can wipe off that grin, I know where you've been, it's all been a pack of lies..."

Such had been the case with Noriega, Milosevic, Pablo Escobar, Muhammed Farrah Adid, Saddam Hussein, Sheik Khalid Mohammed, Abdullah Mohammed Abdullah, and Abu Nidal. The list was endless. The mind bending hours of intelligence gathering, analysis and planning, the countless miles in the cool night air gave Chief time to process that which he'd been unable to while responding so often to mission requirements.

There were mandatory steps to process through any given situation that a human being endured. Grief, for example, had seven phases or steps that a human was required to go through before resolution and peace could be obtained. There were no short cuts. The longer one put off a step, the harder it was to accomplish and the longer the final resolution would take. Some people got stuck at different steps. Some took longer than others to get through them all. But regardless of what an individual "wanted" it was mandatory to go through each individual step until completion.

Chief was learning a very hard lesson. He too was a human, subjected to the same rules. He didn't get to take shortcuts. And although he was learning that now, the surgeries, the extended recoveries and the piles of heavy narcotics had done a lot of damage by keeping him in denial. He was way behind the power curve when it came to the psychological healing he needed. He didn't get to just push things into a box and stash the box in a closet. Eventually, everything in that box, everything in that closet would mandate an answer. It was completely up to him if he wanted to control it when it came out, or ignore it and get bit in the ass when he least expected it. That concept was just as foreign to Chief now, as learning a new and foreign language had been in the past.

The grief Chief felt in his heart was compounded by the deep denial he used to control it. He lost his friends, his Warrior Brothers, his true family, but he lost so much more after the explosion, after the divorce and the Courts Martial. He lost his ability to trust, especially those closest to him. He lost his ability to look to the future and to hope. He lost himself in the process of fighting to preserve the very thing he now realized he never wanted back. That guy he was trying to get back to being. Chief didn't like that guy. The guy he used to be. Instinctively, he tried hard to recover himself. After all, it was easier to go back to what he knew, then to go forward and re-invent someone he didn't know.

Chief was coming to the conclusion, that he lost his own innocence by witnessing over and over the very worst mankind could do to each other, watching humans participate in the most despicable conduct in the name of God, or some fucked up religion, justifying their immoral conduct through their own version of reality. His body was ravaged, almost permanently destroyed. The longer he was off the narcotics, the more his brain came back and demanded processing that which tore his soul to pieces. He was so exhausted with the physical disabilities he endured on a daily basis, yet he knew how lucky he was to have recovered as far as he had and not been a decrepit vegetable on life support in a bed until he expired. The brain injury alone could have done that to him, never mind the seventeen spinal reconstructions he endured to date. Chief was the luckiest man on the planet. And he knew it.

The physical recovery was nearly done. Bones were stable now. Grafting was solid although perforated by scar tissue and residual damage from malpractice. Over the twelve years of surgeries and recovery to his physical body, there had been no time to mourn the loss of his men or to heal the Moral Wounding Chief had endured. No time to do anything but block out the anger or the rage, the perpetual agony that he dealt with every single day. For the past twelve years, he was in surgery, then recovery, then the "Awe shits" from the medical world followed directly by the abandonment and betrayal by his own wife and family.

Betrayal by those closest to him felt much more like treason. There was a trail of damage and disaster behind him now. And it was time to put it all into context and begin the mental healing process. It was time to say goodbye to his men, goodbye to the man he'd been and count his blessings for the man he was to become. It was time to praise God from the highest peaks that he met his new partner and soul mate, now his wife. The first wife he ever really had that lived up to the name. He'd come through the toughest trial anyone could endure in life and survived to tell the story. Now SHE was a major reason for his existence, for his very survival. No man makes it through this world alone. Chief truly was the luckiest man on the planet. These were important lessons to understand, digest, fully embrace and comprehend. The struggle now was to find others who were awake, aware, willing to bare their heart in order to foster an environment where truth could survive. Chief has to find the few strong warriors who survived the unspeakable trauma that life dishes out and come out the other side of the storm wiser, more compassionate, more determined to change the world and stop the madness of the gerbil wheel. Those were the ones Chief sought now, the ones who knew the "Moral wounds of War" and were trying to overcome the consequences. There had to be more of them out there. But when one is standing on the leading edge of a Samurai Sword, the population is pretty thin. Finding those that are of similar mind set is difficult. Finding those with the same strength, the same character, and the same staunch belief structure are genuinely few and far between.

Life was about balance and Chief had to find the balance between who he'd been, and who he was becoming. The rage in his soul was a major obstacle to happiness and peace. That was just beginning to become clear. His entire soul had been irreparably insulted. *Forgiveness was a major component of healing. But how does a man forgive that which he doesn't recognize or understand?*

There was a lot more healing to be done. And there was no guide book, no instruction manual and no mentor to show him how. It was up to him to figure it out while limiting the disaster his path could inflict upon the ones in his life that he truly loved. His wife and children were more important than anything in his life. Because he truly believed, *"Life is about what you do to other people!"* Things were so much more complicated with Step-Children now. Relationships were hard enough, but dealing with his own disaster on top of keeping his new family together was more than problematic.

Tears welled up in his eyes as Chief tried with almost super-human resistance to restrain himself from breaking down and crying like his soul depended on it. He needed to cry. He fought emotion, under the shocking realization and recognition that he was on the verge of completely losing it. But old habits were hard to break and Chief still suffered from that old male warrior syndrome. Nothing was registering in his brain. What the hell was going on? There was nothing to cry about. He was home. He was walking again. He was married to the woman of his dreams and had an incredibly wonderful family. Yeah, there were problems, but compared to what he'd lived through, what he'd been through, what he'd seen in his short lifetime, there was absolutely nothing to cry about. He was the luckiest man on the planet. And then it struck him. That's exactly what he was crying for. The fight wasn't over yet. He faced so many more surgeries and recoveries before he would truly be out of the woods and back on his feet. He was out of the loop for way too long. And he felt useless, tired and seriously weak.

Commanders at the highest level depended on Chief for his intuition, his character, moral compass and Intelligence Analysis to conduct foreign policy and prosecute so many missions, so many different war efforts. Those who knew him had nothing but outstanding referrals and good things to say about him. But Chief softly wondered in his mind now if they would have the same respect, the same encouraging words for the man who had changed so much. He'd gone through hell and come out the other end not a broken man, but a well worn, hardened Samurai. A wise man with the patina only the inferno of so many missions could provide.

There was an aura of recognition that accompanied that combat patina, those scars and that 1000 meter stare. The antique patina wasn't complete yet, but the final result was coming. It was time to find his purpose in life. The reason he'd survived. To find and justify through his actions, that reason for surviving when so many others had not. The reason for coming home, and getting through those infernal fires of hell. It was time to reflect, digest, regroup and set out on a new course in life.

As he sat in awe of the incredible nature surrounding him, sudden movement and nearly silent foot steps caught his attention and brought Chief back to a different level of consciousness. A small group of deer, bedded down during the 103 degree heat of the day were now up and active, munching from place to place in their daily dance of sustenance, nibbling on a smorgasbord of plants, grass, trees and flowers. These creatures were the perfect example of what "man" no longer was. Sustainable with the bare minimum to exist on. They drank water, but didn't need volumes of it, nor to store it. They had to eat, but they did so in a pattern of wandering that left the plants unharmed and able to recover. Watching those deer reminded Chief so much of his Special Operations warriors. Silently traversing hostile territory in the shadows of daylight and dark of night, leaving no foot prints, no markers, no indicators that they'd even ever been there.

Quietly, Chief chuckled to himself as he remembered something he told his boys one night, a night near Halloween when they couldn't sleep after watching a scary movie. It encompassed every mission he ever went on, the warning to the Bad Guys who thought they were "Billy Badass".

"When you're all alone at night, and you don't hear anything at all, don't worry. It's just me."

There had to be a reason he'd lived through the horrors of seven combat tours and over 180 covert Special Operations missions. He'd lived through such a long journey. The explosion, surgery, wheelchair, recovery, divorce and rebirth. His "Alive Day" delineated his life into two distinct segments. Now he was at a place he never expected to be. A place of honor. A calm corner of Earth where he knew he still had something to give, another mission to accomplish. Something driving him every day to get out of bed and go "do" something useful. He wasn't exactly certain what that mission was yet, but it included reaching back to the younger men just now coming home, teaching them what he knew. Mentoring those who were conscious, in his grid square and willing to listen to the old Grey Haired Warrior.

Every soldier Chief had ever known, especially those who spent so much time down range, couldn't wait to get home. They all hated being down range in the heat, hated the goat shit, missed the comfort of their loved ones, and their home. The first month home was usually a celebration, a re-orientation both fun and emotionally fulfilling. Yet within three months, an itch started. Something deep within their brains made them feel uncomfortable about being home. As if something was missing. Unfinished business of some sort kept them remembering things that didn't have any real importance in their lives. Jokes about the sand, the heat, the goat smells commonly caused them to romanticize their time in the sand box. These feelings of inadequacy, questions about what they really did over there and why we lost so many good people to such a shit mission constantly came up as they tried to re-adjust back to American society. A group of civilians that proved life went on without soldiers even coming on their radar. The longer they were gone, the worse it got when they came home. And six months after coming home, it comes to the fore. They just gotta go back. Chief was a civilian now, but he knew exactly what all these guys were feeling. He didn't need to prove anything. He didn't need the money, nor the recognition. Yet the urge to go back was stronger now than ever.

There were two call signs most people knew Chief by, back when he was on Active Duty. These were much more than just "legendary names". To Chief, it was his entire reason for living. Those who knew him had deep respect for what he'd accomplished and what he was living through. Within the Inner Circle of Tier One Warriors, Chief was respected as the "go to guy" for not just dangerous missions, but for impossible missions that no one else would do. Yet with all things, time passed and Chief knew he too would eventually pass with that time, into oblivion, into a time and place that had no reverence, no respect, just part of history not worth repeating.

On missions Chief accomplished doing good and getting people to safety, the missions no one ever heard about, hostage rescues and the like, his call sign was "Arc Angel Six"! And everyone knew when Arc Angle Six and his Team were in the grid square, things must be serious. On the other hand, when Chief was out doing take downs missions, guiding his Team to excellence to extinguish evil and sending bad guys to see their maker, taking down drug dealers, Cartel leaders, war lords or just plain bad guys, the call sign everyone knew was Chief, was "Bad Karma Six." Every operator, pilot, support Team knew when they heard this callsign, they were part of something bigger, historic, worth a shit and they did whatever they could do to be involved in that mission.

Chief was a different person now. His body was broken, disabled, and dangerously close on multiple occasions just mere steps away from permanently checking out. After years of surgeries, recoveries, mind numbing boredom and intentional five meter targets, Chief had actually recovered to some degree of functionality. The writing was on the wall though. Eventually he needed to quit. To walk away simply because those involved were more worried about Chief and how bad his spinal condition was, how bad the pain was, instead of the keeping the mental focus on the mission.

Chief recognized how much everyone on the Team worried for him. And he knew that eventually, it was his professional task, his honor that required him to eat the bullet and just stop. It was up to him to just draw the line and do the honorable thing. Because too many more good men were at risk because he wanted to keep being superman. Walking away was the hardest thing Chief would ever do. Simply because he knew his Team cared. They loved him. They would do anything to protect him on mission that should have been about the hostages, the bad guys, and doing whatever it took to bring the mission to "Zeus".

When Chief finally realized "he" was the problem, "he" was the "dog with the biscuit", Chief knew instinctively it was time to fall on his sword and make things right. It was time to walk away. Time to retire and let the next generation take over. The reality hit him extremely hard between the eyes. He was never going to be the super human door kicker he used to be. That concept alone was still elusive and contributed to his depression and denial. His brain was seriously impacted not just by the immense and intense concussive forces of the explosion but by the years of surgery, anesthesia and narcotics he was fed to deal with the pain. Compounding the situation was the protocol of the Veterans' Administration, pumping over thirty different types of medications into his body. These included sleeping pills, anti-depressants, serotonin re-uptake inhibitors (SSRIs), pain medications, diabetes medications, and prophylactic drugs on the VA protocol template. The combination caused side effects requiring more medications to treat. Chief's body was a disaster from the medical malpractice, the constant gerbil wheel of surgical intervention to fix the bone grafting and the failed fusions. There were now over ten sets of hardware that failed, causing him to go to the next step in pain intervention. They all wanted him on the Morphine Pump, a continuous subcutaneous drip of Morphine directly into the epidural space, directly into his spinal cord. Yet every person he ever met who had one installed was a zombie. Not something Chief was willing to put up with. So he opted for the Dorsal Column Stimulator implant, a new system of embedded battery and computer programs that electrically shocked his cord and interrupted the pain signal going to his brain. Anything was better than more narcotics. He was a train wreck and his body needed more time to heal. He was fed up with the gerbil wheel of doctors, not ever coming to any real resolution. The continual shoulder shrugging when he asked questions was really pissing him off.

"How much longer is it going to take?" Was his common question, his intention lost on the very people he was asking? He wanted to be well enough to go back. To pick up where he left off and continue the mission. Yet now one understood that basic concept. All of the medical personnel assumed he was just content with where he was. They just didn't get it. They all wanted him to "take it easy" and give everything time to sort out and heal. That time was now over in his mind, no matter how detrimental it was to reality. The continual Gut Check led him to his current state of "self introspection and evaluation".

To Chief, too much time had passed since he felt like he did anything "worth a shit". Regardless of how damaged his brain and body was he now he had to do something with what he had left. He couldn't just sit by and watch evil thrive. ISIS was on the rise. A pseudo replacement terrorist group for the Red Army Faction and Abu Nidal, Slobadan Milosovic and Usama Bin Laden, using Islam as a basis for their warped ideology. They were murdering people in the most heinous ways, calling it "Allah's Will" and doing things against humanity that God Alone would wretch over.

The names changed since Chief's time in Europe and Italy when Abu Nidal was king, but the tactics and the motivation were still the same. These assholes were worthless thugs, going no where fast, wrapping themselves in the flag of righteousness. Nothing new. Just a different generation with the same sick agenda. America was going to war in Yemen, Saudi Arabia, Libya and Syria. Chief had to do something useful. There was no "expiration date" on his Oath of Office, to protect and defend the Constitution of the United States of America against all enemies, foreign AND domestic. The frustration was building and Chief had to do something with his life to make him feel like he was actively participating, not just surviving. Whatever was going on within his soul, the motivation was more than he could explain.

As all this and more swirled through Chief's brain, like two squirrels chasing each other around a pine tree, the cell phone in his right rear pocket interrupted with a specific ring tone letting him know that someone from the home landline phone was calling him.

"Daddy, there are some scary men here that want to talk to you". Suddenly, the muffled sound of a handset changing hands ceased and a strange male voice with a thick Arabian accent spoke.

"Asalamu Aleikum" muthafukur!

A searing hot pain shot through Chief's stomach... and life again changed in thirty seconds.

ABOUT THE AUTHOR

Samuel Hill is a pen name. The Author's true identity is by law, and subject to non-disclosure agreements, classified until 2085.

The author served from March 1976 to July 2006 including both enlisted and officer time and was awarded, in ascending order:

((all classified awards have been redacted))

Southwest Asia Service Medal

Kuwait Liberation Medal

National Defense Medal

Achievement Medal for Heroism

1 Army of Occupation Medal (Berlin)

4 Good Conduct Medals

Army Commendation Medal with 6 oak leaf clusters (seven awards)

(one with Combat "V" device for Valor)

3 Meritorious Service Medals

2 Legion of Merit Medals (One for civilian operations)

Additionally, "Chief" was cited as the Intelligence and Security Command, Commander's Trophy for Operational Intelligence Achievement (1st Runner Up) after only three years in service, for operational Intelligence 110 miles behind the Iron Curtain during the Cold War.

He is now 100% Permanent and Totally disabled, currently writing the series, "Six Days to Zeus" which has been optioned by Phoenix Pictures to become a Hollywood movie.

He founded "Tier One Tranquility Base" in 2010, a non-profit for PTSD and the Moral Wounds of War.

Printed in the USA
CPSIA information can be obtained
at www.ICGtesting.com
LVHW041251151023
761121LV00001BB/70